With the Tiger

Inez Baranay is the author of nine published books. These include the novels, *The Edge of Bali*, *Sheila Power* and *Neem Dreams*; a prose collection, *The Saddest Pleasure*; a nonfiction title, *Rascal Rain: A Year in Papua New Guinea* and *Sun Square Moon: Writings on Yoga and Writing*.

WITH THE TIGER

HarperCollins *Publishers* India
a joint venture with
THE INDIA TODAY GROUP
New Delhi

First published in India in 2008 by
HarperCollins *Publishers* India
a joint venture with
The India Today Group

ISBN: 978-81-7223-717-2

HarperCollins *Publishers*
A-53, Sector 57, NOIDA, Uttar Pradesh-201301, India
77-85 Fulham Palace Road, London W6 8JB, United Kingdom
Hazelton Lanes, 55 Avenue Road, Suite 2900, Toronto, Ontario M5R 3L2
and 1995 Markham Road, Scarborough, Ontario M1B 5M8, Canada
25 Ryde Road, Pymble, Sydney, NSW 2073, Australia
31 View Road, Glenfield, Auckland 10, New Zealand
10 East 53rd Street, New York NY 10022, USA

Typeset in10.5/13 BakerSignet BT
S.R. Enterprises

Printed and bound at Thomson Press (India) Ltd.

To Julie Brumlik

Contents

Acknowledgments

Research and early work was made possible by a Literature Residency in India in 2002 granted by Asialink and funded by the Australia Council, the Federal Government's arts funding and advisory body.

Most of the work of a first draft was enabled by a Writing Fellowship from the three Canberra Universities in 2004. I am grateful to everyone who was part of my time at ADFA, ANU and UC.

Thanks also to Jenny Pausacker and John Paramor for critical readings of early drafts.

Thanks to the librarians at the Queensland State Library. Thanks to Tim, Joanne and Loma for finding the title.

Author's note to reader

This novel is closely based on Somerset Maugham's novel *The Razor's Edge* (1944). I have followed Maugham's structure exactly and named my characters for his. The title of each of my sections is a line used by Maugham in that section. Some other phrases in my text also correspond to his.

The action of *The Razor's Edge* begins in 1919 and is mainly set among Americans in Europe. *With The Tiger* begins in 1979 and its main characters are Australians.

PART I

If I call it a novel

If I call it a novel it's because I don't know what else to call it.

I've often been asked: is *your* work true, based on a true story, based on anyone *you* know? Truth is fiction, we writers reply, and fiction is truth. We all live among stories, we turn fragments into stories when we dream, we get to know each other by telling stories about ourselves. The songs we hear contain stories. Commercials tell stories. These days we call politics, law, religion, history, family life 'narratives'. We turn on *The News* for the latest versions of old myths.

My own first novel was treated like an autobiography, yet I've told more secrets about myself in works with characters and themes more distant from my own experiences. My second play was based on a well-known real-life scandal, and it was largely discussed in terms of whether the events in the play exactly depicted what had in fact once happened.

As soon as we begin to imagine them, the people in a novel or play are characters, quite separate from their models. That's what writers say: they are ours, we do what we like with them, as if we were gods. Or perhaps the characters are using us and, how about this, maybe that also makes us like a god. The characters are also yours, dear reader, we all know that too: acts of reading create the text.

I thought about disguising my characters for this book, perhaps making them American, or living in another time, turn blondes into brunettes, men into women. But no, it doesn't work. They must be the people they are, as they appeared in my life.

As I begin to write this, the arts pages of the weekend paper of choice are featuring a piece by a writer who has been made into a character by a novelist, a friend she introduced to the situation he wrote of, someone she had once thought would at least remain a friend. He wrote a bestselling novel, and all she's got is this story to tell. It's like he won. A supplementary page treats us to a survey of various novelists who have lost friends by depicting them insufficiently disguised. Is it truth or is it construal the lost friends resented? Appearance or representation? The rueful author of the feature article admits that the triumphantly bestselling author of the novel has the right to turn anyone he knows or doesn't know into a character – for what writer does not? – but cautions that there should be some kind of limit. And cautions that if people knew how ruthless some writers were they might not admire them so.

I am going to write this, this novel as I must call it, because of a conversation I once had many years ago. It was with a young man, someone I briefly knew, first when he was still a boy, not yet twenty. We had a few other encounters over the next twenty years. I could try and find out what happened to him since I last saw him but I don't want to. I feel that one day, one way or another, I'll find out.

It's not very likely that he'll become famous, though I wouldn't be very surprised. More likely he'll leave only unobtrusive traces. Or he may attain a moment's celebrity, that dazzling mutation of fame, and find himself with admirers and imitators; snapped or stalked; some disputing his worthiness. He might give interviews freely or exclusively or not ever. They may talk of the influence of his past, his journey, his reinventions. And all that might be in some obscure specialist journal or some small-time cable TV show. If he were the kind to become to any degree well-known this would be read by the world that is interested in him. But far more likely, my novel will be read, if at all, for any of the reasons we read novels.

Memory has its own time zones: some of the events that involved us both are clearer in my mind than more recent ones. But who knows where invention begins. One memory leads to another and some memories provide details.

Let's see if that makes a novel.

I had known Elliott Templeton for over fifteen years

First I have to tell you about Elliott.

In 1979 I had gone up to Brisbane for the first time since I had escaped, as I used to put it, in the early sixties.

I hadn't been back to Queensland since I had fled the repressive Deep North over fifteen years earlier, a typical refugee vowing never to return until the state was free, I was a success and my torturers had died.

But since then I had calmed down, got on with my work and made a life in the liberating air of the south. I had arrived to live in Sydney during its golden age. Still, eventually I came to think it was high time I went back up north, just a visit, just to show myself it didn't have to be a big deal, and what better opportunity than this, the Sunshine State's very first production of a play of mine.

They could go on ignoring my plays in Queensland when they were produced by small theatre companies in Sydney, but those new small companies were getting new big audiences, and several times had extended their seasons and moved into bigger theatres, and the small companies' plays were taken up for new productions by large, subsidized companies in other states.

But it was not a happy cast and crew I met in Brisbane. They had just returned from the regional tour that preceded the city opening, and the media in the small towns of our northern state had not been particularly appreciative. They had pointed out that they had better actors in their own local amateur or semi-pro companies, and their own directors who had better taste than to inflict a play that might be all very well for southerners who blasphemed, expressed insupportable views and offered no redeeming values.

I had been asked up to Brisbane to see if I couldn't turn a couple of lines here and there into something that might go down better in these parts. No one had given any indication that I would ever be asked to join them outside the rehearsal rooms. I was treated with a mix of respect and resentment. In those days they still talked about how you had to go Down South to Make It, or how you didn't have to. While down south they talked about you had to go overseas to make it, or you didn't. The theatre's PR person had kept for me some local press cuttings disputing whether I could really be counted as a Queensland writer any more, whether my play was in any sense a Queensland play and whether a state-funded company should be spending Queensland money on one who chose to live elsewhere. Some crap local journo, but no one wanted to publicly disagree with them.

I was briefly interviewed by the local paper, which had minimal arts coverage, and asked, 'When are you coming back to Queensland?'

'I'm here now,' I said.

'To live?'

'I've never been anywhere that I want to live forever,' I had said, but the paper reported me as saying 'hopefully'.

They asked me why I had left Queensland, I said to have the career I have had by leaving it. They asked why I couldn't have had that there, and I said, 'Do you really have to ask?' None of that got into the paper. But I also had to fend off invitations from the city's social set, the ones who subscribed to the theatre to mark themselves them as cultured people, and who seemed to expect me to cheerfully attend their gatherings, marked by the self-conscious formality of the provincial. Over-dressed women – in too much floral, too many aquamarines, too determined a mood – urged me to confirm that things up here were better in important ways and to confide what I knew of the secret lives of certain actresses and weather girls. I'm working, I began to say, not untruthfully, as an excuse to avoid any more of these evenings in suburban hell. Forgive me, dear reader, I know things are different now.

In my hotel room the phone rang. I hesitated but picked it up and heard an unexpected voice say, 'Didn't think anyone out here knew *you*, did *you*, you suddenly famous little tart?'

'Elliott?' I said. He was one of those people who never announce their names when they call. His voice was unmistakable but still, it was annoying. 'What are you doing here?'

He was visiting his sister. I hadn't known he had a sister.

'Come to lunch,' he said, and gave me directions or perhaps orders, for Elliott commanded all who had fewer years, less money or less authority than he. Actually he probably always had commanded everyone all his life.

I had known Elliott Templeton for over fifteen years. I'd met him soon after I'd arrived in Sydney. I'd gone to Sydney with a sense of wanting to be where The Sixties would arrive soonest, and began writing anything and everything I could, putting on little sketches and scenes in art galleries, theatre foyers and the street, and letting anyone and everyone know about them.

I'd known that Elliott originally came from Queensland too, though I understood he had slipped away quietly when he'd been the age I was when I decided I'd better flee.

Once I had got over the fact that I really could remake myself and start a new life, I began to write about what I'd left behind, and eventually that turned out to be the right first book at the right time. It was an Australian coming of age and coming out story, ending with a dream that men of my generation would be the last to ever feel they had to try to be straight if they weren't. It was produced at the cultural moment when the dream of endless liberation was flourishing.

By then I was already involved with the theatre, and working with a company that had become a new family, one of my new families.

Somewhere along the way I had come to know Elliott, at first a little, then well enough for him to phone me now.

He was in his late fifties then, an elegant man who dressed with much care and to great effect in expensive Italian clothes he had learnt a great deal about, bought in Melbourne, Milan and New York. He knew certain designers, knew their work, knew them personally.

Knowing people was Elliott's forte, his metier, his vocation, his *raison d' être.* Rich and famous people, that is. And he kept account of what was going on in their lives: who their agents were, what deals they were making, who they were sleeping with, who they were wearing. He knew old money and new money, people famous in tabloids and famous in art journals.

He had affected grandeur and mystery. *Such an operator*, they said of him, *what a hustler*; in Sydney these were admiring terms. In past decades he had been the live-in companion to an antique dealer, a high-rating radio announcer and a show business entrepreneur, and close, therefore to their circles of acquaintance. He had achieved his ambition of becoming known to some of the people who were on so-called A-list invitation lists and gave parties to visiting celebrities from abroad – royalty, rock stars, returning expatriates. If he was not as indispensable to or familiar with these circles as he liked to make out, well, no one cared as much as he did.

I don't suppose people he met asked 'What do you do?' His reputation always preceded him. In the papers he was described as a 'professional man about town'.

He was not an interior decorator, but had been called upon to advise the newly rich what to buy in the way of antique or designer furniture, rugs and decorative objects, some of which he obtained for them. He was not a sommelier but he had arranged for the occasional company or corporate head to have a wine cellar they need not be ashamed of, and he talked up these commissions so much that fresh commissions came. He was not a couturier but if you knew how to ask, he would take you to two or three boutiques or tailors he knew and make sure you bought the right suits, frocks and accessories – and make sure you understood you had got a good price, for he understood retail. You were also to understand he sometimes got his own threads here. He connected people: he was someone for whom knowing people and doing deals was second nature. He never referred to people as clients, but for all these services there were recompense, commissions, percentages, spotter's fees, little thank yous, tokens of appreciation, favours owed.

He'd do anything to know certain people and be asked to their parties. This anything at one time had involved him in some lucrative dealings of a less than legal nature (this is the kind of language he'd use) but by this time Elliott had long retired from procuring banned drugs or experienced temporary companions. Rumour had his beginnings as a teenage whore, a plaything in the most corrupt circles, a toy boy, a young kept man, but I don't know whether this part of his past had been long buried or recently invented.

He had either been lucky or had chosen his paramours well and early on had begun to acquire a portfolio of investments as well as the enviable *objets* that could be shifted from his harbour-side apartment to yours, under private arrangements. As he attained maturity, he became known as a 'society walker', an escort for a couple of wealthy women, who favoured him for his perfect manners, reliability, discretion and just enough outrageousness to guarantee some laughs. He was neither too camp nor too straight-acting to seem a threat to the patriarchal ascendancy. He in effect had given himself a second upbringing by queens to have this very life.

Did I say he was discreet? While he never divulged the exact nature of his services and rewards, he was also a shameless name-dropper, social-climber and, to use a blunt old-fashioned word, a snob. A colossal snob, actually. He found real value in a person's celebrity or wealth, a value he never questioned or modified. He lived to know the people gossiped about by those who never met them, people whose launches, openings and cruises outsiders dreamt of or schemed to be invited to, though sometimes a lot less than Elliott liked to think.

His own background, something he never mentioned nor let slip, was a country pub in the northern state. The town grew, his family had prospered, and, in the Australian way, joined the middle class in one generation, the children growing up aware of their right to distant horizons and endless opportunities.

Elliott was successful in his reinvention of himself before self-reinvention had become a cliché. He'd discarded all trace of a

Queensland accent long ago. His parents were conveniently deceased and could never surface to cast doubts on the hints he had begun to make of renegade Lords in a First Fleet ancestry. (Other people were beginning to claim descent from First Fleet convicts but that wasn't Elliott's style.)

There were no other relatives, at least none Elliott cared to find or own up to, but for the younger sister who had married well and who was the reason for his visit to Brisbane.

Apparently the younger sister had recently been widowed, an event that had worked to bring the siblings together again.

When I first met Elliott

When I first met Elliott, I had been as ambitious as only a provincial émigré to a big city can be. I began self-publishing some short stories and sketches, handing them out at theatre and art gallery openings, the kind of thing, I found, where Elliott was always to be seen.

I had known of him, of course; to the extent I had had a circle back in Brisbane outside of my home and school life, Elliott had been connected to it. To the extent he knew anything about me, he knew I came from there too. He began to say hello to me after a couple of my plays had been produced. In the early days, no one could have known that they'd be taken up so eagerly by a new middle class hungry for a new national theatre. I've had my detractors but I think the audiences largely felt that if they could be observed that well, someone thought they mattered.

The new audiences were ready and pleased to hear Australian accents on the stage – indeed, many of the well-trained actors had to learn to speak in Australian accents, for much of the work of drama schools back then was in eradicating all traces. Announcers on the ABC still had to sound British.

I came to realize it was clever, the way Elliott at first greeted me; he could declare as little or as much acquaintance as he chose, he could in future drop me or take me up. He was keeping an eye on me, as he kept an eye on other new arrivals of talent. He never went so far as to be the first to patronize any of the young painters, actors or writers he kept tabs on, for he left to others the judgement of their worth, but he was in a position to claim prior knowledge if and when he chose. I was never pretty or glamorous so he never had that kind of interest.

My first book, when it finally came out, its appearance delayed as the small alternative press struggled for funds, the publication often postponed, might have remained a very obscure thing but for some good timing out of my control. And the novel getting banned in Queensland was, of course, the kind of publicity even money couldn't buy.

One day I had received a hand-written invitation from Elliott. He had just bought the apartment right on the water at Elizabeth Bay, and I was far from immune from a desire to see this fabled demesne. Elliott let it be known its acquisition marked a new phase in his life, a kind of semi-retirement.

It was a large party, and I actually knew a few people there, actors and directors and a couple of other playwrights, and though I was even more shy in those days than I am now, I was also more bold, and managed to circulate and participate to a respectable degree before my usual early exit.

I did get a feeling that was my audition for a part at smaller, more important parties. My play took off, the season was extended and other productions of it were scheduled in other cities. I suddenly had a whole lot of new best friends. I met Elliott again in Melbourne, and he seemed impressed that there I already knew some of the same people that he did.

Elliott had just bought a flat in St Kilda – he lived in both cities for a few years in the mid-seventies before moving back to Sydney. Anyway, he asked me to a lunch party there, a much smarter party I guess than the first. It was a seal of approval of sorts. My little success and our common acquaintance gave me a little more cachet. We saw a bit of each other over the years. I don't know if I would have called him a friend exactly. He only took an interest in people according to how much status derived from knowing them, or how useful they were. By now, he was someone a lot of people wanted to know. He was such an operator that even people who said 'he is such an operator' wanted to know him.

He was a stylish host and took much pleasure in the pains he took to give his guests a good time. He never stinted on hospitality: he'd served excellent wine and spirits even at the large informal party I had first gone to. He did have several different kinds of parties; the large informal kind, buffet luncheons, drinks parties (never the vulgar 'cocktails', as I learnt to appreciate) with sufficient waiters circulating with trays of drinks and finger foods; and after-theatre suppers for a smaller selection.

And then there were the most exclusive and desirable parties of all, those everyone longed to go to even if they pretended they did not, even if they pretended they didn't know about them, even if they were unqualified for invitations being women or heterosexual or too evidently puritanical. At these parties guests were sometimes required to appear in themed costume. The waiters generally wore only tans, and tiny Speedos and lifeguard caps. This kind of thing was already passing into legend once I was becoming better acquainted with him. I think he had begun to mention his Buddhism around now.

Ah, the price of such connectedness, such desirability. 'Oh my god,' he'd say when he called me, just a hint of a moan, 'people can be so inconsiderate.' He'd go on to tell me that some people he knew, from the United States, or England, or Italy, would have given his number and address to some friend or relative of theirs who was coming to Australia on business or a holiday, clearly in the expectation that Elliott would treat them to some of his famous hospitality or access to the invaluable data in his famous address book.

If he could get away with it, he'd just give them a quick call, send them a basket of fruit, tickets to something, maybe an itinerary he'd drawn up for them according to their taste.

Sometimes he'd feel he had to ask them to lunch, and though he had moaned about these very people to me, he had called to ask me to come. And I'd accept.

'So-and-so absolutely loves your work,' he'd tell me, 'and knows everything you've written,' but then when we met so-and-so would tell me she particularly loved something or other of mine – *The Removalists*, or *The Tree of Man*, the former being a play by David Williamson and the latter a novel by Patrick White.

It caused him pleasure to give

I hope I haven't given the wrong impression of Elliott. This book was never meant to be about him but my story must start with him and he will inevitably reappear, and I don't want anyone to think I thought him contemptible.

Meanness is contemptible, and Elliott was a generous man. Though he might have given you gifts to win you he continued to do it when you were of no use to him. It caused him pleasure to give.

He served only the best wine and food at all times, for everyone, and not just to impress; he wasn't a bad cook himself and always got excellent caterers.

At some of his parties you would be beckoned into one of the guestrooms where lines of coke were laid out on a glass brick, and the joints that were passed, discreetly or blatantly depending on the composition of the gathering, were large and stuffed with the best quality sensimilla. I don't think it ever occurred to him to keep any of this for himself, or to dole it out charily.

Though people gossiped about Elliott Templeton, and a lot of this gossip was mocking, some of it malicious, no one turned him down. The guests at his parties were a mix of ages, professions and backgrounds. I soon came to realize that this is what characterizes the best parties and that most other gatherings are marked by the sameness of their members.

Though Elliott himself had a malicious streak, and liked to exhibit his insider knowledge, no one could resist trading gossip with him, even to the extent of admitting their own latest forays into business deals and personal affairs, for in turn he always told them something it thrilled them to know, though they had to pay by betraying every confidence entrusted to them, every sworn secret and every slight suspicion.

Around this time, Elliott took up Buddhism and began his successful career as a Buddhist, one tiny moment before it became so very fashionable, and he took credit for steering many people on that flexibly defined path.

He brought a Rinpoche on a tour to Australia, and was active in organizing a benefit for Tibet. On a prominent wall he exhibited a thanka of impressive dimension and a photograph of himself bowing to the Dalai Lama. He later was to begin referring to His Holiness in a tone of special intimacy, as one of the special confidants in need of Elliott's assurance if not quite guidance.

Elliott's own humble background had been obliterated and had not the effect of giving him any special sympathy for the downtrodden or the struggling. Elliott did not believe anyone laboured under real disadvantages that could not be overcome by sheer will.

That was not my impression of how the world worked, but we didn't really discuss it. We'd talk about people we knew. Elliott gave good gossip. He'd seen an early play of mine about a wedding party that disintegrated into bitter exposures and revelations, and consequently would feed me scraps of story and dialogue from similar domestic and social disasters.

He knew perfectly well, I believe, that many people accepted his invitations for the sake of a free meal or to meet someone whose name they could drop; he knew some of his guests were stupid and some fraudulent. The larrikin tradition of Australian manners meant that parties inevitably arrived at the stage where the drinking would get out of control, decorum was shattered and conversation degenerated into brawls.

Still, the glamour of certain names blinded him to some extent: they were the people in magazines. He lived for special and intimate moments with them, and to relive them, time and again. I think there was a kind of romanticism in Elliott, he saw in celebrity a kind of democratic aristocracy.

And a lot of people really liked him; I was one of them. I've gone on about him quite a lot, I know. Let's get on with my story. I've got to get you interested in someone else.

I don't think it matters

I had just shaved and was choosing a jacket, for in spite of Brisbane's hot climate I knew what to expect, when there was a knock at the door.

'I thought I'd better pick you up,' and Elliott sashayed in, 'or you'd get lost. We're early, we can walk along the river for a bit, then take a cab. So what's this hotel like?' He looked around to see if anything had become world standard. It hadn't. It was pretty basic.

Of course I would not have gotten lost at all, but Elliott wanted to be in charge, or to talk to me before we turned up at lunch, or make sure I didn't get there first. Probably he wanted, at least partly, to ensure that I adopted the correct position, namely his, on the great issue of the day.

His recently widowed sister apparently was about to redecorate the conjugal home, and Elliott was very concerned that she do it with the right decorator. I was instructed to insist no one else would do. I surely had heard how fabulous so-and-so's renovations had turned out?

The home, now his sister's, had belonged to the family she had married into. Evidently she had always shared some of her brother's own determination to rise above her origins, and in her own way been as successful. She had met the late Mr Bradley when he had come on some business to her home town. He had been some kind of property lawyer with a city firm. He made money, bought a house in a desirable area of Brisbane and sent their children to private schools. Apparently Elliott's late brother-in-law had disapproved of him so much that it had kept brother and sister apart, but feeling he was entering some new stage of life, Elliott was finding the ties of blood quite compelling. He also saw that this style of house was ready to be cherished in real estate markets.

'She and I are quite close,' Elliott told me, 'though of course she doesn't know everything.'

I understood. I had been picked up first by Elliott also to ensure I understood the limits of his sister's knowledge of Elliott's life, or, as we were saying by now, lifestyle. And the knowledge of her children. They got the general idea but not the details.

Mrs Bradley had been a widow for long enough to begin taking charge and, Elliott emphasized, also to spend a little money on herself. It was his fraternal duty to support this new independence of hers. Her son and daughter had finished school, the son had a job in Hong Kong and the daughter had begun university nearby. It was time for all of them to look at the situation. I gathered that Elliott had stepped into the role of paterfamilias, and fondly intended to keep a close eye on developments, beginning with the choice of decorator.

Although houses right on the river were becoming desirable around now, the family home was old enough to be situated in the erstwhile preferred position on one of the city's ridges where one might hope to catch a breeze on a sweltering day.

It was a large timber house, set high on stilts in the local fashion, a 'Queenslander' they call them. I recall that at the moment of turning into this street I first really saw how elegant and charming the style of house is; I had finally been away long enough for a disinterested appreciation of the city's domestic architecture. On the spacious veranda – the length of the house and almost as wide, looking onto a vast lawn bordered with jacaranda trees – sat pretty rattan furniture, the large table covered with a crisp white cloth; and set for about eight or ten people.

'Elliott tells me you live in Sydney, does Nell really like it there?' Mrs Bradley asked me, referring to a newly famous ex-TV weather girl, now a model, celebrated for her sporty 'girl-next-door' look (though few of us live next door to statuesque young women with excellent deportment). She was also known for her unlikely origins in this very city, which professed to be very proud of her, although when she had lived here she had been told she was too large to be a model yet ill-advised to leave Queensland. (Whatever became of her?)

'I don't know her,' I replied.

'Why not?'

'Authors don't normally hobnob with models.'

'But she's really nice!' said Mrs Bradley, as if I were being perverse in refusing to know her. 'Isn't she?' turning to another guest, a white-haired man in his sixties who had been in the same law firm as Mr Bradley.

I had already been feeling some nervousness being back here, in the bastions of support for the state's infamous regime and its rampant police brutality. Only a few years earlier, a police commando-style raid had been carried out on a group of people living in a remote part of the far North Coast, living peacefully by all accounts, hippies and drop-outs, going about their properties naked, growing vegetables and attempting, in an ages-old tradition, to create a utopian commune at the greatest possible distance from urban centres. Helicopters had dropped police onto them, many of them had been bashed, their houses and gardens had been razed, yet none had committed any crime more serious than smoking some of their home-grown marijuana, a crime in this state treated with more abhorrence than, say, murder. I dreaded being asked why I didn't live here, as if to leave the state amounted to a kind of treason. The head of state, who was known elsewhere as 'the hillbilly dictator', was in his home state regarded with tolerance and even affection, for Queenslanders knew one thing: they were different from the rest of Australia.

Mrs Bradley and her guests did not disapprove of me or Elliott, as we were family and clearly tolerable human beings, but in general they would never have thought to utter an objection to, say, the bashing of demonstrators on the streets the previous year. Even the liberal-minded said the same thing about their home-grown dictator: 'He's done so much for the state.'

'Where's Isabel?' asked Elliott. I was glad we were going to talk about someone else.

'With Larry. They'll be here soon. Shall we have a drink?'

'Without delay!' Elliott turned to me and explained, 'Larry is a very old friend of my niece's.'

'Her fiancé,' corrected Mrs Bradley.

'Yes, well…' said Elliott, his dry tone conveying that they would have to see about that.

We were served mango daiquiris, or perhaps margaritas, in any case one of those cocktails that so suit the anticipation of languorous luncheons on wide verandas in the sub-tropics. Pimms maybe, stirred by crunchy celery sticks. I suppose we inevitably chatted about the weather, fresh enough in the early spring to make sitting outside pleasurable, especially on the well-ventilated deck. Clearly no one was going to venture onto controversial topics. I would have expected nothing more than to pass a few hours thankfully away from the hotel room and anxiety about the play. Elliott was toning down his usual schtick, I was interested to notice, out of respect for his sister's attaining her place among the bourgeoisie, and to keep the company charmed.

The French doors leading into the house, closed to keep the air-conditioned living room cool for later, suddenly were flung open and a girl came out onto the deck, followed by a boy.

They were both young, radiant with exuberant energy, glowing in tan skin and white tennis clothes. Isabel was a tall young woman, her skin a golden sheen. She had lovely eyes, full lips and wonderful skin. The harsh Queensland sun might eventually harm that clear glowing skin, but she was young, no visible damage. She gave an impression of fierce healthiness and strength, an Artemis. The young actresses I had met early that day cultivated pallor and thinness, they had trained their expressions to sullenness and jadedness, and I suddenly recalled them as seeming pretentious and sickly. Isabel was a bit tubby, her sporty clothes doing nothing to conceal a plump girlish belly and rather fat legs. But her lovely exuberance and naturalness made us all feel our years. I had been the youngest person present until then, and though I was only in my early forties, which seems young enough to me now, I felt stale and musty. Elliott's elegance suddenly seemed tired and contrived and his sister drab and old. Isabel seemed so vivacious, with an innocent libidinous energy. In a way it was a shocking moment. It marked the very instant in my life when I realized my own youth had well and truly passed and hereafter everyone young would seem enchanting and distant.

They'd been playing tennis, and glowed with energy and smelled of after-game soap and shampoo. Isabel and Larry. She was a bit of a knockout, and in his own way, so was Larry. Enchanting and distant.

We were seated at lunch and a cold soup was served.

'Now isn't this lovely!' Elliott began. It transpired that the veranda had been extended and redesigned according to his dictates: the floorboards polished, wooden ceiling fans installed, the romantic rattan furniture. He had begun leaning on his sister – Louisa was her name, I've just remembered – to appoint the interior decorator he recommended to redo the whole house.

'You've had the same furniture since you got married,' Elliott remonstrated.

'You tell her, Uncle Elliott!' Isabel enthused. 'I would love the lounge room to be done up all in white, white walls, white furniture, everything white! Why not!'

Mrs Bradley did not appear to seriously consider this option for a moment, and seemed reluctant to embark on much redecoration at all. 'Maybe just the walls,' she said uncertainly, 'though I'd have to move everything.'

I didn't speak much and the young man, Larry, said even less. Larry was sitting near me and I found I kept looking at him. I learned at some point that he was almost a year younger than Isabel but where she looked womanly he looked very much a boy. You could glance at him and take him for a youth who had not begun to shave. He was tall and thin, with a kind of loose-limbed grace of easy movement that I had noticed when they had come in, as if he were a dancer or did something like karate. I kept noticing the way he sat, the way he ate. He had graceful hands. When we exchanged some remark, I noticed his eyes; not only deep-set with thick long lashes but remarkably dark, the iris as black as the pupil, and this gave them a peculiar intensity. He seemed to have no affectations, appeared neither shy nor arrogant, and at some point, like that picture that looks like a girl seen one way and an old woman seen another, suddenly he seemed old for his years. He hardly said anything yet he seemed part of the conversation. I don't remember anything we said to each other but in my memory we communicated. Once I noticed that he and Isabel exchanged a glance, tender and affectionate. They were in love, young and in love, with the blessings of all around them. Though I've always been a long way from believing a marriage made a happy ending, there was something sweet about it, if also perhaps a touch of preposterous naiveté. Isabel and Larry were no doubt considered a perfect young couple, having everything they could want to start their life together. There seemed no impediments like family opposition, social opposition, poverty, overwork, or vast differences that made being a couple such a fraught endeavour for the less fortunate, yet I felt a pang I still remember, knowing that even such charmed desire would inevitably arrive at tough times. I already had a reputation as a cynic, yet this fleeting sadness of mine might have been embraced by an ardent sentimentalist.

There was a tiny moment then, Larry glancing at me, seeming to catch my curious, momentary observation, to uncannily read it correctly. He couldn't have. But there was that odd moment when he seemed to perceive exactly what kind of thoughts I was thinking.

'What do you think, Larry?' Mrs Bradley was asking him, for the main conversation had little deviated from interior décor and Elliott and Isabel's zealous promotion of an entire makeover of the house's interior.

'I don't think it matters whether you change it or not,' he said.

'You shit!' Isabel cried.

'Aunt Louisa likes it the way it is, so what's the point of changing it?' he said.

I laughed suddenly; it was such a simple, sensible remark.

'Don't encourage him,' said Isabel to me and 'Don't grin like that, that wasn't so clever,' to Larry. He only grinned some more. His smile lit up his face, until now seeming usually grave. He had very white teeth. Isabel looked fondly at him and I thought that her love for him had something of the maternal in it, as many kinds of love do: partly a protective feeling, I guess, and partly a desire to steer him on a superior course, one which she knew better than he could or cared to.

'Don't take any notice of him,' teased Isabel, 'since Larry went to India he wouldn't care if we all sat on the floor and ate with our hands!'

'You've travelled in India?' I asked him. He nodded. 'You look rather young to have done that.' Though they were off on their travels at earlier ages, young Australians, fewer of them headed straight for England, more set off for Asia.

'He was much too young,' said Isabel, who had turned her attention to me, leaving discussion of holland blinds versus venetian blinds to the others. 'He dropped out of school and took off with just a rucksack. When he came back he looked so thin and wise that I just sat on his doorstep till he promised to marry me. There was major competition...'

Larry said, 'Don't believe a word.'

I thought I was so lucky because they were talking to me.

I left with Elliott a couple of hours later.

'They're far too young to marry,' he said.

'Oh, I dunno, it might be fun to be that young and really believe in it and make a go of it. Do it when you're young, we're all too cynical and cautious later.'

'No, it's mad. She's twenty and he's only nineteen, he hasn't got a job, he has some tiny income from some investments he was left, nothing much. Louisa isn't rich. She has some decent assets, but she can't do that much for them.'

'They can earn their own living, surely.'

'Larry is not even trying to get a job. He is trying *not* to get a job.'

Elliott told me that Larry hadn't done anything since he got back from India and that was several months ago. He had been mad to go, anyway, not finishing school, but suddenly dropping everything and taking off.

And we suddenly dropped that topic, for our taxi stopped at a curio shop where Elliott had spotted something his discerning eye told him was a great bargain. I was encouraged to go in with him and observe him at work.

The following evening

The following evening I made my own way back to Mrs Bradley's house (I was still calling her Mrs Bradley) for the party for Isabel. When she'd invited me, before we left the lunch, I might have had a suspicion how glad I'd be to have somewhere to go. No one from the theatre company had extended any invitation to me; I didn't particularly want to go out on my own, not in this town; I was studiously avoiding the arts-patronizing socialites; I didn't want to spend the night in my hotel room. I showered and put on the same linen jacket, thankful for same-day dry-cleaning service.

Mrs Bradley greeted me, dressed in a floor-length shift made of some Indonesian batik. Something else matching, maybe a short jacket.

Elliott was already there, too, dressed in a pale blue linen suit with a T-shirt of the same colour underneath. (He was dressing like this before anyone had even heard of *Miami Vice*.) He shook my hand. In Sydney he would have kissed my cheek. Perhaps the suit was already audacious enough.

It was a small-ish party, about twenty guests. I had a general impression of a group of young people whose names escaped me as soon as I had been introduced. The only one I really noticed was a boy of particularly massive build. 'Built like a brick shithouse,' they'd've said where I came from. Isabel was pretty in a white dress, and Larry, too, was dressed in white, in cotton drawstring pants and an embroidered white shirt. His clothes looked Indian but too spotless and new to be relics of his trip. They were a group of polite, shiny-clean young people, not much like the few students I knew in Sydney who wore slashed jeans and razorblade jewellery and were rather keen to displease their parents, especially parents who lived in what appeared to be the complacent conservatism enjoyed here.

I'd already seen Elliott in a number of different social situations but this was a new side of him, and so far seeing this new side had been my main interest in being at the house in Acton – that and my lack of other diversions.

I didn't usually meet families. In Sydney we had been talking about creating our own families. I was one of those for whom friends were a compensation for the family you'd been born into, and who expected nothing from blood relatives. I had begun work on my play about just how tightly bound and loyal people could be or were expected to be when they had eschewed conventional family structures. Ha, little did I know just what resonance this would have in the coming decade.

There was punch served out of a large bowl set up on the veranda where we'd had lunch.

The kids seemed nice, all around Isabel's age, a couple of years out of school, most of them students I think, a few already working. Some of them had left Brisbane for universities or jobs in the southern states, but clearly had not made the never-coming-back vows with which I had once departed, and were visiting in their term break. I just couldn't wait to leave home and this state when I had been their age, and never regretted doing it, having made others besides myself unhappy in my ill-fated attempt at 'normal' relationships. But there was no sense of the same desperate longing among this lot. They all seemed sure of having the life they wanted: you decided whether or not to go on living 'at home' and it didn't make much difference as you did what you liked anyway. As the offspring of the haute bourgeoisie of a conservative little city, these kids knew few restrictions on their choices, and getting away from here was no big deal.

Larry was unusual in that group, having already gone travelling. If any of the rest of them had been overseas it would have been on short cruises or holidays in Fiji or Bali.

The caterers seared steaks on a barbecue and set out salads, seafood and roasts on a buffet table. I helped myself to some grilled prawns and looked for a seat. There was space next to a young woman who indicated that I was welcome to place myself there. She was unexceptional, at first glance on the plain side perhaps, only she did also have that sheen of youth that I was beginning to find so captivating and moving, making it impossible for any healthy happy person of her age to seem quite ordinary. She wore a longish dress in a small floral print and her ash hair was scraped back, held by a velvet bow at her nape. She gave me a shy smile.

'How do you like it up here?' she asked me graciously. Do I now recall an incipient vivacity behind her modest demeanour? We exchanged a few remarks and I told her my connection to the gathering: that I had met no one here besides Elliott before yesterday.

'I know who you are,' she said. 'I'm Sophie.' We said once more that we were pleased to meet each other, for I had been introduced of course earlier, me retaining no names. 'I suppose you know everyone,' I said, trying to find something to talk about with her. The others were talking among themselves.

She did, and proceeded to name two or three of the young people around us, a trainee radio producer, a couple of law students. I wasn't really learning anything and I did wonder for half a second how long I had to sit there.

'And who is that young man?' I asked, indicating the brick shithouse I'd noticed before.

'That's Gray Maturin,' she said. 'He's mad keen on Isabel, always has been. But she thinks of him as just a friend.'

Now we were getting somewhere! Quiet, shy little Sophie, I suddenly saw, doesn't miss a trick. Trust a wallflower to really see what's going on. Thank you goddess of social intercourse for sitting me next to a decent gossip! I made all the encouraging, interested sounds I could. I suddenly saw that I'd underestimated her.

'Well, Isabel of course only has eyes for Larry. She knew she was going to marry him even when we were all just kids. When Larry went travelling, Gray hung around more than ever, but Isabel didn't seem to notice how he thought of her.'

Gray was not exactly handsome, but somehow striking: an effect of his size, along with an unmistakable sensual quality, a quiet smoulder under the sports-jock exterior, with a sense of determination about him. He had a lot of black hair, bright blue eyes, the kind of face they call a map of Ireland. He obviously kept himself fit, football, I would have thought, running, that kind of thing, maybe even the gym, although this was before working out became the universal imperative. For all Larry's thin, intense charm, he looked puny next to Gray.

'Couldn't Gray have made her notice?' I asked.

'Gray and Larry have been friends since they were little. Gray would never go behind Larry's back. Larry trusts him.'

'You've all known each other a long time,' I asked, looking around me.

'Most of us have been friends since school, primary school even.'

'So what does Larry do?' I asked, somewhat mischievously as I remembered what Elliott had said.

'He's just Larry. He didn't go to uni and he doesn't work. He's probably just working out what he really wants to do. That could take a while. He's kind of complicated.'

'And that's all right with Isabel?'

'She loves him.'

'Only I thought Gray would seem the better catch.'

'Most of the girls here would give anything to go out with Gray. But he's so in love with Isabel no one has a chance. And he won't compete with Larry either, as long as Isabel feels the way she does. Gray has a code.'

'He's a student?'

'Engineering. His father owns this huge development company and he works there part time, he'll go into that. He's a good catch all right.' But she said this with a hint of irony, a tone that made clear she wasn't one of the girls who'd give anything. 'He's even offered Larry a job there,' Sophie added, 'but he just said no.'

'Travelling to exotic places at a young age can make you realize there are more possibilities than you might once have thought.'

'Larry only says he hasn't made up his mind what he wants to do. But he is engaged to Isabel.'

'And what do you do?'

'Veterinary science. I'm repeating second year.'

Later in the evening, as trifles and pavlovas were being served, and the younger set turned up the music, I took my coffee with the older folk. The conversation turned to the offer made to Larry by Mr Maturin, and Larry's refusal. Mrs Bradley was putting it down to Larry having been spoiled by indulgent parents as a small child. There was a Dr Nelson there, not a medical doctor I suppose, the man I'd met there the day before, who was Larry's appointed guardian. There were a couple of women friends of Mrs Bradley's.

'I can't tell him what to do even if I wanted to,' said this Dr Nelson. 'He's had a few offers and he says no thank you, very politely mind you, but it's no thank you every time.'

'He can't refuse, that's all there is to it,' said Elliott.

His sister gave him a thin smile. I guess she'd been well- acquainted with this laying-down-the-law side of her brother. 'He has refused,' she said. 'You can't make him take a job he doesn't want. He's got enough money to live on so there's no urgency.'

'His parents left him a trust fund,' Dr Nelson explained. 'It's been his to do what he wants with since he was eighteen.'

'Why doesn't he want it?' I asked, though I could imagine that a job in an engineering firm or whatever it was wouldn't suit that sensitive-looking boy.

'He doesn't really give a reason,' said Louisa Bradley.

'He goes on with a lot of crap about it has no meaning for him,' said Elliott irritably. 'Someone please tell him the meaning of life: make money, get yourself in a good position, set yourself up. Then you can think about the meaning of it all.'

'It was that trip he went on,' said Dr Nelson. 'Going to India. I think that did something to Larry. He didn't come back the same person that he went.'

'He was lucky he didn't come back sick. People come back from India with amoebic dysentery that turns them into skeletons and they finally get rid of it in about twenty years,' said Elliott.

'It's a fascinating country,' I said, 'and a lot of people feel changed by their experience of it.'

'You've been?' asked Louisa and Dr Nelson.

'Only one very brief trip, a couple weeks stop-over coming back from Europe, but enough to see why...' I didn't go on. Why people go back over and over.

'I ask him about it, he says there's nothing to tell. I'm just glad he came back in one piece,' said the doctor.

'He hasn't even told Isabel anything about it. Did he see the Taj Mahal, did he see an elephant, did he bring anything back? Not even a sari for Isabel. Not even a toe-ring.'

'Ah, well,' said Dr Nelson, signalling his departure. We said our farewells and he shuffled off to his car, and the other older guests left then too. But Elliott and his sister hadn't finished discussing the desirable destinies of the young. I wondered if I should make an excuse to leave, it wasn't really any of my business. Elliott was leaving town in the next couple of days and clearly wanted to thoroughly workshop this whole theme.

'We can talk in front of Will,' he said. 'He's discreet – aren't you, precious – and anyway he's got other things to gossip about back home. Where's that lovely Armagnac I brought you? Let's have a drop.'

'Well I might as well tell you the rest,' said Louisa to me. 'You know Gray Maturin is mad about Isabel. And he has made it clear he wants to marry her.'

'She should marry him,' said Elliott firmly, as if his certainty might bring it about. Oh, hadn't he said twenty is too young? It was a different story now. I only listened.

'And he's also Larry's best friend. Larry even asked him to go on that trip with him.'

'Which Gray very sensibly declined.'

'Are young people really meant to be sensible?' I did ask at one point. It seemed to me that they were meant to be not sensible, to try things out, take risks, experiment.

'That's all right for some of us,' said Elliott grimly. 'Isabel's best chance for a good start in life is a good marriage.' Ten years after Stonewall, this was, nine after *The Female Eunuch* came out, and two weeks after Elliott had hosted a party that involved a demonstration of fist-fucking. It was family values when it suited him.

'They are young,' I persisted. 'Very. What's all this rushing into marriage?'

'She's an old-fashioned girl really,' said Louisa warmly. 'She's mature for her age, she's always known what she wants. She's not like a lot of them these days, women's libbing and carrying on.'

'She should marry Gray,' said Elliott. 'Have a big wedding, go on a fabulous honeymoon, they'll start off with a beautiful big house and no worries. Have a couple of babies while they're young. Once that's all out of the way you can still have a bit of fun and cover your tracks.'

'You can't tell girls who they should marry, Elliott.'

'You should be able to,' he said. 'Let's face it, you don't know what's good for you when you're young. She'd be...'

'You do know what's not good for you,' I murmured.

'...set up for life. Face it, Louisa, you haven't got much to leave her besides half this house, and I intend to kick around on the planet for a good while yet and indulge myself completely. I'll always help out of course but the Maturins are loaded, they know all the power- brokers in this state. It's perfect. Things were done much better in the old days,' he said grandly. 'They knew what marriage was all about.'

If Mrs Bradley thought it odd for her brother to be pontificating about marriage she gave no sign. Elliott would be known simply as a 'confirmed bachelor' in the town of his origins, and he had already indicated to me that he didn't inflict knowledge of his 'lifestyle' on his sister. He might have thought she'd take any explicit reference by him to his own preferences as 'rubbing her nose in it'. Elliott had never been much interested in the 'liberation' movements.

'It's like we're in a Jane Austen novel,' I said, but I was only speaking to myself.

'People do marry for love, for passion,' said Louisa.

'That's their mistake,' Elliott retorted. 'Look at the dreadful result of that particular delusion. Marriage is for social reasons, and once they've settled down, he can keep a mistress in a flat somewhere and she can discreetly take a lover occasionally and everyone is happy.'

'You've been away from Brisbane too long,' his sister said.

I'm very ignorant

The next day I didn't have to go to the rehearsal.

I decided to go to the State library which in those days was in a colonial building in the centre of town. I wanted to read some journals and look something up, something new I was working on.

And there, at one of the spacious polished round tables alongside the bookshelves, I saw a young man I recognized. It was Larry, in blue jeans and a striped shirt, reading, clearly absorbed. I hesitated. I wanted to say hello but should I interrupt him? And just as I had decided to leave him alone he looked up and saw me. I went over and said good morning.

'What are you reading?' I asked.

'A book,' he said with a smile, and it didn't sound rude.

'It was a nice party,' I ventured.

Larry nodded. 'We had a great time. You should have stayed for the dancing. I didn't get home till five.' I blinked slowly – it was still morning. But when you're that young you can stay out all night and go on into the next day unaffected.

'Nothing shocks me,' I said, not quite truthfully. 'So, what is the book?' remembering reading banned books in this very library, where, it occurred to me, people might have come, many years after that, to read my own first book.

He turned it over so I could have a look at it. It was a translation and commentary on the Yoga Sutras of Patanjali. It was the last thing I could have expected. There weren't even any pictures. Or conversation.

'What's made you read this?' I asked.

'I'm very ignorant.'

'You've also got your whole life ahead of you.'

'I'm also very curious.'

'Hmm,' I said, for I too had once not only been ignorant and curious but had also known that I was. 'I wouldn't have thought this would interest you.'

It had taken me a long time, too long, to begin to seek out the books that would tell me who I was and what I wanted to know. First I had had to get to this city, and then to this very library.

I had sought books out here too, I had begun to know what kind of thing I wanted to read more of, I had begun to keep lists of titles and authors and wonder why they were not easily found. I had begun to be awed and grateful for the invention of libraries, free and open, available to anyone who made the slight effort. I had become aware that far more literature had been banned in my home state than in the rest of Australia, and this continued to be the case at this time.

'What does that mean?' Larry asked mildly and reasonably. I didn't know if I meant that he was too young for the book (I would never say that), or if he should be outside kicking a ball around (which I had never done). I had also been a young man who sought out books in libraries, because I'd had a glimmer that there were many other ways to have a life, that you could break free and, though you hardly could hope or imagine, be among people with whom you were what you wanted to be.

But I didn't think Larry was looking for the reflections of the same kinds of forbidden, denied and unknown experiences that I had longed for, literary experiences and life experiences. I was sitting next to him now and we talked quietly a while, with no one else nearby.

Larry began telling me that when he'd come back from India his guardian and everyone else too wanted him to go to university, but he didn't think he'd learn what he wanted to know there.

I said, 'It's none of my business, but do you think they might have had a point? It can save you a lot of time. As a student you're given direction, and there are people who know about the things you're interested in, and you meet other people who also want to learn...'

'Maybe you're right,' said Larry, 'but I don't mind how long it takes.'

'How long what takes? To become educated?'

'To find what my life is for.'

'What is any life for?'

'That's just it, I don't know yet.'

I had some sympathy, of course, for a boy who'd rather come in here and read than do what the others were doing, for a boy who thought there must be something he wanted to do that no one had yet told him about. Who still didn't know who he was going to believe.

'I remember,' I said, 'the amazing realization that books were written by people, by writers, and that I could become a writer.'

This must have been where I really had allowed myself that thought, allowed it, that is, with the sense that I could and I must make that happen now, that it was now or never.

'I don't have any talent,' Larry said.

'Doesn't stop a lot of people. So, what are your plans?'

'Just muck around.' The way he said that wasn't as if he was trying to be funny, he wasn't defiant or apologetic.

But I couldn't help smiling. I didn't think he was living in the best city for mucking around. 'Ohhhhkay. Good luck with it.'

I went and looked a few things up, read the Sydney papers, read a couple of journals. As I was leaving, I passed by where Larry had been and there he was, reading.

I had a late lunch, and, returning, detoured slightly to go past the library again. I went back inside and there was Larry, still in the same chair, still reading, still quite absorbed in uncommon concentration on the same book.

He's going to be away for two years

'Come to lunch,' said Elliott. He was on the phone and we'd been talking for at least an hour: he'd squeezed every last detail about the theatre mob from me, and then thoroughly rehashed the current main theme of his life: the question of his niece Isabel's options. Once Elliott decided to take someone in hand and shape them, he threw himself into the project.

I remembered another Isabel, the subject of a novel by Henry James: a young lady of spirit whose marriage choice among several choices provided material for a long account of its many consequences. She hadn't chosen well, that Isabel, for reasons found in the themes of *The Portrait of a Lady*, and in her day there was no simple calling-it-a-day, you lived with that choice forever, that or unthinkable scandal, especially if you were a real lady. A century or so later here we were. You might have almost thought there had been little change. It was an effect of coming to the Deep North again, I thought at the time, this rather quaint, it seemed to me, obsession with making a good marriage. It amused me to see Elliott absorbed in this.

'At your command,' I replied, glad enough of the invitation. It was my last day in Brisbane and I found this diversion of Elliott's diverting enough. One doesn't often meet the source family of one's friends, or see them, not after a certain age anyway. Not, that is, if you're the kind of person who doesn't live near their family, geographically or metaphorically. Absorbed as I was in the notion of a family of friends, it seemed a timely opportunity to observe the dynamics of loyalty, hierarchy and power in a blood family. Writers are always assessing situations as material.

When we arrived at his sister's house, it was to find Gray Maturin and his father waiting. Apparently Elliott had arranged for their presence, and for Isabel's absence. I felt we were a very strange combination, but I guess Mr Maturin didn't think he was having an intimate conference with two flaming queers from down south, he thought he was discussing matters of import with the uncle of his future daughter-in-law and his friend, a famous writer, for so I was introduced. They were quite evidently proud of each other, the father and the son.

The delicate subject was Isabel's giddy preference for marrying Larry, one it was important to alter in Gray's favour.

'He wrote us a letter,' said Mr Maturin of Larry.

The letter had politely but firmly turned down the offer of a job, a job with a long career path and no ceiling.

'What reason did he give?' I asked.

'He didn't give a reason,' said Maturin senior. His son looked uncomfortable, and never said anything, maybe under orders.

Elliott exploded. 'That is the best, by far and away the best, opportunity a boy like Larry will ever get in his whole life. If he's turning that down he's out of his mind.'

Mr Maturin senior quite agreed, and the bond between him and Elliott was forged.

And as Elliott was saying that – he said it all several times over, as people do when they want to make a point, repeating himself, changing his phrases slightly to emphasize his meaning – we heard the door, and Isabel came in. She might have heard what Elliott said, in any case when she came in, and stopped and looked at the gathering, I saw that she knew at once what it was all about, why the Maturins were there, what had happened.

The Maturins didn't stay much longer, and then the subject was rehearsed some more among us.

'There is no way known,' said Elliott, 'that that boy is ever going to be given an opening like this. And he either knows it or he doesn't know it. In either case, saying no proves he is just not quite stable, not quite all right, Isabel, and I advise you to avoid being over-entangled.'

'I want you to be happy,' said Isabel's mother, 'and you cannot be happy if you don't feel secure. Gray Maturin is the kind of boy who actually asked his father to offer Larry a job, knowing that if he did take it, Larry would still be around and have a chance with you.' She seemed to be choking back some tears at the thought of how noble and romantic Gray was.

'You do not want the life of some gypsy hippie fantasist or whatever it is Larry wants to be,' said Elliott. 'Look at you, you love nice things, you want a nice life, darling, it's all ahead of you.'

'There is nothing better for a woman,' said Louisa, 'than to know that the man she loves can always protect and provide, and then you have your shared values, your friendship, compatibility. Gray has all that. And honestly, the way Judith was eyeing him the other night, she said if she was twenty years younger…'

Isabel did not argue very much. I saw that she thought that what they were saying made sense. But it only made sense to her head, and she wanted to follow her heart, which said something else. Or maybe she liked the *idea* of following her heart more than really being the kind of person who did.

'You know what would be lovely,' said Louisa Bradley, 'if you go down to the Coast tomorrow and check on the unit. And take Larry with you.'

'Nice thinking,' Elliott told her when Isabel left the room. She was going to call Larry and arrange the trip. 'Pack them a picnic. Champagne, pâté, camembert, peaches…Those two have to have a talk. If he loves her he'll change his mind and if he does it quickly enough, he can still take up Mr Maturin's offer.'

I narrowed my eyes at Elliott and he just gave me a bland stare. I suspected that Elliott was quite sure that Larry would turn Isabel down, but wanted to show how kind and open he was.

I heard all about it from Elliott later back in Sydney. If I may fracture the chronology of this story a little, I will tell you now what happened next. In the order in which it happened, that is, not the order in which I learnt of it.

At the end of the next day Elliott was at the house again when Isabel returned from her trip to the coast with Larry. This time, when she came home, she went straight to her room. Eventually she came out, red-eyed from crying.

'It's sad, pumpkin, but it's for the best,' said her mother.

'There is all the difference between liking someone and marrying them,' said her uncle.

But they were not to be quite satisfied. 'What we decided,' Isabel told them, 'is that Larry is going to go away and do his own thing for two years and we'll decide everything after that.'

'If he goes away for two years you'll be deciding all kinds of things that have nothing to do with Larry!'

'No,' said Isabel, 'I'm going to wait till then.'

'He's going to be away for two years!' her mother said.

Elliott could hardly believe his otherwise rather captivating niece was not sticking to his script. 'What about Gray? Is he meant to wait too?' he asked acerbically.

'No,' said Isabel. Gray could do whatever he wanted, she said, she herself was going to wait for Larry. 'I've got uni, I've got my friends, I've got tennis, I've got a lot on, Larry's free to do what he wants and I'm free to do what I want and we'll get together again in two years. We're *young,*' as if she had to remind them.

'And what is Larry intending to *do* wherever it is he's intending to go?' inquired Elliott.

'Just muck around,' Isabel told him with a faint smile.

When Elliott began to speak his mind about exactly what he thought about that, Isabel told him to mind his own business. She didn't use those words and she did it very sweetly and charmingly of course, but she was telling him it wasn't his decision, it wasn't his life.

'She said it was something she had to work out for herself,' he reported. 'And now that I've thought about it, it will all work out for the best. Larry's only nineteen or twenty, that still is young, he needs to get around a bit, what happened to that old idea of you sow wild oats and then settle down? Larry needs some experience, an older woman for a start, Isabel will be only too happy about it one day.'

'Does it have to be a woman?' I remarked.

'True, you never know these days, do you?'

We left it there, but I thought for a while of how I had seen myself in the boy who had chosen to spend a Saturday reading in the library.

I saw your young man

'Just rang to thank you for all your kind hospitality,' I said, 'and to make sure you got the tickets. I'm hoping we'll get the chance to say goodbye that night, I'm going back to Sydney the next day.'

'Oh, we were just saying we must have you here again,' said Louisa Bradley. 'Don't just disappear.'

We chatted for a couple of minutes, then she said, 'Isabel's just here, I'll put her on.'

'Thank you for the tickets,' said Isabel. 'Can you come over again before you leave?'

'I'm not sure, but why don't we go out after the play? I didn't get a chance to tell you,' I said. 'I saw your young man the other day, the day after your party. He was in the library, reading the whole day long.'

'That's Larry,' she said.

What do you think of Larry?

The play went off as well as could be expected and I met my guests at the end.

'Well, that was very interesting,' said Louisa Bradley politely.

'I see what they mean, it is really more of a Sydney play,' said Elliott.

'I thought it was wonderful!' said Isabel. 'I loved the characters and what they said and the ideas in it.'

I invited them to come to the closing night party, but Louisa said she was tired and Elliott said he would accompany them home.

'I would love to stay and go,' said Isabel, 'Mr Maugham will see me into a taxi later?' turning to me and I said I would be delighted. I was too. Going with her was a lot better than going alone.

We saw them off and then Isabel said to me, 'Actually, I was really hoping I could have a bit of a talk with you.' Not going to the party at all was also an acceptable option.

After all the bits of business, where to go, deciding to go over to my hotel, where we could have a drink in the lobby, going there and finally managing to order some tea, and I recall, a milkshake for Isabel, after all that, it was time for her to tell me why she wanted to talk with me.

She said, 'First I have to ask you, why did you tell me about seeing Larry?'

'I thought you'd like to know what his idea of just mucking around was. In case you were worried about it.'

'I know Uncle Elliott has told you everything. He didn't tell me he told you, I just know. Can I ask you something?' A beat, so I would know it wasn't a casual question. 'What do you think of Larry?'

'It's hard to say,' I said carefully. 'I've only just met him. He does seem very nice, if that's not too feeble a word. He has an attractive quality, and he's obviously strong-minded. He's interested in the wider world. He's not a typical Queensland boy.'

'You would know a lot about people, being a writer.'

'I'm prepared to invent anything about people, being a writer.'

'Well, Uncle Elliott says you are really observant. He says you pick up on things others wouldn't notice and that's why you're a good writer.'

'I don't know,' I said dryly. 'Talent would be more useful.'

'I can't really talk to anyone else. Mum can only see it her way, she really believes in her idea of a good husband, someone who'll give you security.'

'I think that's what mothers are supposed to want for their daughters.'

'And Uncle Elliott can only see it from the social side, it's all who you know. Living in the right place, having the right things. And my friends, well, they think Larry's a bit strange, some of them.'

'That would be a bit hurtful.'

'They're nice to him but they think he's a bit of a joke.'

'Is this about what other people think of him?'

We had the hotel lobby to ourselves, seated in a little area got up as a lounge bar. There'd been a few people here during the day, but the rather drab few armchairs were rarely employed this late.

Isabel proceeded to tell me about their day at the Coast, and I encouraged a detailed account. She and Larry drove down in one of Louisa Bradley's cars, found the estate agent, and did a quick check of the apartment that was rented out to holiday makers when the family wasn't using it. It was a bright sunny day and though it was getting a bit hot at this time of year they decided to eat outside. They bought a couple of beers from the bottle shop and fish and chips from the fish and chip shop and sat under a tree at a picnic table on a grassy bank looking onto the sea. It was a clear, bright day. The taste of sea air added flavour to their food, seagulls hopped around their feet scavenging for scraps, there was a slight breeze that tempered the midday heat, surfboard riders skimmed along perfect waves and children and dogs played at the water's edge. Everything spoke of the life of ease and pleasure. A few tall buildings cast long shadows on the beach, not as many as there soon would be as coastal development flourished.

Then Larry said to her, 'So what did you want to tell me?'

'What?' she asked disingenuously.

'Come on, Isabel, your mother could have done that business on the phone. We've been sent out of town for a chance to be on our own and talk about exactly what we're going to do.'

'Well, that wasn't too hard to figure out.'

'And your mother and your uncle and probably you too want to know how serious I am and if I deserve you and how I'm going to prove it. I don't really blame them. I suppose they told you I turned down the job Mr Maturin offered.'

Isabel tried to keep things light. 'Gray would have been disappointed too. It would have been nice for him to have you in the same office.'

'It is just not what I want to do. Can you understand that?'

'I'm not sure I can, Larry. I need to know more about it.'

'All I know for sure, Isabel, is I love you and I want to share my life with you.'

'I love you too, Larry.'

'Why can't we just say, all right then, we can live together, we can do that now, you've got your scholarship and I've got my money, we can get married as soon as you want if that's how you want it…'

'Doesn't marriage mean anything to you?'

'What it means to me is I can prove to you I am serious about my love for you and wanting us to have a life together. We can do that, we can do that as soon as you want.'

'And what do you want to *do*?'

'Muck around.'

'Please don't try and be funny.' She had tears in her eyes and a sob in her voice.

'Hey,' he said softly, taking her hand. 'I don't want to make you sad. Don't cry.'

She couldn't stop the tears running down her face, but she dried her eyes and said, 'We have to work this out. Today.'

'What I want to *do* is what I am doing and what I will do. Read amazing books and travel and meet all kinds of people. We've got enough to live on if we're careful.'

'How long do *you* think we can live like that, like backpackers, they all have to come back and face reality and decide on the future. Look, if *you* want to take a year off and travel, I would do that, once I finish uni and *you've* got something to come back to.'

'Isabel, we can find out what's really worth doing, where we really want to go, by not tying ourselves down too soon, by being free, by exploring the possibilities that come up…'

'Larry, that might sound lovely but people need to work. Everyone needs to do some kind of work. Women too, *you* know I want to get some kind of job, even if it's part-time or some of the time or whatever.' Until there were children, she meant. 'It's good to work.'

'What is good about it?'

'Self-respect. And making a lot more money than some basic little income where *you've* got to always live like a student. And being part of something. And having a future, knowing what *your* life is all about.'

'Money doesn't really interest me,' said Larry. 'And I want to know a lot more before I decide what kind of work I want to do. I might need to create something of my own. Whatever I do,' he said, struggling to articulate something she could accept, 'I've got to believe in it, it'd have to be something I'd do even if I didn't get paid. Maybe there is work to do that I don't know about *yet*. Maybe I'd rather be a mechanic or make furniture.'

'This state is really going to go ahead,' Isabel said, repeating the Maturins' credo. 'We can be in on it, contribute, be rewarded.'

'And everyone in on it will get richer and richer.'

'Why not?'

'That just doesn't interest me. I know *you* can't live without money. I'm lucky enough to have enough to live on. That's what gives me the freedom to do what I want.'

'Just muck around.'

'Yeah,' he said slowly.

She looked at him a moment. 'You've really changed since you went to India,' she said.

'Have I?

'Yes. Don't you think you have? Mr Maugham said the other night that India changes people. You've never really talked about it. Only things you'd write on a postcard. What happened?'

He sat silent for a moment. 'A lot, really. I had a lot of time to think. I saw a lot of a life that seemed so different from what I'd known it shook up my whole idea of what was possible. And then, I found out how dead a dead person looks.'

'You saw a dead person?'

'A guy who'd become a really good friend died, in front of me.'

She gasped and took hold of his hand. 'God! What happened?'

'I don't really want to talk about it. It just happened. A lot of people die every moment.' But the look in his eyes, she told me, wasn't as casual as his words. She saw the anguish that was still fresh in his mind.

'Oh, Larry,' she said softly, 'are you depressed?'

'No,' he said, and smiled. 'The only thing I'm not happy about is that I'm not making you happy. Look,' he said, taking her hand again, 'I just have to find some peace of mind, some kind of answer. It's all so hard to put into words. Sometimes I think, why should I think I'm so special, why don't I do what everyone else does and what everyone wants me to do, what's wrong with that. And then I think of a guy who was having a great time and had a lot of things to look forward to and suddenly he's dead. I just can't help asking myself…what life is all about, just that, whether it's about anything at all or just blind fate and chaos. I want to make my decision out of some kind of knowing.'

Larry was always moving when he spoke like that, I already had been given a sense of that myself at the library. He had a lovely voice, soft but not weak, unpretentious but not rough, well-spoken but not posh. In some ways he sounded quite mature, old for his age, in some ways quite childish or naïve. It wasn't easy for him to articulate things he would rather not even try to say, but he made the effort for her sake, not giving up, with such anguished sincerity that for a while Isabel could say nothing.

'That could have been me,' said Larry.

'Jesus,' said Isabel, 'I'm glad it wasn't.'

'But why wasn't it? Was it just pure chance, nothing but luck? Is that what rules our lives? If not, what does? I began thinking about all that, and I want to find out everything I can about it.'

'Everyone has those thoughts,' said Isabel. 'It's all very interesting but no one really knows the answer. People believe what they want to believe.'

'Does that mean there is no ultimate reality? Nothing anyone can prove about what life is *for*?'

'Larry,' she said, 'don't go sounding like you took too many drugs.'

'Don't forget that one reason to take drugs is to know more about reality,' he said.

'That's just a delusion, or an excuse,' she said. 'I like a drink, if a joint is going around I'll have some, but I don't pretend it's making me wise or giving me amazing insights or anything. Don't tell me that what you want to do is just take drugs.'

'You know that's not it.'

'No, you couldn't spend all day reading if you did.'

'Oh, he told you he saw me,' said Larry. 'That's more the kind of thing I want to do. I want to spend the day reading, a lot.'

'Oh, Larry, I'm sorry but that sounds so immature. Everyone wonders what it's all about but there's just no point in thinking about all that too much. We're lucky to be Australians and get good jobs and live a good life.'

They sat close on one side of the picnic table and looked out to sea. They moved together, put their arms around each other and gazed out to the horizon. They turned to each other and kissed. The kiss turned into another kiss and another. Their temperatures rose and their blood surged and they began slipping their hands into each other's shirts, but then they stopped and moved apart. They might have driven to a motel, abundantly provided in the district for lovers with no common home. But they agreed without a word not to act on the lust they aroused in each other, sensing it would leave the issue even more confused and unresolved.

'What can we do?' asked Isabel.

'Do you want to break up?' he asked.

'Do you want to?'

'No. I told you. But I do want to just explore, leave it all open for a while. I want to get back to India, but more prepared this time.' He looked at her. 'It doesn't look like you want to do that too, but I don't want to lose you.'

'Okay,' she said, 'how about this: two years.'

He looked back at her. 'Two years.'

And they agreed that she would wait to see what he wanted to do two years from now, and he would be free to go wherever he wanted, explore whatever path lay open before him, walk through any door that opened to him. At the end of that time he would come back and marry her, or come back and tell her that he wouldn't.

'Do you think I did the right thing?' she asked me in that strange little hotel lobby that night, her face flushed, her eyes wet, her voice a little hoarse. I had encouraged her to tell me her story in detail and I'm sure it happened just the way I've told you. A writer remembers the telling details, the precise phrases that enable a complete recollection; we can distil the words we were told, to create a dialogue that is truer than speech, stripped of embellishments, repetitions, distractions. By now the lights had been turned down and the hotel shut to non-residents. The last staff member to appear had checked I had a front door key so that I could see my guest out myself. We asked for a taxi to be called and required it to wait.

'You've done the only thing you could do. And you've been wonderful, I think, you've been generous and understanding.'

'I never really thought of him as a boyfriend before he went away, but when he came back, I fell in love with him. I do love Larry, I do want him to be happy. And, well, it will be better for both of us if he's away from here for a while. I can't stand everyone criticizing him the way they do. The worst part is, I don't know, I can't help sometimes wondering if everyone's right.' She sighed. 'So I'm not all that generous, and I'm not really understanding. I want the time for myself as well as for him. I don't understand him at all.'

'Do *you* know that saying, the heart has its reasons that reason does not know? It sounds better in French.'

'Can you say it in French?'

I obliged. She repeated it. 'Not bad,' I said. 'I can tell you went to a good school. Look, why don't *you* go away with him for a while? Go and be a seeker *yourself*?'

'Oh, I'd love to. But I've got uni, and Mum, and I don't know, I'm scared I wouldn't like it, and also, I think Larry would be better on his own for a while. It's like he'll get himself together somehow and come back and make the right decision.'

If I mixed with young women her age in Sydney they had shaved heads and pierced nipples and thought it normal to be stripping, fighting or weeping at 3am in bars. Isabel accepted the principles of her upbringing. She was a conventional girl from a conventional home. She lived in a city from which those who sought an unconventional life fled. Isabel wasn't unaware of the liberation movements of the decade, even if they hadn't made much of a visible mark on this city. If you knew where to go there was even a punk group in Brisbane in the seventies, so I learnt later, but you had to know where to go, or want to. I don't suppose Isabel did. If the word feminism had come up she would have pointed out that she both liked men and believed in equality. She also loved the idea of being a wife and of having a newer, better version of her mother's life, a life that had caused Isabel little distress or criticism. They doubtless left certain subjects unexplored. Her mother might have guessed but would not have wanted to have confirmed that Isabel wasn't waiting for marriage to have some sexual experience. She was of her time, but casual sex was not thinkable, she wanted romance, love, commitment. She had every intention of keeping her own name, earning her own university degree, carrying her own in conversation –

of claiming the rights she wanted a right to. And she also wanted for herself what her mother wanted for her: a good marriage, a husband to be proud of, a husband who would be proud of her, realize she was an ornament, a prize, a trophy, a power in her own right. Isabel, as I said, was pretty, and possessed the confidence of young women who have grown up with the unconditional approval of well-off families, a circumstance that bestows an attractiveness mere prettiness doesn't come near. She was a prize all right. I loved it, I admit, that she sought me out to confide in me, to know what I thought, to see if I could advise her. Girls like her had never wanted to know me at that age, puny little sissy that I'd been. I hadn't been bold enough to speak the thoughts that at least would have made them notice me. But I had gaped at glamorous actresses in old movies on TV and dreamt of being surrounded by beautiful women who loved me for my mind. (Sadly for me I dreamt of boys who loved me for my body.)

'It's just that I don't understand Larry,' she said. 'I love him but I don't understand him. I don't understand what he really wants. If he wants to try things out for a while, all right, I know once he commits he'll be very true to that, I would trust him completely.'

'He probably doesn't understand himself,' I said. 'He probably couldn't tell you what he's looking for. And some experiences can have a very profound effect on you, sometimes it takes time to know just how profound. Seeing someone your own young age die would be one of those. Travelling, when you're young and free, will do that too. You have a whole new sense of who you are or might be, people see you only as you appear to them at that moment, they don't know who you know or where you went to school or where you got your clothes. They take you as they find you and you get a new sense of yourself.'

I said some of that or something like it to Isabel that night.

I don't want to make some kind of big mystery out of what happened to Larry on his first trip to India, exactly what happened to affect him so profoundly. I don't think he ever fully told anyone about the experience at the time. But many years later he did tell a man, Josh Rouvier, who Larry and I both knew, about the German boy who had died, and I'll tell you now, as best I can. I didn't know all this at this stage, but a novel has its own specific chronology.

Larry had begun smoking marijuana in the year before he dropped out of school and bought a ticket to India. It affected him greatly; he wasn't the kind of boy who got stoned and went driving round with the car radio volume at max looking for chocolate bars in the middle of the night, no, he was the kind of boy who felt an awakening sense of mysticism or wonder I suppose, who was enthralled to notice how everything shimmered and connected.

He longed to make sense the more senseless it was, sense and meaning had become puzzling and fascinating, he wanted to know how people had tried to express these states of wonder, and he began reading the Beat writers and then the Eastern writers they had turned to, began listening to modern jazz and Indian music and Philip Glass, so far all so standard.

Soon enough he decided, as Allen Ginsberg et al had decided before him, that he had to go to the source, he had to go to India.

In Bombay he soon hooked up with other young travellers like himself, with battered paperbacks of Hermann Hesse or Zen Buddhism in the pockets of their rucksacks, exchanging tips on cheap hotels and quality bhang. There was a German boy, Dieter, a fun-loving, adventurous guy who had already spent several months in India, had been to the mountains and the sea, had talked with sadhus and swamis, had been to small villages as well as other cities.

Dieter was popular with the young travellers, bringing people together, giving things away, joking about their anxiety and trepidation, and displaying no fear or disgust at the filth and poverty around them in their absurdly cheap rooms. They were mainly well-off young white people, the travellers, who had more or less easily raised the funds for a bit of mucking around in the East, where their sports were seeing just how stoned they could get and just how little they could pay for a room or a meal. Just being in India was spiritual, they told each other.

But Larry found that Dieter had another side, sober and serious, intense and intelligent, well-read and questioning. He could be silly and playful and switch to an intense mood, and attempt a discussion on the workings of karma. He noticed similar kinds of things, the leper without feet or hands who had been left on a cloth to beg in front of a bank, and spent his time singing. Singing! The way you had to learn, being here, to let things unfold, let things be tardy and unreasonable. The many shrines and icons that showed you that here, here people were so naturally part of a deep and ancient belief, one that had them singing even in adversity, one that had them seeing something different where Larry and Dieter saw adversity.

Dieter and Larry began to exchange books and to have long conversations about what they were reading, and about the religions of the land, about what they might believe or seek to believe. They exchanged their burgeoning snippets of knowledge about karma, maya, shakti. It must be rebirth that made sense and justice out of such capriciousness and extremes, they told each other.

The two of them went on the road together, travelling in rickety, crowded buses or rattling, crowded trains, learning to fall asleep as they bumped along with their heads on each others' shoulders. And all of this was flavoured with hashish, which was plentiful and cheap if you knew how to get it and Dieter knew how. They read Watts and Leary, they talked about ultimate reality, knowledge, experience. They pointed out to each other the beautiful smiles on people with few material goods, the truck drivers who'd cheerfully share their cigarettes after ten hours straight of hot, hard driving in dirty vehicles with ruined suspension. They found charm and beauty in the simplest things: Indian matchboxes, coconut shell spoons. Participation, they discovered, is what India wanted of them, to be with others and do what others did, not to stand apart and only observe. They had their foreheads smeared with ash in temples, they ate strange things at street stalls, they bought homespun shirts in markets.

They smoked some heroin.

And next time, Dieter pulled out a fit, a needle and a spoon, and showed Larry how to cook it up and how to inject himself with heroin, promising him the experience of nirvana.

Which it was.

He felt like Jesus' son. He wanted it again.

'Delhi, two days away,' said Dieter.

They reached Delhi and found a cheap hotel in a cluster of cheap hotels. Dieter disappeared for a while.

That night there was a party on the roof, with music not quite up to date, a random mix of cassette tapes that had survived various trips by fans of various bands. Various drugs were passed around. On the roof smoking and snorting took place in the open but Dieter beckoned to Larry and a couple of others he had sussed out and they went down into the dingy little room they shared. Dieter cooked up the heroin he'd bought that day. Larry tied a belt around his arm, pumped up the veins.

Dieter injected Larry, then the Swiss boy injected himself and his friend and then Dieter injected himself.

The needle went in, Dieter sat still for a moment, his face looking rapturous, no, stricken, and then he fell to one side.

The others, off their faces already, just looked at him for a while. It took them some time to work out what they had just seen.

Larry sat immobile, having shot to a state of sublime indifference, as they all did, as Dieter died in front of them.

He had just turned eighteen.

The day after my talk with Isabel, I went back to Sydney and soon after that I left Australia for eighteen months.

PART II

A thoroughly undesirable young man

Near the end of the following year, back in Sydney, I caught up with Elliott again. We talked about all kinds of things that have nothing to do with this story. And I remembered the events of the previous year, and asked after his sister, and Isabel, and Larry.

I think I'd heard before I went travelling that Larry had moved to Sydney soon after he had made his arrangement with Isabel, but Elliott had long lost touch with him.

'There was no point at all. I invited him to all kinds of things at first, but he never accepted, not once, he'd always say he didn't have the right clothes or he didn't go out at night or he didn't go out in the day. I gave up on him, he had no idea what some people would give for the same opportunities. I don't know what he was trying to prove. One time I asked him to lunch – he could have met Gordon H. Gordon – and he just said he never had lunch!'

I couldn't help smiling, to Elliott's displeasure.

'He's just a thoroughly undesirable young man,' Elliott pronounced.

Larry was simply a social failure as far as Elliott was concerned, and he never expected to see any more of him. Gordon H. Gordon by the way, was known for liking to find raw talent in the form of comely, intelligent youth and ripening it if it in any way could contribute to his advertising and media empire. In this town, where you breathed raw ambition, a lot of young men would give anything they had to be asked to lunch by Elliott to meet Gordon. I was amused at the thought of Larry's lack of interest. I remembered the way he looked and spoke and wondered how many of Gordon's protégés were of Larry's calibre.

A few weeks later I went up to the North Coast. I'd rented a place near Bangalow to write in and was working on the screenplay adaptation of my second play. One day I was doing something in Byron Bay – bank, post office, best baker – and there's some tall and tanned and young and lovely boy saying my name and it took me a moment but that's who it was, Larry. He looked fit and relaxed.

We asked each other what we were doing here, writing I said, reading he said, and I said why didn't he come and have lunch with me one day and he said all right.

'All right!' I repeated, teasing him. 'I thought you didn't have lunch!'

'Oh, you've seen Elliott,' he smiled. 'I'll have lunch with you tomorrow.'

Pleased but baffled

As usual I wrote all morning, then drove into town and met Larry, as we had arranged, at a café near the beach.

I don't know why he agreed to have lunch with me. It's not that it was a strained conversation, just not much of a conversation at all. When I asked him where he was staying, he was very vague about it. We talked about the area, how popular it was becoming – though with hindsight I can now remark that we had little sense of just what it would become.

Byron had long been a kind of mecca for the surfers and surf culture, of course, and nearby Nimbin, the location of a pop music festival about a decade earlier, had become a hippie and drug-tourist mecca. And those great houses near the unsurpassed beach you could once rent for so little, they were still to some extent available, though their owners were fast selling them or finding they had to logically and justly raise the rent. Managing the area's growth was already an inevitable topic whoever you got talking to. New kinds of people were scouting around looking into a new life here.

The lunch left me a little pleased but baffled. Larry didn't seem to want anything from me, and although he asked me quite a lot about my work and the house I was staying in, I had a sense it was to keep the focus of our talk away from him. He did say he'd been going to some yoga classes, and in 1981 or '82 this was pretty unusual, especially for a man. There was an elderly – Larry's word, but I gathered aged about seventy – woman who had been teaching for about twenty years and I might have got the impression that he had moved up here to do classes with her. Or he might have come to study with someone else and that's how he met her.

There was already a bit of a scene going on up here with the drop-out professionals starting new clinics, communes growing vegetables and workshopping their hierarchies in the surrounding hills, ageing surfers setting up factories or turning grazing land into fruit farms.

But I didn't get from Larry a clear sense of who he might be mixing with, of what his social life consisted. He didn't seem particularly lonely, not that you can always tell, but I wasn't sure what kind of people he was seeing.

I asked if he kept in touch with Isabel. He said of course, although they didn't write very often. He seemed to think that they would meet again soon, but I can't remember how I got this impression.

I didn't mind in the least that I had come out for no evident purpose but that of relaxed somewhat idle chat for the mere sake of it, with this sweet-natured, lovely looking, smart and unusual man, who, though so young, had had the poise to arrange our lunch so gracefully. We looked out upon the glorious beach in shaded comfort, being served lots of that fresh, light, delicious food they were getting known for around there. I wish I could remember more. We probably talked about where the salad vegetables were grown and which markets we liked. Where you could see old art movies in someone's disused cow shed, now a make-shift cinema saloon, bring your own cushion. Whether there had been magic mushrooms before cows had provided their breeding grounds, and how the deplorable ill-effects of beef and dairy farming were ever-diminishing with the changes we were seeing. The consequence of this lunch was a sense of my having a particular connection or relationship with Larry, apart from our mutual acquaintances.

I'd probably come into town the day before because I needed to break my routine a little, or enough errands had piled up to make it needful, so maybe I'd also been looking for a little fresh stimulation, a little change of scene, just a short one, a mood that would have you tootling over to Byron and glad to run into someone you wanted to have lunch with.

I wished him all good things, told him he could find me if he ever needed to, and ambled home with the windows down along what was in those days a slower road, no doubt my mind already on the pages I was coming home to.

It would only make Isabel obstinate

I wasn't in Sydney when Mrs Bradley and Isabel arrived the following autumn, so I am filling this in with a bit of help from imagination added to subsequent intelligence. I'm tempted to point out here that completely invented parts of my plays are the parts which have people claiming to be or know their originals. You find out a lot by simply imagining.

Elliott told me that he had made elaborate plans to take his sister and niece, when they came to town, to buy clothes and meet all kinds of people – in that order of course. Off they would go to Double Bay, to swish little boutiques of exclusive couturiers and imported fashions with in-house stylists.

And they would stay with him, at his flat on the water in Elizabeth Bay, there was plenty of room.

The day after Isabel and her mother arrived, ring ring at the door, who could that be, it's Larry.

Imagine the look on Elliott's face. What was *he* doing *here*? And not having phoned first.

Well, Isabel had asked him to meet them there. No one had told Elliott, and it didn't look as if Mrs Bradley really had known the extent of it, but Isabel and Larry had been keeping in touch, and had made plans to meet.

'We have an appointment at eleven, or we'd offer *you* coffee,' said Elliott pointedly.

'You must meet us for lunch, Larry, mustn't he, Uncle Elliott?' said Isabel.

'I've been given to understand that Larry doesn't do lunch,' said Elliott dryly.

'I'll do lunch tomorrow,' said Larry, so pleasantly that even Elliott couldn't go on being rude to him, and Larry, as I knew, could be so disarming, so unassumingly self-assured, unapologetic with no apparent arrogance. In his generous and showy way, Elliott at once began to make a reservation at some fashionable restaurant or brasserie and invited three or four other people to join them.

Without Isabel present, her mother and uncle discussed the situation. Gray, back in Brisbane, still wanted Isabel; he often called her, took her out sometimes, made it clear he was hers any time she said so. He had no guile, would never have played hard to get or tried to make Isabel jealous, not that it would have worked. No, Isabel was still waiting for Larry to come back to her. She had promised her mother that she would immediately break it off with Larry if after the two years he didn't immediately agree to marry her, but Mrs Bradley and Elliott had both said it was mad for Isabel to be waiting in Brisbane where she could end up stood up and have nothing to do. Sydney was the answer, Elliott had space for them, all the connections, and if Gray didn't work out either, he knew of a very eligible heterosexual-enough boy or two he would hook her up with.

But they hadn't factored in Larry also being in the same city, and Isabel so keen to see him.

'Don't think of trying to exclude Larry,' his sister warned him, 'it would only make Isabel obstinate.'

Elliott had now fashioned himself as a man who cared about his family, was close to his sister, took special care of his niece. He saw that his sister was right, he had seen Isabel display her will. He would have to plan his strategy more carefully.

Larry came to lunch, and though he was more casually dressed than anyone else – 'jeans' reported Elliott with a shudder, 'but at least a decent jacket' – he was considered by everyone there to be adorable. To think of all the people he could have met already through Elliott! He evidently had a charismatic personality thing going on, Elliott conceded, 'for some people; I never could see it I'm afraid.' Elliott placed him between a magazine features editor and a dealer in rare icons. People were still having long lunches then. It was considered heroic, in those days, rather than self-destructive or unthinkable, to keep lunch going until cocktail hour.

Elliott was nothing if not calculating, and his invitations and placements had very much taken into account the relentless and usually successful designs for seduction of Larry's lunchtime neighbours.

The editor and the dealer each paid Larry a lot of flirtatious attention, Elliott noticed, and, to his great gratification, each of them later told him they had discovered he strictly swung the other way. She said, 'Why didn't *you* tell me he only liked boys?' and he said, 'Why didn't *you* tell me he only liked girls?' This afforded Elliott considerable glee, of course, yet even more exasperation with his niece's not-quite-fiancé. In a town full of fiercely ambitious young people who'd have killed their grandmothers for chances like that, Larry, though perfectly sweet to everyone, had clearly not thought any of this was a remarkable opportunity nor gave any indication that he knew he was a good-looking boy where looks were a precious currency.

'So what do you think?' Elliott asked me when he related all these titbits, 'Is our Larry perhaps exploring even further fields? Is he dedicated to rough trade perhaps? Does he suck cock? What does he *do*?'

'Elliott dear,' I replied, 'I think he is one young man who spends his time on pursuits this town does not discuss.'

I'd like to think I said something wittier, but if I did I can't recall it.

I could not work out how calculating or even aware Larry was of the effect he had on people.

Anyway, Elliott's friends loved meeting the young people, Isabel looking fabulous in her new clothes. She was having the time of her life, starting to be asked everywhere, to more events than she could possibly attend. She was saying yes to as much as she could say yes to. But as it soon became clear, without Elliott having anything to do with it, neither she nor Larry seemed to have any intention of trying to include Larry into Isabel's new world.

More answers than questions

The day came when Isabel could no longer avoid her mother's questions. One afternoon she came home from a charity fashion show and her mother said, 'Sit down, have a cup of tea with me. I know it's not two years yet, but Larry must be giving you some kind of indication.'

'Not really,' said Isabel. She and her mother had been in Sydney for a month, and Isabel went out every single day. She'd seen Larry some of those days, not many of them. He encouraged her to have her own life, find her own version of the sparkling town, to accept all the invitations from Elliott's circle; he seemed to be busy with things of his own.

Apparently he had enrolled in some kind of course in philosophy, and was also going to a meditation class. He must have enrolled in other courses, as he seemed to go to a lot of classes.

Isabel was really enjoying her new life in Sydney, and I don't think it even occurred to her not to go to every party and opening she was asked to just because Larry had no interest in going, not that he was usually asked. They had agreed to put the question of their common future on hold, and Isabel, I imagine, was enjoying the fact that she was free and single and able to do what she wanted, and that Larry was close by and not apparently involved with anyone else.

The older ones didn't understand it, Isabel realized, but that was because they were old.

But Mrs Bradley had become increasingly puzzled, and decided it was time that something was declared.

'Elliott thinks Larry must be up to all kinds of things,' said her mother. 'Experimenting with drugs and alternative lifestyles, living with who knows what kind of people. What is he doing? It's as if he has some kind of double life.'

Isabel laughed. 'I know Uncle Elliott thinks it's all very unromantic and strange,' she said, 'but Larry and I are good friends, and it's all fine. Don't worry.'

Her mother and uncle didn't understand that while it was nice to see Larry sometimes it was also nice to see a new world without him, and that did not mean that he was not good enough. Isabel decided that Larry believed that couples did not have to do everything together, and that this was further proof of his perfection, and a further sign of the successful partnership ahead of them. And she would be perfectly happy to be seen out with him, anywhere.

And her mother and uncle, in spite of their concern over this, were pleased to see her thriving, become a woman, and partake of the pleasures of a great and beautiful city.

But her mother's words had awoken a new uneasiness in her. Or perhaps made her acknowledge an existing uneasiness.

'Larry,' Isabel said next time they met for one of their dates in Sydney. The weather had been glorious and they often met at the Quay, and took a ferry to Manly, or the zoo, or Watson's Bay. 'Larry, why haven't *you* shown me where *you* live?'

'It's just a little room,' he said. 'It's nothing much. It's not somewhere to go, I only sleep there.'

She thought there was another reason. They only met, and stayed, in public places. He took her hand sometimes, sometimes he put an arm around her, but mostly he didn't and even when he did it seemed fraternal rather than romantic. She thought that if he took her back to his place, one thing would lead to another, for he could never have forgotten how it had been, the two of them, what he had been to her, what she must have been to him, not something *you'd* want to give up. She was certain he wasn't sleeping with anyone else, she felt strongly she would know, perhaps at some time he had, perhaps in India, perhaps here, but he was like her, sex was not a casual game. They got on as well as they always had, their compatibility was undeniable, the way they could talk about anything at all, it never had to be about anything much, the way they could be silent together. He liked hearing about the art gallery openings and the first nights at the theatre and the charity luncheons she was being taken to, the famous people she had been introduced to, what she was finding out about Sydney, the things you heard that explained a lot or the things you'd never have guessed.

'My Sydney is different,' he had said once, and she knew it was, but she had seen him at the lunch, and he was the same Larry, everyone liked talking to him, he could get on with anyone, he would always be able to have his own interests and still be charming in her world. She hadn't set out to test him but when she had seen him at that lunch, getting on so well with everyone, she thought, *you've passed that test.*

'I want to see where you live,' Isabel said.

They took the bus – Larry always walked or took public transport. It didn't mean she had to, but she went along with him for now, he always made it interesting, pointing out people and buildings she wouldn't have noticed, and she did get to see the kinds of clothes worn by people who couldn't afford to take taxis everywhere but still had interesting style, and who would be copied by designers who got their inspiration from kids on the street who shopped in op shops or made their own clothes.

She and Larry reached a row of large terrace houses. As they stopped an elderly man stuck his head out of the ground-floor window to see who was there.

Larry opened the front door that hadn't been painted in many years and they went up the stairs. He opened another door and he hadn't been kidding, he lived in one room. He shared a bathroom down the hall, she didn't want to know who with. She knew he could see it in her face, the shock, just how basic it was, a single bed, a table and chair, a wardrobe.

'I told you,' he said gently.

'You can afford better than this.'

'I don't need anything more. It's handy, I can walk to all the libraries I use, and everywhere else I go.'

She walked over to his table. Two or three small books and notebooks sat on it, and a large volume she examined curiously.

'It's a Sanskrit dictionary,' he said. 'I've been given permission to go to a lecture series on the Vedas at Sydney University.'

She sat on the chair and he sat on the bed. 'And where are *you going* with all this?'

'It's the path, not the destination,' he said, and smiled at her expression. 'All this might lead to knowledge,' he offered.

'What will you know that you don't know now?'

'That's what I'm trying to learn.'

'When are you coming back to Brisbane?'

'I don't know, I haven't thought about it.'

'I don't *get* it, Larry.'

He only looked at her. He had no resentment nor defiance, not even sadness. His attitude to her remained tender and she didn't get that either: he wasn't trying to persuade her, win her to his way of thinking. He seemed to think they could go on, side by side, although their lives were becoming so different.

'Tell me,' she pleaded, 'what you're trying to do.'

He said, making the effort to find a true answer for her sake, 'I want to know whether God is just an idea, and why there is evil, and what my soul is, and if death is the end of us, I want to know what prayer is and the way we should live.'

'Larry, if there were answers to those questions we'd all know them.'

'Maybe,' he said, 'but maybe the point is not the answer but to go on asking. There are more answers than questions.'

'Then what,' she asked, prickling tears of vexation in her eyes, 'is the *point*?'

'I also want to know, more than anything, why some people have found answers that they find satisfying, convincing, answers they can live by.'

'I don't know,' she said, 'it all seems kind of, well, juvenile. Most adults can put all that aside and get on with living, having the best life they can have.'

'I'm lucky to have enough money to live on, and I don't have to put it all aside, I can focus on it, and that's what I'm choosing to do.'

'You could have a lot more money, and do so many more things, and you can always do some reading or study in your spare time.'

'All my time is spare, and Isabel, I am so grateful for that, I feel I have to use it well.'

'What if,' she asked, making her best point, 'what if everyone thought like *you*?'

'Everyone doesn't think like me. You don't think like me.'

'No, I really don't. I don't want to stay in cheap places, in small bare rooms and not even your own bathroom.'

'I travelled in India like that, and had a ball.'

'I want to have babies, Larry, you used to want that too.'

'We can take them with us. I saw people travelling with their children. We can teach them to read and they'll learn more about the world and other people than staying...staying in one place and going to schools with uniforms, lining up and saluting the flag.'

'Children cost money! Honestly, you ought to find out how much it costs to have a baby. It all costs a packet. It's just how things are, Larry, you say you're lucky to have enough to live on, I say we're lucky to have the opportunities to create a really good life. We could live in really nice places and our kids could go to really good schools, and we can still travel.'

'Isabel, I don't want to go on two-week holidays with itineraries, I want to stay in places for as long as we feel like being there, and get to know people who live there, and find out from other travellers about new places to explore.'

'Well, I just don't want to know a lot of unwashed drop-outs who just can't make it, there's nothing to talk about with people like that. Oh,' she sighed, 'you think I'm awful.'

'No, I understand what you're saying.'

'See, if you were staying poor and studying because you had a plan and you were just starting out, I'd support you, I'd be there for you, but I have to know you're going somewhere.'

'I can't tell you where I'm going, because that's what I want to spend my time finding out.'

'And meanwhile I do what, wash our clothes in a river?'

'You have no idea how interesting people are, people *you* meet on the road, people from all over the world.'

'I love meeting interesting people! I'm meeting interesting people all the time right now.'

'Yes, dressed like that, in clothes by famous designers, meeting people the world already has told *you* are the interesting ones.'

'And *you* want to go slumming; admit *you* feel superior because *you* don't *have* to be in the cheap hostel or local bus, *you* can leave it all any time *you* want to.'

Then they sat silent for a while in his little room, some traffic noise penetrating. There had not been any hostility or rejection of the other in their argument, but there was no way to defend the idea of making a life together from such inharmonious desires.

'Does this mean,' Larry then asked, 'that *you*'ll only marry me if I come back to Brisbane?'

She couldn't answer at once. She wanted him so much, she wanted to leap onto him as he sat on his abstemious bed, she wanted to make him say he would do anything for her, but after all they had just said she wasn't sure she really should.

'That's what it means,' she said sadly. 'Larry, believe me. I'm not going to throw my life away. I know we're still *young* but I also know we'll never meet anyone we will ever feel the same way about. You want to know the meaning of life, for most people the meaning of life is to find the right person to share *your* life with, and how lucky were we to find each other that early, to know each other so well, no one will ever replace that. We've got the same friends and everyone wants to have *you* back. We'll be able to come back here to Sydney and go overseas and we'll be able to have a big house where people can come and stay, we could have the best life there is. Most of the world would give anything to have what we have and can have. How can it be right to throw all that away? How can the best way to live be to turn *your* back on everyone who loves *you* and wants to support *you*? How can it be right to reject everyone who has cared for *you*?'

'Isabel,' he said gently, 'I can't go back to Brisbane and do that job. It would be…like dying, a kind of, I don't know, letting myself down, not living up to my ideals…'

'Oh, what does that mean!' she broke in, suddenly exasperated. 'That's just so self-indulgent. It doesn't mean anything.'

'Listen to me, I'm trying to tell you the reason–'

'That's not reason! That's completely unreasonable! If *you* loved me, if you did really love me, *you* wouldn't do this.'

And all that remained was the sad conclusion that they were no longer engaged to be married.

She wondered if that's what he had really wanted, to force this issue, to make her break up with him.

'No,' he said, 'what I really wanted was for *you* to want what I want.'

After a while she said, 'I suppose I'd better give this back to *you*,' and began tugging at the antique ring they had chosen together.

'Keep it,' he said, 'please. To show that we'll always be friends.'

They went back down and as they went out the front door the ground-floor window opened again. Isabel turned and waved to the old guy. 'I don't think,' she remarked, 'that that old sticky-beak would believe we've only been talking.'

You're well out of it

'You look great.'

'You look wonderful.'

'You are the most beautiful girl in the room.'

Yes, thought Isabel, exultant, this is who I am, this is where I am meant to be.

The party Elliott gave at his apartment that night was full of people in taffeta and raw silk, drinking chilled vodka and champagne and gossiping gaily about scandals and triumphs in theatre and politics. She thought it was fabulous, she adored being there, she was thrilled at how she was treated. People seemed to her wonderfully sophisticated and civilized, and if some of them were pretentious, well that was wonderful too, they were pretentious in the interests of being stylish and interesting and fun. To Elliott's friends Isabel appeared fresh and lovely; she was the youngest person there and even those not much older than her felt worn and strained at the sight of her luminous skin and shining eyes and expression of unaffected delight.

She wore a rustling, knee-length skirt made of layers of black silk taffeta gum leaves over a black lace leotard and black satin ballet shoes. She moved like a dancer, she was the new girl in town, everyone wanted to know her.

'You make us feel so old and decadent,' said a woman in a silver organza gown. 'You don't even smoke, do *you*? Come here, Maggie, just look at this girl's skin. Don't ever go out in the sun, will *you*? Are you an actress?'

A well-known photographer whirled around the room snapping the decisive moment, ignoring those posing for him and clicking where people were momentarily unselfconscious as they laughed or drank or munched crudités and tiny quiches, or looked sideways at someone.

There was a group of boys dressed in tight vinyl frocks and fish-net tights, slashed and safety-pinned, in massive platform-soled shoes, green and pink Mohawks plumed on their scalps. They'd been paid to appear and stood together in a corner snarling and swearing, then mimed to some punk music. Later an opera singer performed an aria and a dancer did a dance of the seven veils.

Isabel thought for a moment of Larry's shabby little room and how indifferent he would be to everything she thought glorious and gratifying here, and knew she had done right.

Much later, when everyone else had gone, Isabel said happily, 'That was a fabulous party, Uncle Elliott, those punk drag boys were hysterical, and that *Vogue* woman is going to send me a ticket to that new Dance Company show.'

In which the two lead dancers had a special something between them not only on the stage, Elliott felt moved to reveal.

'I didn't get a chance to ask you,' said her mother, 'how was your day?'

'Good,' said Isabel casually. 'I went for a walk with Larry and we made a big decision, we called off our engagement.'

'You broke up?' asked Mrs Bradley, suddenly alarmed in case Isabel's evening-long good spirits would suddenly turn to hysterical grief. 'Are you all right?'

'Of course I am.'

'You broke up?' said Elliott. 'Larry might have called me, he was going to come to a sit-down lunch on Friday, who am I going to get in his place at this late stage?'

'Larry will still come,' said Isabel, 'it's only our engagement that's over, we're still friends.'

'You intend to keep seeing him?' asked her astonished mother, looking closely at her. 'What's that on your finger? Aren't you giving that back? I don't know, it's all very unconventional.'

'Maybe,' said Isabel. 'But not as unconventional as staying engaged to him would have been.'

'I'll tell you what I think, I think you're well out of it, Isabel,' said her uncle.

Marriage is a serious matter

A couple of weeks after that I was back from my travels and spending some time in Melbourne, and so far I knew nothing of what I've just told *you*.

Some mutual friends of Elliott's and mine told me that Elliott had just arrived in Melbourne as well.

'Taking his sister and niece shopping,' said our friend, 'being Eleanor Lavish and enjoying a climate that needs a leather jacket.'

We were reconnected. Elliott rang me, he wanted me to arrange good theatre tickets for him. He told me what I had already heard, that Mrs Bradley and Isabel were with him, he'd brought them down to spend a week shopping. He'd certainly thrown himself into the brother-and-uncle role.

Elliott asked me to lunch with his sister. Isabel was otherwise occupied and we talked about her a lot of the time. She already had a couple of beaux here in Melbourne, and was out that day with the heir to a cleaning products fortune or something.

'She is very much in demand. Princess Isabel,' said Elliott proudly, 'is taking the town by storm. She's been asked out by a promising young stockbroker and by the *Cleo* centrefold. I tell her to have as much fun as she can while she's *young*. Just be careful, I tell her.'

'I hope she doesn't need to be too careful,' said Louisa. As is often the case they were using me as a third party to rehearse their differences over what they thought Isabel should be doing.

Elliott had brought them to Melbourne to put an end to Isabel's connection with Larry. Apparently she had gone on seeing him in Sydney and couldn't tell them why, only that he was her friend and here they were in the same city.

They found these excursions strange enough to be worrying. How on earth could Isabel get serious about anyone else if she were still going on endless harbour cruises with Larry? They weren't sure if it really was only a case of manners these days having become so different. Either way, it was a great relief to them that Isabel seemed quite delighted when the Melbourne proposal had been put to her.

'I think she must realize she needs to really pay attention to the options we are looking at here,' said Elliott.

'Oh, it was odd behaviour,' said Louisa, 'and I don't think she quite understood herself, or she would have told me, I think she would try to tell me. But it is lovely to look around down here, and the clothes are rather special, and Isabel has met some really interesting people.'

'She's a beautiful, smart, educated girl,' said Elliott, 'and it's such an asset to a career to have a wife like that.'

'Marriage is a serious matter,' said his sister; 'we want her to be happy.'

'It is a serious matter,' said Elliott, 'we also want her to be set up for life.'

We were in the lobby of the Windsor, finishing our coffee, when a young woman in fabulous clothes, radiant and confident, came towards us – that's what registered a split second before it registered that it was Isabel. I hadn't seen her for quite a while, remember, and was knocked out. She had taken to wearing designer clothes since her time in Sydney, although we may pause to notice that every garment on earth in some sense was designed by someone. I mean designer, not merely designed, and of course we were all noticing how Design was everywhere. Designer clothes were as if made for Isabel, and though I'm no expert on fashion I could tell that she had enough innate sense of style to have started putting things together in a distinctive way of her own. She had freshness and glamour, very fabulous combo.

'I hope you'll allow me to take the three of you to the opening night of my play,' I said, knowing I could get a couple of extra tickets, and that the advance publicity for the play, and the promise of an extravagant production, ensured that having seen it first would be negotiable kudos.

I do believe that the women were about to say how lovely that would be, when Elliott began saying how they'd have to check the date and how much was going on, everyone was in town, and so on. But after sufficient demonstration that I had better not presume further availability, we agreed that they'd love to come.

'We're inundated,' confided Elliott, 'you're lucky to get us so soon.'

'I am indeed,' I said, 'and you may be lucky enough to meet the director, who happens to have a pair of genuine Tibetan monastery doors for sale.'

'Oh, I have procured genuine Tibetan monastery doors already, didn't I tell you, these ones are particularly rare.'

I said, 'Oh, I only thought if you didn't want them you'd know someone who did.'

Show him to act so snobby to me now.

Elliott had to put up with me, because Louisa and Isabel seemed keen on the idea of the theatre. And I was only too glad to have someone with me who hadn't been involved with the production all along.

But Elliott managed to remain lofty. 'I no longer concern myself with the desires of others in this transient world,' he said, as if he had never needed a commission in his life. 'Some people are beginning to notice what some of us had known for quite some time.'

You've done right for you

After the night at the play, I didn't see them for the next couple of weeks. I was working and, well, I was seeing someone, someone who kept me in Melbourne, and kept me from thinking very much about other people.

Elliott had been gloriously extravagant, wanting to dazzle the women with the something else of Melbourne that you had to admit Sydney didn't have, so they were having fun dressing up in a more European kind of city, and I saw them next at a gallery opening.

I thought we'd just have a quick chat and keep moving about the room, but Isabel made sure the other two had moved on and she turned back to gaze upon another canvas or two at my side.

'Remember that time in Brisbane? When we talked in the lobby of your hotel, and I had a milkshake, and they were cleaning up and turning off lights around us? That was so nice of you. I've never forgotten how good it was for me to talk with you. I would love to have a talk with you again,' Isabel said disarmingly, having waited for a moment where no one else could hear.

'Name a day, and I'll take you to lunch.'

I wonder why she did seek me out. She really did want to know what I thought, and gave me the impression that she would consider whatever I said, take advice from me. She was making big decisions about the direction of her life, and I guess she looked at me and at her uncle and the differences between us as she considered her options and made her allegiances. There were plenty of older women around who were also interested in Isabel because she was Elliott's niece and also because of that eager, vibrant, fresh quality of hers. It was a competitive little world, Elliott's world of socialites and the movers-

and-shakers, as people said then of people of influence and initiative, and of the wannabes, and Isabel was astute enough to perceive that women who offered to mentor her and train her, to make her a stylist or a journalist or a production assistant, also wanted to score her, to acquire her as an asset, and so, as she was being asked to serve their interests first and not necessarily her own, she wanted disinterested guidance. And she had seen that I would not say no.

It is a truth universally acknowledged that the best asset for a bright ambitious girl is a gay uncle, so if you really want to succeed, have two gay uncles. I was an alternative Elliott.

Isabel's ambitions were always going to veer towards Elliott's own ambitions for her. Still she was curious about, even attracted to, my own take on things. I'm trying here to see what Isabel wanted from me. In my own way I had a very good life. I travelled quite often. My work was pretty well recognized – my plays were produced, I published other things, I did pretty well out of them, my name was known, she'd know all this, and the Hollywood adaptation was by now in the works. I had begun my literary career seen as a writer from and for a gay ghetto, but eventually my plays began to be produced by mainstream theatres for mainstream audiences. This of course brought about particular criticisms, with the gay press often accusing me of not having enough gay characters and the mainstream press sniffing at my inherent limitations in depicting non-gay characters or at my supposed coded messages. But all of that only attested to the fact that my plays were produced and noticed and enjoyed. Writers are by nature dissatisfied and, though it didn't entirely satisfy me, I took some pleasure in knowing how many people came to my plays and even how envious and disparaging some of the literary people were about it. If my plays had run for three nights in some backyard toilet with six people watching they might have said they were good. I didn't have Elliott's wealth or his contacts, but there were people Isabel wanted to meet that Elliott didn't know as well as I did. She might have wondered about the doors that were closed to him and open to me.

Isabel knew very well what her mother thought, but she didn't want her mother's life, she wanted to really live. Isabel was of her era, even if she tended to the conservative. She looked very contemporary, with her great haircuts and clothes; she liked her generation's music, whatever it was then; the occasional recreational substance was not unknown to her; she felt she had a right to sleep with a man if she wanted to (though she didn't feel exactly free to do so, with her condition of romance and commitment); she had done her Arts degree and was open to the right job: is this what makes a young woman *of her time*? Still she wanted to marry, she might not have said that a woman's business was finding the right husband but she had known from the earliest age that she wanted to marry, and marry well, just as I had always known, it seemed to me, that I would be a writer.

It might have been because I was a writer that she sought me out. Sometimes people will say, just as Masha says to Trigorin in *The Seagull*: I'm telling you all this as a writer. You can use it. Or people suppose you are not going to judge them, that shock or disapproval are not in your nature. Of course people told Chekhov things because he was a doctor, but these days you don't need to be a doctor to have someone feeling they must share with you their most intimate experiences. I'll listen to anyone for a while. In general I like to hear people's stories. Anyway, I don't recall that Isabel ever did mention my occupation as a reason for her confidence.

'So what did you want to talk about?' I asked, as if I couldn't guess.

I'd proposed a drive out of town and took her to the Dandenong Ranges. We had to pass through an urban wasteland of furniture warehouses and used car yards, and eventually began to wind our way up through ferny bushland and tall trees, and past several self-consciously rustic cafés where you could have tea with the obligatory scones and cream. It was horrible weather, grey with a constant drizzle, but I'd hired a good car and we went along steadily. We began speaking on the drive there, stopped to inspect a so-called antique shop, and finally reached our destination, resuming our talk when we were served our meal. I had imagined lunch under the trees in the pleasant garden, listening to bell birds and smelling the gumtrees, but the rain kept us indoors. However, it did help create an atmosphere of intimacy.

The day was the turning point in our relationship. Or, I think, it was where our own independent friendship really began. It marked a kind of commitment I made to her, to be her other uncle, to be her confidant, to speak frankly to her.

Isabel told me all that had happened since I had last privately spoken with her. That's how I've been able to write all this. I simply listened, making encouraging noises, asking the occasional question, sometimes steering her back to a point from which she had digressed.

And when she had done, she asked me, 'What do you think about it all?'

I said, 'Larry, with his so-called mucking around, seems to do more work than a lot of people with jobs.'

Doing the kind of work Larry does, the reading, the study, the thinking, having the desire and the drive and the dedication and the discipline to do it, can't be explained by the motivations that make most people choose a certain career, take a certain job.

'I understand that, being a writer,' I told her.

'But you make money from what you do,' she said, 'you get recognition, you give something to others.'

'I didn't when I began, and there were no guarantees that I ever would. I've been lucky, it took a while but not as long as it does for a lot of other people. But I could have been working away for the last twenty years without my plays being produced, or I could think myself lucky to sell a few thousand copies of a novel like most writers. But I would have kept on going, even if it meant living like a poor student, like Larry does, taking odd jobs to keep myself going.'

Well, you might say that was easy to say and maybe it was.

I meant it, but I also found it hard to imagine how I could have kept on going if no one had been interested in my work – the right interest, the right people. Plays aren't completed until they are produced, until actors act them and audiences watch them. I had learnt how audiences respond by having audiences to respond to my work.

I had observed the lives and careers of other artists. I knew that those who never made much money or got much respect for what they did were sometimes unable to go on.

Some of them had others to support, and though they might have suffered penury on their own, could not ask partners or children to suffer deprivation along with them. There's an opinion around that a real, true artist will never put anything or anyone before their work but this is as unreliable as any other universal generalization. Artists can also be faithful, loyal, tactful and unselfish to people close to them, even if, according to some, they will thus betray their art, and they can be as prone to unrewarding obsessions and self-defeating choices.

Some succumb to bitterness in disappointment, some have to work at other jobs that take over their lives or drain them. And some kind of success on the other hand often does work to make a writer or other artist more productive, whether through its material or morale-boosting effects. That is, of course, if it doesn't destroy them with the new weight of expectation.

So, while I might have had some sympathy with Larry's ability, or insistence, on doing work that brought no such rewards, I was confronted with the likelihood that I might not have been able to do the same.

We returned, Isabel and I, to the subject in hand, what happened to Larry in India, why it had had its effect on him.

'I really want to understand him better,' Isabel said.

It is difficult for a lot of, maybe most, people to understand anyone for whom economic benefit and the approval of the majority are not part of their motivations.

'Something happened to him in India,' she said. 'I know some friend he met there died, and I know that must be awful, but that doesn't explain it.'

'I don't know India well,' I said, 'but I know how much it affects people. The extremes of poverty and wealth there are, well, they are very extreme, and none of it is hidden away. If you're a young Westerner from a comfortable background, it can be a very alarming experience, to be the foreigner, to see lepers and beggars on the street, not to share the cultural references and common knowledge around you, to find everyday life so unfamiliar and unpredictable.'

'Well, all right, *yes*,' said Isabel, 'but what is Larry trying to do now? He won't say, or only says *mucking around* then goes and does more courses than any uni student I've ever known. I think he doesn't know how to tell me, and I can't really work it out.'

'Maybe he wants to find God,' I said.

She made a sound, a tutting and a sigh. Finding God, it implied, was something you ought to keep to yourself and was insufficient reason to cause so much vexatious perplexity.

'He's never even said he believes in God,' she said. 'He doesn't go to church or anything. I haven't gone myself, not for years.'

'Is God found in churches?' I said, not really asking.

'How does a person *find God*?' she said impatiently.

'Oh, I have no idea, I only thank God I'm an atheist.'

'Are you really?' she asked intently.

'Yes,' I said firmly, 'always have been.'

'I've never really talked about all that with Larry, a bit when we were really young, before he went away, we didn't have any real convictions. I still sometimes went to church with Mum, he didn't.'

We had a little chat about how irrelevant and unsatisfying church-going seemed to us, and yet how curiously it had never died out as a cultural practice. Its appeal, we surmised, was in the sense it gave to some people that there was an ultimate meaning to life and that it could be known. Or that in attending they were doing one good, right thing.

'Some people think there is such a thing as a meaning of life, out there, something you can find,' I said.

'You don't?'

'I think that to be human is to make meaning. That's what humankind is, a meaning-making animal.'

'So there's no meaning?'

'Of course there is, all the meaning that has been made.'

I don't know if that's what she had to stop and think about. After a while she said, 'What I don't get, I do love Larry, and I just know he loves me. But he's been making choices that mean we won't be together...'

'Here's one thing I know,' I said, 'given to me by years of being around. You can love someone and not be able to make a life with them. You can love someone and want quite different things. People can love each other and still find themselves growing apart. People can love each other the same way for a while and then one of them begins to love in a different way.'

Ah, love, I had given it some thought as who hadn't. When you tell someone about love you are telling yourself. Of course, I maybe should have just told her bluntly that Larry clearly didn't love her, or not enough.

'I know,' she said slowly, 'that all of this makes Larry the good guy and me the bad guy. He's the one with the ideals and I'm the materialistic one. Mum thinks I've made the right choice, and so does Uncle Elliott of course. What do you think?'

'What does it matter what I think?'

'You're not really involved, you're objective but you know us all, please tell me what you think.'

'I think you've done right for you,' I said.

'Yeah, so why don't I feel better about it?'

'Why don't you feel better about it?'

'I know I did right, but I can't help feeling people would think if I really loved Larry, if I was a good person I'd go with him.'

'What about if Larry really loved you?'

'I know he does, but men always are the ones who decide what kind of life you're going to have, that's how it's always been. That won't ever change, not for a very long time.'

It kept raining outside, not heavily but enough to make it nice to stay inside. There was a big couch near an open fire, and we sat there for a while, looking into the crackling flame, drinking coffee and eating chocolate desserts.

I wasn't sure she was right, and I could have said that things never would change if all women thought like her. But Larry had shown there was something he wanted more than to marry Isabel, even if it was a way of life that did not seem well thought out to her.

'There are so many ways to love a person, so many kinds of love,' I insisted.

'Are there? Can *you* love someone even if you get annoyed and infuriated?'

'Oh, *yes*,' I said.

'No, I don't know,' she said at last. 'I think if *you* really love each other *you* want to be together, and *you'll* compromise to do it, because we all have to compromise. And I thought he'd do what I wanted to do because basically he's weak.'

'How can *you* say Larry's weak? He's gone and done exactly what he wants to, with no one encouraging him to do it.'

'I could always make him do whatever I wanted. He was always like that in our group back home, he just did what everyone else wanted to do.' She looked at me a moment, then said, 'I'll tell *you* something, but don't be shocked.'

'I severely doubt *you* could shock me.'

'Well, *your* book shocked me! So I can't tell *you* anything worse than that!'

I remembered saying to Larry that time I'd seen him in the library in Brisbane that nothing shocked me, but it isn't true. People think because of what I've written, and seen, that I can't be easily shocked, but in fact I am shocked all the time.

'Well,' said Isabel, 'I got Larry to spend a last night with me in Sydney. We got tickets to the Cold Chisel concert, it was fabulous, and went to Kinsellas afterwards. He looked hot, too. He really gets into it if *you* can get him to go out to things, I don't know why he doesn't do it more. We were in a great mood, and drank champagne. My plan was to stay with him that night, to seduce him. I know I could have done it. We had kind of decided not to sleep together again till we got married, but once…before he went away…it was really lovely and special for both of us. But back then, we weren't ever able to spend the night together, living at home, being so young. Then, you know, after he came back, we were engaged and we said we would wait…I thought that was sweet, and I thought we'd be married soon and have a honeymoon. I was planning it. Anyway I knew I could get him to go to bed with me, and I had it all worked out. I looked great that night. I would later say I was pregnant. And he'd have to marry me, and everything would work out.'

'And…?'

'I couldn't do it. I just couldn't do it to him. We had a bit of a cuddle, then said goodbye.'

'Do you regret it?'

'I don't know, yes and no, I didn't even consciously decide. I just didn't go through with it. Might have been my higher self taking over.'

'Maybe.'

Before we parted that day, I said my piece about the effects of time, that time changes things so very much. When you're young and in love you think you'll never get over it, but eventually you do. All kinds of wounds are healed by time, and they are healed by distance, too. The quickest way to get over love-gone-wrong is to go somewhere new. So enjoy Melbourne, go to everything.

I was going to take my own advice, as it happened, and was making plans to go away again. I only saw Isabel a couple of times more, among crowds at parties, and not long after, I was packed and departing.

PART III

For ten years after this...

For ten years after this I saw neither Isabel nor Larry.

Every now and then I'd see Elliott. As usual we'd run into each other at things when we were both in town, or sometimes have called each other first. We'd have lunch, usually with other people as well, but we'd always go and have a huddle *a deux* and run through the names we asked each other about – how about X and have you seen X and are X and X still together – and once in a while I'd get around to asking after Isabel, and suddenly get a vivid flash of her. Of course being gorgeous at twenty-one doesn't mean it'll last, but apparently she was looking good.

All the news about Isabel was good.

But as for Larry, Elliott was dismissive. 'Well, I don't really think so,' he'd say, if I asked if he ever heard about Larry, as if a bit affronted that I would think he would know or even remember such a loser. 'I have no idea what kind of world or what Larry mixes in. I doubt we would cross paths.' I think Elliott could never get over the fact that Larry hadn't tried to impress him. People showed off for him and he wanted that from them at least.

I spent time with a fair few people in Sydney, and in other places, that Elliott would have dismissed similarly. But I never came across Larry anywhere either.

I don't know that I thought I necessarily would. It would have depended. He could have turned up among the young students or artists I met, or – though I still didn't know it was as likely – among the young trades workers you also come across, or, who knows the way people change, he could have turned up having turned to anything you might think of, wearing a suit.

Or maybe there was no way he would turn up. There were, now, suddenly and increasingly, many young men, men of all ages, who were no longer around. Someone you hadn't seen a while, someone you had once had not so long ago had those sweet times with, talked with, danced with, looked at things together, shared what you've felt like, or nothing but smiled at one time. You found out that they were very sick, that they were dead. These were the plague years, the advent of the new disease. There wasn't a cause, there wasn't a cure. There were scary rumours and bad news.

Many years later, Larry told me what he did those years. But I'll tell you now.

No, I'll tell you when I get around to the time I finally met him again and he told me his version of the decade in which none of us had seen him. A reader should not know more than the narrating character does. Not even a narrating character who is the author. Not even if the author is veiled in fiction.

No, I'll tell you now. You know I didn't know all this yet, but I think you should know some of it now.

He told me so much, eventually, anyway, that I had better start recounting it now.

We are all accustomed to multiple chronologies. I was just watching a television show, I suppose you'd call it a documentary, with scripted 're-enactments', plus a voice-over narration, plus present-day interviews with the people who'd been involved, plus archival material – at least three time frames in a mainstream prime-time 'current affairs' show. So here it is, in some sense a flash-forward (future Larry relating this), a flash-back (what past Larry had been up to) and the present moment in which I take a breath, recall all the details available to me and begin:

Not long after we had all last seen him, Larry got work as a builder's labourer.

He found a job on a construction site on the Gold Coast, working on a big new shopping mall that, in an irony unavailable to anyone at the time, was one of the projects making Gray Maturin rich.

It was hard physical work, dirty and at times dangerous. Larry carted bricks, swept floors, lugged bags of tiles, hauled pots of paint and lengths of timber, and carried everyone's garbage to the skips. He sweated, he stank, he ached, he was covered in grime, he took orders.

If he had thought it was work that might leave his mind free, he soon found that there was little time for any reflection or contemplation. He helped erect slabs for the cement pourers, he worked with chippies and sparkies and plumbers and roofies, he learnt to keep out of their territorial disputes and the bickering, and even fights, that arose when one man's work, or tardiness, impeded another's. He turned up to work every day for a couple of long seasons, and earned his reputation for being a good worker, reliable and strong.

'Why did you do that?' I asked him.

'So many people had been telling me that work gave meaning to life, that everyone had to work. I wanted to find out if that were true.'

'Usually work-as-meaning means work best suited to your abilities and likes.'

'That's what this was. You mightn't think it to look at me but I've always been pretty strong, and liked the outdoors and physical exercise.'

He didn't ever talk any more about his motives in choosing this kind of work. I wondered if he might have wanted to prove something, to Isabel, to everyone, to prove that if he chose not to get a job it wasn't because he was afraid of hard work or unwilling to do it.

Maybe self-fulfilment, a career path, networks, opportunities and all that were part of a labourer's job but not necessarily, and the first thing that kind of work was, was *work*: toil, exertion, drudgery. Occupational health and safety was not conscientiously considered and people did get hurt in industrial accidents of varying severity that you weren't meant to make a fuss about. Things dropped from heights, supporting structures gave way, back muscles tore.

There's a kind of romance bookish types have had with labouring man, a romance about the most basic labour, and then there's the fetishized look of muscles and tatts, work boots and blue singlets. I'm not immune to it, but I do realize that it's largely a fantasy, and we want our Village People hard-hat types to be musical when it's after hours.

At 'smoko' three times a day the men stopped for tea and food, and Larry got to know his workmates a little. Some of them had worked together a long time, while there were always some who were new to the site, and the rotation of short-timers. Some were supporting families, some were supporting habits, some took pride in doing a job well, some did as little as they could get away with. Once Larry had been around long enough for anyone to have an opinion on him, he was deemed an all-right bloke; he didn't mind giving someone else a hand, moving something out of the way or carrying a box for them, even if he didn't have to. Sometimes, if there were spare moments, Larry would take a book out of his pocket and find a quiet corner to read a page or two while he could.

I wondered if taking on this job had more to do with his break-up with Isabel. It might have been harder on Larry than he'd been prepared for. While he had been determined on following his own path and not doing what everyone wanted him to, and while he had accepted, finally, that this meant losing Isabel, he might not have realized how final that would be. He might have wanted it all, freedom to follow his passions or his whims and also a devoted partner, marriage to the childhood sweetheart he never stopped loving. Many of us want to have what doesn't go together: freedom *and* commitment, safety at home *and* adventure abroad, vanilla *and* chocolate…

Larry might also have been here, working as a labourer, to test whether the esoteric stuff he'd been reading – the old yoga texts, the volumes of philosophy – was, as some had suggested, all right for the comfortably off, the 'middle class'. He had heard people say that all that kind of thing was an indulgence, a luxury. Isabel had accused his search of being 'self-indulgent', as if she, and everyone, believed that he was doing no one else any good. Being part of the work that created a massive new building made for the happy business of commerce and social interaction had the satisfaction of a tangible result.

Anyway, Larry began to notice one of the other men there, an older man, who, he eventually found, had been an immigrant from Jordan via several years in Germany, and, like Larry, worked hard, kept to himself, and was seen sitting alone with his mug of tea reading a book in his breaks.

He was far less inclined to interact with anyone else, but after a while he'd look over curiously to see what Larry was reading, and finally they began to talk.

He was reading something called *The Aquarian Conspiracy,* while Larry was reading something by Castaneda.

They began tentatively to talk about the ideas in their books: about paradigm shifts and transformation of the self, about the limitations of words and the limitless power of the mind, about new discoveries in consciousness and physics, about sorcery, process, new ways of healing, new ways of educating, new communities, and how spirituality got corrupted to religion.

'I only read metaphysical books,' his new friend told Larry.

What these books were telling him was that reality was a matter of what you believed it was. Heard of seeing is believing? Forget it, believing is seeing.

'It's all my mind making it up, everything I experience in my life,' he told Larry, 'that's one thing for sure, what I learn from these books, the mind is powerful and you can create anything you want with mental discipline.'

They discussed the various disciplines that enabled you to direct the power of the mind to whatever it was you wanted to be, whatever it was you wanted to do.

Sometimes Larry worried that maybe that was the easy part, and the hard part was knowing what you wanted. Or, as an ancient text from India had it, what we had to do in life was to do our duty. But how, in this world of unprecedented possibilities, could you know what your duty *was*? Larry was worrying at how you knew what was good and right, how you made correct choices, how you ensured that you were ethical, what you did about evil.

'Evil is as divine as good,' his new friend told him. 'Everything is part of the divine. Everything we know is a manifestation of the divine. It's all just ideas, anyway.' Then he'd abruptly leave Larry, and avoid any more talk along these lines for the rest of the day, sometimes longer, remaining taciturn and unreachable, until suddenly he'd sit himself besides Larry with his mug of tea and say, 'Have you read *The Tao of Physics?*'

Some of the other men talked a lot more among themselves, sport and women and TV.

Sometimes Larry and Jamal began to find more opportunities for a bit of a discussion, just the two of them, taking up where they'd left off. It was always Jamal who'd suddenly make a sound of disgust or annoyance and suddenly there was no more talk. But it all excited Larry tremendously, to realize that there were people all over the world also excited by these ideas, that not only ages-old texts but some of the latest writings might offer him direction.

Once in a while they'd go and get a drink together after work. They'd have a couple of Cokes somewhere cool and quiet, especially on the hottest days, when they didn't want to wait to get home to cool off.

Jamal did not like to talk about himself very much, but Larry learnt that he had gone to university in Germany, acquired some qualifications, and managed to immigrate to Australia.

'I could not really imagine his life in Europe, let alone before that,' Larry told me. 'I knew nothing about the part of the world he came from, or what religion if any he had been brought up in.' Jamal never asked him about his personal life, either, and their talks became more relaxed and intense when it seemed that it had been tacitly agreed that he never would.

Larry gathered that he did not care to utilize the qualifications that had gained him his residency status here. He got the impression that Jamal did not care to spend his days inside an office, nor to commit himself in the long term. He, like Larry, might have been able to find employment that others deemed more desirable, or perhaps the widespread racism endemic in the country had made that virtually impossible. But this work suited him too, it was straightforward, he liked the exertion, he wanted the experience, and no one bothered you. Which was a point at which, again, their conversation came to another abrupt end. Larry never knew if Jamal would talk to him again.

'What I got out of this, above all,' Larry told me all those years later, 'if I were to sum it up, was one very exhilarating and inspiring notion: we had to lose our old habits of thinking. Jamal said to me, "You are looking for something new, you want to think in a new way, you have to have a new mind." I set out to try and create for myself a new mind.'

I was only just twenty-three

The night, a long time afterwards, that Larry told me all of this, he put me under a kind of spell. He spoke to me for hours, eloquently, as if he had been waiting for the opportunity to summarize his experience. He spoke with equanimity, as if no emotion could disturb or distort the frankness and thoroughness of his account, yet with warmth and flashes of telling precision in the details or words he was recalling. As in my earliest meetings with him, he seemed to switch suddenly from appearing young for his age to appearing almost uncannily mature. The relaxed accents of his Australian English had become tinged with various expressions, pronunciations, intonations and odd bits of vocabulary he had picked up in his travels and through his close contact with a wide range of people.

Sometimes he would be absorbed in the telling, but suddenly would look up and straight at you, look hard and see that you heard him. When I made a comment or asked a question he always listened and responded, giving the impression that he respected and enjoyed your interest.

One day at the building site, Jamal told him that he was going to leave and go travelling in South-East Asia for a while, and asked Larry if he wanted to come too. In a few weeks they had tickets and visas, and landed in Bangkok. They took a bus to the south of Thailand and found themselves a simple hut on a quiet beach, in a still undeveloped area, among many other travellers, who congregated under a large thatch roof, in an open-sided structure where they ordered endless dishes of the most delicious food Larry had ever tasted, flavoured with lemon-grass, ginger and fish sauce. They drank Mekong whiskey and passed around joints of impressive quality. It was searingly hot, and though they'd sometimes go and splash about or swim in the clear lagoon-like sea, or, once in a while, go inspect the market in a nearby village, they mostly lazed about in the simple restaurant, bar and meeting place known as John's.

Such an ambience was conducive to long raves about existence and meaning. Many of the travellers were students and readers. Some of them though wanted only to 'get wasted' and found such talk 'bummed them out'. They migrated down the beach to a similar open-sided restaurant, known as John's Two, where loud music was constantly played and discussion discouraged. In John's One a kind of non-stop symposium was held, that went on through days and nights, with people arriving and leaving. They passed around their books and talked endlessly; sometimes it became a little silly, ghost stories and accounts of prophetic dreams and irrational knowledge, and sometimes the discussion was as focused and rigorous as that at any formal class Larry had ever been to.

It was here that an American man of around thirty told them that although he had read widely and deeply all his life in philosophy and mysticism, he had finally arrived at the deepest knowledge of himself, the realization of his powers, and the ability to make his life whatever he wanted it to be, by having attended an exacting and exhilarating three-day personal development seminar known as The Process.

'I've heard of that,' a couple of people said, 'I want to do that, I'm going to do that.' Begun in California, it had been taken up by some famous actors and writers, and was becoming available around the world.

'You can't change your life in three days,' someone posited.

'You can,' said the guy who'd done The Process. 'I was stuck in a bad relationship, a job I hated, and felt undressed if I didn't wear a suit and tie.' He was tanned and wearing only a relaxed grin and a sarong, and everyone laughed.

Not everyone; Jamal didn't laugh. Jamal, Larry found, became difficult in this group. He either harangued or sulked. Although he had never touched alcohol back in Australia, he began pouring Mekong into his morning coffee here. While he had seemed to enjoy having in Larry a friend who shared his interests back when they'd worked together, here he seemed resentful of those who had plenty to say on the kinds of things he had been reading. And he clearly had a huge crush on one of the girls there, a Dutch blonde, whose somewhat clichéd utterances were the only ones he would nod at and encourage.

But, though he didn't want to see it, the girl liked Larry. Larry tried to include Jamal in their exchanges when she contrived to sit next to him.

Larry shared a simple little thatch hut on the beach with Jamal. With their passports and money buried in the sand under their beds, they, like everyone, kept the door open to relieve the heat.

Late one night Larry was drifting off to sleep, Jamal snoring in the other bed, when he became aware that someone else was there. It was, of course, the Dutch girl, who woke him with a deep, exploratory kiss, lying next to him, and shedding her sarong.

'What did you do?' I asked.

'I did what she wanted,' he told me. 'It would have been very rude to refuse her, and I didn't want her to get upset and wake Jamal. She slipped away afterwards, thankfully, and I lay there a while wondering what on earth to do. I only hoped Jamal hadn't woken. He usually slept like a log, after drinking all that whiskey, but I couldn't be sure.

'I was only just twenty-three,' Larry said.

'It took me only a moment to throw my things into my bag. I found someone up in the restaurant, paid them for the room, and, with only the light from my torch, walked as far as the road. With the dawn light a bus came along, just one of those little vans where a couple of old women made room for me among piles of produce and a few chooks they were taking to the market. That took me to the village where I got another bus to the next big town, and then a bus to Bangkok.

'I spent a few nights there, then went up to the hills, planning to explore and then go on to Vietnam. But I kept thinking about that American guy, who looked so happy and free and had changed his life so radically.

'Eventually I went back to Sydney, and in no time found out where I could do The Process.

'It was an intensive session of three days, long days from early morning to late at night, during which we had to undertake to have no contact with anyone outside of the workshop. No caffeine, no tobacco, no drugs. Two hundred of us sat in rows on hard chairs in a room with no windows. There were only a couple of short meal breaks and bathroom breaks, and the pressure on us was intense.' They were taken through many exercises, Larry told me, from which they discovered, or were endlessly told, in many ways, that they each had created every aspect of their own lives and always would. At first it seemed that they were being insulted, ordered about, disrespected. Scepticism, disappointment, boredom and rage were common. But then they began to see that something was working, something that just might give them what they were here for. There were clever processes which made them divulge all their most intimate experiences and feelings, and even more cleverly made them realize that things had not just happened to them, they weren't passive in all of this, but everything had been a choice they made. Some people cried, fainted, vomited, had hysterics or wanted to. Memories were unlocked, unconscious drives were acknowledged. It was like years of conventional therapy squeezed into the space of three days. At the end, everyone felt not only exhausted but transformed, radically liberated from everything that had prevented them from the full potential of their beings, and about to embark on new lives of limitless energy, accomplishment and reward. It might have been like brain-washing, except that they felt free to express their own truths, and they all felt joyous and light, full of light. Everyone came back to the follow-up session, and many of them went on to do more of these courses.

'It was the experience I had wanted when I had become fascinated by notions like paradigm shift and a new age. I did all the post-graduate courses The Process offered – that's what it was called, The Process, or TP. After months of that, I went over to LA to train as a trainer. And I then guided many hundreds of people through TP. I saw the results of what I judged then to be the most effective, brilliant and sufficient method of gaining something I even called enlightenment.'

Larry's charisma no doubt made him especially effectual, bringing shoals of new adherents to The Process.

People gave their joyous testaments, confessing the suspicion ('brain-washing'), resistance ('I'm not going to clap every time someone speaks!') and resentment ('arrogant trainers') with which they had embarked on The Process, and affirming that, at some point, maybe during TP, maybe not till it was over, they 'got it' and 'it' was nothing, a blissful, energizing nothing, and this nothing was enlightenment. After doing TP, everyone suddenly knew that they were perfect, everything was perfect. It was sartori. People turned up to their jobs and suddenly shaped up or suddenly were so brilliantly, brutally able to speak their truth that everyone around them shaped up. Or they suddenly quit. People left long marriages. Other people made fresh commitments. People who thought they couldn't sing began to sing. Shy people accosted strangers. Aggressive people got in touch with their inner humility. People began to dress differently. People who had needed medications, therapy, walking canes, spectacles threw them away. Bearded men shaved. Salespeople's sales went up and up again. Arachnophobes acquired pet spiders. Teenagers cleaned their rooms.

Graduates brought their friends to Introduction Evenings, signed them up, and The Process grew. Everywhere you went people claimed that we all 'create our own reality' and everything that happened to you was because you chose it. You even chose your parents. How powerful is that! You chose your traumas and your tragedies. You chose your disabilities and your disappointments. Perfect! You chose them perfectly! Now choose again! Believe you can and you will. Visualize it well and it will come to pass. Create an intention and you have created a new reality.

I had heard this kind of talk myself, thought of it as part of a fashionable psychobabble from which I could mine choice phrases to round out a character's dialogue. I recalled those far-off days when one was liable to come across actors, for example, who spoke a jargon about creating your own reality and choosing whatever supported them in their choices. Some of them seemed rather smug about it.

And there Larry had been, so young and so authoritative, in the thick of it all, guiding hundreds of people at a time to the paradox that they were the source of all their experience, that they never had any control, that they acted out of ideas and notions they were free to discard, that they were machines, that they were God, that they could have and do anything they wanted if only they realized that having and doing came after being, so all they had to do first was to be.

All of that kept Larry occupied for quite some time, but then it no longer gave him the answer he lived to seek.

After some time, but as if quite suddenly, Larry felt trapped. He carried out a three-day 'training', and at the end, with people weeping with joy and relief, hugging each other and proudly and gladly and bravely stepping into the first day of the rest of their lives, as he was being thanked and congratulated over and over, he felt as if he had done the whole thing on automatic, his heart hadn't been in it but no one knew the difference.

He realized that he was in danger of ending up in what he had always wanted to avoid, the equivalent of a religion, where ritual and belief took the place of experience, where questions had to be framed to fit the answers already available. This in spite of the central insistence of The Process that it was all about the experience, that belief disappeared in experience, that all you had to do was get out of your own way and let your life work, that once you realized you had never had a choice only then could you freely choose, that all TP did was show you that you could be what you really were.

'It all started with one question,' he told me. 'Why did my friend die and not me? If it was an accident or a random event, why isn't *everything* accidental, random? If there was a purpose to it, whose purpose was it and how could I know it? Where can there be a line between the random and the inevitable? For a while I thought The Process was answering all of this. But it wasn't. There was no meaningful way that I could say my young friend had chosen to die. The value I got was in realizing I could choose what to *do* with the experience of seeing it happen, that it meant what I chose it to mean. So I was back where I started. I still did not know enough, I still wondered how others had made sense of existence.'

Graduates of The Process all routinely joined in a meditation on a vision of a better world, but as they adopted the belief system of TP's anti-belief system, they were liable to say that poverty and disease were choices, individual choices. Asserting over and over that they took responsibility for their own lives, they were liable to deny they had any responsibility for life as a whole. If anyone suffered any ill fate they could happily dismiss it as a message from the universe. Poverty, they were liable to say, came out of poverty of desire, poverty of spirit. Victims of cruelty had to take responsibility, they were liable to say.

Larry began to be alarmed that, no matter how much it was never intended that way, not by him, the idea of endless choice had become just another way to compete for more points, to bring about proof that you were choosing better than the next guy. And no matter how much The Process was about finding that everything was already perfect, it easily found perfection in people's choice to sign up – and pay – for the next training, and was not inclined to acknowledge as perfect any refusal.

But still, it seemed as if he had made a powerful choice anyway: that of coming across, and listening to, several people who lately had begun to tell him about an amazing guru from the Himalayas, a woman, not like any guru you ever heard about, for she did not require silence, study, obedience nor obeisance from you, but gave you ways to express yourself, explore yourself, remake yourself and find greater pleasure in life.

'Someone said to me,' Larry told me, 'and this was someone who had been a trainer with The Process, had trained trainers in the States and then had left: "The Process still depends on mind games. You say it's all about getting past beliefs and the games we play about cause and effect, but it's still something that depends on taking up new ideas. And just look at the mind games people play when they're into it. With Auntieji there's none of that, you never ever talk about what happened when you were three or what kind of mother you had or why you want to quit your job." In The Process we'd repeat slogans like "understanding is the booby prize" and "it's about what you experience" but it suddenly all looked to me as if that wasn't really how we operated. I dearly wanted to get outside of concepts, ideas, mind games.'

Larry quit The Process. He didn't give anyone a chance to even think about how to talk him out of it. He got rid of everything he couldn't carry and departed at once for the mountains of India.

Remember, he's telling me all this ten years after it happened. In those years I might have forgotten Larry except that seeing Elliott and asking after Isabel kept reminding me of him, and I'd wonder what happened to that beautiful, unusual boy who had been offered what so many people wanted and wanted something else, had been offered security and money and connections and a marriage, and gave it all up to follow his own way. And ten more years have passed since that long talk.

Twice as rich

When Elliott Templeton's niece Isabel Bradley married Gray Maturin, it was the biggest, most lavish affair Brisbane had ever known. Not only Brisbane. Between Elliott and Mr Maturin there was a guest list that made headlines, social pages, gossip pages, history.

It was a display of wealth and power, it was a party to usher in a new decade, it was the Maturins' announcement that they were major players. She was radiant, he was beaming, the families were thrilled, the guests had the time of their lives. It was an immense production and everything went off smoothly. There were palatial marquees, there was champagne flowing like a river, there was sumptuous food, there was a cake an architect designed, there were ice sculptures, there was music and dancing, an old-fashioned band for one age group, as well as the local rock band that was the one anyone would get if they could get anyone they wanted. The guests received gifts.

The dress itself was newsworthy. Its basis was a vintage gown of awesome provenance made of silks and laces no longer available. Isabel gave it to a museum afterwards.

The event marked also a sort of marriage between Elliott and Mr Maturin. They had formed their alliance in their common determination to eliminate Larry and champion Gray in the quest for Isabel's hand. Each was used to getting his own way, and respected that in the other. It must have seemed such an unlikely alliance, Elliott and Mr Maturin, Camp Decadence on one hand, Moral Majority on the other, but they acquired esteem for each other, for they were both self-made men, with an instinct for capitalism and making useful connections. The times suited them.

The Maturin name was beginning to be known of course even in the southern states as one of the country's biggest and most entrepreneurial property developers. New meaning was given to 'exclusive' and 'expensive'. Gray brought vision – that was the word they kept using – to the firm, and now sat at the right hand of his father. They were a team. Gray had respect for what his father had achieved; his father had respect for Gray's 'new blood', 'fire in the belly', 'contemporary flair'. I don't know who put these words in his mouth. The famous Rapture Resorts began to be built, very much under Gray's eye. Isabel was quietly credited with having considerable influence. Gray saw the potential of high-end tourism, pushed the Rapture developments, and then sat back as the media became breathless reporting how lavish and splendid the new developments were, no expense spared, the extent of the pools and waterfalls, the palm trees and the imported marble, the suites and the condominiums, the artworks and the chefs lured from Paris and the furnishings and fittings and the stars that would stay, and Queensland really on the map.

Gray and his father were already becoming known as The Maturin Team. Senior had established a property development firm twenty years earlier and Junior had been prepared all his life to come aboard with all that new blood, hunger and flair. Unlike some of the entrepreneurs who were also beginning to make a name, Gray had had a privileged background; it was his father who was the self-made man. But Gray had plenty to prove, that he could outdo the others, that he was worthy of Isabel, that he had as much cunning and flamboyance as anyone in the new decade of prodigious display of wealth. Nearly all of it was loans but everyone consented in treating illusory money as real. It was a time of a kind of mass hallucination.

Mr Maturin bought and renovated a house for the young newlyweds on the river at West End, just before it became fashionable, *making* it fashionable, on enough land for a village. It had decks and pavilions, atriums and courtyards, wings and extensions. There was a jetty, swimming pool and tennis court, rolling lawns, gardens and orchards. Inside, there were many bedrooms and even more bathrooms, en suites and built-ins, flowing spaces and defined areas, designer this and heritage that, everything that opens and shuts. Elliott would happen to have a glossy, scented magazine upon his person when I saw him, and show me Isabel's house featured yet again, or sometimes she was featured, an example of a woman of style, fresh and contemporary, a supportive partner yet with her own interests. Isabel finally got to create that all-white room, this vast sitting room down the length of one wing of the house, white walls, furniture, cushions, rugs, lamps, shutters, white everything, opening onto a deck also all white.

She began a bit of a craze for it. You'd see people doing all-white living rooms, all-white bedrooms, all-white studios. People would say 'I'm going to have an Isabel Maturin room.' Later that decade when a famous American designer bought a hotel in South Beach, Miami and created all-white rooms therein, people would say how he got the idea from her. He'd been a guest at one of the Maturins' splendiferous parties. Isabel met a lot of people, rubbing shoulders with fame, infamy, notoriety, celebrity, accomplishment, recognition. And then they bought that white painting.

They paid several million dollars for a painting that looked like a blank white canvas. But no, if you looked closely you could see that white came in several shades and so you were made to question your notions of absolutes, which made it worth every cent. Or, no, being all-white it said volumes (and volumes have been said) about oh, serenity, or snow, or Zen, something else beyond price. There was awe and there was ridicule. We were reminded that the public laughed at Van Gogh, we were reminded that there's one born every minute. The purchase was worth every cent for the publicity.

Then Alan Stock bought a real Van Gogh for many millions more, more than anyone had ever paid for a painting or for much else either.

Maturin Team's parties made news. Possibly the most lavish one was held when they bought a television station, in an audacious move that left few without interest in what they were up to. Maturin Senior had had his grave doubts but Gray, no doubt after discussing it with Isabel, won him over. It was possibly the high point in a career of high points. A new legislation banned cross-media ownership, the ownership of TV stations by entrepreneurs in cities where they already had a considerable newspaper interest. This meant that a media mogul had to sell a station. The Maturins bought it. There were strikes, there were resignations, ratings plummeted, advertisers withdrew, media commentators commentated their hearts out, vast amounts of money were lost at first – and then the Maturin network, as it was now, 'bought' a couple of the most watched, most listened to, most influential media stars in the country.

The media stars' deals with the Maturins were to set them up for life. They were offered contracts they couldn't refuse: salaries, perks, condos at the Rapture. Advertisers began flocking, people began tuning in, and the Maturins began hobnobbing with heads of state. At some point a small private jet became a main means of transport. Profiles of Gray and Isabel were commissioned by editors. Sometimes Roman emperors were mentioned. People I knew in media and publishing talked about it. Some deplored it all heartily. Some hoped for a bit of that Rapture.

Anyway, the party to usher in this new era was, in Elliott's words, an extravaganza. Guests came from business, stockbroking, merchant banking and the media, both the media's stars and the media's owners, of whom the Maturin Team were now one. There were movie heart-throbs of yesteryear and upcoming pop stars. More marquees, even more champagne, chartered planes for the guests, limousines to drive them around, jugglers, clowns, bands, choirs. There were oceans of champagne and mountains of fresh seafood. Chicken stuffed with pine nuts and wild rice, duck stuffed with mangoes and macadamias. Trolleys of desserts. Everyone partied all night.

There was the all-white party – the famous all-white party, I nearly said. Our idea of famous by now was not removed from tabloid celebrity. Anyway, apparently everything was white at this party. The musicians not only wore white, they had specially made all-white instruments, there was a white dance floor, the art-directed decorations were white, everyone wore white, and Gray gave Isabel a white Rolls Royce.

I think it was at this party that the notorious Sydney underground cult personality Mistress Stiletto was one of the trophy guests, dressed in a leather ball gown and leather tiara.

I think they really thought it would go on like that forever, that wealth accumulated without end.

I'd get news from Elliott from time to time. The young couple had honeymooned in the Balearic Islands. The young couple were very happy. The young couple were meeting very famous people. Gray had helped thrust the Maturin Team right into this new age, and their developments were the talk of the city, all the cities. The famous resorts with the no-expense-spared aesthetic, their miles of swimming pools dotted with decks, wet bars, spas, the plethora of palm trees, the vast marble lobbies. And the apartment blocks in the city. And the renovations of the grander Queenslanders. A formerly provincial city with a dead city centre was becoming 'on the map', 'very liveable'. The Maturins were lionized in their home state.

No one who was making that much money in Queensland could do so without being on good terms with the state government, and if there was one thing everyone knew about the Queensland government, it was that it was a kind of tin-pot totalitarianism. But they loved their avuncular dictator up there, police brutality notwithstanding. 'He's done so much for the state,' remember. Queenslanders knew they were different, and that outsiders could not be trusted.

I still had no intention of going back there if ever I could help it, the place scared me. None of the refugees I knew from the state would go back until there was a change of government, which didn't look likely.

Isabel and Gray had a baby, then another, sweet babies, perfect babies and everyone was even happier. They were very lucky with the nanny. Even when Elliott wasn't showing them to me over the years I came across photos of Isabel, in huge sunglasses, bouffant hair layered to the shoulders, something sparkling at the neck and ears, in wildly colourful outfits, sometimes accompanying Gray, sometimes not. She looked happy, if you could tell. Elliott said she was happy.

It was the age of excess. The age of 'greed is good'. Entrepreneurs became heroes to the public. The most famous of them, Alan Stock, bought football teams, islands, breweries, newspapers, TV networks, and that painting. Everyone was getting rich. Oh, except the people who weren't, but you never heard about that, certainly not from Elliott.

Elliott was happy about all that, and also about the fact that, so he told me, without stirring a finger, he was nearly twice as rich in 1986 as he had been in 1978.

'Someone's finger must have stirred,' I said, 'at least that's how money is made where I come from.'

'Mr Maturin just tells me what to invest in and I get it done,' said Elliott, somewhat smugly I thought.

'I *should* be rich by now,' Elliott said, 'being in the middle of middle age.' The definition of middle age had been shifting over the years. Anyway, he was in his mid-sixties now.

He was looking good, too. He ought to, he worked at it. He began going to health farms and spas, and never stinted on massages and a range of what he called his 'wellness therapies'. He twiddled at bits of metal the acupuncturist stuck in his ear, he showed us the cupping marks on his back, the burns where the moxa stick had been applied too close. He often announced he was feeling sore or superb after reiki or shiatsu. He had mixtures of herbs made up for him, he brewed up foul-smelling Chinese potions. He got vitamin injections from a doctor and tonics from a homeopath. He ate only fruit in the mornings. He was as robust as ever, and always toasted noon with a glass of champagne.

He always had new clothes, and still made trips abroad just to go shopping. Since Mr Maturin had become practically his brother and made his money 'work for him', as they put it, Elliott didn't have to work any more. Although he had no financial need to keep up his introducing and acquiring and procuring and advising and connecting, he kept it up a bit anyway. It was his vocation. He was born to be the man about town.

Yet, as years passed, somehow Elliott didn't seem any longer to be quite of the times, quite in tune with the contemporary.

Things were changing.

Young people were different, young people always are. The hedonism of the 70s had suited Elliott. Now there were different moods around, many young people were sober and money-mad yuppies who wanted to own their own home before they travelled, and had never got around to having the kind of chaotic wild sex that older people were beginning to be nostalgic about. Artists talked first and foremost about agents and deals and their image.

Elliott didn't always seem so fabulous. He didn't understand raves, he didn't understand Ecstasy.

He didn't understand just how safe or just how reckless sex had become.

Elliott began to talk about how things used to be better.

Older people should resist the impulse to talk about how things used to be better. They've always done it, so how can it be true?

The advent of sunscreen, faxes and MTV were insufficient to make Elliott look kindly on the times, in this, his mood of general disappointment.

Elliott raved on bitterly to me one night in a corner at the party after a concert, about what this new generation would never know, as if it were their fault.

I couldn't tell at first what had brought this on. Then the name Paul Barton came up.

Paul Barton had called Elliott 'some old queen who used to be around' and someone passed it on to Elliott.

The very same Paul Barton whom Elliott had befriended when he'd been little nobody from nowhere knowing no one. Paul Barton had been the newest kid in town, but not just any kid, a good-looking kid with a smart mouth, baby-faced with the bod of a god, a sweet grin but steely ambition, and Elliott had swooped upon him and taken him up and become his mentor and patron and friend and who knows. He kept Paul for a while and though Elliott had always said that he knew he was being used and would be deserted when he was no longer useful, he was mad about the boy, and only meant that he wanted to one day become a very special kind of ex, one who remained a trusted, esteemed friend, an advisor and confidant, someone who would always be acknowledged for what he had done, someone that Paul would continue to value, be proud of having known, defer to.

'I befriended him. I showed him around town. I took him to get his hair cut and his back waxed. I introduced him to everyone he is now so sickeningly proud of knowing.'

But Paul Barton stopped returning his phone calls, and if Elliott ever saw him Paul was always rushing off and had to be somewhere and gasping about how busy he was, how flat out and overbooked. He stopped saying we must catch up. He began to pretend to barely know Elliott, and spoke of him only with dismissive disparagement, said he was a snob and a social climber and a has-been.

Elliott still entertained lavishly, and sometimes he had to invite Paul Barton, it would have made such a big deal not to. But he resented it bitterly.

Elliott was adaptable, up to a point, but he had just about reached the point.

'It's not the same city any more and I don't want to leave Australia and live the life of an expatriate, not after I have survived everything that I have survived in this dear nation of ours, so why leave the country now, not for good anyway. I'm going to Salzburg next month for *The Ring* but I'm coming back and I think it's time for change, capital C change.'

The beauties of nature, most splendid period

Elliott was always a step ahead. He had long ago decided to buy a property in Byron Bay, and had snapped up a vast bit of land on the beach years earlier, and now he was going to build on it.

It was as if he had long known what would happen to the classical sleepy small seaside town surrounded by farming properties where for so long, apart from the local residents, the only people who went there regularly were surfers. The beach was magnificent, the waves legendary. Hippies followed, then their children, the ferals, though for a long time they were more likely to frequent the hinterland. Ferals favoured rainforests over beaches and you didn't find cow-pats with gold-top mushrooms on the beach. Later, general tourists and backpackers followed, and, a decade after Elliott's move, an increase of the 'can work from anywhere' crowd, with computers and modems, faxes and satellite dishes, and the useful profits from selling up their city flats. They settled near the beach and in the hills to write screenplays, self-help books and weekly magazine columns, to open juice bars and sushi bars, surf shops and furniture shops, to run a bed-and-breakfast or a massage clinic with isolation tanks and aromatherapy.

Byron was not that far from the border with Queensland, a couple hours' drive south of it, bit more before the good new road, but what a border it still was. The idea of running up to Brisbane to see a show or buy household goods simply did not exist. It was as if you might risk your liberty or your integrity by going there, and what could you possibly want anyway? You drove ten hours – fifteen or more in those days – south to Sydney instead. Or flew.

'I'm ready for a much simpler life,' Elliott told me. 'I want time to enjoy the beauties of nature.'

Elliott of course had his own idea about what constituted simplicity, or, indeed, nature.

Having made so much money through the Maturins, it wasn't hard for Elliott to find a spare half-million dollars to construct his new abode. 'So simple,' he would say, 'influenced by Asia and the Pacific, very appropriate to the new lifestyle.' This was Asia-Pacific plus appliances, lavish styling, and landscape gardening. From the house's surrounding wide verandas, guests gazed upon pavilions and pools, the Balinese garden, the Japanese garden, the Australian Natives garden.

It was made for the best parties on the North Coast and that's what Elliott gave. It didn't occur to me then that Elliot's career at the time was somewhat like Isabel's, distinguished by giving parties.

Property developers and film producers came. The property developers, by the way, were soon advised in no uncertain terms that the area would always defend itself from the ghastly sight of high rises, franchised fast-food joints and un-aesthetic intrusions into the tasteful constructions that blended with the natural beauty of the area. Stars on huge Australia-wide concert tours came to Byron for some 'down time', Elliott gave parties for them. CJ Lonoff at the height of her recording and video-art career bought property there. Elliott gave a party for her. (It was a long time before she managed to return.) CJ Lonoff's long-time personal assistant, Rye Bread, semi-retired, moved to Byron, Elliott gave a party. The moon was full, it was the solstice, it was the first day of spring, Elliott gave a party. Easter, Anzac Day, the Queen's Birthday holiday, the Melbourne Cup, Elliott gave a party.

No one had orgies any more, not at Elliott's place anyway, all that was long past, and if people took drugs now they'd brought their own, but Elliott, as ever, catered copiously with carefully chosen wines, boutique beers, and lavish spreads, which these days featured local fresh produce and plenty of choice for vegetarians and vegans.

Once Louisa Bradley came to one of the parties. 'We met his sister,' people would say proudly, 'which was sweet.'

Of all his fabulous visitors, Elliott valued none so much as someone he called Rinpoche, a Tibetan monk. The first party Elliott gave was for the blessing of his new house, featuring this Rinpoche. Isabel and Gray came to that one. 'We met Isabel and Gray Maturin,' people mentioned whenever they could, 'they're actually rather sweet.'

For by now Elliott's Buddhism was part of his profile, and his new front door had once opened in a monastery in Tibet.

And before all the other parties, there had been this joyous day of ritual. The house was bedecked with garlands, and an altar with his very best Buddha statue was erected. The Rinpoche came and gave blessings, fragrant smoke wafted everywhere and bells chimed. And then, something Elliott had not quite foreseen, the Rinpoche called for rice, and went about not only the area around the altar, but all over the house, where the polishing of the floorboards had only just been completed, strewing handfuls of rice. There was rice in the swimming pool, rice all over the garden, rice all over the decks. 'We're still picking rice out of mats and couches,' he told me later. 'But,' he said with satisfaction, 'we got rid of any past energies,' which meant the undesirable psychic shadows of previous residents on the land or of, longer ago, any disgraceful business of dispossessing any people who had been there first.

'I heard he got in some kind of eastern magician to purify the place,' said the woman who sold me bread and milk.

'They're saying the land is worth three times what he paid for it,' said the man who filled my car with petrol.

I knew more about all this than normally I would have because, around the same time, quite independently, I had decided to buy some property of my own, and got myself a bit of a shack at Brunswick Heads. It was a writing retreat, a retreat from social life and social demands. I went there for some seclusion, solitude, but when Elliott knew I was in the area, I had to come to the party for the Equinox.

Parties of Elliott's I didn't go to I heard about. Everyone in the area gossiped about Elliott, and when I talked with him, over a drink or on the phone, he gossiped about himself even more. And of course from time to time I asked after Isabel, and was occasionally treated to images of her with her big hair and big sunnies.

Around the time Elliott told me he had become twice as rich through the Maturins, an investigative current affairs documentary series on television revealed incontrovertible proof of corruption in the police force in the northern state. We saw police enter gambling dens and brothels they swore didn't exist. We saw them take bribes. We saw proof of the government's collusion. Consequently we began to hear more of the scope and extent of the corruption.

One of the other high-fliers, one of the entrepreneurs, the highest flying one of all, also had bought a television station in Queensland. Alan Stock was the most famous of them, for he was 'mates' with the prime minister and had foreign heads of state over for a barbecue, he kept company with film stars and sports stars, and so on, he exceeded the Maturins and all the others in the immensity of the amounts of money he spent, the extent of his flamboyance and visibility, the enormity of the effects on workers of his purchases of media, sporting teams, breweries and bakeries. The reported sums of money associated with his activities would have been boggling even with a couple of noughts removed.

He was a popular hero for a while, most of all when he had had built for himself some kind of fresh design in racing cars and this car had won some American car race that Australia had never won before, and this was meant to prove that the entire nation had been vindicated of any hint of minor importance or negligible influence or inability to produce world-class competitive machines and men fit to drive them. Workers gave themselves a holiday to celebrate, people sang in the streets, yuppies were served champagne (domestic) with their breakfast lattes, and politicians fell over themselves to offer him honours.

Ah, but it wasn't so very long after that Stock's image began to be tarnished as people became aware of how very much some hard-working people had been hurt by his purchase of a long-established chain of bakeries that had started as a family business. No one who had created the foundation, the goodwill and the good reputation of the brand was compensated or even thanked, and before long a great deal of fresh unemployment, destroyed livelihoods and righteous resentment was laid at Stock's door.

And then one day, the news broke. A certain bank had collapsed, and this was the bank that had provided so much of the funds to Alan Stock, the most famous and flamboyant of the decade's entrepreneurs. Then other banks crashed.

Meanwhile the famous Inquiry into corruption in Queensland had been set up. Day after day, week after week, the Australian public read the evidence: a police chief heading a police force that took bribes as a matter of course, a premier who required deposits into a special fund from developers wanting to operate in the state, a government that did not protect or provide for most of its citizens, and turned a blind eye to the corruption, coercion and brutality that marked most of its police force's daily operations.

The downfall of Alan Stock cast suspicion on the honesty and decency of all of the celebrated entrepreneurs. The new mood was nervousness, denial and backtracking. The deregulated banks, which had been, as they say, 'throwing' money at the Maturins, suddenly decided the party was over.

And suddenly the Maturins were tainted with scandal and entirely broke.

Trousers of startling colour... singlets of contrasting hue

It took me a while to catch up with all that news. I was travelling, and for a while didn't see the papers or anyone who'd recently been in Australia. But it was front page for several periods over a couple of years. It was the end of the Age of Greed, they began saying, ostentatious display was over, opulence became the style of yesteryear and you could no longer find anyone who had a good word to say about making fast money through massive borrowing and speculation. The flamboyant entrepreneurs who had been popular heroes were now roundly vilified high and low. Huge numbers of Australians had been badly hurt, some of them referred to as 'little people', what politicians called 'mums and dads', whose savings and superannuation had disappeared with the collapse of banks, corporations and investors. The pollies and stars who had chummed about with Stock quickly realized they would lose votes, jobs or fans if they didn't distance themselves from him fast, and distance themselves they did, from him and anyone who could be seen as of the same ilk.

I heard the rest it when I got back, and eventually returned to the North Coast in the summer, the last summer of the decade, and caught up with Elliott.

Elliott blamed the Maturins' ruin on Alan Stock, 'an outright crook,' he said, 'who's given all entrepreneurs a bad name,' even the good guys like the Maturins, who would have been able to make good if they had been allowed, but the banks had pulled the plug on them, ruining them completely. The Maturins had not only had to contend with the big rises in interest rates, but also a pilots' strike that had effectively halted tourism for a couple of years and meant that their new luxury resorts for far too long lay almost empty. Imagine those palatial, sybaritic spaces, readied for the jet-set, the international party people, lying silent and unpopulated like opulent ghost towns.

Well, all right, the Maturins had over-extended but so had everyone and the banks had green-lighted all the schemes and if everyone now was saying it had all been folly and madness, that the profit margins had always been too low to cope with vicissitudes of interest rates or any unforeseen setback – well, easy to say now, wasn't it, the way things had turned out.

Now they were saying Gray had been too young to be allowed to make the decisions he did. When he'd been the young god of high flying his youth was said to be part of his advantage.

And yes, Mr Maturin had contributed to the premier's fund, that now infamous fund, but you simply had no choice in order to do business in the state, and it did not mean that he was corrupt, as some very malicious people were saying, who had not been pure themselves if you wanted to know, and the fury and the shame Mr Maturin felt had affected him very badly, he'd had a heart attack and had not been the same since.

A few properties around Byron were auctioned off or changed hands, for several people in the area had been involved in investments and speculations that were undone by the corporate scandals, the collapse of the merchant banks and a stock market crash a couple of years before. I thought Elliott might have suffered, remembering that he had pretty much handed over his financial affairs to Mr Maturin, but he gave no sign of it, it didn't look like his parties budget had shrunk in the least, and he went on entertaining and acquiring art works.

When Mr Maturin died, there were some very nasty rumours. Some had him commit suicide, and some had him collapse while trying to flee the country to avoid his creditors and the fall-out from his embroilment with the fast-failing state government.

But as for Elliott, the new era was one of his most spectacular periods.

He acquired a tan, cut his hair very short, and began wearing intense, outrageous colours. He got himself a whole new wardrobe, having embraced the lifestyle of leisure and freedom in his new locality. He bought Italian and French resort wear, and a line of amazing clothes made from Indian fabrics, designed in New Zealand and sewn in Bali. Elliott now was resplendent in trousers of startling colour and singlets of contrasting hue. He had a personal trainer come round to guide him in a new blend of Tai Chi and Pilates. In turn he grew some kind of health-giving mushroom in dishes in his kitchen, bought costly bottles of a juice from a Tahitian plant that would keep him young, and stored up liquid oxygen for its particular invigorating properties. He had his body stretched and strengthened on the latest machines. Elliott always seemed to be the first to take up these things, for by the time everyone else had, he'd moved on to something else.

Everyone told him he looked wonderful, he looked amazing, he looked young, he looked great.

Elliott also wore his new North Coast clothes when he went down to Sydney; although he found himself going less often he now never missed Mardi Gras, held in that wondrous sensual Sydney season, the late summer-early autumn, the nation's party of the year. Besides the parade and the dance party for thousands that went on into the next two days and beyond, Mardi Gras had become a season of its own, an arts festival of queer films, performances and exhibitions, and people flew in from Europe and the States for the time of their lives. We both went down to Sydney that year, Elliott and I, and had a drink one evening, the air sultry, marvellous looking boys and men happily milling about in shorts and muscles, everyone, it seemed, in a mood of celebration, for having made it into a new century, for being alive and free and proud to party.

'Come with me,' Elliott said, 'this will interest you.' He took me to the studio of a restorer and framer, where a picture of the Dalai Lama had been installed into a special frame carved out of Himalayan teak.

'It's something His Holiness wanted me to have,' said Elliott shamelessly.

I think it was on this occasion that Elliott divulged that the collapse of the Maturins' empire had not affected him. Not very long, but long enough before it all happened, he had withdrawn his investments from the care of Maturin senior, and placed them in blue chip investments and real estate property. And why? On the advice of his Rinpoche. Elliott had asked the Rinpoche for some advice, and the Rinpoche had said something like, life is a matter of endless cycles, nothing remains the same, all is impermanence. This, to Elliott, was a clear and unmistakable message, and he immediately withdrew his money from the so-far spectacularly lucrative yet speculative investments where it had been breeding. The meticulous timing of this advice had assured his faith in the eternal wisdom of the East.

Back in Byron, Elliott bought some more land and began the grand project of planning the construction of a Buddhist centre.

Byron was suddenly full of Buddhists, often with colourful pasts. For most of them, apparently, Buddhism seemed a cool substitute for retirement, a chance to do whatever you felt like, a way of aligning yourself with the spiritual against the religious, a badge of credibility and good character.

When Mrs Bradley died, Elliott went up to Brisbane to help take care of things: direct the funeral, dispose of worldly goods. I think his nephew, Isabel's brother, who I never met, might have fleetingly repatriated on this occasion, but he liked living in Hong Kong and intended to remain there. Louisa Bradley's house was sold, and everything in it. And so was Gray and Isabel's house.

Elliott laid down the law to them. Gray couldn't get any kind of employment in Queensland, after what had happened, and there was no point in staying there, they needed a big change. They got rid of everything in Brisbane and he brought them down to Sydney. There he installed them in his own harbour-side flat, with his own housekeeper kept on staff.

'Go and see them when you're down there,' he instructed me.

'I'm making this my main home anyway,' he told me in Byron. 'And they wouldn't want to live up here.'

Probably not, and Elliott wouldn't necessarily want them there, they might have cramped his style.

Still, say what *you* might about Elliott, and people said plenty, not all of it kind, not all of it undeserved, for he was, as we said in happier times, a celebrity-fucker, but you had to say this: he was genuinely good-hearted, caring and generous.

PART IV

You haven't changed

Next time I went to Sydney, at Elliott's suggestion I called Isabel. By then, she and Gray, with kids, nanny and Vuitton cases, were installed in the apartment Elliott had kept at Elizabeth Bay.

Sounding pleased to hear from me, she asked me over at once. I was pleased in turn, very curious to see the woman she had become. It had been over ten years.

She answered the door herself, with a warm eagerness that charmed me. For a moment I thought she had just thrown a cardi over a slip – no, not really, but when I looked at what she was wearing I saw that she had acquired a new minimalist style, the slip was a black dress of emphatic simplicity, beautiful cut and soft fabric, the cardigan of silk and cashmere with exquisite little onyx buttons, and the ballet slippers were beautifully made shoes of the softest leather. She'd had her hair cut very short, in a severe little bob that flattered her eyes and cheekbones.

Isabel had always been pretty and now the addition of maturity and elegance made her beautiful. The slight gap in her front teeth and the slight cleft in her chin emphasized rather than detracted from the effect. She'd been bouncy and vivacious and a bit tubby, now you'd say her vitality shone through. She had acquired new self-control and up-to-date stylishness.

Vitality – that was one of the words used by the journalists of those glossy and less glossy magazines Elliott used to show me. 'Class' was another, and the beauty of the girl from Queensland was, and here's another term popular in Australia, world-class. Even given Isabel's natural assets, it took a lot of work and time to look that good, not that there's anything wrong with that.

'You look wonderful,' I told her.

'Don't look too bad yourself.'

Those ten years meant she couldn't be called a girl any more. She called me Will now, rather than Mr Maugham, and as we began to resume a conversation begun long ago, it was with no reference to, or much consciousness of, our age difference.

We sat in the living room overlooking the Harbour, looking much as it had when Elliott had entertained here.

'You haven't done the all-white makeover here yet,' I teased her.

'Bit over it,' she said, 'but it'll come back.' Elliott's stuff of course was never going to be replaced. This was the stuff, the style of furniture, the kinds of objects, the colours of the walls that Isabel was going to live with and, in a sense, fit herself to.

She'd asked me over at an odd hour, four, smidgen too early for a drink.

'I'm bringing back afternoon tea,' Isabel said, and indeed the housekeeper soon brought in a silver teapot and china cups, the whole tea service, and some dainty sandwiches and cakes. In case I don't mention it later, afternoon tea became a bit of a social craze in the next couple of years. Hotel lobbies were renovated for the purpose of afternoon tea. There was that 'afternoon tea' series on the radio.

'So,' I said, 'Sydney.'

Isabel said, 'Well, you know all about it, what wasn't in the papers Uncle Elliott would have told you.'

'I don't see much of the papers but do get the general drift. I understand you are utterly ruined,' I said with some irony, looking around the palatial apartment with the most desirable view in this city.

'I know,' she said, understanding my point. 'We are lucky to have this. But we haven't got a cent of our own, really, the banks would have let us keep our house but we couldn't afford to keep it, if you know what I mean, the rates and staff and everything, so we sold that too. Bloody banks,' she said with a moment of bitterness, but quickly recovered, showed she did not want to pursue that line. Banks were being eloquently and widely cursed without her contribution. She said, 'You know what I was thinking? Isn't this funny: remember when I wouldn't marry Larry because he had so little money? We've got less than that now.'

'Yes, pretty funny,' I said dryly. 'So what happened to Larry?' I asked, curious. 'Where is he?'

'No idea. We haven't heard a word in nearly ten years. His legal guardian died, you know, he was the only other person close to him. He did go back to India, I heard that.'

We sat for a moment, thinking of disappearances and deaths.

Then I said, 'Do you ever think you should have married him?' No point in being polite or tactful, I often thought, if you want to know something, ask. She shot me a look, taking that in.

'I've been really happy with Gray. He's been, he is, the best husband you could wish for. Even when everything was going pear-shaped he tried not to bring it home. I've been fortunate.'

Which made me wonder if they might have broken up, if it hadn't been for the drama of wrecked reputation and lost fortune. Marriage was another country, especially when children and property were involved, you didn't just say, now it's time for me to move on without you.

I'm speaking as an observer, of course, of that happy state. Falling in love and staying married are different things (forgive me if I'm quoting one of my characters).

There was a sound of juvenile homecoming. The nanny had brought the children home from school. The two little girls came in for a moment, kissed Isabel on the cheek, solemnly shook hands with me.

'How was school today, darling?' Isabel asked each of them.

'Good,' each said in turn.

They hadn't come rushing to Isabel but they liked her, I thought, and were perhaps a little in awe of her. They'd been very well-trained – brought up, I mean – with good manners and neat clothes. Anyway, they were too young to be interesting. Soon they left, to be taken to ballet or a birthday party or do their homework, whatever privileged little girls do of an afternoon.

'Sweet. And how is Gray?' I asked when they'd gone.

She hesitated. 'All right. It's all been very hard on him. I mean, it was really horrible when it all happened, like it couldn't be happening, it didn't seem real, it was really hard to deal with. There was a period when I didn't know if I could keep on going, when it was clear we were going to lose absolutely everything. I didn't think I could bear it. In a funny way, that's what kept Gray sane, and alive. He struggled to keep it all together. He felt really bad for the investors who lost money. Sometimes he gets these massive headaches, migraines I suppose, he's in such pain and it goes on for days. The doctors can't do anything. He's had all the tests there are. It's one reason we came to Sydney.'

I said, 'Sometimes a complete change does wonders in itself.'

'There's also the fact,' she said, 'we are totally busted stone-broke bankrupt.'

I looked around. 'That must be frightful to bear in an apartment like this with a Harbour view, costing you a total of nothing at all while you can cover your starving bones with Armani.'

'Akira actually,' she corrected me, then giggled. 'You haven't changed,' she said. 'But honestly, if it was just me, I wouldn't necessarily have accepted this. There are quite a few things I could do. I got over that hopeless feeling and would have found something new. But there's Gray, and the children. I accepted Uncle Elliott's offer because of them.'

Gray returned as I was getting ready to leave.

I was surprised to find how pleased I was to see him. He looked older than Isabel now, and though he retained his bulk on that large frame, he looked kind of haggard, and, well, grey. 'Has Isabel been making you drink tea?' he asked genially after we had greeted each other. 'Have a real drink, won't you?'

'I can't just now, but let's do that soon,' I said.

We found ourselves promising to see a lot more of each other, and meaning it. I don't think any of us had planned to.

Something unexpected happened

For the next few weeks, I would often see Isabel. I was living in Potts Point, my little flat facing the other way from her, over the wharves and the city.

'Afternoon tea' became our regular date, nearly always at her place. I'd cross over Macleay Street and walk down the old stone steps that led to Elizabeth Bay, the Harbour suddenly visible as the steps take a turn halfway down. A couple of times we went out, to the state art gallery or a couple of the small commercial galleries.

I was staying in Sydney for a while working on a play and a screenplay. Once in a while I'd have lunch with the producer and a couple of directors, but I didn't tell many other people I knew I was in town so I could concentrate on work.

As usual I'd write all morning, and if I weren't going out to lunch, look forward to seeing Isabel. There weren't that many long lunches any more, anyway, these days. The work generation was ascendant, work becoming the new sex, the new black, the new way to spend your youth. There were fewer restaurants and more cafés. A well-known chef said he now made more money providing sandwiches for people to have at their computers than catering restaurant lunches.

Isabel didn't have many friends in Sydney, though she would have had a lengthy list of acquaintances, many of whom had enjoyed her and Gray's lavish hospitality in the old days of eighties' excess. She was making a new life for herself, slowly beginning the charity work she'd become known for, planning events to raise money for children.

She treated me as if I were a friend of her own generation, and I found her relaxing and pleasant to spend time with. The fact that she was easy on the eye and wore impeccable clothes didn't hurt. Like many women, Isabel was reaching her peak in her thirties. It was a beguiling recreation just to look at her.

We'd talk about all kinds of things, art, movies, fashion, books – she read literary best-sellers. I'm not saying it was intellectual talk, rather gossip about people who made and sold art, movies, fashion, books. It was an easy, relaxed friendship, with much of convenience and timeliness about it.

So we were having a cosy, lovely time, then something unexpected happened.

You don't remember me

All the big cities of the world contain many worlds that don't necessarily connect.

There are some places where many worlds do connect. The steam rooms are such a place. They bring men of all kinds together. Men with manicured hands, men with rough hands, the young and the old, the lucky and the generous, the comely and the homely, the observers and the participants. A model of democracy.

Such were my happy thoughts late one night as I sat relaxed over a last drink, having stopped on my way home because it was a lovely, lively night. I was in a bar near Taylor Square, sitting by the open window.

A man walked past, paused, walked back, stopped in front of me, and said 'Hello!'

I barely glanced at him. He was tall and thin with a beard, not one of those stylish goatees the boys were wearing around now but a ragged beard of the kind worn by men who can't afford razors or have some beatnik, refusenik, unreconstructed hippie thing going on. He was dressed in clothes that looked like they came from an op shop or even a bin.

I knew a young man who did find clothes in the bin, but he lived in a very desirable new apartment block in a great part of town and was blessed with unfailing serendipity, charm and eccentricity, and the clothes tossed at the bins by his neighbours were absolute finds, so when he turned up to a very smart party and mentioned that everything he was wearing, even socks and underpants, was found in the bin, he was thought adorable. That's all by the way, this night on the other hand I was reminded more of the increasing numbers of the destitute on the city's streets.

I hesitated, expecting this barely apprehended apparition to ask me for my spare change.

'You don't remember me,' he said.

I'd have sworn I'd never set eyes on him before, though there is that swift moment of your mind darting through many crowded occasions in those better days of yore when there were faces you never quite saw or too many of them. And people changed. And memory failed.

'Larry,' he said.

'My God! For God's sake sit down! What are you *doing* here? No one knows if you're alive or dead. What do you want to drink? How long have you been here? Where have you *been*?'

He'd been in Sydney a few weeks, he told me.

'And on the breadline, are you?' I said. 'They don't do much in the way of food here but...'

'Do I look as if I need feeding?' he said, amused and also surprised.

'Your clothes look like they came from Vinnie's,' I said. I saw that they were perfectly well cared for, but it was an odd effect in Oxford Street, among boys who could tell you the difference between French seams and French cuffs to see this no longer boy, but still very young looking man, poised and lovely, as you could only see if you had a reason to look closely, dressed in some clothes he'd had for years and some clothes he'd somewhere along the line picked up as the only thing available.

'I suppose they do,' Larry said, with a smile as if the sudden realization was rather entertaining. 'I've been meaning to get something that would be better for around here, but I just haven't got round to it.'

'I can lend you any money you need, it's really no problem,' I offered.

His look was that same surprise, not wounded dignity. 'No, it's not that, really, I've got more money than I can really use, I've spent so little.'

I recalled the inheritance that had allowed him to take up a life that rejected or redefined ambition and opportunity.

'So where on the planet have you been mucking around?'

He'd just come from India, he told me.

'I did hear you had gone there, Isabel told me.'

'You talked to Isabel?' he asked eagerly.

'I saw her yesterday.'

'Isabel's in Sydney?'

'Certainly is. Remember that apartment of Elliott Templeton's? She and Gray are living there.'

I was watching him closely during this exchange but saw no evidence of any complicated emotion, just a nice surprise at hearing of an old friend you've always liked.

Larry knew that Isabel had married Gray, but knew nothing of her subsequent life, the limelight, the crash. I was amazed until I thought about the fact that Larry had been out of the country for many of those years, and mainly in India where you would see no news of Australia in papers and magazines if indeed you ever saw papers and magazines which, I gathered, Larry usually did not, not seeking them, though he might have picked up the occasional weeks or months-old copy of *Time* or the *International Herald Tribune* at some chai stall frequented by Westerners. Of course I didn't think all that then.

I briefly filled him in.

Elliott, since Larry asked after him, was not in Sydney at this time; he claimed to be 'slowing down' and was off at some health spa.

'And how do Isabel and Gray like life in Sydney?'

'Pretty well, I think, but why don't you ask them?'

'I would love to see them,' Larry said.

'I don't have the number on me, but directory assistance will. But Larry, a quiet word dear, I'd do something about the facial forest unless you want to scare the children.'

'I will.' He took a good look at what I was wearing, and looked carefully at a couple of guys in the place, not seeming to notice that they looked affronted that this derro seemed to be cruising them. The music pulsed over us. Larry asked me, 'Where do you get your clothes?'

I told him, and told him as it was in Melbourne it wasn't much good to him. We went on talking about Isabel and Gray, how they'd stood by each other, about the children, things like that.

Nearly an hour passed. It was way past midnight, and the street was still lively. I felt too pleasantly tired to go home to bed.

'I'm going to get something to eat,' I said, 'would you join me?'

'Not this time, thanks,' said Larry graciously, 'I'd better be off.' And he was suddenly gone.

Same as ever, I thought, always a bit mysterious about where he lived and just what he was doing. I wondered how much of that, how much else about him, was a kind of pose.

How could you stand it

I phoned Isabel the next day. 'Can I come over for a cup of tea? I want you to guess who I've seen.'

Gray was there too that day. 'What was that about seeing someone?' Isabel asked, pouring whichever blend of tea she was featuring that week.

'I saw Larry last night,' I said.

There was a split second of utter stillness as they took it in and then they asked me everything at once, where and how, what was he doing, how did he look, where had he been, why hadn't he called, where was he right now and call him this minute and get him over here.

'I never got his number,' I admitted.

I remembered how he didn't like telling anyone where he lived, the effect was that you didn't like to ask.

'I can't believe you saw him last night and today you don't know where he is!'

'I'm sorry, but he was definitely very thrilled to know you're here and if that's the phone that's probably him now.'

But it wasn't him, and a couple of days later when I saw Isabel again there was still not one word from Larry.

'You made it all up! You did not see him!'

'I did so. He sat down and we talked for nearly an hour. I told you, he recognized me first. He's grown a beard.'

'I hate beards! Unless they're only those little new ones like this.'

'He'll be in touch, there was no doubt.'

It was another two or three days before she called me and said, 'Please say you're free, can you come over? Guess who just called?'

'He didn't? What did I tell you?'

'He's coming over now, can you come?'

'Don't you all want to catch up first?'

'We all would really like you to come over too.'

When I got there Isabel was still shrieking and laughing, telling him what a shit he was for not getting in touch at once. If I hadn't heard her first I wouldn't have seen at once that the man she was hugging and punching was Larry, and Gray was hugging and punching him too, all of them beaming.

Old friends, always happy to see each other, even after all this time. Much earlier in life than I ever had, they had made friends they'd have for life.

'Mr Maugham told me I looked like a dag so I flew to Melbourne and got some clothes.'

He had shaved off the beard, too, and the clothes were fabulous yet very understated. The look in his eyes and the intense impression he gave of boundless equanimity gave him an air of maturity. But he looked so young, too, and thin and self-possessed and as adorable as ever.

You wouldn't have picked Larry and Gray as contemporaries; Gray now looked middle-aged. They were all very warm and affectionate together but Larry had something about him I might call, and I'm not sure this is the word, detachment. But not cold. Extra aware but not spacey, aloof but not up himself.

Gray had opened some champagne, and I noticed that Larry drank his very slowly, not finishing his glass.

The children were brought in, Amanda and Kristina or Samantha and Jessica or something, and Larry was good with them, kids can tell if you like them. So it was all about the children for a while, Gray and Isabel very proud of them. I didn't mind them but I could tell Larry was genuinely interested and made them giggle as they told him the doll's name and their favourite story and agreed their mother was beautiful. Then the children were sent off to have their dinner.

'You'll see Uncle Larry again, won't they, Larry?'

'Quite likely,' Larry smiled and they smiled back at him and obediently went away.

'We'll have adult dinner here at home and you both must stay.'

Gray and Isabel insisted: it was no trouble, there was this and that in the freezer and this was a good time to open that wine someone had given them and get something sent over from the best Thai restaurant in town.

'Have you gone vegetarian, Larry?'

'I prefer vegetarian food if it's available.'

She looked pleased with herself for guessing.

It was mainly Isabel and Gray's story over dinner, the house on the river and the children, and some of the exciting development projects, and the recognition Gray had received and everyone who had called him 'visionary'. And then the effect of the entrepreneurs who had broken the banks, and how it had all collapsed, the inquiry into corruption back in the home state, and the aftermath. The death of Gray's father and how it had all knocked him around. They had lost everything, and Isabel and Gray were trying to keep the tone of the evening upbeat but there was no way to conceal what it had meant to them.

Larry had said he'd drink water only with the meal, but when Gray made a bit of a point of what an excellent wine he was opening for the occasion, said in that case he would have a glass. But I noticed he only took a few sips. I wondered if India had done his liver some damage.

'Tell us about you now, Larry,' Isabel said. 'Where have you just come from?'

'India.'

'Well, tell us! What were you doing there? Did you have a good time? Is it really amazing? We're all wearing pashminas now.'

'I stayed in one place for most of the last three years.' Everyone was looking at him, going 'go on'. 'In an…ashram.'

'What is an ashram exactly? It's the name of a day spa I've been to in Woollahra.' This was the moment I registered that day spa was the new term for beauty parlour.

'An ashram is a retreat.'

'So, you did the whole spiritual trip thing? Is that all for real?'

'Well, I really did spend that time in the ashram,' Larry said hesitantly, as if it were difficult to answer her question exactly.

'No, I know,' she said, 'but what is it really, isn't an ashram a place where they go to do *yoga*?'

'Some people call it *yoga*, yes.'

'They make a lot of money from Westerners I suppose,' said Gray as if he were being witty. Larry smiled politely.

'And don't you have to bow down to some guru?'

'There are many ashrams in India and I don't know what they do in all of them. We had no rules about bowing to anyone.'

Larry spoke as he always did, with a voice any radio broadcaster might wish for. He made a sincere, unpretentious effort to answer what he was asked. Though some of Isabel's and Gray's questions could have sounded as if they were challenging him, he was unruffled by any of their implications. They also seemed to be driven by an affectionate curiosity and, come to think of it, a curious affection. No matter how different their later choices were, clearly they'd enjoyed those shared early formative years, and enjoyed recalling them, years that in my own life, as a puny misfit, were not untainted with fury and despair.

Larry did not volunteer much, or do much more than provide an answer. He wasn't inviting an expansion of curiosity or questioning.

We asked if he'd met any Indian film stars? Or any artists? Or anyone really interesting?

'I did, I met all kinds of people, I made sure I did, I travelled around the country quite a bit before I ended up staying in the ashram, and I had conversations with people everywhere.'

'In English?'

'Often in English, many people speak English, especially in the cities, but I also learnt some Hindi and some Tamil, enough to talk with people a bit.'

'So what was this ashram like? Aren't those places very commercial now?'

'This one wasn't.'

We dragged out of memory yesteryear's stories of the excesses of the glamorous gurus, sex scandals, corruption, fleets of luxury cars, scheming factions, brainwashing. The reliance on the devotion, and financial resources, of Westerners. For gurus as well as speculators had come undone as the Age of Excess ended.

'Not where I was. It was all very simple.'

'Who else was there? Were there many Westerners?'

'A lot of people had travelled a long way to get there.'

'And everyone stayed in this ashram place?'

'Increasingly, people began to stay in guesthouses near the ashram, as the residential quarters were always full.'

'So it was all tourists?'

'There were many Indians there.'

Larry answered all our questions with serene readiness.

'So there was what, a guru at the head of it?'

'Some people called him a guru, or a spiritual master, or a fully-realized being, things like that. He never claimed to be at the head of it.'

'But he was the reason everyone was there?'

'He said the reason we were there was not him but our...the word means something like spiritual practice, but it's a more common expression there. That, he said, was what we came for, not for him. But he was a kind of focus, or unifier.'

I don't think all that many people out here had heard of the saint at this time. Some people went to India to track down gurus and faith-healers, and some of them had found their way to him. When reminded, we think we might have heard about him: one of those ones they go to in India; the one that had lived in silence in a cave for many years and then for a long time the only thing he ever said was 'be good'. That gave plenty of people plenty to be going on with, apparently.

'What did you do all day?'

'Whatever we wanted – meditation, reading, sitting, or doing your...the word means your job, your work, your duty.'

'So, this saint guy, he'd what, would you see much of him?'

'Most of the time he sat where anyone could go and sit near him, if they wanted to. So you could go and sit with him, and you'd find you'd been there for hours.'

'While he did what?'

'What we all were doing.'

'Did you have a nice room? Were the bathrooms clean?'

'I slept in a very simple, clean space. There were people cleaning everything all the time. Most of us did some cleaning work at some time.'

'How could you stand it for, you were there *how* long?'

It seemed to me, looking at Isabel looking at Larry, that some kind of realization was coming to her, that Larry was not the same Larry. Maybe she had wanted him to make her feel she was the same Isabel. But he had changed, gained experience and knowledge, you could see it. But then, you don't see someone for the longest time, and it's not the changes you see but how they seem just the same. He retained the open, even-tempered quality he'd always had. Larry never tried to persuade others to his point of view, but he'd explain it as best as he could if asked to.

Her eyes were all over him, checking out the clothes, the way he wore them, how he really looked up close (nice, casually confident, really good).

I don't know how much she took in of what he was telling us, she was sizing him up. Feeling a mix of things, looking upon him as an old friend, as someone she desired and could have married...and there was, still, again, something maternal in the way she looked at him, tender and protective, amused and proud and anxious. Isabel had lost him once, and just as she thought she might have got him back she saw, what, that she hadn't really got him back, that she could lose him again.

'So what was he like, this saint?' Gray was asking.

'Medium height, medium build, medium dark, early thirties.'

'No, what was his attraction? To you?'

Larry took a moment, then said, 'I think I could call it saintliness.'

'Which is what?'

Larry didn't answer at once.

'Do you mean someone very charitable?'

'It isn't quite the right word. It really means something like, someone who has received spiritual illumination. It doesn't have exactly the moral meaning we might put on it.'

'What did you get out of it?' Gray probed.

Larry blinked slowly. 'Peace.'

No one went much further along those lines, it would have begun to sound like an interrogation.

But there was plenty to chat about, their memories of tennis games and parties and the time I had first met them all, the old house and Mrs Bradley. How I'd become their other uncle, being Uncle Elliott's friend. We told each other the story that says 'this is my life with you in it'.

You did it yourself

I'd promised to take the three of them out. I knew it would be nice for them to have something to do together and it would be nice for me to have their company. I got house seats to the play – the audiences were loving it, and it would also be nice for my young friends to see that.

I made a booking for supper afterwards in the Desirable Nightspot du Jour. We would see and be seen.

So I was wearing my very best jacket when, after a drink with my agent, I turned up as arranged at Elizabeth Bay. We were all going to have a drink there before going to the theatre together.

Isabel answered the door. 'Weren't you screening? You weren't answering and Larry didn't leave his number. We can't come tonight, Gray's got one of those headaches and I can't leave him.'

She wasn't dressed to go out, and she looked pale and a bit tired.

'Don't say anything,' she warned me, 'everyone thinks of something to try or some cause and we have tried everything and are having every test under the sun. I'll have a drink with you till Larry comes, then you two go on, *you* must go anyway after all your arrangements.'

It was ghastly for them and not so great for me and I was mentally regrouping when Larry arrived.

'Can I see Gray?' Larry asked when Isabel told him what she had told me.

'Be really quiet, I know you will be, but everything is agony. But he'd like it if you just quickly said hello,' and I was included in this.

We went into a big bedroom, it was like walking into a magazine page, everything was very neat, no clothes on a chair or book open on the floor or anything like that, and Gray was lying there with a cloth over his forehead, which you only just made out because there was one lamp on, dimmed down low.

I felt a bit awkward, suddenly it all felt very intimate and they knew each other better than I did, but Larry just went up to Gray, who had opened his eyes and turned his head to us and was managing an obviously painful and genuine grin. Larry said softly, 'Isabel told me. Do you want me to try and help you? I think I might be able to.'

I don't think Isabel or I dared to look at each other.

Gray croaked out his assent, and Larry sat down on the bed.

He said softly, 'Gray, lie still, close your eyes, allow your body to relax. In one minute from now, you will find that your arm is lifting, this one, the right arm, and you will keep it raised for fifteen seconds, then lower it.'

Isabel and I sat down – there were very nice chairs in their bedroom. And were very still and silent.

I wasn't counting but it felt like sixty seconds and Gray lifted his arm and after a second or two I began counting and it was all about exactly what he'd said. It didn't look as if Gray was making an effort to lift the arm, it looked as if the arm were being lifted for him, by some invisible force, gentle but strong.

Gray tried to say something, something about feeling his arm lift though he had not tried to lift it.

'Good,' said Larry very gently and slowly. 'Now Gray, just stay there, lying still. I want you to visualize the pain in your head. Feel the pain there and look at its colour, and its shape, and how big it is. Look at its edges, with your inner eye look at all its edges. Now see all those edges growing closer together and smaller as the shape gets smaller. Watch it get smaller and smaller, as if the pain was just a balloon of that shape and size, blown up and now slowly all the air is being let out of it and it's shrinking, shrinking until it's so very small you can't see it any more. Now you are going to sleep. You will sleep deeply for two minutes, then wake up refreshed, alert, with no headache at all.'

For two minutes Gray lay there still, breathing. Then he opened his eyes, turned to look at us, smiled uncertainly, smiled certainly, and said, 'I feel great!'

He sat up, 'Larry, Isabel, everyone…'

Isabel said, 'Really, really, no more headache, oh my God!'

'Larry, what did you *do*? I've never found anything that could help.'

Larry said, 'You don't have long if we're going to get to the theatre on time.'

Isabel said, 'I will be dressed in record time, I had everything ready.'

Gray said, 'She probably had everything ready for me too.'

We even had a mouthful of champagne before we rushed off.

There was no interval, it was the length of a movie, sit down and listen for eighty-seven minutes give or take variations in timing and, er, feedback. It was a very good house that night, and everyone relaxed and got the jokes. Anyway, I'm sure it was very distracting. Quite a bit later, when we were eating and drinking, and had talked about the play and they had asked me this and that about writing it and about the actors and the theatre, though Isabel kept stealing glances at Larry, then…

And then there was that quiet moment when we all just paused and looked at each other.

'What about before?' said Isabel.

Gray said, 'Larry, what did you *do*? Those turns are bloody agony, and it's always here we go, it goes on for *days*.'

Larry said, 'It's just a technique I've learnt along the way. As you saw, it was very simple.'

'Did you learn that in India?'

'I did.'

'But what did you do?'

'You saw what I did.'

'But you cured me,' said Gray.

'You did it yourself,' said Larry, 'really.' And said it in a way that we were being told to now talk of something else.

'No, just one more thing,' said Gray. 'Can you teach me how to do that? Can you come over tomorrow?'

I've never loved anyone else

Larry went to see Gray the next day, and spoke to him alone for a while. Isabel assumed Larry was coaching him in the technique he had used. All Gray said was that Larry asked a few questions about the headaches. Gray wasn't the kind of man to say more than that, it was up to Isabel to see that the two men's quiet little talk had left Gray oddly thoughtful for a while. I don't know whether Larry and he talked about his headaches again. Larry came around a couple more times, Gray was fine. A couple of weeks after the night at the theatre, Gray was struck with another headache. It wasn't as bad as the previous one, but he was certain that if Larry were there it would go. He wanted Isabel to get hold of Larry, but Larry had never given them a phone number, he said he didn't have the phone on. Gray tried to use the techniques Larry had shown him, but he really needed Larry.

Why? I'm not sure how you'd explain how Larry had cured Gray, whether you'd call it a kind of hypnosis. You see exactly how it's done, in front of you, but you can't necessarily do it yourself.

Larry turned up the next day, and sat with Gray, and the headache went away. Larry again told Gray he could do to himself what Larry did to him.

'I think I was close,' said Gray, 'but I still need you, coach, just while I'm training to get back into form.'

'At least tell us your address!' said Isabel to him. 'It's mad that we can't get in touch with you.'

Larry gave her a private mail box number in Surry Hills, said he checked it daily, and that was his address.

'You don't live in a mail box!' said Isabel. He only smiled at her, as if she were enchantingly amusing, and she found herself unable to force him to tell her where he lived.

'What is all this mystery, what for?' she said to me as we were having our tea the next afternoon. 'Remember when we were all in Sydney before, Larry wouldn't tell anyone where he lived, and then I went there and it was just a little room, there wasn't anything mysterious about it.'

We agreed Larry wouldn't be in the least ashamed if ten years later still all he had was a similar little room.

'Anyone else, you'd think all sorts of things.'

'You wouldn't think them of Larry,' I agreed.

'Then why?' Isabel asked me.

She really did expect me to come up with something, and I said, 'I think Larry has a sense of privacy, something quite deep, a privacy of his spirit.'

'What can that mean!' said Isabel impatiently. 'Isn't that a bit pretentious?'

'Some writers and artists feel like that about the space they work in, it's space dedicated to their work, so they like to keep it reserved for that, it's not a social space or even a space that others can enter, it's consecrated.'

'Well, I'd like to see this so-called work Larry does.'

'I think we did see it.'

'Oh.' Gray's three-day headaches were not a scenario she wanted to revisit. 'Does he heal other people, he's so good at it he should be, I don't know, doing something with it.'

'How do you know he isn't?'

'No, I mean really get some recognition.' Perhaps she imagined him on a televised tour of inspirational lectures, books and tapes on sale. She only wanted to talk about Larry that day. 'Why is he so, well, strange? I mean, I've known him just about all my life. He always was a bit, a bit like that, as if he was thinking of other things, but he didn't miss a thing that was going on either. And now, he still is a bit strange isn't he? What *is* that?'

'I think it might be something quite simple.'

'What?'

'Virtue.'

'Oh, for God's sake!' she frowned. 'Don't say such weird things.'

'Why is that weird?'

'It gives me the creeps.'

'Do you mean, perhaps, a heartache?'

'Fuck you,' said with no exclamation.

'Do you want to show me the door?'

'Stay right there,' she said grumpily.

'Thank you, it is such a pleasure to gaze upon you, even when you are cranky and confused.'

'You're one sick bastard.'

'Thank you.' She did look all lit up because this is what she wanted to talk about and I think I was the only one she was talking to about it.

'Be nice. Why am I so obsessed with trying to work Larry out?'

'If you are really asking me, I think you're still in love with him.'

'Fuck you.' But then she added, 'I've never loved anyone else in all my life.'

There, she'd said it.

'I see,' I said slowly. 'Presumably you don't favour Gray with this confidence.'

'God! Look, I do love Gray.'

'Well, you did marry him.'

'I had to marry someone and he was perfect, actually. Mother really wanted me to marry him, we had the same group of friends, he was really going places. And we have had a really good time, he's always been good to me, and he is a wonderful father. You say Larry has goodness! Gray has always been kind and generous and always done the right thing.'

'Even if the Inquiry doesn't think so.'

'Those bastards, everyone had to come down because of a couple of crooks. No, Gray never did anything that wasn't ethical, and anyway, I'm talking about what he is as a husband, I can't complain about any aspect. You're so cynical, everyone knows that, but he really is just what you see, a lovely man.'

'Sounds like Mr Right, Prince Charming, the Perfect Match.'

'Why *are* you always so cynical? Gray and I have been very happy together.'

I just looked at her.

'I never forgot Larry, but as I never saw him it didn't bother me, we didn't know if he was alive or dead or what, it wasn't like it would be if I had to see him. And now I do have to see him,' she said, her voice changing.

She should have been an actress, I'm not saying she didn't mean any of it, just how she looked, how moving emotion is. She was always ready for her close-up. She could never be had for the price of a cocktail like a salted peanut.

'Do you remember,' she said, 'you once told me something like you can get over someone easier if they're really far away, if you don't have to see them?'

'You don't *have* to see him. If it's that hard, you could manage not to.'

'I couldn't not see him when I can! You know what I mean. And he might just suddenly vanish again, you know he might.'

'Would you think of separating from Gray?'

'I've got no reason to.'

'Being in love with someone else?'

'You know perfectly well you can love more than one person, didn't you write a play about that?'

I don't know if she ever read me, but she read my critics, anyway, or listened to them at parties more likely.

'Oh, women want a man to be everything in the world, best friend, lover, provider, gorgeous hitchhiker…are you going to find it all in one person?'

'I know Gray doesn't say much but believe me there's more to him than you might think.'

'I don't underestimate him, I think there is a lot to him, I've seen how he is with you, he really loves you, he thinks you're beautiful and amazing and he still can't get over having you, and he adores the kids. More than you do.'

'What, so now you don't think I'm a good mother?'

'I didn't say that, you are a good mother, you give them everything they need, consideration, encouragement, milk, ballet. But Gray dotes.'

'I've never thought it was good for a woman to have no life of her own, only husband and children.'

'Husband and children is not a life?'

'I can't believe you're saying that,' she said.

'Look, I'm with you, there's more to do than that, but for some people that is a life.'

'And the girls do adore me,' she said.

'They do, they're kind of in awe of you. You are the kind of mother I, unsettlingly, have suddenly realized I had. An air of aloof yet charismatic glamour.'

'Actually, they worship Gray,' she said, 'and why wouldn't they. He's very lovable.'

'So are you,' I said.

'Darling! Another cup?'

For a while we talked about Gray, about how the Inquiry had affected him, how shattered he had been to find himself publicly linked to all those greedy criminals and corrupt pollies, he had never thought he was linked, he just was very good at business, great timing and vision and boldness and people skills. It devastated him to know, Isabel told me, that he could have kept all the businesses going if he could have done things the way he had planned, he always knew what he was doing, he believed in himself, but suddenly the plug was pulled, loans called in, banks fall, rates rise, and there's Gray ruined, he feels so bad about it, a lot of people felt very let down, and a lot of them think it's his fault, and he does feel it is, so there is all that guilt and feeling sorry for people.

Later we went back to the subject of her marriage.

She would never divorce Gray, she told me, she couldn't do that to him, and she didn't want to. They got on well, they never fought, they agreed on the kids' upbringing. 'And you know what? We always have great sex. We've been married for ten years now and it's still always really good. I know you wrote that play about how monogamy doesn't work but it does for us. You mightn't think so, but he's, you know, he's really good.'

'I would so think so.' Isabel had an obvious attractiveness. Gray's sensuality was also apparent, people just didn't usually look for it. Or they saw pretty quickly that Isabel was the only one for him.

'I've never wanted to cheat on Gray.' And maybe could have, but we didn't go there.

'So do you ever think you should have married Larry when you could have?'

'No way, it would have been a disaster. What I do regret is I didn't go away and live with him, we'd have had a great few months, and I would have totally got him out of my system.'

'Or you might have found yourself very deeply involved and unable to leave him.'

'No, it's always been mainly a physical attraction. The best way to get rid of a temptation is to give in to it, right? Right? Those things don't last, they burn themselves out.'

'Maybe. But I don't know you'd have gotten over Larry in three months. You're the kind who wants to be needed and adored like Gray does and Larry never would have, you'd never ever really have all the attention you get from Gray, and you'd have gone on trying to get it, to make him go through hoops for you.'

'You think you know so much,' she said, and she really was miffed. 'It might be different for two men but if a man comes back to a woman once he'll come back as often as she wants him to.' She had decided that Larry had 'come back to her' when he had come to Sydney to meet her all those years ago.

'Where did you pick that up, *Cleo, Cosmo, Women's Forum*?'

'I meet all kinds of people from all walks of life if you must know.' She smiled at me in a provocative way.

'Give me a chocolate biscuit and tell me about the walks of life.'

'Do you know who Vivienne Kertesz is?'

I should have known. Isabel reminded me. Also known as Mistress Stiletto, she had performed at one of the Maturins' parties back in the good old days.

Quite a cult figure, once notorious for her outrageous shows featuring black leather bondage gear, she gave glamour and visibility to the fetishization of whips, restraints, masks, all that kind of thing. Sado-masochism, or the pretence of it, had emerged as a fashion, but by now it had been some time since Mistress Stiletto had performed at small clubs or big dance parties. She used occasionally to be photographed in her private dungeon, dressed for designer torture, hanging off a sling or making repairs to some rack. I hadn't heard of her in a while but apparently she now had created a line of up-market lingerie and sex toys, and was cultivating her well-heeled shopaholic acquaintances at the kind of social event Isabel went to.

'I saw her again at a fashion benefit thing. I went right up to her and told her she looked fabulous and I'd always been sorry we hadn't had time to really talk when she did that appearance for us in Brisbane. She had a whole different look going on now, so I might have reminded her of a good time, a nice part of it to remember. She was a bit suss for a while, but I just raved on and I really did know the designer she was wearing who she also knew, blah blah, we had a good talk, so next thing I'm going round to Vivienne's studio, invited into her adjoining apartment, looking at her new camisole designs and playing with her samples of fur-lined handcuffs.'

Isabel went on to tell me about the groovy girl-talk they had had, for she had ordered a few things and gone back to collect them, bringing a bottle of champagne with her, and urging Vivienne to tell more of what she knew.

'I could write a book.'

'Why don't *you*? It could be the self-help book of all time. Let's think of a name for it.'

'You think of a name,' she said bitchily, and I smiled at her and we sat in silence.

'I wonder why Larry really asked you to marry him,' I said after a while.

She glared. 'Can you read my lips? It's called love, ell-oh-vee-ee.'

'Oh, I'm sure there was a kind of love for you, still is. As you say, you'd known each other since you were little, played tennis and went to the beach together, developed those first adult sexual feelings looking at each other, had sex for the first time together, am I right?'

'We were each other's first and it was very beautiful and special for both of us, if you're not too depraved to appreciate that.'

'He would have expected himself to be in love with you, and to get married to you, he would have told himself it was natural. He'd have just thought, you'd go on as before, only be sleeping in the same bed.'

'I've thought so much about what he expected.' Isabel was fascinated of course, as I was engrossed in talking about her, and Larry, and love. 'I know I just said it's mainly a physical attraction, but I didn't only have lust for him, it was love.'

'Isn't lust a kind of love?'

'It's not the same thing. It just isn't, no matter who you are.'

'It might not be the same thing, but only in the sense that there are many kinds of love, and lust is one of them, and sometimes you also have other kinds of love for the one you lust for. And it's not always the same all the time.'

'Well, all right, I had love for him, and I did have lust for him, I was kind of mad with it actually, he was all I wanted. I couldn't stop thinking about it, I wanted him so much. It was a real passion.'

'Was it? Passion doesn't stop to wonder if it's the right thing or will it last or what anyone will think. It doesn't need any reason, it isn't about reason, it's unreasonable, it's its own reason. If you're not already a reckless youth you feel like one. It's destructive, the greatest loves in stories are full of destruction and hurt and tragedy, but you know they'd do it all again.

'And that kind of passion, if it hasn't destroyed you, it dies. If you're not destroyed you end up with the wreck you've made of your life, or you end up with a fool, or if you're lucky you end up comfortable old friends.'

I admit I was going on for a while, as I was working out some ideas about some characters I was writing, and had lost Isabel a while back; she was not going to change her story for any story of mine. But what she came out with was:

'Do you think Larry is sleeping with anyone?'

'I have no idea but as he's an attractive single man in his thirties I would think he has plenty of opportunity.'

'I know he isn't.'

'He told you?'

'Of course not! I just know. I can tell. Feminine intuition. Do you want to know what I really think? I don't think he's slept with another woman since he left.'

'What about a man?'

'Come off it, Larry isn't that way inclined.'

Well, there was someone I knew who thought different, but I didn't mention it. It was time for me to go. Isabel and Gray were going out and she had to get herself dolled up. I wandered out into the still summer Sydney night, with the tang of the Harbour in the balmy air.

Isabel had made me think of Josh Rouvier, and I wanted to hear more about what I'd recently heard from him. Josh had just moved into a new studio in Surry Hills, and a cab was coming along. I took it, and went to see Josh.

He was repeating himself

I mentioned Josh earlier.

I'd known him for over ten years now. He was another of the young boys that make it to Sydney in a mood of that-or-die-trying. One good thing about a small town, you know you want to get out, as Lou Reed sang. It's not that there's no one who'd understand, it's that you don't know how to find them. Big city, you do know. Josh had learned a few skills back in Woop-woop: changing tyres, ironing shirts, fellatio. But he had longed for the wider world, for everything the small town did not have, the masses and the glamour, the intensity and anonymity, the possibilities and prospects. Back there, there seemed to be nothing in store but re-enacting the endless cycles of limitation and pettiness. He poured over copies of his mother's *Women's Weekly* for glimpses into a richer world.

Until at school he began art classes, where he got his best marks, though he did not for long imagine he would be an artist himself. He picked up some notions through reading novels based on artists' lives: *Moulin Rouge, The Moon and Sixpence, The Agony and the Ecstasy, Lust for Life, The Venetian* – anything his teacher mentioned and he could get out of the library. Josh and I had once hilariously recalled such novels together. He'd suffered a mild dyslexia that meant each book took months to get through, but he knew them by heart. By then he'd given up novels and sought out films. Anyway, he had the natural assets of good luck and a good eye. He knew he needed to be around artistic talent. Off to the big city he would go.

He had come to town in about 1980, and did it tough for a while – had his stuff stolen, no fixed address, a hard time getting a job. But soon enough, helping out with the cleaning work somewhere, Josh was picked up by Adam Douglas, and soon thereafter was employed as Adam's studio assistant. Adam had been to New York, where the new breed of star artists were employing studio assistants, so he wanted one too, though he was not making that kind of money yet. Josh was paid in free board and training. His initial brief was a vaguely defined 'help me keep track of things'. Josh took on more and more responsibilities: housekeeper, secretary, companion, confidant, even advisor. He became an intimate of Adam's inner circle, part of the scene, though he always worked beyond the call of duty, and cleared up after a party, or at least first thing next day.

Adam painted in oils, onto sheets of corrugated iron or old doors or slabs of siding, imitations of the graffiti, that, along railway lines, on public buildings and buses was deemed a criminal eyesore. Adam had gone to New York to study the graffiti art there and finally found a gallery in Sydney to show him. To call vandalism art upset certain critics, for whom the avant-garde had been adequately defined by the past. Adam went on to paint canvases, with inspiration from Basquiat and Haring, and also worked in linocuts, but that would have been after Josh's time with him.

Adam's great friend Benjamin Trust moved into a new large studio with him.

Ben, who began making jewellery out of plastic shapes and found pieces, was beginning to create extraordinary costumes, mixing natural skins, furs, leather and woven cloth with nylon, vinyl and rubber; he created adornment with feathers, shells, beads and a range of found objects from nuts and bolts to toys, cutlery and used lipstick cases; he constructed highly decorated robes, headdresses, staffs, luggage. He was a distinctive figure around the inner city, wearing his own creations, pushing his studded leather shopping cart, his hip-length hair plaited with beads, feathers and leather straps.

Both were serious and dedicated artists whose work and forms were too long treated as marginal frivolities. They mixed art, craft and fashion, agitprop and popular culture, the influences of nascent hip-hop, punk and the kind of drag queens who not so much changed gender as added a gender or two. The work referred to, and interacted with, cultures marked by recreational drugs and sex, gay liberation and identity politics. They made unique pieces of rare materials, and also ran off T-shirts, posters and postcards, employing nationalist and cult icons. Their studio shows added to all this music and dance and performance. It all seems so distant now, so fresh. In those early years the dominance of entrepreneurship and the aesthetics of commodities still had not extended their firm grip. Theorists were someplace else, learning a new post-structuralist vocabulary, moralizing and hesitating. I knew them slightly, Adam and Ben, introduced by an actress friend who was close to them and took me to their studio parties.

Ben began using Josh to model his stuff, and when Adam went on a trip back to New York, which was the fount and holy grail of inspiration for this little group, with its downtown do-it-yourself art scene, its vitality and bravura, so much of it expired before the decade ended amidst drug overdoses, AIDS, violence, the star system and real estate gentrification – when Adam was gone, Ben took on the employment of Josh, who had become indispensable, gently keeping things together.

Josh, though not particularly handsome, even well into his twenties looked like a boy and wore hand-painted T-shirts over torn jeans, his hair a different colour each week, sometimes streaked, sometimes creating a leopard or tiger effect or he would shave a number or symbol onto his skull. But he seemed to do these things not out of narcissism but as part of his innate desire to please. He was sensitive, caring and appreciative. He liked cleaning up but he knew what to leave alone. He had taste and discernment and never stinted on praise and encouragement. He happily shared his employers' beds at times, with them and with others; relationships then were indefinable, fluid, elastic, capable of many permutations, and their shared experiments in erotic possibilities increased their shared affection.

Still, eventually Josh left Adam and Ben, I don't know why, who were at the time still thriving.

He was next employed by a sound artist, whose studio was filled with esoteric instruments and electronic equipment. Josh looked after the artist and his schedule diligently for a year or two, but eventually gave his notice.

'I've always been in visual art, so I missed that too much,' Josh told me. 'And he just didn't really inspire me any more, and if I felt like that now everyone else would feel it soon enough. He was repeating himself. I had to move on.'

Necessary to break with the past

When Josh left the sound artist, he soon found employment with our mutual friend, Robert Grossmann, whose installation piece was the talking point of the Sydney Biennale that year. Robert had had people talking a couple of years back with his installation called *Nothing,* into which people were admitted one at a time to find themselves in a cube-like room painted matte white containing nothing, not a thing. Most of the complaints were that one was not allowed to stay there long enough. Long queues formed of those keen for the experience, or to repeat it. He had a great instinct for controversy, Robert; a gallery had been raided and briefly closed down with charges of obscenity laid by the police – later dismissed, as no member of the public who had actually been to the show had ever complained – for a piece of his combining installation and performance, in which two men wearing only black leather chaps, studded leather bands and chains were strung up in a rack and a sling. Observers were told they were free to inflict torture, though not so many of them did.

Robert's new piece was called *Garbage,* and reproduced a pile of trash found at a dump in the outer suburbs. It included some decaying organic matter that filled the space around it with an inescapable stench. Emptied cans, smashed bottles, soiled plastic bags and so on made up the rest of the potently suggestive detritus.

He made his reputation with this one, and acquired Josh as his assistant – this time Josh received an allowance as well as board.

As with Adam and Benjamin, Josh became more than an employee, he became Robert's intimate companion, he became indispensable.

When Robert was unwell for a while, Josh took an extra job, but he stayed with him. I'd seen Robert get well again, and was away, travelling, at the time he suddenly got very sick again and died, and only knew about that months later. When I returned, Josh had vanished from the scene for a while.

So it wasn't until a couple of years later that I saw Josh again. By then he had taken a job in an art supply shop and rented a studio of his own.

He'd found it necessary to break with the past, he told me, and establish himself as an art worker in his own right.

Josh had a new acquaintance, an art dealer, who admired my plays. This dealer got Josh to invite me to one of his openings, so, after a long time in which we had not met, Josh got in touch with me. I was invited to come along before the opening began and we all had a drink together, the dealer and Josh and I.

I then kept in touch with Josh, and from time to time had a look at his efforts as he set about making art of his own. First he painted his studio walls with images taken from those illegally scribbled onto walls; later he shopped and hunted for vintage clothes, discarded household items and scrap metals and refurbished them into somewhat unwearable apparel and personal decoration; and later again he erected a panel of knobs and handles, each of which emitted a different sound when touched, and you could touch as many as you wanted at a time.

He imitated each of his former protectors and mentors in turn, and, at the time we reconnected, was making an installation piece of a larger than life mannequin with an elephant head made of papier-mâché, swathed in Indian fabrics. I had yet to learn from what influence this derived.

I never knew you knew him

I was having a coffee with Josh in Darlinghurst Road after we'd been to a movie about Andy Warhol at the Chauvel.

Josh suddenly went 'Oh my God!' interrupting his own monologue on mechanical reproduction and the unaccredited work of assistants in the world of art and called out 'Larry!' and lo and behold that's who it was coming in to the café, Larry. This was not long after the astonishing night when freaky bearded Larry turned up on the street, and just after he had turned up at Isabel's in his new clothes, which he was wearing now.

Josh rose as Larry approached and they kissed each other on each cheek.

Well!

Then Josh took it in that I knew Larry too, but Larry seemed unfazed.

'Mind if I join you?' he said. 'I think I'll get something to eat.'

'The pasta is good here,' said Josh. 'Larry, how long has it been? Where have you been? No one has seen you for yonks. Not even a postcard. And you didn't tell me you knew him! You did not need to lose weight,' and there was a split second of *oh no*, but, 'but you look well,' said with much meaning.

'I am,' smiled Larry.

'You didn't tell me you knew each other!' I said to them.

'I never knew you knew him. We go way back, don't we?'

'Nothing should surprise me,' I said.

Larry ate his fettuccine pesto and Josh told him how fantastically his career had gone since they had last seen each other.

And looked at me for substantiation.

'It's interesting work,' I confirmed. 'There's a lot of interest in Josh's work.'

'I live off it,' Josh wanted him to know.

'That's great, Josh,' said Larry warmly.

'You must come to the studio, I'll show you what I'm working on, and you must come to this.'

Josh pulled out a flyer, advertising the forthcoming group show that was to include his new piece. Larry put it in his pocket, and pulled some money out of his wallet.

'Don't get up like that as if you were going!' said Josh.

'I am,' smiled Larry. And suddenly, he had, he'd slipped money under the plate, smiled at us with one of those sweet smiles of his, and disappeared without any memorable exit lines.

'Where is he going in such a hurry at an hour like this?'

'Might have someone waiting for him,' I ventured, thinking of those late night dates with someone finishing their shift in a theatre, restaurant or taxi-cab.

'I don't know whether to pity them or envy them and...' Josh paused to make sure I was paying attention and added, 'I should know.'

'What makes you say that?'

'When I was so much younger and naïve, I had a moment of wanting to live with Larry for the rest of my life. I am seriously grateful to whatever fate stepped in, come to think of it, it was Larry himself, who suddenly was going somewhere else right now this minute, no former warning.'

Josh of course liked nothing better than an audience for his stories, the telling of which owed nothing to discretion.

'So where on this planet did you meet Larry?'

'Well, I'm not sure it was on this planet. It was when Robert was dying. Larry knew him. He wasn't like some of Robert's friends, it was all too much for them, they didn't want to know, everyone is just so busy with so much to do and what's the point of visiting someone's who's dying, what's in it for you. They'd either been through it before and didn't want to go through it again, or just couldn't face it.

'And I had given up work to look after Robert, there was no one else to do it, and he was very sick, and sometimes he would be really horrible to me, I knew he didn't mean it but it was awful. And no one was looking after me, so I was not in a good way, broke, sick, taking too many pills, going what am I going to do now? Then one day Larry turned up to visit, and he began to come and sit with Robert sometimes and Robert would always sleep peacefully then. And Robert died, and all that was horrible, and Larry just said to me, 'You look like *you* need to go out for a nice long lunch,' and he got hold of my arm and took me right to Watson's Bay, and we sat by the water and he ordered everything, and just let it all come out, I was broke and rundown and scared and I had to change my life bigtime and the way I looked no one would even buy me a drink let alone make sure I moved in. All of Robert's money had gone on hospitals and drugs and carers and then his mother turned up after he was dead and took everything that was left, all his work and stuff, I just didn't count, and I was homeless. I didn't think I could go on. Larry! He was so easy to talk to, though he never said much. We spent the whole afternoon there by the Harbour, I felt he'd brought me back to life. You know what, I even told him that I wanted to do my own art. He was the first one I really said it to.

'"What do *you* need most right now?" he asked me. I just went *ahhh*,' and Josh shook his head at me, 'I could hardly say, I needed to get away, have some time, go somewhere different, become what I wanted to be, and Larry just seemed to understand all that and said, "I was thinking of going to Pondicherry. You should come with me. As my guest. If *you* really do just want a quiet time."

'"Larry," I said, just to make sure, "I'm not up to doing anything at all."

'He realized what I meant. "No, no, as just friends. It would be good for me to have someone with me who wanted a quiet time."

'I didn't have a clue where Pondicherry was. I realized that Larry was making it easy for me to accept by making it sound like it would be good for him to have someone around, keep other people from intruding. Probably it was. When we were there, I would see people looking at him when we were out together, having a meal or going to lectures or to do group meditation. Doesn't sound like a usual kind of holiday, does it? People would be looking for a way to talk to him, but he would just talk to me, and I was kind of his buffer zone, 'cause he likes to go round in a world of his own. Not that he misses much.'

Pondicherry, as Josh soon found out, was a quiet little city on the east coast of India. Larry arranged their visas, assured him he didn't need vaccinations or to buy a thing, and in what seemed like mere days, they flew via Singapore to Madras, and from the airport took a taxi to Pondi, a few hours drive down the coast.

Pondicherry had once been part of the French empire and distinctive traces of its French past remained in the graceful architecture of the old town, the names of the streets, the elegance of the foreign visitors, the baguettes and brioches you could buy at the bakery. They stayed at a guest house on the eastern side of town, at the southern end of a long wide boulevard that ran alongside the sea. It was one of a number of lodgings owned and run by the Ashram that dominated the area, its various buildings painted a distinguishing pale grey.

Exhausted, unwell, and never having been out of Australia before, feeling so frightened and weak he even wondered if he might die, Josh spent the first days barely venturing out of the guesthouse, sleeping in his room, sitting in the seaside garden, picking at toast and eggs and fruit salad in the dining room and then going to lie down again. As he began to feel stronger, he began to listen to the other guests talk among themselves, chatted to the staff, kind women in blue saris who did not speak fluent English but seemed to communicate warmth and uncanny insight. He picked up books and newsletters in the dining room, and began to wonder who The Mother was, and who Aurobindo was, and to form some idea of what kind of place this was, and why people came here.

Each room had a name, a word on its door, such as Peace, Surrender, Abundance, Forgiveness. Josh's room was called Spirit and Larry's room Knowledge. An Indian couple he talked to over tea one day said that there was always a meaning to the room you had been assigned, and that one should reflect on this.

'Larry was always reading, it was always something strange, spiritual stuff, philosophy, history. He was interested in Aurobindo,' said Josh, 'that's what he'd come here for, to find out more about him.'

Sri Aurobindo, fleeing prosecution by the British and perhaps with his future calling already clear, moved south to Pondicherry and began the spiritual work that would be the focus for the rest of his life. Here he met the French woman who would become known as The Mother. The Mother and Aurobindo formed a unique alliance. Josh sketched a few of these facts, and I would hear more about all this from Larry much later.

What had interested Larry most was the relationship between the political activism of Aurobindo's early life and the spiritual focus of the later years. Was it a matter of progression, or retreat? Did the latter pursuit negate or affirm the former? What could he learn about the relationship between political activism and the spiritual life? Larry spent a lot of time in the Ashram's library, studying in those cool, high-ceilinged rooms, or seeking out people who could talk to him about these matters.

Josh, content to have but a dim apprehension of Larry's project, began in time to venture out of the safe, serene grounds of the guesthouse, walking along the *Rues* and peering through high gateways into courtyards to the solid, elegant, cream or pearly grey buildings of French schools, hospitals, and hotels as well as the Ashram's various quarters: residential, workshops, clinics. Bright bougainvillaea cascaded over fences, and he stopped to watch some girls kneeling drawing elaborate geometric designs in chalk on the pavement at a doorway. What were they doing? Were those mandalas? They must have been taught at a young age to draw such elaborate, perfectly balanced designs so swiftly and neatly. He began to notice them in all the streets. What did they mean? He bought a notebook and copied some of the designs. Bit by bit he made his way north to an octagonal park where he sat upon a bench and watched workers and tourists walk its paths or rest in its shade, children play, gardeners tend the flower beds. He marvelled at his own nerve, though the first excursion so many blocks from the sanctuary of the guesthouse left him so weak that he took an auto-rickshaw back there. As he grew well and strong, his confidence and curiosity growing, he crossed the canal that divided the town into the quiet, broad, well-tended, European-influenced avenues on the eastern side and on the western side the narrower, far more teeming, bustling Indian streets that stretched into an infinity of Indian urban life that he found daunting to even contemplate. This was a quiet Indian city? Good grief, what must a busy noisy one be like! He had to pick his way over pavements of broken stone, dense crowds and roadside businesses. But he found that if he relaxed and smiled, it was easier. If you smiled at strangers you found the ones that smiled back! A gay man should know this! 'Australia! Coming from Australia,' he answered everyone cheerfully. One day he found himself at the main market, and was lost there for hours, amazed to see the colourful, unfamiliar produce of the food section, the astonishing varieties of banana and coconut, the piles of spices that the stallholders let him curiously sniff at as he attempted their local names, and the narrow aisles packed with stalls selling cloth, baskets, bangles, mehendi, kohl. He was struck by the pyramids of fine powder in brightest colours, gold, hot pink, blue: what were they for? Ah, for the patterns the girls drew on the ground. Something profound was awoken in him, something to transform him, that he could not yet name or comprehend.

Larry took him one evening to the group meditation that was held in the grounds of one of the Ashram buildings. People, many people of all ages, mostly Indian but many Westerners too, left their shoes at the gates and fell silent as they passed barefoot through one courtyard into the large courtyard where a large black tomb, the tomb of Aurobindo, sat in the centre, already covered with petals of jasmine, champa and rose. They walked in a procession with tiny shuffling steps around the tomb, some falling to their knees to press their hands or their foreheads to its cool marble surface as if to pray or to draw into themselves some mysterious energy. Sticks of incense added a smoky fragrance. Everyone seated themselves upon the carefully swept grounds around the central tomb, moving up next to each other, sitting very close in rows so that they might all fit there. A bell rang out, the lights were dimmed and all became completely silent. Everyone sat still. Josh was not sure he was meditating correctly; for a while he felt thrilled and puzzled to be part of this, then he began wondering how long it had been and how much longer it would be; then his mind wandered here and there and then he began to feel stiff and sore and wondered how people could sit on the ground for so long with no apparent discomfort. He had heard it was good for you and that the adoption of chairs accounted for widespread troubles with hips and knees in later age. He didn't think meditation was for him, though it had all been very nice to experience, in spite of his embarrassing struggle to get back to his feet and shake out his pins-and-needles and his cramps. Anyway, afterwards, Larry told him that all he had to do was to sit, and that the stillness of his body would help to still the mind, and what he could do was to observe his own breath, just watch the inhalation and the exhalation, and release any other thoughts that arose. Josh did go back, and tried that, and when the bell rang at the end of the twenty minutes, he found to his surprise that he had not seemed to think of anything at all, but only to experience the scent of the flowers and the agarbatti, the sound of his own breath, the soft swirling shades of darkness behind his gently closed eyelids, the sense of a vast unified consciousness that might create a great peace if only it were more widely and often entered. He and Larry went to group meditation night after night.

I could barely have imagined the place Josh was describing to me in Darlinghurst that night, but since then I have been to Indian cities and found even in their miasma and cacophony these beautifully-tended oases of stillness and loveliness. If only, they make *you* think, all our cities contained these spaces dedicated to silence and contemplation.

When they left the Samadhi grounds, they would stroll in the gently lit streets in the warm air, keeping hold of the silence they had experienced, as if staying a while in a transitional zone as their senses took in the sights of the promenade on the esplanade, the lights on the gentle sea beyond the stone wall, the statue of Gandhi, the families and couples and groups of friends sauntering along or stopping for snacks, the children with their new balloons or bamboo flutes, the sellers of newspaper cones of roasted channa or peanuts. Then they would often have dinner at a garden restaurant, where they ate grilled fish and *pommes frites*, sometimes an onion soup or a cheese soufflé, and maybe a glass of wine. Larry then would begin to talk, opening up and relating some of his experiences of India to a fascinated, even besotted, Josh. On one of those evenings, Larry told Josh the story of his first trip to India, the story of his early adventures and of the friend who'd died, the story I've already told you.

On other occasions, Larry would take him to eat at the Ashram dining room, where a crowd of mostly Indian pilgrims lined up for an extremely cheap meal of rice and vegetables, deliciously spiced but not too hot, eaten with the hands – right hand only! Larry instructed him: sit on the ground, no lingering once you're done, take your plate to be washed.

When Larry disappeared for hours of the day, Josh knew he had gone to read at the Ashram library, or to visit people he wanted to talk to. Josh had no interest in accompanying him, nor did he have much of an idea of what Larry's pursuits consisted; he had enough to do, he told me, with recovering his health, forming some new determination, and simply being where he was.

Josh encouraged Larry to read to him. 'I loved hearing that stuff.' Josh became sentimental as he told me this, and carried on for a bit about the way Larry read: 'He didn't put much expression into it but it was so calm and clear, and these beautiful words. I know, it sounds over the top, but I do not regret a moment.'

'I still haven't heard of anything for you to regret,' I said.

'Larry had got us two rooms,' Josh said. 'I would have shared a room if he wanted to, to save money or whatever, but he said he sometimes read at night and I was there to have a holiday and should keep my own hours. We'd always meet at the end of the day, sometimes I'd see him during the day, sometimes I wouldn't.

'Sometimes he'd give me a hug when we said goodnight, and I wanted to go on holding him. Finally, one night, as he was letting go of me, I did just hold on, and run my hands down his back and said, 'I could try and be very quiet,' or whatever I said. We made sure all the windows were closed and then, and let me tell you he is too thin now and he was thin then but he was not bony, he was strong, just naturally slender but hard and smooth and round. Anyway, the earth moved, what do you want to know?'

'Anything you tell me!' I said.

'I thought I'd better go back to my own room afterwards, it was all a bit quiet and ashram-y there, they had a curfew and they only had single beds, and I paused and looked back at him as I slipped out the door, and he was picking up an open book, beginning to read it again, and I was forgotten.'

I couldn't help smiling. Yes, a perfect image of Larry, I thought. 'What about the earth moved part?'

'Oh, he was kind of straightforward, no frills, the basic suck and pull, kind of like someone very young would be, vanilla all the way, but not shy at all, not uncertain or anything. I mean, he was really into it, and he was gorgeous. But, basically I had just given him a little break from his reading.

'Yeah, you can grin like that!' Josh grumbled, but then grinned himself.

'Anyway, act mean and keep 'em keen, not that he was mean, he wasn't mean at all. He was as sweet and generous as anyone could be. But for him, I was just there and one day I wouldn't be, and it wouldn't make much difference to him. But I was hoping he would want to keep me round. Like, really, really hoping. I was waiting for my chance. I wanted him to think he needed me. I thought I was good at that.

'And then one day he just says, "Look, I'm leaving now, I've paid for your room for the rest of the month and I'll give you this," and he hands over rupees and dollars, "so you can get a place when you go back."

'I thought, what have I *done*? Was it anything I said? I was devastated. I wanted to beg him not to go, but I couldn't say anything, no way, he didn't have to look after me, he'd always been lovely, whether we had sex or not was always up to me, but I had no idea why he was suddenly leaving or where he was going. I soon realized it had nothing to do with me, that he knew I could look after myself now. There was something new he wanted to do. He confirmed my return flight and then basically didn't need to think about me any more. He had gone, really, before I could even think what to ask him. I thought, just as well I didn't really have any huge expectations. Lucky for me, 'cause, really I had no clue.'

We must have talked of other things too, but before we parted that night Josh asked me, 'What do *you* think of him? You haven't said.'

'You know,' I said, 'not many people can claim that they always do and say whatever they want to, but a lot of people would like to. Larry is the only person I know who really just does whatever he wants.'

This didn't really satisfy Josh, who said, 'He does, but you only can tell what he wants to do at any given point in time, I could never get to what he overall basically really *wants*.'

That, I said, was the mystery of Larry.

PART V

It was on that night we met

Autumn is a good time to be in Sydney. I wasn't in a hurry to leave, and was able to stay. I had work to do, people to see, and time to enjoy the carnival atmosphere of the prolonged yet freshened summer, the bare-limbed bodies on the street, the impression that everyone spent most of the bright blue days on the beach or the Harbour, or could. The enjoyment was mixed with nostalgia, excitement and detachment. I was feeling my age. All enjoyment is tinged with nostalgia in the later part of life. I'd be mad not to just make the most of this benign season, catching up with all kinds of people I'd once known, walking around the dear old streets and the dear old neighbourhoods and the memories they unlocked, memories of various shades of the past, past times, good times and sad times. This was not depressing. *Carpe diem*, we all said so often, and do it now.

Once in a while I'd be part of a foursome with Isabel, Gray and Larry; there was a very nice car and we went to lunch in the Blue Mountains and we went to lunch at Palm Beach. There was a holiday mood on those days. That's what their presence in my life and mine in theirs signified. It was all very much a deliberate kind of holiday mood, it was all very much about Gray recovering his spirits. Gray wasn't going to be put on medication and Gray wasn't going to talk to any counsellor and we wanted Gray to want to get well, and we saw that he was beginning to, very much so.

Gray wasn't someone I could imagine even having one drink with if he did not have this oddly intimate place in my life. I never talked with him about anything much but we got along easily, and he provided a kind of focus for our little group. He loved having us all around him, he loved doing his best to make sure we all had a good time, mostly because it made Isabel happy. She wanted me along I think for some kind of balance, maybe to take attention away from her intense attention to Larry.

I'd watch them and wonder and think about them. What I saw was that it really was a case of Gray adoring Isabel, being a little dazzled by her power and strength, adoring his family and wanting all that to be as perfect as he could make it.

I would recall the wondering remarks of a dear friend who said, whenever he saw a heterosexual couple, 'What could they *talk* about, what on earth could they possibly have in *common*?' It interested me to see this little unit in operation. I felt the occasional rush of sadness and pity for the very young man I had once been so long ago, a boy who tried to be a husband to a girl, in a short but disastrous period of my attempt to be what I thought I had to be. I admitted very soon I had made a mistake, and soon extricated myself and travelled away to where I would find liberation, but I had caused grief that became bitterness and enmity. This young couple, though, Isabel and Gray, had matched their desires to the desires of those around them.

Unlike Larry. Sometimes Larry drove, especially after lunch, as he never drank more than a mouthful of wine, while the rest of us had whatever we wanted.

We wanted quite a lot of good wine. We'd become quite animated over lunch, but drowsy and silent in the car on the way back to town.

I noticed Isabel once as she turned in the seat, she was in the passenger seat next to Larry, and she turned and gazed at him, looking close at him, quite unselfconsciously lost in gazing at him, her expression kind of glazed, her mouth open. There was a kind of intense wonder and desire mixed in her stare. Gray was dozing or looking out of the window, not that she seemed to have any caution. It was a strangely unguarded moment she couldn't have realized I was noticing. I wondered whether she would be extra warm or extra cold to Gray when they got home.

All that was a nice little time had by all but it suddenly got very cold for a few days, I didn't need to be here any more and I began planning to move back up north.

Elliott had some time since returned to the North Coast; he let Isabel know that he was investigating a couple of places up there that she and Gray could go to for a few weeks over winter. I don't think Larry had revealed any plans of his own, though there was some talk of us all seeing each other again up north in a few months. Larry's position with his friends seemed odd at times, a kind of *cavalier servante* of romantic myth, content with attending, assisting, diverting.

Anyway, Isabel had been saying she'd like to go out one night before I left, do something special, go somewhere new. So I had invited them out on my last night in Sydney.

I got theatre tickets and made a booking for supper. Isabel indicated that she expected us all to be in for a long night. There was talk of checking out a certain club afterwards. She said she wanted to see the nightlife of the city, to see something different.

It was on that night that we met Sophie Macdonald.

I never understood what he saw in her

We couldn't say we hadn't been warned. We weren't going home yet, not after the show (a hit musical we were destined to enjoy), not after dinner (delicious, great service, glamorous room); not after some ghastly yuppie nightclub with self-conscious people all in black, a tiny dark dance floor and robotic music; and not even after I took them, because Isabel insisted, to a gay bar on Oxford Street, for a drag show.

I did not really want to turn up at the Astor with three tourists, as my friends might be perceived; and with the passing of the years, I no longer knew the bars all that well, not many of them, and some that I did know there was no way I could take them to.

But we got in at the Astor, because no one looked as fabulous in a black dress as Isabel, and she wore amazing high heels manfully, and she was in a mood to be irresistible. I fancied for a moment that Larry and I would be taken for a couple. It was packed, and the mood was raucous and good-spirited. We were entertained by a few gaudy little shows, and we were all in the mood to find them great fun and fascinating.

How drag shows had changed; once the performers enacted fantasies of glamorous divas, and created illusions of opulence with a plethora of frills, miles of sequins and clever lighting. Not any more. Now post-punk it was all deconstructions of gender: frocks with moustaches, tits with men's suits and a deliberately slutty aesthetic of torn clothing and bits of leather. This had become known as irony.

None of this of course was usual entertainment or venue for my three young friends, not even for me though of course I had spent more time in the vicinity, even at this very pub though in earlier incarnations.

It was getting ridiculously crowded near closing time and we had to go outside to breathe, but we still couldn't go home, Isabel wanted more, Gray was thrilled to see her have the night out she wanted, Larry seemed to be quite content to accompany them, though he barely drank, as usual. If the rest of has had drunk as little as he I don't know if we'd have been so keen or so swept along in the mood. I can't say it was a mood of hilarity and great enjoyment, not any more, now there was a touch of grim determination about it. We consumed quite a bit of champagne, of increasingly diminishing quality. Began early with the best French and now down to some local bubbly. So now that everything was closing down and it was that darkest hour before dawn, I took them to The Blue Room.

There was really not much love of tourists here. If you didn't feel at home you might not be welcome. And you had to know how to find it, which dark alley and un-signposted staircase to take. The Blue Room didn't open until after midnight and mainly catered for people who got off work at around 3am, and badly needed to unwind, or to wind up more maybe. Performance art was second nature to many habitués. Drag entertainers ending their shift, musicians, taxi drivers, truck drivers, waiters and bar tenders, dealers, hookers, people still discoing. Actors ended up here after the party on the last night of the show, or in times of not working. You'd see the occasional local writer, in need of a drink at some ungodly, or researching a screenplay. The un-pretty sight of someone who'd taken too much speed was not uncommon. Border skirmishes broke out at times, and the bouncers never got bored.

I got us a bottle of something sparkling, why stop now, a brandy here would be just as bad, and found a table. I drank fast, hoping that they would too, as the night suddenly felt as if it were going in a downward direction. I didn't like the fact that I'd been made responsible for bringing us here. I suddenly had a sour little thought that I had been set up as Isabel's key to some kind of slumming, something to make Isabel feel deliciously groovy and edgy between charity luncheons.

She really was so bourgeois, as if I hadn't known. I felt we had come too close to a part of my life I kept separate from them. I had been known to turn up at this sleazy little dive in long gone days, it was always in a mood of should have gone home long ago. But it was also in the days when we made sure wherever we went we made it look like fun.

Suddenly we hear '*I don't fucking believe it*!' The woman saying this is coming up to us, a young woman looking extremely amused at the sight of my friends. She also looked very drunk, not only drunk, I don't know what kind of drugs she was on but they didn't make *you* mellow.

'Sophie?' said Gray, with a mix of wariness and warmth. 'What are *you* doing here?'

Isabel gave her a frosty 'oh, hello'.

'Hey, Larry!' said the girl, in her throaty voice. 'And who's this?' she said seeing that I was with them.

'You remember Will Maugham,' Isabel said coldly, in a kind of quasi-introduction. 'You remember Sophie Macdonald,' I think for my benefit so that I'd know I was meant to recognize her.

'I remember *you*,' said Sophie looking at me, 'bit up yourself weren't you?'

'Could be,' I said mildly, with no clue.

She had on a very short, very low-cut shiny dress over fishnet tights, with a red bra and pushed up breasts clearly visible, giving a voluptuous edge to her thin body. She was adorned with straps of studded black leather and rows of rings through her earlobes, and she wore an emphatic amount of makeup. She was dressed for sex, with a kind of vivacious obviousness that had its own sense of style. The roots of her hair needed doing, and strands of red and orange hair were randomly pinned up or gathered in bunches. Her heavily outlined eyes had an unnatural sparkle and the whole effect was weirdly attractive and feminine in spite of the sluttishness and dishevelment. I'd never seen a drag queen get this look down.

'You don't seem too pleased to see me!' said Sophie to Isabel.

Isabel just raised her eyebrows. 'Heard you were in Sydney,' she said distantly. I nearly laughed at just how outraged and disapproving she looked. Nothing she'd seen that night had remotely raised that look on her face. She had gone all thin-lipped and censorious.

'Sorry I was out when you called,' said Sophie sarcastically. 'How are you?' she said to Gray, 'Heard you went belly-up, took a few people down with you.'

'So you're living in Sydney, Sophie?' said Gray gallantly. He sensed Isabel's frostiness, and seemed to understand it, but seemed more inclined to be pleasant to someone they'd apparently known a long time ago.

'Yeah, they kicked me out of Brisneyland,' said Sophie. 'My in-laws, protecting the family name. I disgraced them and I had to go. So here I am.'

Larry never said a word, just looked at her.

There's someone suddenly by her side, a hard-looking man, the wiry bulging-muscled kind, whose tattoos weren't a fashion statement but carved without anaesthetic into flesh with blunt knives and ballpoint pens, and he was saying, 'Soph, these people bothering you?'

'Old friends of mine,' she said.

He didn't like the look of us, he didn't like her talking to anyone else. 'Come on, babe,' he ordered her, 'get back over here.'

'You're the one bothering me,' said Sophie.

'Come on, you're out of it, get over here,' he said, beginning to pull at her.

'Fuck off,' she said, trying to shake him off. He only took hold of her harder, evidently painfully, in a way that demonstrated he had no qualms about bullying, forcing or abusing anyone who made him feel like it.

Gray just stood up. That's all he had to do. This tall, this wide, he still looked like a footballer, and he'd been working out again recently. He just towered over everyone and though I'd never known him to be in a fight I had no doubt he'd get into one if he felt he should, and do some damage.

The guy let go off Sophie's arm with a violent movement, as if throwing her to us, growled, 'Cunts, y'll keep,' and moved away.

'Thanks, Gray, I'll pay for it later but it was worth it,' said Sophie, who wasn't going to go away yet. 'You haven't said much, Larry.'

'I never did,' he said mildly.

'I wonder why you're here. Are you living in Sydney too?'

'Just for now,' said Larry. He hadn't stopped looking at her.

Sophie drained whatever she was drinking, and held out her glass. I filled it with our frothy wine.

'Better go or I'm really in trouble,' she said. 'Though he's the kind of trouble I can't live without, hurts so good. Been really excellent to see you all.'

She went away and Isabel said, 'Let's go.'

'I wouldn't mind a hot drink and something,' said Gray.

We went to an all-night café in the Cross and ordered hot chocolate and tea and raisin toast. 'So who was that?' I asked.

'Don't you remember? You sat next to her that first time you came to dinner at our place in Brisbane, that party we had.'

I did remember then, because I remembered the name. Sophie, I'd used the name for a character. 'Was that really her? She told me she was going to be a veterinarian I think.' She had been such a quiet, even ordinary young girl, though I recalled also her sharp eye and insightful remarks.

'Ha. She had a baby really young, some band came to town and next thing she's off with one of the musicians, who knew quiet little Sophie was such a groupie. Then she gets pregnant and the poor bloke comes back to Brisbane to be with her. Actually he started up a new group there and they were supposed to be getting quite good. He could have had his pick of girls.

'I never understood what he saw in her. When the baby came they got married and acted like they were more in love than ever, the two of them always together, always with the baby, always just so into each other they hardly spoke to anyone else, it was a bit of a joke really. She'd take the kid and go to band practice. They'd be holding hands and all over each other everywhere they went. Anyway one night he's driving, there's an accident, a head-on, not his fault, some drunken idiots, she's the only survivor. She was unconscious for a long while, critical, and then she came to and they had to tell her and she had hysterics and on and on and on it went, she went a bit insane and stayed in some kind of nursing home for a while.'

'That's horrible. Poor girl.'

'Girl! For God's sake she's at least thirty-something now.'

'What happened then?'

'Oh, suddenly she stops shrieking and carrying on but she just turns into a total slut, she was always off her face, began just going to bed with anyone, she was mixed up with that sleazy scene in the Valley. She was arrested a couple of times, being disorderly, obscene.'

'And it was still a small town.' The Valley was a mere block or two of red-light and late-night venues, since those days becoming quite trendy as such districts do, with expensive new apartment blocks replacing warehouses and thrift stores, and new inhabitants who lodged complaints about after-hours noise though they had moved there to be near The Action. The Valley was Brisbane's own metaphor for criminality, perversion and staying up all night.

'It was. When she was arrested, well, couldn't have that, respectable family. They gave her some money, we heard, and she's got some kind of income from the insurance, all she's got to do is stay away. You'd think she'd want to do something with her life, it's never too late to go back and get qualified, she was going to finish her degree when the baby got older.'

'I can't help feeling sorry for her,' said Gray.

'I'm not sucked in,' said Isabel. 'She must have always been a bit like that, people don't change that much.'

'Come on, Is, she lost her husband and her baby.'

'Yeah, I know, but look, Gray, I love you but if I lost you I wouldn't turn into what she turned into. Come on! Would you want me to?'

'No, sweetheart,' said Gray, the only time I knew him to even try and be witty, 'even though it might be good for my ego to think you'd throw yourself on the funeral pyre, I'd be glad to know you could pull yourself together and take up bridge or Tai Chi.'

I could barely rally to even think about the varied and unpredictable ways that great loss and grief were enacted. People fell to pieces, we all lose a piece of ourselves when someone close to us dies, someone we love, someone who's been part of our lives, but mostly we are put together again, maybe with the joins showing, maybe with visible gaps or ill-matched patches over the empty spaces. Suffering doesn't always ennoble us; sometimes we behave badly in grief. Friends and work and time do their healing work. Some people get glued back together a bit more successfully than others. Some bend, some break. If love is very new or very old perhaps it's a little easier to bear, harder for some. If the loss comes in love's early maturity, maybe that is the hardest to bear, who can say. There are so many ways of being left and death is not always the worse.

And as I write this, it occurs to me that Sophie would have been given painkillers and sedatives for a long time while she was in hospital, and that's how some addictions begin.

'It's dreadful to lose your one great love,' I said, or something that feeble.

'Oh, it was that mad kind of young infatuation that would never last.'

Larry had not said a word.

'Larry,' said Isabel, 'say something. Hey, you used to be quite friendly with her once, didn't you?'

Larry said, 'When we were all in about year nine or ten, Sophie and I used to talk about books. She read all kinds of things. Neither of us knew anyone else to talk to about all that. She wrote too. She used to show me some poetry she'd written.'

'Oh God, I bet it was drivel.'

'No, it wasn't what you'd expect, it wasn't sentimental girly stuff, she really played with words and ideas. She was into music and her poetry had a musical quality. She read different poets, and tried to work out how they wrote. And she got interested in the environment and Third-world debt, and we used to talk about that. She was really idealistic, and wanted to make a difference.'

'I didn't realize you'd been so close,' said Isabel.

'We were that year, especially in the holidays when you'd all go away. I didn't really belong there, and nor did she. We'd both lost parents and didn't have rich families. I think she must have been very happy with a real musician.'

'Yeah, only because you wouldn't think of her that way,' said Isabel. 'She was probably after you, couldn't you see that?'

Larry just shook his head, more to say it wasn't like that than he couldn't see it.

'Yeah, no, but when Larry came back from his trip,' said Gray, 'all the girls had a big crush on him. Sophie probably did too.'

'Get the bill,' said Isabel. 'We're going home, I'm going to bed now.'

He was desperately afraid

The next day I went up to the North Coast, settled back into my little house, and after a couple of days visited Elliott. He was full of plans for the Buddhist centre he was building. He had found yet more Himalayan monastery doors through an art dealer and showed me pictures, plans, blueprints.

He didn't look all that well, suddenly, not that I mentioned it. Although Elliott had some complaints, they weren't about his own health. No, he was at pains to have it understood that he was fighting fit.

If only they knew, if only people knew, of course some people knew but a lot more people really should know, Elliott felt, just how much he was giving to everyone: this centre, and the most rare and valuable art, and his very special association with His Holiness, with whom Elliott had met again – he had the photograph capturing this meeting framed – for 'this,' he said, 'is the greatest spiritual leader in the world today,' and His Holiness at least had fully understood what Elliott was all about. So, said Elliott, who had entered some kind of manic, bitter phase, and was beginning to make plans for his demise, plans that were aimed at self-aggrandizement and revenge as well as the distribution of some very lovely and wonderful things, so, he opined, if only people generally were a little more enlightened they might realize how Elliott was supporting their spiritual practice.

Look, I don't know of what Elliott's Buddhism consisted. He didn't offer me any of his views or beliefs about it. Once he said something like it was more of a philosophy than a religion, then another time he said it was the world's fastest-growing religion. And I'd heard him tell someone that he realized he'd really been a Buddhist all his life. Somewhere in the last few years he had begun using phrases like spiritual practice. As far as I knew, and that was never very far at all, let me be the first to say so, the key themes of Buddhism were kindness and detachment, and so that's what you'd expect to see in its followers. But one might say the key themes of Christ's teachings were tolerance and forgiveness, draw your own conclusions. I was never averse to picking up wisdom wherever it came from, but having never been called, as it were, to Buddhism, I knew not its charms and spells, and only was inclined to see how detachment so often was achieved where kindness was not among some so keen to embrace the four noble truths and the eight something and the five something else. Later, Larry was to tell me that Buddhism maintained that our essential nature was Buddhahood, meaning, I suppose, enlightened perfection, whereas Christianity, for example, maintained that our essence was original sin and we were in need of salvation. Believing *you* are basically a Buddha is of course the more attractive option. Maybe that's what had appealed to Elliott. That, or the sheer fashionable cred of it all. In another era he'd have been a Roman Catholic and cultivating acquaintance with the bishop and name-dropping the pope.

Anyway, Elliott was only in his early seventies now, but he'd been knocked around by a broken rib, acquired he told me, when he had insouciantly told a young, I guess somewhat buffed, friend in a moment of warm and exuberant greeting that surely he could hug him a little harder. He was suddenly old, suddenly he was looking old and feeling old and feeling close to the end, but not, he knew, the end of time, the hereafter was here on earth and it was your objects and your wishes and your influence, these things that lasted after you had gone, that were your part of the progressive future.

Apparently we all want, we humans, to have some part of us live on after us, which is why people have children, often suddenly in older age, and 'you,' people have said to me, 'have your books.' This perhaps is a life after death, but it's not immortality, far from it, books fall apart eventually. So that's of little real comfort so far. Others might leave a garden or a good example or a gift, but they say we are hard-wired to want to leave a mark upon the world, driven by the drives of our genes. If you don't have children, you leave other stuff.

In any case, the broken rib had caused Elliott great pain, and not only that. He had arthritis, he had a prostate problem he would not name, he had infections that were taking too long to heal, but he still went to parties if there were parties to go to. He wasn't up to actually giving the parties so very much any more, was up to organizing nothing more than seeing one or two people for a cup of tea. It was other people's turn, he said, but he was beginning to be disappointed in his expectations that his own past lavish hospitality would be returned.

People had so many things to go to now, there were new people and new parties, new fabulous homes being created, and CJ Lonoff was finally about to come to spend some time in her house near Byron. She was giving interviews about her new spirituality, and how much she was looking forward to living somewhere so spiritual. There was going to be a party at her house, a party that Rye Bread was arranging. Everyone was saying that parties were more low-key these days, much smaller, but if there was one party he wanted to get better for, it was that one. Elliott only hoped that Rye knew what he knew about the available caterers.

He so wanted to be in the loop, closely connected to whoever there was around who was being currently celebrated. Books of photographs, small art films that won overseas awards, political biographies and self-help books were now often launched in the North Coast area these days, little local events that made national news, and Elliott made sure he got wind of these things and made sure he was on the invitation list. He called in favours and presumed his inclusion with a breezy, forceful assumption that if he needed his name put on a list his name got put on. But it was up to him. No one was looking for him. I felt sad as he told me of his efforts. I couldn't tell if he realized he wasn't all that interesting to many people any more, he no longer possessed much advantageous influence, he didn't really know who was doing what or were they any good. He scorned much of the new. But he did know who was currently getting the kind of attention and money that validated them totally as far as Elliott was concerned. Such success for him was apparently the sweet side of existence, and he liked being connected to it.

Elliott kept talking about all the famous people he had met over his life, as if this were the greatest validation of his career. He'd tell stories out of the blue to drop the names of dealers, directors, artists and businesspeople who had benefited from his advice, or about whose private personality he knew a thing or two. It did not seem to occur to him that any of this was futile.

Elliott dragged himself out of bed to get to a performance of a touring string quintet. He fell and broke that same rib again and was carried out of there in an ambulance.

Even so he would not be deterred a few days later from a literary luncheon in the area's most fabulous restaurant, for its views and its food and the chance to hear a bestselling author talk about the fraudulent book that had made her half as famous as her later confession made her.

Listening to the glamorous author reveal the childhood insecurities that had led to her claiming fiction as factual account, Elliott swayed and drooled in a chair, his eyelids heavy, having been unable to eat, and having ingested the increased dosage of highest grade painkillers he had had prescribed for him by a doctor who agreed you could take this alternative stuff too far, there were some things western medicine was good at, pain relief being one.

But he only reported that the author knew someone that he knew even better, and that what she had to say was important – for her book was still selling well.

Elliott was desperately afraid, I saw with a shock, afraid of being left out, afraid of being no one, afraid of dying.

That drunken slut

Winter passed, and when the weather became warm enough down south, Elliott began planning a trip to Sydney. He wanted to see how Isabel and Gray and the kids were, and to go to the opera, and to some chef's new restaurant. He didn't want to fly, and began to express a preference for a leisurely trip by road.

'Aren't you due to go to Sydney?' he asked me.

In fact, I had been thinking it was time to see a few people. 'Face time' still worked best with agents and directors, and besides I'd suddenly become a little restless after having burrowed in for a few months, hardly seeing anyone and getting a lot of writing done. I was ready to show my new work to a couple of people at this stage, and to enjoy some city life again.

So I drove Elliott to Sydney. We took a couple of days for the journey, in his gorgeous BMW convertible, though we mostly kept the top up. He insisted on paying for everything, and had chosen where we would have lunch and where we would stay the night. He was in fine form and made every effort to be entertaining. And the countryside was wonderful to see after the rain.

We got into town the next afternoon. I left Elliott at the new apartment he now rented, and went to the same studio apartment I had had before.

There was a message there from Isabel. I called her and the first thing she said was, 'Uncle Elliott's not with you, is he?'

'No,' I said, wondering if she was concerned about him. 'I've just dropped him off. He's fine. He's probably having a bath and a nap before calling you.'

'Good, don't tell him, will you, but please can you come down, please come now, I have to talk to you.'

'What happened?'

'It's too horrible, I have to tell *you* the whole thing.'

Is anything really too horrible to say on the phone? I wasn't pleased, having my own plans for the next few days, but I had never heard Isabel sound like this. I wondered if Gray had relapsed, and why she seemed to think I was the best one to talk to. I quickly made a couple of other calls, then I hurried through Potts Point down to the bay.

She flung open the door. 'Where have you been?' she almost shrieked. She really looked overwrought, and I'd never seen her so dramatic.

'Isabel, what is it?' I said, following her into the sitting room.

'I have to say, I blame *you*! What the hell was that all about, taking us to that sleazy little dive?'

'What are you talking about? What is the *matter*?'

'Larry is going to marry Sophie Macdonald.'

'Who is that?'

'Don't act dumb, that drunken slut we ran into at that disgusting place you dragged us to that night.'

'Come off it, Isabel,' I said irritably, 'you were the driving force for that particular excursion. Let's not rewrite history and tell me exactly what the problem is.'

'The evil little bitch got hold of Larry, and God knows what kind of victim act she put on for him, but bloody Larry, he can be just so naïve, that's the other side of that nice side of him, he is taken in by her, and next thing she is completely and totally dependent on him, and now she's got him to promise to marry her!' Tears gushed out of Isabel's eyes, she sounded furious rather than bereft, she was raging.

'How about some tea and a shot of whiskey?'

'She would have to be the most manipulative little slut on earth. Apparently she's got Larry believing he's going to save her and reform her and cure all her addictions.'

'How do you know he can't? Look at what he did for Gray and his headaches.'

'That is different! That is completely different! Gray wanted to be cured.'

'How do *you* know she doesn't?'

'Jesus Christ! Are you kidding? She's just evil, she doesn't care who she destroys to get what she wants.'

'Isabel, could that be fair?'

'You have absolutely no idea! I know what women like her are like! Listen, *you* have to talk to him. Larry really respects *you*, he says he likes talking to *you*. He'll take notice of *you*. You have to tell him not to do it!'

'Isabel, really, I am not going to tell a grown man, or anyone, what to do.'

'You have to help me help him not destroy himself! I've always helped Larry, and *you've* got to help me now. He wanted me to marry him but I didn't want to stand in his way, I knew he had his own ambitions and his own path to walk.'

'You gave him up for the sake of waterfront houses and a limitless credit card. You wanted security, and the familiar. You got everything *you* wanted, and now *you* can't work out why *you're* not happy ever after.'

In reply Isabel threw a vase at me. It went past my head and smashed into the wall behind me, shattering.

We both went rigid for a split second, as it was a heavy crystal vase and had flown pretty close, but she wasn't going to say anything but 'pick it up'.

'You pick it up!' I retorted.

'I don't know why I asked *you* to talk to me. You are so cold and arrogant.'

'And you are a spectacularly lovely woman whose beauty is enhanced by the flushed cheeks and brightened eyes of fiery emotions.'

She was like her uncle, telling new versions of the past and seeming to expect you to believe them. Funnily enough, while I was the fiction writer among us, this always slightly shocked me.

I can carry on about the blurred lines of fiction and truth at some length, but in everyday life I do attempt and expect facts, consistency and literalness. I've known a few mythomaniacs and a few people who habitually embroider and recut their accounts of events, and it's annoying that I cannot tell to what extent they really do believe themselves.

Isabel glared at me but she didn't mind the flattery and began to calm down.

She finally sat down, then moved over to sit right up against me, partly apologetic, partly forgiving, and then bestowed a kiss upon my lips, which charmed me, as those days many straight people wouldn't dream of kissing a gay man on the lips.

Her fury had expired, her mood quite altered.

'But you do see why I'm upset?' she said more calmly. 'It's a disaster waiting to happen and I have to do what I can to avert it.'

'There's no point in trying, Isabel,' I said. 'Larry's motivation is far stronger than yours.'

'My motivation is real love,' she said.

'Real love has less power than other motives,' I said, 'such as self-sacrifice, which I suspect is Larry's, or the desire to change someone for their own sake, also maybe not unknown to him.'

Yes, I went on, while she, Isabel, might want to save Larry from himself, or from Sophie, what he wanted was a mission and a cause, to be useful and devoted, to bring about improvement and salvation. He would have been about thirty-three, it occurred to me, an age known most likely for self-sacrifice, think for example Jesus Christ.

Isabel wanted to keep Larry close, keep him exactly as he was, the single man, the family friend, the best friend, who is there, waiting, in case she ever needs him. She too was maybe waiting for some right moment. She wasn't going to give up anything for him, but she liked to think he still wanted her and lived in hope of her.

'I'm too unselfish,' said Isabel, 'I'm the one who really loves him, because I supported him in finding his own path.' She was crying again now, and had to look for some tissues.

I knew a little of Larry's lost years by now, not nearly as much as I knew later. I knew he'd been travelling, and done a lot of reading. His 'research' Gray had called it. Gray had once said Larry should write a book and Larry said he might and since then Gray made sense of everything Larry had done by seeing it as research for a book, which apparently I was advising him on. Larry was hungry for knowledge and experience, I surmised, to which he would add by getting married to help an old friend. Maybe the adventure of marriage appealed to him, or of having a kind of disciple, or a cause, or fulfilling some need to be really needed.

I was quietly immersed in such thoughts when Isabel dried her eyes and said sarcastically, 'Thanks so much for your kind sympathy.'

'Look, Isabel, you can tell me anything, you know that, but you can't expect me to give you the responses you want. I'll tell you what I think, but it mightn't be what you want to hear.'

'Give me some advice then. What can I do?'

'You have to be nice to her. This is the woman Larry is going to marry. He's your friend, but if you're mean to her you'll lose him because she'll be his wife.'

'Oh my God, it's too late, I said really horrible things to Larry. You're right.' After a while Isabel said, 'You've got to ask us all to lunch or something. Please. I can't be the one to ask first after what I said to Larry yesterday.'

'I don't know… you will have to be very, very nice to me. A bribe is not out of the question.'

Isabel wanted me to arrange it at once. She brought out the number – yes, the couple had already moved in together and had a phone – and I telephoned and it was Sophie who answered. I briefly said I'd heard the good news, offered my congratulations, and invited them to lunch with Elliott and the Maturins, saying that I'd confirm the date with Isabel, then reconfirm with them, while Isabel was giving me a silent thumbs-up and a 'thank you'.

Again Isabel's mood had shifted.

'Thank you, darling Will!' she said. 'You are very special to do this. Let's have a drink before you rush off.'

She suddenly seemed oddly satisfied, as if the situation had turned in her favour. 'What are you thinking?' I asked suspiciously. I knew I had been spectacularly manipulated.

'I'm only wondering what Sophie will wear,' said Isabel, 'even Larry wouldn't let her look like she did that night.'

And was now going to marry Larry

Whether or not it was because Larry wouldn't let her look like she did that night, Sophie turned up to lunch looking very different.

So different that if I hadn't been expecting her, I would not at first have recognized her. It wasn't just what she had on, though that was part of it. They were new clothes bought all at the same time. These days we'd call it a makeover. They didn't look particularly expensive nor particularly cheap, but their newness was evident. The shoulder pads looked especially unconvincing. It was all trying too hard. She looked older than she had in the Blue Room that night, and thinner; and there was no sign of that spirit, that sexiness. It's as if she was trying to look like every other thirty-something yuppie, yet the clothes denied any sex appeal at all. Sophie looked like she was going to a lot of meetings, praying for courage, serenity and wisdom, taking twelve steps, or maybe doing some equivalent in a self-help program exclusively designed and administered by Larry. Larry and she sat closer to each other than the rest of us, partly because she needed to feel his encouragement, and partly as a demonstration of their status as a couple, a statement about their seriousness. Her hair was now an even brunette, cut to a single length that needed trimming or growing out. There was no colour any more. It looked like the old quiet Sophie grown older in a way she was trying to live up to.

She hadn't taken a drug or a drink in some time now, and she was not even smoking cigarettes. She was not-drugging and not-drinking in the way of an addict. Looked like a statement more than a preference.

She fidgeted constantly, her fingernails scraping her ragged cuticles, every now and again trying to stop herself.

I had arrived at the restaurant early, some spacious tiled Italian place in Darlinghurst, chosen by Isabel who had specified the table. She and Gray arrived just before Larry and Sophie, and everyone was still saying hello and how have you been and have you eaten here before and so on, all a bit tense under the surface, Isabel checking Sophie out, no doubt making judgments of the too conservative, too neatly matching outfit, and Sophie no doubt perfectly aware of it and also suddenly aware that she hadn't really realized how she must look now. These people knew her, kind of. Elliott arrived just when we had exhausted these preliminaries, and everyone made much of his well-timed appearance.

Elliott didn't know much about Sophie, only that she was a childhood friend, tragically widowed, and was now going to marry Larry. If he wasn't quite sure why he needed to be called upon to commemorate this, to him, rather indifferent news, he was quite pleased to be an essential part of the occasion. His cherished niece's oldest friend, after all, and Gray's too. And Larry these days had become a perfectly acceptable luncheon companion. Heavens knew what he saw in the quiet young woman in those awful clothes, but he at least was decently dressed and reasonably sociable. Elliott while never quite warming to Larry was now inclined to view him as some kind of benign eccentric rather than a complete no-hoper.

'So,' said Elliott genially to Sophie, 'where will the honeymoon be?' I hadn't realized this would be an inevitable question.

Sophie looked at Larry.

He only smiled.

'I always think it feels special to go overseas,' Elliott persisted, 'even if it's only to Fiji or Noumea. Bali is thoroughly ruined, don't go there.'

Various global holiday destinations were discussed, and Isabel and Gray obligingly reminisced about Barcelona and Majorca.

While we studied the blackboard menu, heard what they were supposed to do especially well here, and hesitated over the critical decisions we were obliged to make, Elliott swept about the room a little, had a little chat with the maitre d' with whom he appeared very cosy, and returned to the table followed by a waiter with a tray upon which sat six shot glasses filled with a clear liquid.

It was some especially marvellous new vodka that was being promoted on these very premises, they were having a reception to launch its entry the next evening, and these drinks were offered compliments of the establishment.

'How lovely!' said Isabel enthusiastically, taking one of the drinks. 'Divine, so cold.' She sipped. 'Oh God, this is special!'

Gray, Elliott and I took our drinks. Sophie shook her head, and Larry said, 'Not for me.'

Elliott said, 'Sure?'

Isabel said, 'Uncle Elliott, what is the name of this? It's divine. Isn't it, Gray? Go on, have some, Larry.'

'Thanks, not for me,' Larry said again.

Larry usually had a very small amount of whatever the rest of us drank. I guessed he was refusing in support of Sophie.

'Are you sure?' said Isabel, rather making too much of a point of it.

It was some kind of vodka infused with some herbs and spices, I made a polite noise or two about it, and next thing, we were all going to have another one.

Isabel said, with a lack of tact so uncommon in one known for her gracious manners: 'So, Sophie, what, *you* never drink at lunch?' I looked at her sharply but Isabel avoided my gaze.

Sophie said softly, 'I'm not drinking at all. I'm taking it one day at a time, and today I'm not drinking.' She sipped from her water glass. There was no obvious trace of the spirited woman who had carelessly sworn at us the last time I'd seen her.

Far from tactfully changing the subject, Isabel called the maitre d' over, chatted with him about the vodka, and animatedly offered her happy confirmation of what he told her about this miraculous new beverage. It was infused with traces of this and that by some new process or new combination, it had hints of, I don't know, apple peel and sea air, or was it moonbeams and the Eiffel Tower. Anyway, it was not like any vodka ever tasted before, or so we were enthusiastically told by Isabel and Elliott.

This came mostly from Isabel with her occasional appeals of 'Isn't it, Uncle Elliott?' or 'What is that other lovely taste of something?' I thought she was rather desperately trying to perform, and he, pleased that his little added touch to the celebration was such a success, allowed himself to be encouraged to further paeans.

What a pair.

Elliott of course had no idea how curious Sophie's recent transformation was to the rest of us.

'Can you buy this yet?' asked Isabel eagerly, still on about the vodka.

'They have it here, I'll get you a bottle,' said Elliott.

'Oh, you darling! That would be fabulous. You are the best uncle, don't I always tell you?'

From time to time during the lunch, I looked at Sophie, though she hardly said anything. Larry answered questions put to them with a kind of definiteness I hadn't really seen in him before, I supposed arising from his role of decision-maker for the couple. He was more than that, too, but I wouldn't know what to call it. Sophie's transformation was all his doing, you could say, but she had freely chosen to put herself in Larry's hands. Subdued as she was, something timid and uncertain about her, picking at her cuticles, then clenching her fists to stop herself, I could only regret the disappearance of her bold vivacity.

As we ate the witty and elegant Italianate dishes, and made well-behaved conversation, Elliott said, 'Larry, I hear you're writing a book. Do tell us about it.'

Larry only said, 'There's not much to tell, I'm afraid.'

Gray said, 'Larry could become very famous. He should write about how he learned his healing techniques. I've got those headaches beat, and I'm feeling very ready for new goals.'

Gray warmly gave an account of how Larry had cured him and then trained him in a technique that bestowed a sense of clarity and relaxation and renewed energy that was helping him begin to formulate new plans of action. Theirs was an interesting friendship; on the surface they had nothing in common but the past, yet this was sufficient to keep renewing their affection and loyalty. Larry wouldn't be drawn out, though, and let the subject move back to the forthcoming marriage.

'We're not sending out invitations,' said Larry. 'It's just the registry office and we hope you'll come as witnesses and we can just have,' he turned to Isabel, 'afternoon tea.'

I was not going to be in Sydney for a while, so wouldn't be one of their witnesses.

Before the subject was extinguished, Isabel asked Sophie, 'What are *you* wearing to get married in?' I had not predicted this inevitable question either. It was one that Larry couldn't answer for her, and Sophie gaped a little, having no ready answer, and Isabel said at once, in tones of much warmth and goodwill, 'You know what, for *your* wedding I am giving *you* a new outfit. Come with me after lunch, I'll take *you* shopping, I know where they've got lovely things that will really suit *you*, please say *you*'ll let me do this.'

The others were beaming at Isabel. Sophie looked as if she was choking down some words and searching in vain for others, and tried to refuse, but how could she.

When lunch was over, I wished them all good things, as *you* do. It felt like a farewell, the end of an era.

Made up for lost time

I'd gone to Melbourne and Elliott turned up there a few weeks later. He was buying what he referred to as 'investment properties' and told me things about them that I forgot as he was talking.

Finally when I could get a word in I asked him about the wedding.

'It never happened,' he said.

'What?'

'Sophie disappeared.'

'What?'

'Larry came home one day, she'd packed a bag, left a note that said nothing, and hasn't been heard of since.' Elliott was pleased with the effect this news had on me. 'They'd been getting on well, they never had any words, Larry had no idea at all why she just vanished in a puff of smoke like the magic dragon.'

Evidently Isabel had told Elliott all about it.

Elliott said that Isabel had taken Sophie shopping for her wedding gift frock the afternoon we had last seen them.

How sweet that was of Isabel, she didn't have to do that, how well Isabel knew clothes, what dreadful things Sophie had been wearing.

Some alteration needed to be done and Isabel had asked Sophie over to pick up the dress a couple of days later. On the day, there'd been some emergency with one of her daughters, who had to be rushed to the dentist, and Isabel left a message for Sophie to wait for her. The housekeeper had let her in and made her comfortable, but when Isabel returned home soon after, Sophie had gone. She thought it a bit odd, but assumed Sophie didn't want to wait.

When she phoned Larry, he didn't know what she was talking about. He had not seen Sophie, and assumed she was still with Isabel.

Larry went looking for her high and low.

About three days later, returning home after another search, he found that she had been back to their flat – it looked like she had made sure he would be out – and taken a few of her things in a bag. One of the other tenants in the block had seen her, and she had been alone, and had said she was moving out. There were no signs that anyone was forcing her to do anything she didn't want to.

'And no one's heard from her?'

'No one, she didn't phone or write to Larry, just disappeared.'

'How is he taking it?'

'I haven't seen him. Isabel said he was pretty upset. But he wouldn't really talk about it, which would not have helped him much. She tried to help him, but he was as strange as ever. I suppose he just went into denial.'

'And what does Isabel say?'

'Isabel is very sorry about it all, but she's a realist, a very practical girl, and she knows it wouldn't have worked out.'

'Really, Elliott, if there's one thing no one knows…'

'All very well if you're writing plays, dear, but in real life there are some partnerships that are going to work and some that aren't. Isabel understands Larry very well, after all she's known him the longest and he was in love with her once, probably still is. He was never in love with that unfortunate girl…'

'Sophie.'

'Sophie. She was a kind of subject for him, a client or test case for that healing type work he was trying to do. It might have worked on Gray's headaches but Gray was always basically all right. This…Sophie was a bit of a lost cause from the start. He's well out of it. She'd been a drunk and a drug addict and wasted years of her life,' Elliott pronounced, 'and she couldn't give it up.'

I could just see Isabel putting on a show of sympathy while feeling considerable satisfaction. I had a certain anticipation that whenever I saw her again, she would find some charming way of saying, I told you so.

But it would be nearly a year before I'd see Isabel again

By then I could have told her a thing or two about Sophie, but as it turned out I did not feel like it.

When I left Melbourne I flew straight up to the North Coast without stopping in Sydney. I'd had a very busy and stimulating few weeks that at the time took up much more of my thoughts than the story I'm telling you here. I went back to my strict and isolated writing habits to finish the play I had worked on over winter. That done, I had to go to London.

I purchased a round-the-world ticket, as I also had people to see in Los Angeles and New York.

And once I'd done all that, I knew, I would really need some kind of break, somewhere new, time off, and remembered how often I'd said I'd go back to India one day, spend longer there.

I don't know why I hadn't gone back before this, but now I could.

A few faxes later, I even had promises of interesting introductions in India, if I felt like exploring the possibility of professional connections there. I decided to stop off in Bombay on the way home, and got my travel agent to book that route.

It was an earlier era Bombay I saw, and I loved it. No one was calling it Mumbai yet and this was before internet cafes, no one had cell phones, even in Bombay you pretty much only got Indian food, fabulous food if you like Indian food, and I liked it.

I stayed at the Taj hotel and though its palatial lobby was a marvellous world of its own I wandered around Colaba, along the esplanade and back to the Gateway of India, and then among the backstreets with their souvenir, handicrafts and curiosity shops. I inspected street stalls of cheap watches, belts, bags, shirts. 'Change money? Hashish? Girl, boy, what you like?' was hissed at me from doorways. I studied the film posters at the old cinema. I took my first, exploratory peeks inside the Jehangir Art Gallery and the Prince of Wales Museum. I gave my coins to beggars and found among them some bright and talkative children, whose future I found unimaginable. 'If you write about India please don't say there are beggars,' my new Indian friends said to me, 'that is all that foreigners ever say.' We were sitting in the area's most famous café, one of those places that stays open late and 'everyone' goes to, on the Causeway, which was made of reclaimed land, somehow appropriately; Colaba had once been an island. It was expensive for these parts, a roomy space crowded with wooden tables, with posters of Hollywood stars and European cities on the walls. It was made to cater to Westerners and Indians with Western tastes, though most of the people there were foreigners, and stared at us. One of my group, not a fan of the place, said you could go there to find out how it must have felt in pre-Independence days when Indians were not allowed into certain places. You could get anything from a beer to a cocktail to herbal tea, eggs and bacon to sweet and sour prawns, tandoori or vindaloo. Later I was taken to see other parts of the city, and felt that it was a place to which I would happily devote a lifetime had I only one to spare.

Three time zones, as it were, come into play as I recall this: the present in which I am writing this, with a recent history of several trips to India; the visit I am telling you about, in which I was discovering the matchless pleasure of Indian companions; and the time I was remembering then, that long ago short time stopover, where, among the richness of impression and stimulation, I had made myself a promise that only now I was redeeming.

In a dizzy-making no-time-at-all, I was invited to accompany my friends to Goa, a few hours journey down the coast. Goa, once a Portuguese territory, from which many Indians of some Portuguese ancestry hailed, was now an established centre for the alternative traveller, and already becoming known for being the place drug-takers headed for and for the full-moon rave parties where thousands of people danced with well-fuelled abandon to music created by globally popular DJs – not, I should say, the reason my new friends were taking me there. There was an old family home, and it still gives me pleasure to remember the interesting people I found there, their charms and histories, and the revelations of the marvellous cuisine of the region. But all that is germane to this story is to relate that one fine day, just before we were to return to Bombay, I was being taken on a drive and we passed by an area famous for the market held there, which was a meeting place as much as a shopping place, with most of the stall-holders and performers (jugglers, fire-eaters, musicians) being foreigners rather than Indians.

It had its origins, I was told, in the seventies, when travellers who had run out of money but wished to remain in the opiated bliss of Goa created a flea market to sell off their jeans and rucksacks and guitars, their old paperbacks and music cassettes and watches, laid out on the ground, maybe under make-shift awnings of sarongs tied to trees. Later, inevitably, Indian traders joined in with crafts from Gujarat, Rajasthan and Kashmir, and now proper stalls dotted the grounds. I found it quite entertaining, far more so than my friends, who had not a little disdain for the 'scene' in these parts and for whom an outdoor market and a colourful crowd had not a whit of exotic appeal. I knew they had other things to do and it was arranged they would go on, and send the car back for me in about an hour.

I wandered around a little, looking somewhat out of place I suppose, for the other foreigners were inclined to affect the international budget travel style that mixed trekking gear with the booty of local hunting and gathering – beads, Indian shirts, mirrored cloth bags and so on.

I looked about for a place to have a drink, and maybe indulge in some profitable eavesdropping, and made my way to a kind of café or tea stall, open on three sides, with wooden benches and tables under shade.

And I saw a woman I recognized. From Australia. Who looked different from the last time I'd seen her. Sophie.

She saw me at the same time. A grin began to play on her face. I went over and shook her hand. We made 'small world' and 'what a surprise' kind of faces at each other.

People moved along to make space next to her. 'Mind if I sit here?' I asked. 'Can I buy you a drink?' That would have meant some tea or a bottled soda.

'Achha, yeah, no worries,' she said genially, shaking her head in assent. She looked tanned and very relaxed, still rather thin, dressed theatrically in a long brightly coloured circle skirt, a long maroon-coloured muslin shirt over that, her hair tied up in a colourful scarf.

Her eyes were made up, the black lines no doubt homage to the Indian custom, and she wore a bindi between her eyebrows and huge gold hoops hung from her ears.

'Perfect weather for this sort of thing,' I offered.

'I suppose,' she said, 'I should ask you how everyone is.'

'Last I heard you were missing in action,' I said. 'Do our friends back home know you are alive and kicking? I haven't seen them since the last time I saw you.'

'Well, I never got married to Larry.' She pulled a beedi out of her embroidered shoulder bag and lit it, discarding several inadequate matches until she managed to set it alight. She inhaled the smoke deeply.

'I heard that. Why didn't you?'

She exhaled and looked around her, smiling. 'This is where I am meant to be. This is where I am me. This is where I do what I want and it's just fine, or it's not, and that's fine. I dance with Krishna, I have visions of huge scarlet serpents, I give thanks all day long, I love this land of intoxication and godhead…and whatever I am is what I am.' She gave a hoarse little laugh, as if in delight at this obscure insight.

'And you did not want a life with Larry?'

'Ahhh, Larry. Larry will have to save someone else.'

'So suddenly at the last moment, you what, what changed your mind?'

We took our bottled drinks, a plain soda water for me, some coloured thing for her.

'Yeah, you want to hear this?' she asked. 'Okay. Well, when I saw you at that lunch, I had been sober for seven weeks. No drink, no gear. I did it cold turkey with Larry talking me through it, and being with me when I howled and cursed and tried to tear the place apart. I could only hang on and go through with it because Larry was there.'

I noticed her heavy-lidded eyes, the pin-point pupils. She was using again.

'Isabel offered me a new dress, in front of everyone so I couldn't refuse. Everyone knew what she thought of me but she was trying to be nice to me for Larry's sake, that's what it looked like. She was only doing it to make herself look good, I knew that. She dragged me off and made me choose some drop-dead designer thing, I just let her. Oh, and I'm in this fucking dressing room in some joint in Double Bay in my cotton knickers, and Isabel suddenly asks me how long I can keep not drinking, and how she's known Larry longer than anyone and she wants him to be happy, insinuating that she's not quite sure he's going to be if he's with me. Then I had to go over and pick it up from her place for some reason, she made them do some ridiculous alteration it didn't really need. I love the clothes they wear here, they are right for every type of body, the clothes fit *you*, you don't have to fit the clothes.'

'So you turned up at Isabel's?' I remembered what Elliott told me.

'And she's not there, there's a message from that woman who works there, the housekeeper, poor bitch, that Isabel said she was terribly sorry but she was held up for a while or something, and I should wait and have whatever I wanted. She sat me in that front room, and brought me tea, and then left me alone. And what was there on a coffee table, with several lovely glasses handily placed alongside it, but an ice bucket with a bottle of that vodka you'd all been raving about at that lunch.'

Elliott had promised to get them a bottle, I recalled.

'I just sat there. Isabel didn't arrive, I didn't dare turn on a TV or try to find something to read, I felt shaky and paranoid. I still would get really stressed if Larry wasn't around. And it was like there was nothing to look at but that bottle. And finally I decided to just have one little shot and you can guess the rest.'

'You didn't stop at one.'

'Man, it made me feel so fucking good so fucking fast. I was nearly choking, laughing, as I threw down shot after shot, thinking fuck *you*, Isabel, fuck everyone, and then I just went, oh fuck, and I raced for it, right out the door, and out in the street I screamed with laughter. I nearly shouted, I'm alive!'

Most alive nearest destruction, always.

'Isabel!' said Sophie. 'I was pissed off, I was meant to just wait for her while she couldn't be bothered keeping our appointment. I thought it was her power trip, making sure I had to go over to her place and making me wait. I never even wanted to go, I was only trying to keep the peace if she was going to try and stay friends with Larry. And you know what, I even thought she might have left that bottle there for me to see, a kind of dare, I don't know if she was daring me to have a drink or daring me to leave it alone. Anyway, once I'd had that one taste, I thought I've done it now, might as well have another, and then I thought it again and again!'

'And if Isabel had come in,' I said, 'you'd now be Mrs Larry Darrell.'

'Yeah, far out.' She shook her head as if unable to imagine it.

How would it have turned out? Did they have, would they have had, fun together, like young couples in love, making meals together, with quick little kisses or bumping hips as one chopped and one stirred, playing favourite music for each other, finding themselves suddenly leaving the half-full shopping trolley in the supermarket to rush home and make love again, watching television entwined on the couch, maybe becoming more like siblings as time went on, knowing each other all too well, with all the abiding tenderness and inevitable resentments arising…

'So did you go home?' I asked.

'Huh!' she snorted. 'I knew Larry would be looking for me before too long, I didn't want to go anywhere he knew about, so I got into a taxi, I had to talk the driver into it, gave him seventy dollars to take me way out into the suburbs, guy I knew out there, he supplied everyone. I wanted what he had, and I stayed out there for, I don't know, weeks I think, I found some guys who really liked to party and we got into it, they supplied the gear and I supplied myself. I made up for lost time all right. But soon I thought, I've got to get far away from here, and got it together enough to get a ticket to get here. Lucky Larry had got our passports up to date. I always wanted to come to India.'

She raved about Goa for a while, and what a great place she was living in, she could bring anyone she wanted there, they were really easygoing, and she knew people here who were quite amazing, and who would never fit into normal society back home, being too wild and free and creative and doomed, being society's losers and shooting stars, she said, among whom she felt she belonged. 'Goa is my destiny,' she said.

Then to my surprise she interrupted her somewhat narcissistic rave and managed to ask me something about myself.

'So are you writing something about this place?'

'I don't think I'll ever know it well enough.'

'I want to read something you've written. Where can I buy one of your books?'

'Oh, not around here, and I don't know if it'd interest you.'

'I do read books, you know,' she said, somewhat sarcastically.

'And do you still write?'

She looked at me for a while. 'He told you. Yeah, when I was a kid I did, but I haven't for a while. But I'm going to get back into it, here. Yeah. Seeing you, see, how about that, you're a message to me. I wish I had your book now, I'd get you to sign it.'

'I've got a copy of one with me. Tell me where you're staying and I'll drop it off.'

'That would be beautiful, what a lovely gentleman you are and I hope having your own lovely time in Goa. But,' and she had been glancing beyond me for a while at a group of people gathered at a little stall selling Indian curios, 'my boyfriend is on his way over, and he tends to be jealous so if you could be a lovely gentleman and bid us farewell soon that would be very thoughtful.'

A man in his forties came over, a dark-skinned, black-haired man in a brilliant red shirt and jeans; I supposed he had parentage of a greater mix than usual. I didn't catch his name, and he only nodded somewhat curtly at me, but gave me an intense stare out of dark eyes. He had a scar down one cheek and there was an unusual bit of silver on a leather strap around his neck.

I got up to go. 'You ought to be careful,' I said to her, so that he could not hear. She evidently had a liking, when she wasn't sober, for what we called rough trade, and I hoped that her notions of some kind of mystical India would save her from taunting fate with her submission. She just looked right at me, so I'd know she had no interest in being careful.

Back at the house, I picked up a copy of my new book, three of my plays with a nice intro. Where I signed my name and dedicated the book to her, I wrote the inscription: 'Gather ye rosebuds while ye may…'

I thought she might know the lines. It used to be in all the old poetry anthologies. I figured she might take it as some kind of validation. If she wanted to live for the moment, she had every right to, and I wished for her a good moment.

Next morning I asked the driver to detour past Sophie's guesthouse. She wasn't there but a woman knew who she was and promised she would get the book.

We were back in Bombay later that day. I went on a short trip over to Madras, and flew back via Singapore.

I barely stopped in Sydney before returning to my home on the North Coast.

The best party

Someone called me on Elliott's behalf to tell me he was very sick. I drove over to Byron Bay to find him propped up on piles of silk pillows on his bed while his two new staff members, young Filipino men, darted in and out with trays of teas, mineral water and herbal mixtures.

Elliott had had some kind of collapse, but he forbade any questions about it. 'All under control,' he said, 'I think I was a bit dehydrated, that's all, and I since found out I was supposed to have plenty of liquids with my new mixture.'

The doctor had come, remember house calls? You could really get anything in Byron. This doctor knew Elliott and had some noteworthy qualifications – certain patients – and had come by and said that they'd do some tests and for now stay in bed for another few days at least, a week even.

I sat with him for a while and Elliott recounted all the local gossip he knew, some of it not up to his usual standards of freshness, but he had heard things about who had bought and sold what real estate for what profit, who had been in town, who was staying at the health spa famous for its detox programme, and whether they had been found sneaking out for alcohol or chocolate.

It all seemed to be quite an effort, this recounting, but he made the effort and seemed to need to perform his unique status as insider, advisor, observer.

And he also talked about what he was going to wear for the big party that was being held for CJ Lonoff in about three weeks.

Even my next-door neighbour and the man in the post office had both made mention of it, for the local papers reported rumours about extra police being sent up to be on duty that night, and that journalism student who had been busted building a platform in a tree from which to spy upon the star's arrival.

A few nights later I went to a reception for a famous animal rights activist and there was Elliott disobeying the advice of the well-qualified doctor, on this occasion preferring to take the alternative advice of a revered spiritual healer who also came to you if that's what you preferred, and had come to the house and done some kind of session, which basically consisted of this person simply sitting with Elliott in a darkened room for an hour and drawing out of him the bad energies that had affected his heart. It was his newly-strengthened heart that he should listen to, Elliott was advised, if he felt like going out, after all there might be someone he was meant to meet that night.

As the latest proof of how amazing this spiritual healer was, Elliott swept about the place enfolded by a gushing shield of the healer's admirers who came to compliment Elliott on looking great. He had dressed and groomed beautifully and was especially vivacious that night, pleased with himself for being there, flushed and sparkling.

He had a relapse after that and once more I went to see him and once more he was in pyjamas but this time he could only talk about the one thing that was making him anxious and querulous.

For now the party for CJ Lonoff was only about ten days away and the very strange thing that had happened was that his, Elliott's, invitation had not arrived, and not only that, who had come to see him but Paul Barton.

Remember Paul Barton? Elliott's ex-protégé of old, nurtured and advised way back when, got what he wanted and moved on fast, showed up years later full of disrespect and denial and disloyalty, too busy for Elliott.

Oh yes, he'd moved up here too, not full-time but he rented something at Suffolk Park and was thinking of buying there.

And now, out of the blue, Paul had turned up, right here at the house, as if an old friendship had not been so lengthily and bitterly interrupted.

And suddenly it's all sweetness and light from Paul, weren't *you* good to me and wasn't I sweet to *you* and weren't those the days, but before long Paul had got to the point, there was that vintage YSL linen suit that Elliott had once lent him (didn't we have fun), which would look even more amazing these days, and he remembered Elliott saying both that he would never throw it out and that Paul could borrow it again one day on another special occasion.

'I said, I just might want to wear it myself!' said Elliott. 'Vintage has it all over anything new. And he gave me this look, as if he knew I wasn't being asked. I wouldn't be surprised if he had told Rye not to invite me. That would be just like him.'

That was not the worst part. The worst part, to me, was how upset Elliott was about all that, how seriously he took it, how much anguish he was suffering simply because there was a party he hadn't been asked to. He actually began to cry as he said, 'After everything I've done for everyone, after having known the Dalai Lama and been Rye Bread's best friend when she was getting her foot into this community, CJ would not have that property if it weren't for me.'

And where was everyone? People knew he was sick, and not even ten people had called this whole time.

'Everyone must know I'm not being asked to CJ's party,' he said, ridiculously. 'And it's going to be the best party of the *year*. Half of them wouldn't know Rye if it weren't for me.'

Elliott surely had heard that they were quite techno, these invitation cards, embedded with some kind of one of those 3D pictures that moves. A hologram, the man in the post office had said. Manufactured here for the first time, my next-door neighbour had learned.

'Unless someone's stolen it,' said Elliott.

'I bet *you* are being invited, *you're* down the end of the alphabet so *yours* hasn't come through *yet*,' I offered, desperate to relieve an anxiety so unworthy of the violence it was doing to him.

'Maybe.' He was a bit mollified, and I felt extra bad for having added to a vain yearning.

'Anyway, fuck them!' I said then. 'It'll probably rain on the night and you know what people are like around here. Half of them won't come and the rest will get washed out.'

Elliott chuckled, liking the vision.

'Or they'll all turn up and tell each other what Rye says behind their backs,' he said.

Rye reliably gossiped without discretion about anyone who wasn't there, but everyone always laughed at and agreed with her betrayals and her slanders, for she had things to tell them you would not hear anywhere else, or not so fast. Somehow people generally enjoy speculation on others' weaknesses, mistakes and misdeeds.

'Anyway,' I said, 'you'll be glad you stayed home where you've got far lovelier things to rest your eyes on in your very own environment.'

'It's a work in progress,' he said, looking around him with satisfaction.

When I left Elliott's place I stopped at a phone booth, and rang Rye Bread's number. Keith answered.

'Keith! Even better.'

Keith had taken over from doing the books a couple of days a week to running the office full time. I'd known him for a long time, from Sydney. He'd moved up here ages ago, and was the accountant for a lot of the new businesses. 'I came up here to semi-retire,' he'd say, 'and now I'm working more hours than ever.' He had red hair and pale freckly skin always reddened by the local sun but he thrived in this climate and went about bare-headed in cars you could take the top down.

He used to get out a lot in the old days in Sydney, and also had a reputation as the most organized, stress-free, efficient business manager you could get, fast and accurate, could manage your books, your budgets, your stratagems.

'And what am I better for today?' he asked me.

'I want to pop in to see you,' I told him.

'Mate,' he said, 'quelle surprise, things around here are somewhat on the flat out and frantic side, but if you just want a quick coffee here.'

I drove over to Rye Bread's office, a converted garage near her house turned into a studio, with a loft bedroom, now the hub of the planning for the big event.

Rye had been CJ Lonoff's personal assistant from way back when they were just two little girls from Little Rock. CJ now had several other PAs but Rye was CEO, as it were, of the Down Under office of a minor industry devoted to the administration of a single celebrity life based on three continents, one that made the only art form to reach all nations of the planet: music video.

CJ had once emerged with cred as an indie star, but her brand name had now been incorporated by one of the few huge global media empires that market nearly all of popular music you hear and see. Her Insurgent label was now but one imprint of a global dominion.

CJ's rise was a phenomenon inextricable from the rise of music video, with its enormous commercial power. The empire's music division was hosting this bash, and the word was that there would be a lot of industry people there, more so than other artists. The district was abuzz with the expectations of the kind of spending that would be going on. People would be flying in from Europe and the States. Hotels and guesthouses were booked out, some people were letting their houses for that week and properties were being listed at real estate agents.

The studio was the centre of operations. It was like stepping into the office of a small arts festival. There was a new security door. Keith presided in the large front office, and I saw a couple of other people at computers and phones in an area at the back. We were able to talk privately.

'To what do I owe the pleasure?' asked Keith amiably. 'I thought you were holed up, so to speak, at Brunswick Head, head down, bum up, over a typewriter of course.'

'Yes, I am working, but I've just been to see Elliott Templeton.'

'Oh yeah? What did I just hear about him? Did he go to that one that draws the sickness out of you with his aura?'

'Keith dear, Elliott is the reason I am here. Look, he really wants to go to this CJ Lonoff party, he is devastated because he didn't get an invitation, is he on the list?

Keith dropped his chin right down on his chest and looked up at me through his eyebrows.

'I know,' I said, 'but you should see him, he is not well, and really looking old, and this could well turn out to be the last thing he wanted. God,' I said, 'he is right, too, that no one turned him down when he was the one giving out the invites.'

'Well, that is true.'

'Out of generosity alone but he has every right to get invited back in turn.'

'He always was such an operator.'

'He deserves this invitation.'

'I don't decide the list, Will dear, I am but the humble secretary to the assistant to the star. Who has her own number of guests and the producers have their own number. Strictly limited numbers.'

'Why didn't Rye Bread ask him?'

'She was trying to cut down, and you know her, if you've got nothing to offer why should she bother. And Paul Barton's got her ear and he's really down on Elliott Templeton for some reason.'

'You should see him. He's devastated.'

'This party may be costing the equivalent of some nation's annual debt, but I do ask myself if that might be the only reason anyone would want to go.'

'I've sent my regrets. Let him take my place.'

'To say he was there and who he has met. Everyone out to impress someone or make a connection or sell their project or find what property might be for sale.'

'You've just convinced me, but Elliott lives to be among all that, and he has been generous to a lot of people who will be there. The truth is, he won't be able to go, he just wants to say he was asked. Keithy, you know what I want. Elliott was always nice to you.'

Elliott habitually extended his graciousness to support staff, too, that was always one great thing about him, he formed friendships with his own staff and with that of places he visited, and did them any favours he could, and whether or not he got any benefits in turn he did it as if that didn't matter, which was more than you can say for a lot of people with more money, and let me tell you old or new money is not the point in any way at all. Keith of course appreciated all this, having been treated like the lord's mere serf in some places and invited to everything along with everyone at other places.

He said nothing for a moment, then said at last, 'Here's what I'll tell you: we got very specially printed invitations printed, not without a great deal of drama, come to me for what designers you want to work with and who not ever. Anyway, let me tell you a little secret, there are a few of these rare and precious documents left over and they are in the box on my desk over there. Now I am going to go and make us a nice little espresso and we do not do decaf. I cannot see my desk while I go and grind some beans and get that steam steaming, so am not responsible for what happens when my back is turned. You don't have sugar do you?'

We had a short and pleasant coffee together a few minutes later, then I told Keith I mustn't keep him and it had been lovely to see him. 'And are you looking forward to the Bay's big bash?' I inquired as I left.

'Joke, right? I mean, we had fun in the seventies. No, mate, once everyone has arrived on the night, guests, caterers, drivers, I clock off,' said Keith. 'And I'm going straight home, so to speak. I'll get myself a takeaway and the video of Batman has just come out. I won't be out after midnight and I won't be answering the phone.'

'I'm sure you'll have a lovely time,' I said and drove back past Elliott's, where I dropped something in his mailbox.

D'you mean to say I'm going to die?

A couple of days later Elliott was beaming at me, as he waved me in to his bedroom. 'Look,' he said, whipping something out from under his pillow.

It was of course a certain innovative little work of art and design.

'Told you,' I said.

'Look at what I'm going to wear,' he said, pointing to a suit laid over the back of a chair.

I had thought it would be enough for him to get the invitation. I hadn't really thought about his actually going, rather envisaging that he wasn't getting any better and wouldn't make it. By now the doctor had been reinstated as chief advisor and Elliott had admitted to the discussion of the fact that he'd suffered a series of strokes. I suppose I thought that if he did go, no one would go so far as to question his possession of an invitation, for no one but Rye would know for sure he had been excluded. At least it would be Keith who would get Elliott's acceptance. Keith would be smart enough to destroy all evidence of an acceptance. There'd be a list of names on a well-guarded gate. Would Keith have to answer for it if Elliott did turn up? Oh dear, and I had indicated that all Elliott wanted was to be asked. What a tangled web this might be.

'You're actually going to go?' I asked.

'My dear, I wouldn't miss it for all the jade in China. And of course the suit will look sensational, better than any new clobber those Johnny-come-latelies can come up with. With that antique brooch, and my new Prada shoes. The boys are going to courier it down to the cleaners this afternoon.'

I did not expect to see Elliott again so soon, but the very next day, when I finished work, there were two messages on the answer phone from his house staff. The doctor had been back, and Elliott's condition was serious. Once more I drove to the Bay. Elliott was sleeping deeply, and there was a new addition to the household, a nurse who had just arrived, a young man who already had commandeered Elliott's boudoir as his exclusive jurisdiction, and I could see that the Filipino boys were feeling territorially challenged.

A combination of his extraordinary will to live and maybe the doctor's medications saw him sitting up again the next day, playfully stirring up the nurse and the house-staff, making obscene suggestions about what they might be up to behind his back, and urging them not to hide it.

'He's looking better,' I said to the nurse.

'He might be looking better,' he said significantly, 'but his next of kin should be here.'

Elliott had not been in touch with Isabel lately and there did not seem to be any other close relations. And there was no sign of the flocks of people who once had made certain to remain in his thoughts. Where there had once been endless drinking and music and riotous leaping into the pool, now there was no one, it seemed, but me, and the nurse and two resident staff.

I had never expected to be the only one to be around Elliott at a time like this. The friendships that last so long and become so significant in our lives are rarely predictable, are not always with those with whom we experienced the deepest and most intimate exchanges of feeling and thought, the most exact correspondences of opinion, not always those who have enchanted us the most. The ones who remain in our lives, through its ups and downs, through our alterations and our ageing, are part of a store of shared experience and common references built over the years, bound to us with invisible threads of affinity. You don't know who if anyone will be around when you die.

I sent messages to Isabel. She and Gray were on holiday, and it would be a couple of days before they could get back.

The nurse called for me. 'I asked him about his spiritual beliefs,' he said, 'and he told me he's a Buddhist. Would he have a priest or something like that?'

As Elliott had been mentioning the spiritual life for some years now, I thought, well, if all that can't help *you* when *you're* dying when can it help *you*?

'Elliott,' I said to him as causally as I could, 'I know that *you're* a Buddhist. Do *you* want to see the Rinpoche or someone like that?'

'D'you mean to say I'm going to die?'

'I would never say that. But *you* did seem to get so much out of everything he's done, and it might be helpful to see him now.'

Elliott lay back on his pillows and did not answer me at once. Finally he said, 'Oh, call up that nice nun,' and I knew who he meant.

I found the nun, and she drove over to the house that evening. I took her to his room and left Elliott alone with her.

I went out onto the back deck. It was a still night, with the half-moon dimly shining through banks of clouds. There was a scent of jasmine and frangipani. No one had switched on the lights of the driveway and pool, but the solar-powered lamps studded around the place created soft pools of light and cast beguiling shadows.

From Elliott's quarters I heard the sound of bells, of chanting.

I wondered about the woman attending to Elliott now. What would it take to lead such a life with its renunciations, vows and duties? I wondered if she ever missed eating meat, drinking beer, having sex, whether she found peace and fulfilment in her role, as she appeared to. What could have caused her to abandon the ambitions of most women and shave her head and don the simple robes? Could this really be a lack of vanity or was it another kind of vanity?

I became lost in thoughts on this human trait. Vanity was generally considered a sign of trivial failing, a need to be thought well of or considered in some sense pleasing or enviable. On the face of it this should be a fault one could eradicate with a modicum of sense or sense of proportion, but on reflection I wondered if it might not be a passion more consuming than love. Time itself cured one of love's terror and servitude, but vanity continued to thrive, being part of all ambition, commitment, desire, integrity, discipline and, who knows, of all humility, sincerity, martyrdom and endurance. All contained a necessary component of vanity. I admit I took out my notebook and forgot all else for a while as I jotted and doodled.

When the nun reappeared, I went back inside with her. She looked deeply moved, and the two boys were crying, and crossing themselves.

'He's a beautiful person,' said the nun to me, 'a beautiful old soul.'

I walked her to her car 'What do you do, if I may ask,' I asked as we reached it, 'with someone in Elliott's condition?'

'I lead him in very particular meditations,' she said, getting into her seat and buckling the belt. 'These inspire the person to think of others with loving kindness and compassion.'

I went back inside.

The last words he spoke

I wondered if I ought to go home, but felt I should stay. I waited for I knew not what in a sitting room next to the bedroom, sporadically perusing some art books and catalogues.

The nurse came in shortly to tell me Elliott had asked if I were still there. He wanted to see me.

I entered his bedroom, where the air was heavy with a mix of incense smoke and the awful stench of severe illness.

Elliott was weak, but managed to croak a little about the nun, how she was the head of her order, and had received particular recognition, and that she had offered him a special guided meditation of notable exclusivity.

'I think in my next reincarnation I might well be a spiritual leader myself,' he confided.

'Oh, perhaps a few more turns on the karmic wheel might be called for!' I said, smiling, trying to make light of it.

'Believe me, few have had such a close association with the important spiritual leaders of our age,' Elliott said haughtily. 'Certain aspects rub off.'

I allowed him to fantasize his choosing his next life according to the respect owed to his impeccable credentials and associations.

He dropped off to sleep. I felt I should stick around, though. The doctor came. He shook his head.

It was afternoon when Elliott called me in again.

'I still haven't replied to the invitation for CJ Lonoff,' he said.

'Oh, I wouldn't bother,' I said.

'The RSVP is due and I always reply,' he said. 'I'll show Rye Bread what class really is. Would you mind writing it for me?'

I found paper and pen, and sat poised for dictation. 'All right, I'm ready,' I said.

He lay back with his eyes closed for a while and I thought he had drifted off.

'Say,' he said, 'Elliott Templeton sends his apologies but is unable to attend as he will be entering a new body.'

He snickered a little. His face was grey, and he looked a hundred. His room was full of that unpleasant smell that made breathing through the nose difficult for me. I'm sure he did not perceive it, yet he had always been so fussy over colognes for his person and the freshest of bed linen and scented candles for his rooms. He was still clutching the invitation card, and grinned horribly at the triumphant snub he would deliver to Rye.

'The little cunt!' he said.

Those were the last words he spoke. He fell back, but though he never regained consciousness he remained breathing for some time. The nurse came in a couple of times as I sat there.

The shutters were slightly open, and at one point, the windows lightened with a rosy glow as the sun set. A full-throated chorus of magpies and currawongs made a racket.

I dozed off in the armchair, but remained alert to any changes in the room. And so it was through a kind of veil, in that mystical state of being between waking and sleeping, that I heard a shocking sound, a choking sound, the sound of the last breath taken, of a human death.

Who could ever know if a last breath is taken consciously? If you drift off to sleep as if there are dreams already waiting, if you begin to dream and so realize you are already sleeping and surrender to it, it's a pleasant moment and seems to have nothing to do with death. But if you are bone-weary, lying in bed wanting too much to sleep, you are too aware as the conscious mind tries to slip away, and become aware of only blank oblivion one breath away. You cannot feel terror falling to sleep but terror is there. Will your body keep pumping blood and breath through you, will you awake with your memory and reason intact? One day it'll be no and no one knows the day. Let us rejoice at having made it this far. You feel grateful when life is good, so life seems good when you feel grateful.

I sat for a while, awed and saddened. Elliott had gone, he was no more. He would go to no more parties, enliven no more social occasions, chuckle over no more gossip, drop no more names, attire himself in no more bespoke suits. He would no longer create connections for people, no longer take an interest in anyone's progress through life. Who can say what any one life has been worth. Some would say his ambitions and satisfactions were worthless, that his life had been silly, useless and trivial. But he had created friendship and beauty and pleasure. He was an old, kind friend.

I felt intensely alive and full of the wonder of existence. I was not able to think at all, and although I felt an astonishing surge of energy, suddenly I fell into a deep sleep, which I only realized when I was woken, stiff and sore in the armchair, by the nurse who came in at dawn. I glanced once more at the empty shell in the bed. How dead a dead person looks. A live body acting the part of a corpse on stage or film never ever really looks dead, no matter how still. I left the nurse to do his job, and went home for breakfast and a long bath.

The next day I picked up Isabel and Gray at the local airport. Then it was up to them to take care of Elliott's wishes in the disposal of his body and to arrange his memorial service.

PART VI

Account of a conversation

The reason I began writing this book was to give an account of a conversation I had with Larry. And now I had better get on with telling *you* how that came about and what he said to me.

It's taken me a while to work out why I'm finding it hard to begin writing this section. You see, having told *you* so much already, pretty much for the purpose of leading up to this, it now seems to me that *you*, dear reader, could well skip Part Six entirely. If *you* did, *you* wouldn't lose the thread of the story, such as it is.

But it is the reason I have written this.

You might have heard that there are only seven basic plots, or ten, or three and that means not only in fiction but in all of life. Good versus evil. Love gone wrong. The quest for identity, for freedom, for revenge, for the Holy Grail. Tears shed over answered prayers. Unhappy families. Crime and punishment.

Still we think that fiction is structured while life is not. What do we do with things that don't fit into the plot?

We could say that everything we want is based on the kind of story we want our life to be.

Though many of the stories of any culture remain untranslatable, the craving for story is universal. We are told that narrative has emotional functions, for we suffer if deprived of it, for example if we are not allowed to dream, or imagine. The study of narrative evolves along with the proliferating mutations of its manifestations. I always thought plays and novels and films could forever satisfy that craving, but apparently for some it's got to be computer games, reality TV and probably things I don't know about.

The search for a story is a story.

So much for that

I was in Sydney again some time that summer. Isabel and Gray were settled back in the apartment in Elizabeth Bay, having long returned from disposing of Elliott's ashes.

The place now belonged to Isabel outright, for Elliott had left it to her. I don't know just what else he did leave her, but certainly he had provided for her very generously and she was looking very complacent about it all. He had also been generous to his staff, and had left a small number of remembrances to a few friends. He left me an extraordinary panel of an Indian relief carving depicting humans and other creatures all copulating together, no doubt an allegory of divine bliss. A great deal of his money went to the Buddhist Centre; the building design had been chosen before Elliott's death and the construction went ahead. Elliott always said Buddhism had great aesthetic appeal (even though his own taste might have been somewhat more rococo).

With the considerable capital now at their disposal, and after a legal victory that cleared Gray of bankruptcy and allowed him to enter the world of business again, the Maturins were preparing for their return to the Sunshine State. News from there was of boom times, for the south-east region had the fastest growing population in Australia. The potential of more shopping malls, housing estates, renovations and all the other bounty of real estate development was accelerating, and Gray was called to contribute his gift of vision. That and a substantial investment.

First, though, there was a great deal of selling off to undertake. They weren't going to keep the apartment, and very little of its furniture and artworks. They'd see the summer out in Sydney. They had tickets to Festival events. But they'd be back in Brisbane in time for the girls to begin their new school up there. One of them was going into high school if I recall.

So much for that.

What I was looking for

When I had asked Isabel about Larry, she only said that they hadn't seen him in a long time. She had an idea he had been planning to go back to India, and thought he could well be there.

She and Gray had made new friends, a couple of other couples, who dated them the way couples date couples, couples go out together, couples have dinners for each other.

The season of our regular foursome with Larry seemed long past, and there was no chance to talk about it even if we had wanted to.

When I think about seeing Larry again, in India, I think it should seem too extraordinary, in a vast land dense with an extensive, renewing multitude of strangers, where the likelihood of running into someone you know must be infinitesimal.

But we do move in small worlds. We live in small villages within large cities, our communities are not geographically based, we don't live where we were born, we don't have a single workplace, we are global souls. While much larger numbers of people might appear in the backgrounds of our lives than in former times, the number of people we really notice seems to have some human constant, as does the number of people we really care about. It's as if the human brain is hard-wired for this. Once it might have been kinship and tribal connections, now it's elective affinities.

And anyway, anything can happen in India.

I had promised myself and my new Indian friends that I would be back and, sooner than I really dared hope, I was. It so happened that my works were assigned to the Australian Studies course at one then another university in India, brought to their attention by an academic who was writing her doctorate on them. Apparently not only academics but general readers were interested in English-language literature that was not only, or especially not, from the hegemonic USA and UK, and the established study of Commonwealth literature had sprouted branches, frequently beginning to call itself post-colonial studies. I was happy to find my work a leaf on such a branch.

She'd been in touch with me, the academic, and all in good time it was arranged that I would come to meet her, and give a talk to her department.

Thus after some delightful times in Bombay and Delhi, further delight awaited me in the charming professor, her family, her colleagues and her students who all treated me with much grace and generosity and took me about Madras, to its sights and monuments, its clubs and hotels. A glance at the professor in the lovely sari she was expected to wear in the institutes of learning might bring to mind an image of woman as ornament, but I was beginning to have my world wonderfully expanded by the likes of her, witty, learned women and men in India who knew far more about the rest of the world, including the minor literature to which I contributed, than it knew about them.

My work was discussed and queried by smart, astute readers who had rarely heard Australian English and never been to Australia. This was just before satellites and economic liberalization brought world television to India. It was not until a later time that I began to meet Indian audiences of Australian TV soaps, from which most knowledge of our little country (all blondes, all heterosexual, clean empty streets) for so long since derived. But for a tiny moment, somewhere on earth my plays were better known than *Neighbours*.

A colleague of my now favourite professor, a theatre director, mounted – that's the word – a production of one of my early plays, while the Indian arm, and I'm not sure that's the word, of one of the multinational corporatized globalized major publishers, steady on the course of takeovers and obliterations that would soon see a handful of these publishers control most of the output and nearly all the distribution of text as commodity, published a series for Indian consumption of Australian plays and a volume of articles about them. This was not so bad because it did include a couple of insightful and appreciative pieces from the far margins of popular culture theory, and that mad interview I did ages ago with a friend of mind who was writing for *Playboy Australia* which let us get pissed and egg each other on to greater displays of frankness and cunning.

Anyway, in this connection I was funded by a government-sponsored foreign cultural exchange body to attend the production and to give some talks.

'You bet I want to go,' I had told my agent, 'even if they don't pay me.'

'I won't tell them *you* said that,' he said, that's what agents are for.

And no doubt as usual if I wanted to be somewhere else it was also partly to do with what I wanted to be away from. India seemed excellent for a distant perspective.

It was my second night in Madras. It was a relatively slower city than Bombay or Delhi, and a gentler one, but still it was noisy and crowded. The river stank so foully that I had to breathe behind the cover of a handkerchief when we passed too close. Apparently some international team of experts in river rejuvenation had been to clean it up and had retreated in defeat, for the depth of this pollution was unconquerable. Public spaces were filthy and unkempt, there were no public parks or gardens in the city centre, and I was told that many trees had been cut down in recent decades. Pictures of the city in earlier times showed quiet, broad avenues shaded by canopies of huge leafy branches – nothing of the kind remained. The city didn't begin to look attractive until I reached the lengthy avenue that ran along the sea shore, the longest beach, they told me, in the country. The waters of the Bay of Bengal lay dark and smooth beyond a wide stretch of sand facing a long series of spacious buildings, institutes of learning and research mainly, it seemed, and at one end the Indo-Saracen buildings of the university, the architectural style a blend of influences and a perfect metaphor for the juxtaposition of communities coexisting in Indian cities. While communal violence of unbearable ferocity and cruelty had been stirred up by political interests, something far from unknown on the subcontinent, what was demonstrated to me was the easy blending of many disparate people. It took me some time to understand that there were great differences of religion, background and caste among the people who cooperated in the endeavours of everyday and professional life. Outside of this little community, perhaps outside of my perception, vile discriminations persisted. But what I saw was a collective effect that was grace personified. I soon perceived that this would become one of my favourite cities.

On my first night I had been taken to a concert, for in this season a festival of the classical music of the region was held regularly. I could not hope to understand this music, but as I followed it as best I could, I became fascinated and felt curiously transported. I looked at the audience, women in saris of sober hue, with tasteful diamond studs in their ears, their dark or greying hair bound in neat buns at their napes, the men in western shirts or lungis and kurtas. Many of them beat time with their hands, though beating time must be the wrong phrase for the supple-wristed yet precise movements they made to the intricate patterns of sound from veena and thambura, from mandolin and mridangam. This was an audience that knew its art form. Indeed in the lobby one could obtain that day's music festival newsletter and the local paper had sections and supplements devoted to the concerts taking place at all hours all over town and the lively critiques they inspired.

Others had gone to a contemporary German play that night, and I gathered that the classical music scene was somehow implicated in casteism and political conservatism, while performed works from other sources attracted an audience more interested in progressive ideas and cross-fertilization.

The drama I had once written was performed in an old theatre set back from the road in a leafy campus that included a small library, in which many earnest people were perusing the crammed metal shelves.

The play, in which one man feels severely challenged when he discovers he has some Aboriginal ancestry, while another invents such an ancestry for the supposed social benefits it will bestow, had fallen into some disrepute back in Australia, where non-Indigenous writers were now required to butt out of these subjects. But here they found it worthy and told me that its themes might be related to the relationships and laws concerning the tribal peoples of India, who were seen as both indubitably disadvantaged and overly promoted through employment and education affirmative action quotas. Furthermore, some believed that an ancient kinship existed between the Indigenous people of Australia and the people here.

Afterwards, I was drinking tea in the theatre foyer, happily chatting to the triumphant young actors and their families and friends, resisting endless plates of cookies and pastries, and looking up, there in the crowd, standing patiently, I saw Larry.

I found myself beaming at the sight of him. The last time I'd seen him had by now been over a year ago.

I introduced him as an old friend. Larry told us he'd happened to pick up a copy of the local newspaper, where he had read of my visit and the production.

'Stick around and we'll go out to dinner afterwards,' I said to him.

I had been put up at a comfortable club which had once been the exclusive retreat of senior Indian officials. It was not far from a colonial-style hotel, once known as the best in South India, still attractive in its proportions and character and promise of comfort. I thought we might go there, but Larry suggested a hotel that lay only a short walk from where we were.

We picked our way along the uneven street, waving away keen auto-rickshaw drivers. Although this was the middle of winter, it was still a warm season, the night almost sultry.

As we walked we chatted about the extraordinary way that Indian English had seemed to work so well in a play written in Australian English, two distinctive and independent forms of the world language, about how the production had made universal what had been written as local, whether hybrid works dissolved or included difference, and so on.

The hotel was a cluster of low buildings set amongst some tree-studded grounds, with the distinction of a well-established reputation as a reliable base for the medium-budget visitor. Its large dining hall stayed open all night in the concert season, and as it happened I had already been here, earlier that day, taken to eat a thali lunch.

I have found, if you spend just three days in a new city being taken out by separate and very different people, inevitably you will find yourself being shown somewhere you've just been. There are always these places that everyone goes to. Larry was greeted familiarly.

We were soon shown to a table and brought a stainless steel jug of cold water which was poured into a couple of steel tumblers. I ordered bottled water but noticed Larry drank the water from the jug.

I told Larry I had seen Isabel and Gray.

'They'll be glad to get back up north again,' he said. 'Gray needed to get back to work again. No doubt whatever he is doing there will be a success.'

'I'm sure he partly has you to thank. He doesn't suffer from headaches now and he seems confident again, he believes in himself again. You did a lot for him.'

'I didn't really. I just made it easier for him to see how he could do that for himself.'

'And how did you know how to do what you didn't really do?'

'Oh, someone did it to me, then I found I could do it to someone else.'

I made Larry tell me the story. He had been on a trek in the Himalayas with an Indian friend, and severely twisted his ankle. It might have been a good while before anyone came along, for this was a minor walking track in a scarcely populated area, where the nights were far too cold to be caught out. They had expected to reach the gompa they were heading for by dark, and didn't have a minute to lose if they were to make it.

Larry's ankle had already swollen, but his friend, a monk whose gompa they were returning to, showed no anxiety, but serenely sat by Larry and patiently talked him through a healing process similar to the one I had seen Larry use on Gray. After falling into a deep sleep, which judging by the light had been very brief, the pain had gone and the ankle returned to walking condition.

'And then, a year later it must have been,' said Larry, 'I was in a situation where I remembered what he'd done, because I thought I should try it. I was with a friend who had a migraine and we couldn't get any help soon enough for him to deliver a lecture and so I told him I wanted to try something.'

'No one was more surprised than me when it worked. My friend had a short deep sleep, woke up feeling fine and finished writing his lecture. He delivered it with aplomb to a grand dinner that night, and was invited to give a lecture in the UK. He had always wanted to go abroad.

'He began to tell people about what I'd done, and they told others. I found all kinds of people turning up at my place or getting hold of me if I was out, asking me to help them. I seemed to have an ability to heal but couldn't explain it, though somehow it worked.'

'Did you ever analyze what you were doing so successfully?'

'It's simple really, we all know that the mind can be very powerful, and it's just a matter of planting an idea in someone's mind. For example, would you be surprised if you poured some of that water on to your own head?'

'I would be surprised.'

'You will. But I didn't want to investigate my own application of whatever ability I had, and I didn't really want anyone else to, and I didn't want to make a business out of doing it.

'Anyway,' Larry said, 'I began to be puzzled by the problem, the phenomenon, of pain. It seems at first glance that its purpose is to alert us to something that's gone wrong, but that doesn't entirely account for it. It doesn't account for phantom pain or sympathetic pain, or different experiences of pain. According to some, the purpose of pain is the healing of the soul.'

'And how does that operate?' I felt moved to inquire.

'It's a religious idea. Pain and sorrow are supposed to be part of God's way of bringing you to repentance and back to God. I looked into ideas about pain to try and help me understand it. In the end it seems to me that the most useful thing to know is how effectively the mind can manage physical pain.'

'You never were attracted to conventional religion as a way of coming to whatever it is you've been looking for?'

'Not really. There had been some standard Christian instruction and observance, inevitably, in my upbringing, but it always seemed more part of the kind of convention that prescribes which fork to use, rather than part of real experience. I never found it convincing. And later, looking at it again, I maintained the same objections anyone does who is prepared to think about it and who requires God to be worthy of one's belief. I expect you know what I mean.'

I did. I said, 'A supposedly good and powerful God who allows evil. One is supposed to think of it all as a test, or part of a hidden purpose you're not supposed to question too stringently. Mencken once said,' and I had learnt this quotation, '"It is impossible to imagine the universe run by a wise, just and omnipotent God, but it is quite easy to imagine it run by a board of gods. If such a board actually exists it operates precisely like the board of a corporation that is losing money."'

I told Larry that even before I thought much about the extent of the world's injustices that this so-called God created or allowed, I had begun to wonder why he needed so much praise and worship. The first thing I ever knew about God was that he demanded to be worshipped, and I tried to imagine this being that required you to regularly sing his praises. I did not care for him. Perhaps that's unfair, for after all he had been supposed to have created the entire world and everything in it, and any creator lives for recognition!

'But as a writer, do you really want to be constantly praised for the work you've done?'

'No. Not to my face anyway! And that's why I am not God!'

'I agree,' Larry said. 'It's one of the reasons I, like most people who question all that, could not accept the idea of God. I could not believe in a supreme being who had to be asked every day to feed us and look after us, to take care of our needs and give us what we wanted, who was jealous and vengeful.'

'Athletes and actors and singers give credit to God for helping them win races and awards,' I said. 'I don't think it makes God look too good, picking winners of races. God won't do too much about poverty and torture, but will get you the Oscar or Olympic medal if you've said the right prayer.'

'And will heal some pain but not other pain. This is where it comes back to the power of the mind. God or no God, belief itself is a powerful force that no one entirely understands. I learnt that you didn't need notions of any god to be able to soothe pain. Emotional pain as well.'

'You just need the right pills,' I joked.

'Yes, difficult feeling or emotional reaction and Western doctors are writing a prescription, but actual physical pain, chronic pain, is under-treated, because the most effective drugs are those favoured by self-medicators, and are the most illegal and demonized.'

'The puritanical tradition seems to be the most powerful one of all.'

We had already eaten a plate of idli-sambar each, rather a specialty of this town where idli were served round the clock, not only at breakfast. We fell silent for some minutes as we ate our dosai. Around us was the clatter and buzz of a busy restaurant.

'Why do you keep coming to India?' I asked him abruptly.

'Because I can,' Larry said. I already understood that. 'And,' he said, 'this is where it all started for me. A friend of mine died, young guy like I was, and I just wanted to keep on asking why till I found something I could live with.'

'These days they'd send you to counselling and dose you with anti-depressants!' I joked.

He smiled. 'Between grief and nothing I will take grief,' he quoted at me.

'Well, I hope it wasn't all grief.'

'Of course not, I also had a good time, a lot of the time.'

Then I took up the tumbler of water, poured some into my palm and tossed it over my head.

I had never thought I was particularly suggestible, often given to formulating contrary viewpoints, but that's what happened. I stuck my tongue out at him. 'Don't think I'll do anything you ask now!'

'I certainly don't,' he said agreeably.

I brought him back to telling me the story of his search for meaning. 'So you began with reading your way through Queensland State Library and then going off on new travels.'

'I was reading certain things. And then when I left Brisbane, I got a job as a builder's labourer, and tried to find out more by talking to more people who'd lived different kinds of lives.'

Larry told me about working on the building site.

'How did you really feel when Isabel wouldn't marry you?' I asked him at some point.

He didn't answer at once. I saw tenderness, sadness and an amused nostalgia for lost times fleet across his face as he thought a moment.

'I was really young, you know. I thought we were going to get married and do everything together. I thought I was offering her something great. I thought it was going to be great.' He laughed a little here. 'But I didn't know how different from mine her idea of a good life was. If I'd had any sense I'd have realized it before making those plans, before making such a commitment.'

After Larry's work on the building site, his short adventure in Thailand, and his involvement with the personal growth workshop known as The Process, he suddenly took off to a place in the mountains north of Delhi where the woman who was becoming known as the Glamorous Guru presided over what was called the Shakti Estate.

In the compound – a large yoga room and several smaller halls, rooms and clinics – the curious and the devoted engaged in a range of activities that led them to experiencing their being and all its occult secrets through exercises focusing on the physical body.

'Everyone was required to do something called Energy Meditation in the large hall every morning. We also did something called Dynamic Yoga and at night we gathered for Freeform. Those were the three activities everyone joined in for, regular attendance at them was regarded as the necessary basis to be registered at Shakti. The rest of the time we signed up for our choices out of a whole range of treatments from accredited facilitators, some in the compound and some in nearby buildings.

'These included a whole range of massage therapies – someone once counted seventeen separate categories – and things like aromatherapy, various movement-based disciplines, things like psychic osmosis, and sweat lodges, steam baths and saunas.'

'What on earth is psychic osmosis?' I inquired, not that I was entirely certain what all the rest of it was.

'It's a one-on-one process where you sit close and opposite to your therapist, your knees almost touching, and you sit there unmoving for an hour looking into each other's eyes. Normally people don't hold each other's gaze for any length of time, often if you look into someone's eyes you quickly look away in shock or embarrassment; and while lovers might hold that look into each other's eyes, or a mother and baby, it would rarely be while sitting still for a whole hour. A great range of feelings and sensations arises during this process, and the therapist is trained to enable these to arise, mirroring then releasing them, all the time holding your gaze so steadily and confidently that you can't look away. Some people apparently found it difficult, even impossible, to stay there for an hour, not because they get bored or restless, but because what arises is so intense, so overwhelming or disturbing.'

To myself I made some silent exclamation but I told Larry to go on.

Treatments and group activities were all licensed by the Shakti Estate, he told me, and Sheela Auntieji was at its centre. She was becoming a recognisable identity in the world of cult figures, with her fiery black eyes, forceful personality, her loose, frizzy black hair and crimson and scarlet saris, her unapologetic scorn for those who asked her for any theory or explanation of the practices she sanctioned or, according to Shakti lore, created out of divine inspiration. 'Experience, only experience, that is how knowledge comes!' is all she would say. Evidently she believed in the centrality of the body in any fruitful inquiry into purpose or meaning, and theory and explanation became the prolific, and profitable, business of others.

As Larry put it, what gave Shakti and Sheela Auntieji credibility was 'the fact of human existence is that it takes place in human bodies. We are embodied, incarnate beings. And yet so many systems of belief want to refuse the body, to hide, deny, ill-treat, humiliate and subjugate the body, the very thing that tells us and shows the world that we exist, alive, experiencing, active beings.

'Our first knowledge of ourselves as separate beings comes from the realization of the separation of our material self from the rest of the material world.

'All experience, profound or superficial, has an essential component of physical sensation and movement, is imprinted on our corporeal beings in some way.

'We increasingly understand mind itself to be part of the physical fact of existence. It's not just a matter of mind over matter, but mind itself being part of matter. This is true in mystical terms and in the terms of recent scientific investigation. Emotions and memory have chemical correlatives in the body.

'In Energy Meditation we would bring about profound changes in mood, feeling and affect by a process so engrossing and strenuous it does not allow for the usual mind games, but is overwhelmingly experiential.'

In this Energy Mediation, he explained, everyone would gather in a room, and on a signal, begin to jump up and down while shouting, without stopping, no matter how breathless, cramped or tired, until the next signal, when all had to immediately stand still and hold that pose, allowing no other movement but the breath through the body; at the next signal everyone had to cry: to make all the sobbing, weeping, howling sounds of crying, whether they felt like it or not, often to find real tears; at the next signal it was time to sit cross-legged, eyes closed and chant a given mantra over and over, and the final signal came with the sounds of drumming, and everyone would dance, dance in any way they felt moved to dance, as long as they danced, and kept it up, until the final signal, an hour and a half after the start of EM, brought the session to an end. No one felt unstirred or unchanged by this practice.

'And what was the idea behind all this? How did people account for its effectiveness?'

'Intellectual or abstract talk was discouraged. We were not meant to make stories out of what happened, but only talk of the sensations in our bodies.

'For example, you might find that a certain kind of massage, or particular movements in DY, brought about tears. Or joy, or anger and so on. You would simply experience that, maybe talk about the feelings and the kinds of tears. You were to focus on that, not on whatever story – past trauma, repressed feelings – you might think accounted for it.'

New cafés sprung up around Shakti Estate to provide its denizens with the best of fresh juices, a range of tea and coffee, salads and cakes. But for a brief summer, it was usually cold there, and other traders made a new lucrative living from selling blankets and ponchos, adding to them, as they became a popular informal uniform, embroidery and appliqués, often in Sheela Auntieji's signature colours of scarlet and crimson. To some of the outside observers, journalists and the like, who began coming to file reports on the Estate, it all seemed entirely self-indulgent, just an orgy of producing sensation and satisfying desires. A great deal of sexual activity took place. Some of the licensed therapists gave instruction in what they called Tantra, others called Sacred Sex: these were therapies that centred on the sexual being and were meant to enhance sexual knowledge and pleasure. Several unlicensed therapists set up in the area and if they got good word-of-mouth, some of the less devoted Shaktiites would frequent them. Tourists began to come to the town, to partake of a holiday program of EM or DY, and as not all of them could, or wanted to, get accredited to do the work on the Estate, they began going to 'Sheela Auntieji-style' programs advertised in the cafés and tourist shops or even the latest guidebooks. I guess it was little wonder that the Sacred Sex workshops got the most attention. Some Indian men began to arrive in town thinking they'd been promised available and willing foreign women, believing the rumours of sex workshops, and under the effect of the illicit pornographic videos that were just beginning to be distributed India-wide. I wished I remembered more of the controversies that began to be scattered through the media at the time.

'Sheela Auntieji said that sexual desire was natural and should not be denied, she said knowing our sexual nature was to know ourselves, she said sex could be a source of joy, she said it was better to experiment than to live with resentful repression; that's all she said and she only said it on one occasion, but books of interpretation and how-to manuals and all these therapies were a result.'

Larry, once he had decided to explore this path, became intensely involved for some time.

'All of this was a great change from what I had been involved with. The attitude to food and sex at Shakti was not like any I had known. And Dynamic Yoga was to me an amazing deepening of a practice of yoga asana that I had begun years before.'

Sheela Auntieji had trained her DY teachers in a series of yoga postures and a method of instruction that required the series to be done in a range of ways.

'Some days we would be given only a few of the poses and made to hold them for a long time – believe me, ten or even five minutes can seem long in some poses, and we did them for longer too, twenty minutes or more, once a whole hour in plough pose. The idea was to keep the mind on the various aspects of the pose, to observe where you had to make an effort to hold it, how the pose changed over time, where you were weak, where you were flexible and where rigid, and so on. Other times we would move through the poses very rapidly, other times do the sequence backwards, other times do a single pose in various ways. This was one of the most valuable practices I did there.'

I would have liked to ask him why, but I didn't want to interrupt.

'The third basic practice was called Freeform, and it was an hour-long version of the final part of Energy Meditation. We just danced to drumming and other music, just moved to music, without stopping for an hour. For most people it was fun, but for some, who did not feel able to dance well or expressively, it could be intimidating, and the requirement of an hour of non-stop movement, especially if you'd already done Dynamic Yoga that day, was considered torture. Some nights, though, there were Freeform marathons throughout the night, with people dancing for hours. It seemed an essential balance, the mental rigour and exacting demands of DY and the spontaneous, expressive flow of Freeform that did not allow for any part of the self to be critical or diffident.'

That, I thought, was a good analogy to the processes of creative work. Larry fell silent for a moment. 'What I learnt from all this,' he said at last, 'was not to ignore the body, and to begin to understand how much can be learnt and changed through bodily experience. It's such a paradox, we speak of "I" and "my body", we feel as if the body is something we inhabit or own, and yet the important and consequential fact is we cannot indisputably separate what we are from our corporeal being, or in fact separate our own physical being from that of the rest of the world. Matter is never entirely destroyed. Tiny portions of air and water and dust pass between all our bodies. And who knows what information they might contain.'

I didn't say anything. My own experience was somewhat different. I had not been an attractive, fit-looking young man and I had always yearned for others to see a 'real' me that was not my body. I had always been a little bitter about naturally attractive, fit-looking people agonizing about their bodies. I had experienced the greatest wonder and gratitude to have still been young in a time and place when for a while all willing bodies seemed equally welcome. But this was only a fleeting thought; I remained engrossed in what Larry was telling me.

'I was lucky to never have significant health problems,' Larry said, 'to have found that the solution to any problems of my teenage years was simply to grow up. I had found that physical exercise cured most depression and much else, and that seemed to me the most valuable single thing I learnt.

'I read everything I could on the body – body and consciousness, the body in philosophy and in religion, the body and fashions – but after a while I was no longer really engrossed in what I was doing at Shakti, and troubled by the self-centredness, as I began to see it, of the pursuits there. I had been attracted to the promise of wisdom, but then, as time went on, I was afraid that I was caught up in a spiral of addiction to greater sensuality, more feats of endurance, excessive self-indulgence. It was too easy to slide from seeking knowledge into seeking more and more sensation, or just a better shape. And then, Sheela Auntieji, who I had admired, was no longer to be seen, and was either secreted in her disquietingly opulent residence or travelling, and everything was run by her deputies, who seemed, how shall I say it, less than admirable or exemplary in their exercise of power.'

Larry did not speak much about his periods of doubt and even anguish. I'm sorry I didn't ask him more about them. It's in these long dark nights of the soul and in surviving them that we learn the most about who we are and what we are meant to do. He never told me what effect subsequent controversies and scandals about this guru had on him, and because in those controversies and scandals Sheela Auntieji was always referred to as a 'guru', I'm not really sure now whether Larry used that word. He told me very little about the discovery of desires, impulses and thoughts that one wishes did not arise, though these too are part of one's nature, of human nature.

'I began to prefer walking in the mountains to going to EM or getting another massage or eating delicacies in Shakti cafés or being offered more and more kinds of sex.'

'Most people's idea of paradise,' I remarked.

'I've found that for me, though sex could be a pleasure, it isn't a need. I've never looked for it.

'After a while I wasn't going to any of the Shakti sessions, although I still lived near the estate. I'd leave every morning and walk a few miles to another town, where I had found a small private library someone had once mentioned. It had been the private collection of a Bengali scholar who had retired to the town and had left it to be run as an adjunct to a small private school. Donations kept the library and school going, but as I only saw one other person there I don't know how they survived. I began to go up there most days to read through as much as I could. There were books of philosophy, travel books, biographies, novels, all kinds of things, many rare and unusual books. Although I've always been able to read for many hours at a time and remember a lot of it, at this time my reading was making me more and more unsatisfied. I couldn't find a thread, or structure, to it all, and it all seemed useless, just another addiction, all of it an escape rather than the real thing.

'And it was here that I met a man dressed in a simple rust-coloured woollen robe that I would learn was the mark of a Buddhist order he belonged to. We were the only two in the library and one day we stepped outside together and began talking.

'He was a lovely man with a huge smile that lit up his face. He had a gift for simplicity, as I was to find out. At first I only thought that he was a simple man. He asked me what I was doing there, and I told him. He encouraged me to tell him more, and we sat for a very long time, on the steps of the library in the warm noon sun of a clear day in the mountains. He kept asking me questions, and I think I told him as much as I've told you tonight!'

Larry told the monk about his childhood. (An orphan has more questions than children in undisturbed families do, and I have since wondered if Larry was so obsessed with his young friend's death because his parents had died when he was still young, but that never came up while I knew him.) He talked about wanting to travel and about the time he was a teenager and went to India.

And that, he told the Buddhist monk, was where he had seen a friend die. And how he felt and how when he came home he just couldn't see the point of what everyone expected him to do. He wanted to know things no one really wanted to talk about, and so he began to read.

'"Tell me this,"' Larry said the monk asked him, '"what have you learnt from all this reading? All these trainings and workshops and self-exploring? What have you got out of it? Where are you now?"

'And I said, "I've got absolutely nowhere. I still don't know much about anything."

'And I felt I was admitting something terrible, how thick I was, how I had wasted so many years of my life, but he just gave me this beautiful big smile, a big friendly smile of approval and said "wonderful".

'"How can it be wonderful?"

'"In the beginner's mind there are many possibilities, but in the expert's there are few."

'He lived in a monastery some distance away and had travelled to this little town to read in the same library. He began to talk about his place. People came from all over to do a ten-day retreat, in which they remained silent, lived very simply and spent most hours of the day in a still meditation.

'For a moment I was a bit wary, for it seemed to me the last thing I wanted was someone else telling me about the newest, latest, most effective path to knowledge. But my new friend said that far from being the latest or newest, this was something the Buddha himself had taught. Some of his disciples had been cut off from the rest of the world in a remote region further isolated by political and military divisions, and so the teaching they passed down had never been corrupted by other influences.

'"Let me go back with you," I said.

'He was leaving the very next morning, he said, as he had to be back in time for all the visitors who were coming for the next introductory course. I said I would go with him. I would sleep where we were, to be ready to leave with him before dawn. I had everything I needed with me, my passport and money and notebook, I would send a message that I wasn't coming back and they could give my bed and few extra clothes to someone else. I was suddenly very sure. I felt that he was a kind of message to me, an opportunity if you like, a test of my faith and intention, I did not really know what, but I knew I had to go with him.

'We walked for two days into the mountains. I was young and very fit, I had good boots, he looked quite a bit older than me and wore cheap flat shoes, but he never faltered. It was glorious. We went on pathways he knew, and saw the most wonderful skies and peaks and valleys, forests and flowers, simple little villages where sometimes we stopped for tea or slept the night on simple beds. The few people we saw seemed to know and respect my companion and there were friendly greetings. I would have been content to know that the sum of everything

I had done so far was to walk those two days in the mountains with my new friend.

'Eventually we arrived at the monastery just before nightfall. To my astonishment, I found that my companion was a highly revered and senior teacher, and was the guide to the ten-day retreat. I was given a bed in one of the dormitories. Everything was very simple and rather austere. The course began the next day. We were not to talk, read or write. We had all agreed not to speak at all for ten days, unless to ask something necessary during an hour set aside for that. Otherwise we remained silent, and were to do as little movement as possible. No long walks, no stretching, nothing but a very slow, conscious meditative walk around the main hall during a break. I found myself anxious about this. I thought I would feel unwell from the cessation of physical activity. Others were more anxious that there was no evening meal!

'Every morning we woke to a bell at four and gathered in the meditation hall half an hour later. We sat still for many hours. We were taught how to sit still and concentrate on the area between mouth and nose, and feel the breath coming and going there.

'Then we were guided to observe each aspect of our being: it could take hours to travel through the body, to observe subtle sensations – itching, throbbing, pain, heat, cold.

'It was a technique for self-purification, and it brought about an intense realization that the seemingly solid body is made up of empty space and subatomic particles that pass in and out of existence. It was the *experience* of the Buddha's message of the impermanent and impersonal nature of existence.

'When it ended I talked a little with the people there. There were a handful of other foreigners, who had been persuaded to attend by people they'd known who had felt transformed by it. One of them was a famous film actor from Bombay, who went on to talk about this in interviews and eventually was a big influence in the growth of the technique. And there were people who went on to bring the ten-day retreat to big companies, schools and even prison. Some, of course, just ticked this off as another experience and departed.

'I knew I would do the next course – twenty days – as soon as I could and I asked if I could stay on at the Centre.'

And so Larry spent the next chapter of his life living at the Centre. He rose at four every morning, and at four-thirty he sat in the meditation hall. Although he became entitled to a solitary room, he preferred to go to the hall, he liked that extra discipline and he liked the hall itself. His life became the routines of the monastery and the endless hours of intense meditation.

Even as the weather became cold, he put on a wool cap and wrapped himself in a blanket and sat in the hall in the dark early mornings. He stayed on during the winter, when there were no beginner ten-day courses and few visitors came, for they were snowed in. He found satisfaction and liberation in the experience of the consciousness that is the ground of all being and through which the illusion of an individual self dissolves. And in time the bitter dark chill of the early hours became tinged with a soft pink warmth and the sound of arriving birds.

Larry paused here. 'By the late spring I knew that I would not spend the rest of my life involved in this, and from that it followed that I need spend no more time here.

'I still had not found what I was looking for. How could I live in the world and reconcile what I had found here: the experience of the insubstantial, impermanent self?'

There were things Larry needed to question, and could do it only at a distance. As outside interest in the practice grew, and it increasingly was taken to and taught in other places, he wondered why there was so much insistence that until the Buddha had taught this technique there had not existed the spiritual wisdom it led to. He was concerned about the new emphasis coming in on the setting up of a research institute and the insistence of the authority of old texts, as if for the purpose of giving the technique a competitive legitimacy in the great marketplace of therapies. 'Most of all,' he told me, 'however much of an illusion my individuality was, I wanted to know, now, if the illusory Larry had anything else to do in the illusory world.'

'I was very afraid to disappoint my teacher and mentor, and went to see him feeling terrible about leaving. Those who had spent years there, decades, said it took years to perfect oneself through the technique.

'I went and sat at his feet, and I did not need to say much at all. He had such compassion in his voice when he said, "Go, go back into the world, only remember your Buddha nature." I cried at his kindness. A few days later I was in Delhi.'

My ignorance was abysmal. But I knew that before.

Larry spent longer in Delhi than he had meant to. He had a couple of friends there now, and through them he met other people. They were involved in an idealistic project, which had its headquarters in a single upstairs room above a shop in the old city of Delhi: it was declared a place for research, practice and conversation about contemporary politics and political life. They were united in their opposition to the prime minister, and in the promotion of the secular ideal on which the new nation of India had been founded not even four decades earlier. As the searing summer approached, troops had been ordered to raid the holiest temple of the Sikhs in Amritsar, said to be the headquarters of a movement promoting a separate Sikh homeland. This, all that had led up to this and all that would ensue, was the subject of much of the talk around Larry. The silent looking within in the remote mountain retreat, and the new appeals to him to undertake more healing work when he ensured that his sick friend became well enough to give his lecture on being a 'critical insider', all that seemed less important than to understand the commitment that his friends demonstrated. Larry realized that he knew too little to add anything useful to the talk around him, even too little to evaluate the claims for and criticisms of Nehruvian socialism, Gandhian technophobia or Ram Mohan Roy's vision of Indian modernity. Anyway, he had to begin to wonder if his own identity, his nationality and ethnicity, disqualified him. He was, like the Indians, a product of British colonial rule, but as a Westerner he was, according to some members of the group, implicated in what they were starting to call the 'epistemic violence of hegemonic discourse'. What place did he have here?

He had come down off the mountain to enter the world, and the world said to him that it ran on politics: everything had to do with power, the exercise of power, the way power is understood. He had once been content to agree with the notion that the personal was political – that it mattered how you behaved in everyday matters, what you called people, who washed the dishes – but he now saw that politics was everyday dynamics, and to claim disdain or a lack of interest for politics was a political stand.

Larry returned to Sydney and enrolled in courses in 'political science' as it was known. Any subject with the word 'science' in it, he remarked, is inevitably a subject unavailable to the scientific method (computer science, home science).

In any case, Larry paid fees to attend a course at Sydney University and, I don't know how, just being Larry I guess, was given permission to audit a post-graduate seminar.

'I mainly learnt that my ignorance was abysmal. But I knew that before.'

As it happened, the lecturer and tutor he saw most of was immersed in the still youthful field of post-colonial theory.

If he studied basic notions of governance, if he studied resistance, if socialism and communism, if free trade and protectionism, if democratic traditions and democratic systems, the examples he was offered to a great extent came from India. His lecturer had just completed a doctorate on Gandhi, and Larry had a few beers in the uni bar with him arguing whether Gandhi's conservatism about caste and women and modernity diminished his standing as one of the greatest figures of the century.

Where did politics interact with the quest for individual freedom, self-knowledge, faith, belief? Larry's inquiry turned to the reconciliation of political reality with the quest for spiritual life. Was there a nexus uniting the political and spiritual as felt experiences or theorized aspects of life? Or was the relationship to be found only in the phenomenon he most wanted to avoid, the subsuming of spiritual experience or inquiry into organized religion?

'It was while reading about the various ways that Indians had opposed British rule and brought about Independence that I came across Aurobindo. He seemed to be a good subject for a research project – how to understand his transition from political freedom fighter to spiritual leader. To research that took me to Pondicherry, where I spent a couple of months with a friend from Australia, a sweet person to have around at the time, very open and real, we were quite close for a while.'

That would have been when he took Josh Rouvier with him, but I did not interrupt him.

'Then after a bit of travel in South India, looking at some village development projects, I decided to go to Europe. I'd never been there, and it was supposed to be the root, the source, of the Western culture I had been brought up in, its political institutions and philosophies, its cultural and religious practices, its art. The idea of my own individual heritage, or roots, had never particularly interested me but I began to wonder what I could learn from it.'

Larry went to Paris, then to Rome, Florence and Venice. I had been to those places, too.

In Venice, with its incomparable allure, he stood one ravishing purple evening at the Salute, its dome glinting gold, the pink and violet lights of twilight over the waters of the Laguna, the gold and rose of the clouds, the palazzi leaning into each other along the Grand Canal, these images mingling in his head with the grandeur of art works and church interiors, and images from a mysterious film he had once seen as a boy; and he wondered what it would be like to capture something of the awe-making splendour he beheld. Rather than just looking, could he also create? Is that the greatest possible apprehension of the divine? He had seen tourists and art students making sketches and watercolours in the streets and *campi*, and sitting before the monumental works of art in the museums, giving them a cold, evaluating stare as they set about making copies. What might he learn from such pursuits? Who could teach him? And not an hour later Larry came across a notice for an art school.

Ah, Italy when you're young! I had spent some weeks in Venice myself as a still young man heady with the beginnings of my career in the theatre. In a captivating little curio shop I bought myself a pair of theatre masks, an upturned mouth for comedy and a down-turned mouth for tragedy; I still hang them over my desk. I had stupidly begun to write a play set there, about a group of foreigners. But I found myself going about in a swoon, dazzled and dazed and even sickened by this highly artificial beauty, the excess of strange loveliness, the famous effect (which I succumbed to) of being in a city built on water. I could not sit still for the long hours writing would take, and once I had left, the spell remained behind. For me Venice stood for art that could not be made and love that could not be held.

'I guess I had a romantic time there,' Larry said. 'I shared a big apartment with a group of students. We had a few parties. Some of them were spending a semester there as part of their degree courses in the States. A few came from other parts of Europe. We all went to daily life drawing and I went to a beginner's class in painting and a course on art history. I'd find English school groups or cultural tourists and sit with them in churches or galleries where they were given lectures on what was around us.

'What did I learn there? Besides the difference between Caravaggio and Carpaccio or Titian and Tintoretto? In learning to make sketches, whether life studies of a human model or depicting buildings and sculptures, there was a more exact seeing that came into play: line, form, relationships, shadow, colour. When I would draw I found there was a sort of necessary dissolving between me and it, the subject or object I was copying. I felt I was learning observation of the world and appreciation for what artists do.

'And a quite amazing art historian and critic from England took me as her lover. She was about twenty-five years older than me, sophisticated and assured and accomplished. She had lots to teach me in all kinds of ways. I was dazzled and proud and very much into her and I admit I wasn't quite ready for it when after a couple of months she told me, in the nicest possible way, that she was going back to London and our time together was over.

'I went about being very melancholy for a while, doing watercolours and trying to write poetry, tearing up my feeble efforts every day.'

Larry did not decide on a life devoted to art. He saw for himself what his glamorous mistress had pointed out, that most of the art students were just bumming around for a while or trying art out or wanting to be commercial, but there was only one, a boy called Jacob, who would have pursued art no matter what, encouragement or none, success or not. He wasn't the only one with talent, he wasn't the only one who was dedicated, he wasn't the only one trying to do something new, but only Jacob was all those things and something more.

'Real artists are born, not made,' was his conclusion, Larry told me, 'and they also have talent that asserts itself early in life. This clearly was not the case for me. But I was glad I'd spent that time there.

'It taught me to see. To draw. To have a slightly improved sense of that cultural heritage. To remember the pleasures of wine, architecture and painting. And, in time, of that amazing woman. I left art alone and went and picked olives for a while.

'But I didn't want to stay in Europe. I still could not stop thinking of India. I decided to go and look at the art here. Of course, as it turned out that was just a rationale for what had no rationality, the desire to return to India.'

It was getting late

It was getting late.

We had had a third snack, of vadai, new to me, and drunk several pots of South Indian coffee, each made our way to the bathroom, and had our attention momentarily diverted by the fresh seating or sweeping past departures of others. A group of German tourists was on one side and I recognized music programs and the music festival newsletter in their hands. They looked as if they might be a group of musicians and maybe critics: professional cosmopolitan people able to pursue a minor interest or even passion. I imagined at least one of them would return to Europe and compose music inspired by what they had heard here as well as their own tradition. On our other side, there was what looked like an extended family, a group of about a dozen of various ages from an elderly woman in a dark green sari to a boy of seven or so. Had I been there alone, or with a less absorbing companion, I would have been happily employed in the observation of the lively room. Waiters in brown uniforms were plentiful and attentive, and young boys wheeled trolleys around to collect used plates and cups and to wipe down tables.

We had been there for hours, but were in no hurry to end the night. I encouraged Larry to tell me as much of his story as he was able and he seemed in the mood to do so. I surmised that he had rarely, if ever, had or made the opportunity to relate his experiences so methodically, to turn the disparate experiences of his life into a cohesive narrative.

His life seemed to follow a pattern of sudden decisions that took him to a new immersion to which he gave himself wholeheartedly until some kind of distancing – not always quite disillusionment but a sense of needing to go beyond – once more set in and suddenly he, almost magically, was led to a new direction. Now that I've put it like that, it seems to me something like the way I wrote.

After midnight there were fewer people there. The family groups departed. A large group of men in business shirts, both Indian and European, took up a table soon dense with bottles and plates. I suppose business deals were being consummated by the breaking of bread together. There were fewer women around now but I was astonished to see three lovely young women sitting together, huge golden paper dosai on plates in front of them, poised and elegant in bright-coloured clothes with matching large ornate bindis on their foreheads. One wore her black frizzy hair cascading over her shoulders. I caught them looking at, apparently discussing, the group of men, but they made no attempt to communicate.

A group of four tourists dressed in shorts and sandals entered and made a bit of a commotion. They seemed to have been drinking and were looking for a place to drink some more. They stood around for a while, calling for the music to be turned up and making it clear that they weren't interested in food. They were shown into another room, which, with a glimpse through a swinging door, looked like a deserted and rather inhospitable extension of the restaurant. A few minutes later they burst out again and noisily swept out of the place, complaining that this was one dead town at night.

Reality by knowledge

Our waiter brought the bill to our table, saying that he was going home but we were please to stay as long as we wanted and another waiter would look after us. I gave him his tip and we ordered more coffee. We lifted our feet so that the floor could be washed under us, but they weren't closing down.

'And so you left Europe,' I prompted Larry. 'What happened next?'

Larry returned to India. He had a notion that he might try to begin understanding more about India through getting to know some of its art, and soon after he arrived his next inspiration came from a conversation that took place in the Crafts Museum in Delhi.

'I liked the Crafts Museum more than the art museum I had been to the previous day,' Larry said. The things he saw there seemed to have a kind of life to them, a greater sense of the consciousness and lived life of people. It seemed to come from the necessity of making something both useful and beautiful – carpets, tools, fabrics. There were terracotta pots, toys, jewellery, metal sculptures, papier-mâché, embroidery, tribal paintings, beadwork, and more. They would have been – were – things that could be admired, could move you, simply as objects, for the loveliness, mystery and skill of their making, but the fact that they also had utility, and in fact many of them were things that once had been put to use, gave them an even more moving quality. They had that indefinable fascination that seems the essence of beauty. And in the grounds of the Crafts Museum was a kind of fair or market, with goods from all over India on sale, and there were studios where the artists, or artisans if that's what they were called, were at work at looms and wheels. 'I was there for many hours that day, and planned to return. I felt awed and a bit overwhelmed at the glimpse into the everyday cultural richness of this country. The art museum seemed to be about the culture of the ruling classes. In here it went far beyond that, to other kinds of power. I was having a rest in a courtyard and somehow fell into conversation with a woman there. She was wearing some magnificent amber beads with a carved amber pendant. She told me she was an art dealer and specialized in textiles and jewellery.

'I told her that I'd spent a little time in India by now but the richness of what was around us showed me how very little I knew or understood the place. She said that the power of the folk art of India was a result of the power of the belief, the faith, that all people here lived every day, no matter how many ways they had of practising it. "There is no individual artist's name on these things," she said. She said – she said a lot of things but she said this, "You want to understand India? Have you been to Varanasi? Unless you go to Varanasi you will not understand."

'I remembered that I had wanted to go there a long time ago. I took a train to Varanasi that night, a slow train. I talked to people and read a little. If you haven't had a long trip on a train in India I highly recommend it. Though you must be prepared to explain why your wife isn't with you!

'As soon as I arrived I went down to the river, taken through dark streets in an auto-rickshaw. It was just getting light as I walked on to Marnika ghat. There was already much activity, and the sound of chanting and bells. There were people washing themselves and collecting the holy water of the river in bottles. A young man took me out in a boat and as the morning sun rose he rowed me along the ghats. It seemed that everyone there was practising their faith, carrying out rituals of bathing in and even worshipping the most holy river in Hindu India – children, women, men. Later there would be smoke from the cremation ghats, and the river would receive the ashes. To the devout, this was the ultimate benediction of life, to make the passage to death right here.

'As always, I was intrigued and fascinated by the practices of faith. Did people believe, and believe in, what they were doing, and what was the meaning of belief? Perhaps we all live by some kind of faith. We all believe something we cannot prove. I knew enough to know that the rituals and practices of faith do not necessarily need to be taken literally to be believed in.

'But if not literally, then how was I to understand it? What was to be gained from the belief of acquiring merit in this life for the sake of the next?

'I found the spectacle there moving, but I was aware, now, that to a large extent this was an aesthetic response. After my time in Venice I wanted to make sketches and watercolours of the scene.

'I found a room and decided to stay there for some time.'

Larry spent many weeks in Varanasi, or Benares as it used to be known and he occasionally referred to it.

He began to make charcoal and watercolour pictures of the place, but then abandoned the practice. He realized that once he began to look at the place as a subject for drawings and paintings, he would 'aestheticize' it: see it through a need for or judgment of its artistic appeal. Although in Venice he had found in the acts of drawing a flow, as he had called it, between him and his subject, an exchange that dissolved barriers between them, he now felt that in Varanasi to be open to the meaning of the ritual practices and the belief system they were based on would be compromised by the barrier created by a sketchbook, or even of a mind-set that looked about him seeking the picturesque. (Needless to say, Larry had never taken a single photograph during his travels.)

He found a scholar who gave lessons in Sanskrit, contestably said to be the oldest language in the world, still used in religious texts, and one he had already some acquaintance with. He also went to classes in the sitar.

'I knew that I was already too old to be any good but I wanted the discipline.'

Larry always enjoyed, I suppose that is the word – he *sought* and needed – mental and intellectual disciplines. With the means to do pretty much whatever he wanted, he rose early, meditated, studied, practised, and attended classes and discourses. He went for walks on the grounds of the university, he went to lectures on the Upanishads. Sometimes he had tea and discussions with other students there, a variety of Indians and foreigners. Most often he went on with his prodigious reading project, making his way through the enormous length of the ancient texts.

And all of this took place within the holy city and the rituals of living, dying and being cremated by the river. If you died in Benares, it was believed, you were freed from the cycles of rebirth. Its waters were meant to provide benediction even if carried from afar, and to purify everything they touched, even to cleanse away the pollution of human ashes, uncremated bodies and waste deposited at the city's ghats.

I knew that Hinduism was too immense a subject to be summarized but I was mostly curious to know whether Larry had formulated any ideas on reincarnation, and whether that might tell him anything to enlighten him on the most basic question of his investigation: why, all those years ago, had his friend died and not him? Did reincarnation offer any answer, any comfort, any conviction?

It occurred to me that the idea of reincarnation by now had become part of the cultural noise, and that in Australia, in the Western world, it was not uncommon to hear casual references to past lives, most often as explanations or evidence for innate knowledge, uncanny senses of familiarity, otherwise meaningless occurrences, strokes of fortune. I had even used the idea in a couple of throwaway lines of a character in a play. But I had never really thought about even thinking seriously about it.

'The idea of reincarnation is central to Indian thought…' Larry began.

'Don't you mean Hindu thought?' I interrupted. I didn't think then to ask him why he had not done any seeking among the Parsis or the Jains or the Moslems. Not that I thought he should be an equal-opportunity seeker, and in India there is a Hindu majority (or so-called Hindu some will say but I can't get into that here).

Larry acknowledged my point. All the monotheistic religions were implicated to some extent in the objections to Christianity we had rehearsed earlier that evening. Patriarchal gods, hierarchies of authority, histories of cruelty and repression, contemporary manifestations of bigotry and hate-mongering, sheer ridiculousness. But it's been said for centuries that Moses, Jesus and Mohammed surely would be spinning in their graves – what better metaphor for being posthumously appalled! – at what has been, is being, done in their names. But on it goes.

Hinduism – and this was in the late eighties and early nineties I should point out – had wide appeal among the seekers of the West, the New Seekers of the New Age, whether for its tradition of contemplation and self-examination or for its many gods and goddesses, one for any human experience. Not to mention the gaudy aesthetic of its popular forms: colourful icons of Ganesha et al, incense, shrines. Even bangles and bindis, even mirror-studded scarves and bags were worn as a kind of reference to or a fond acquaintance with 'Eastern spirituality'. (None of this took into account, by the way, political fascism in the rise of Hindu fundamentalism.)

But Larry and I were still talking about reincarnation.

'Reincarnation,' I said, 'means endless, recurrent rebirth, or at least until finally you're so good you get off the wheel. Is that the idea?' Larry smiled. 'There's a couple things that get me, though,' I went on. 'Where does an individual soul begin?'

'As I understand it, the idea is that there is no beginning and no end. Reincarnation is an answer to suffering and misery: you can create a better life by living your current life well.'

'Who or what created this system? Why didn't she/ he/ they or it create a world free from suffering and misery at the beginning? And why,' I continued, 'is the ultimate aim to have no more rebirths? What is more wonderful than life at its best? What could be a greater reward – greater, I think, than no more human life at all – than a lucky life, one full of pleasure, and a highly developed, ultimately evolved being, wise enough to make the most of it?'

'Even the best of lives include suffering. This is what the Buddha showed us. No life has been free of desire and suffering.'

'Reincarnation still seems to be a system of reward and punishment,' I said. 'Where are people born if they have finally been really good?'

'Australia!' said Larry. 'That really was what one esteemed pandit said in one discourse!' We had a moment of amusement over that, somewhat wry amusement for after all it seems that one thing citizens of our country of origin had in common was a sense of our extraordinary luck: space, peace, resources. Since that night, as we have continued to remain relatively untouched by wars and tsunamis, I have been told by several young Australians that we must have been good in a past life.

'I preferred to see it as karma,' Larry said. 'That there is a consequence to all our actions. This I found extremely appealing: if everything we do has some outcome, some result, and not only in the world, not only in its effect on others, but on our own lives, then there is a way that makes sense to think about evil and injustice…'

'A comforting way,' I said. 'We often tell lies – or create fantasies – for comfort.' The words of a poem came to me: *But is there any comfort to be found? Man is in love and loves what vanishes. What more is there to say?* Where did that come from? But wasn't the idea of karma's consequences just another version of heaven or hell? And didn't it rely on some kind of constant, authoritative system of assigning and measuring good and bad?

'Comfort,' Larry agreed, 'might be part of the reason people believe in reincarnation. There is a kind of *sense* to it. Everything matters.'

'Where I stop,' I said, 'is imagining how it works. You die, you're up for a new life, who decides who you'll be next? Is it like an actor going for a part at the Sydney Theatre Company, with the director going "You're not quite right for this"?'

'Some people think that the soul itself chooses the life that will teach it the lessons it needs.'

'Well, that's very neat.'

'Of course, not being able to imagine or know how things work doesn't stop them from working. And most people believe in it. And some scholars have proven that early Christians also believed in reincarnation, so that it properly is part of Christianity.'

'Most people believing in something doesn't make it true. And here's what else. There are more people on the planet now than there have ever been. Where did all the new souls come from? Does the big reincarnation machine manufacture new souls? What is the effect on the world of most people having new souls? Of course that would explain the general lack of improvement in the general well-being of the human race. A soul is meant to benefit from age, that's why it's not a body. What if we cut the population right down again, would we be all old souls – experienced, presumably wiser, better? Is that what the planet needs? But where would the other souls go?'

'I know,' said Larry. 'I never could understand the idea of reincarnation as a series of performances of a single soul. That would retain the central role of the ego.'

We talked for a while about the idea of a person's soul instead returning to some kind of big soul stew, some universal soul, out of which some new bit of individual soul would emerge to enter a new body. But finally, all *you* can know is that no one can *know*. Delusions arise from faith, belief and trust without proof.

'I'd meet people in India who'd tell me I must have been here before. In a previous life, they meant. I have found myself feeling weirdly at home here, things felt familiar to me, I didn't have trouble adapting to, oh, the food, the manners, the kinds of conversations *you* have. If this meant that "I" had been in India before, who was this "I"? Not the Larry who'd been backpacking there in 1978. Not me, Larry, late twentieth-century Australian layabout.'

'And there's the fact that when people talk about their past lives they always used to be Cleopatra or a shaman.'

'I know. There's no way to really come at it, is there?'

Larry put me to shame. Although we had both arrived at a position of scepticism, I had taken a jet right to the spot, as it were. I had merely glanced down at the faraway ground, content to see it from a vast distance, to pass over it swiftly.

Larry, though, had, as it were, crawled over every mile of it, looking closely at what he passed over, stopping often to examine its details up close.

He spoke in measured and complex sentences, those of someone who read a great deal, spending a lot of time in other centuries and a range of cultures through an esoteric range of texts: works of philosophy and theology, nineteenth-century novels, sixteenth-century poets, works of antiquity, works in translation. He retained his Australian accent, yet it was subtly modified by the effects of his many years in India and elsewhere, by his long periods of silence, by his study of other languages, by his conversations with the learned and the wise, with professors and farmers, with priests and mothers. I'd never really heard anyone speak like Larry. He had the surface charm of one of those rare good-natured creatures that everyone seems to take to, but there was a lot more to him. His search did not make him seem self-obsessed but rather more interested in the world. I admit he never said anything particularly funny but he was far from dull. In any case, the unlikelihood of his attempt at a joke was refreshing when what passed for humour in my other worlds was often just sarcasm, fault-finding, calumny, attribution of base motives.

'I began to think,' he said, 'that the important question was, does this belief have a practical effect?'

In individual lives, maybe it does. And Larry with his much greater experience of the country and I with my small experience had found here great kindness. And yet there was crime and violence and cruelty and bastardry in India as anywhere that claims to believe anything. It's usually the situation that determines our ethics.

'It had a practical effect on particular lives,' Larry said. 'There is a tradition here – or at least there used to be – of renunciation, if not throughout your life, and I know this is mainly for men, then in the final part of your life, where you give up your home and your wealth and your family. My friend in Delhi's father had done this himself. He had been a successful and well-off businessman, but once his children were grown up and married and he felt he was getting old, he shaved his head, called in a priest and a lawyer, and left his home with nothing but a robe and a begging bowl. It's not common these days, but it still is not unknown. No one has seen him since. I had met him once, in the old days when he wore a suit and went to the office, and I fancied sometimes that I would see him somewhere, maybe in Benares, but so far I haven't.

'Anyway, one day I was sitting near the Mosque, thinking about, or just watching, how other religious faiths went about their own observances, and an object caught my eye, something hanging round the neck of a man sitting near me, a necklace with several little pendants or icons hanging in a chain from it.

'I looked at the man wearing the necklace. He smiled and came closer so that I could examine it. The little symbols hanging off the thread included the Om that stands for Hinduism, the cross that stands for Christianity, the crescent moon that stands for Islam, the lotus that stands for Buddhism, a flame for Zoroastrianism, a mysterious small sphere, and even a hammer and sickle symbol and also a dollar sign! It was the first time I had seen it and now was the first time I heard of the saint.

'The man told me that his necklace was a copy of one that had been given to a saint who resided in the south, one who was given many gifts and gave them away but had kept only this one thing. He had taken all religions and made them into none. 'Into one?' I said, thinking that's what he had said. "None or one," the man grinned, as if it were a great joke.

'I wanted him to tell me more, to summarize the thinking behind the design, but he said that the method of the saint was to take *you* to the path of knowledge, which was *your* own inquiry into the Self. The saint had only one message, and that was "be good", and it was *your* duty to find what this meant.

'In Hindu philosophy, the man explained, there are three main paths in the spiritual life: bhakti marga, karma marga and jnana marga – the paths of devotion, action and knowledge. It is said that jnana *yoga* is the most difficult path to follow, and also the most noble. Reason, or the discerning intelligence of humankind, is its instrument.'

'Paths to what, though?' I said.

'Perhaps to define the end is not the point,' Larry answered. 'Perhaps they are paths to more paths. Perhaps *you* could call it the Absolute, or enlightenment, or even God. Perhaps it is what brings peace. For a long time I wanted to define the goal, or the end of the path, and now I don't. I wanted a belief to hold on to but now I don't.'

It was still questions of God and the ego that Larry was grappling with in Varanasi. God, if he had to call it that, was everything and everyone, if it was anything at all, but did this add up to a belief, what were its implications and consequences? If you believed that God was within you, would you end up worshipping yourself? Where did belief end and superstition begin, a conspicuous question in a city where you could buy blessings and talismans, where you could obtain the means to salvation, much like the pardons and favours traded by the medieval Christian church, or current televangelists for that matter. It was a faith carnival, that was one way you could look at it. Larry told the man that he had come to Varanasi to see 'the real India' only to find there were as many 'real' Indias as people who claimed them. He had wanted to find some ultimate Reality, but seemed to come up against the limits of reality.

Larry said, 'I guess there is a pattern emerging. Once more, because of one conversation or encounter out of all the ones I had on any given day, I felt inspired to go somewhere else. As with the woman at the Museum, I just suddenly knew what to do next. Perhaps I would find the limits of knowledge, but I found something wonderfully satisfying in the notion that you can attain Reality by knowledge.'

In many strange situations

I feel I should point out I am not trying to offer any kind of account of all the ways a person might come to an understanding of the spiritual life or the life of the mind. I don't know enough to do that. Larry talked more about those kinds of ideas than I can set down here. It's not what I'm writing this for.

It's Larry himself who is my subject, because of the long story he told me that magical night, in a city where we were both strangers, where he seemed ready to talk and I was keen to hear, where in some mysterious way the ambience and the subtle information all around us created perfect conditions for the telling.

Larry was captivating, I hope I haven't overstated this fact. He spoke with the eloquence and equanimity of someone much older, yet in a natural, conversational way. He clearly had been blessed with several kinds of intelligence as well as that inexplicable quality of charisma, the ability to influence and inspire those about them. He was never unaware of your responses and would not have spoken at such length – and of course I can't set down everything he said, even while I create his words out of memory, using the artifice of dialogue and not the reality of how we actually speak – had I not been encouraging him with my fascination and prompting.

While I longed to know more (it was only not to miss the next part of his tale that I did not more often make him stop and give me more details) he summarized his experiences in such a considered way I knew he had thought long and hard about each one.

We'd all grown up reading dropout heroes, Dharma Bums, Siddhartha, Huckleberry Finn. We were in an age where the spiritual search had become a kind of cliché, a commodified enterprise, and to travel to India not particularly extraordinary. You didn't even need to go to India to feel entitled to a special reverence or a special antipathy for the place.

But India wasn't only one place. One of its places was this thriving city. Madras was a provincial city compared to the movie, business, fashion and crime glamour of Bombay or the government, education and research centres of Delhi but it had the buzz and energy, the sense of history, diversity, tension, tolerance, industry, initiative and miscegenation that great cities have.

Larry, as I have indicated, had cultivated uncommon powers of concentration, and apart from natural lulls and short diversions during his account, he seemed not ever to be distracted by where we were or how much time had passed.

During my what now seems rather long and active life, I have been to most continents, met many people from many walks of life, and found myself in many strange situations. There has been romance and violence, thrills and terror, boredom and angst, exaltation and the abject. Actually lots of boredom. But I wasn't bored when I dined with a famous movie star, was being taken blindfolded to sit and talk with dissidents and outlaws in fear of their lives, took opium in Vientiane and mescaline in New Mexico, was held up at the point of a home-made rifle in West Papua, was at an orgy of five hundred naked men in San Francisco. I've mixed with the most suburban and the most outlandish members of my own and other societies.

But I do not think I have ever felt that I was in a stranger situation than when I sat in a simple dining hall in an Indian city hour after hour while Larry talked of his search for something that mattered more than anything on earth and yet had no real name.

What have you come here for?

There were the usual pauses and interruptions, of course, during Larry's lengthy disquisition. A new waiter cleared our plates and asked us where we were from. We exchanged the requisite remarks about the cricket teams of our countries. I had learnt in India that to nod enthusiastically at the words Allan Border and Shane Warne created an agreeable fellow-feeling. We ordered lassis and another round of idlis. Then Larry began to tell me about the saint.

Many years before Larry had travelled to see him, the saint had arrived from another small town as a young man, a boy really, sixteen or so. Nothing in his past had hinted at what he would become. He hadn't been very studious or religious, he ran around town with some bad boys. Rather than attending school they would often go to a nearby larger town where they hung about on the streets, looking for foreign tourists, and acquiring cassettes of Western rock music and a wardrobe of jeans and sneakers and baseball caps. But the boy began to have dreams, he dreamt of a triangular mountain rising like a pyramid out of low-lying hills, the sight of it filled him with ineffable joy and he would wake up weeping and longing for this place. Then one day he had come across a picture of the place right out of his dream, and it was a real place, it existed. When he came out of the deep trance or ecstasy that the sight of the picture had caused, he found out where this mountain was. Driven by such occult compulsions and his visions of the holy mountain, he slipped away from his parents' house one night, going farther from home than he had ever been, and strangers assisted him with food and transport for the few days' journey. Arriving at a temple at the base of the mountain he had fallen into a trance and could not be roused from it. At first he was fed only by a kindly temple sweeper. Eventually two of his brothers arrived to identify him but he would not answer to the name he had been given. People gave him a new name at some point. At some point he went up the mountain and sat inside a small cave there, silent and almost entirely motionless for ten years. At first few people knew of him. But his devotees grew in number. They brought him blankets and food and water, they planted a garden around the cave, they erected a wooden structure at its entrance, they guarded him and cared for him. They combed his hair and cut his fingernails and massaged his still limbs. His complete silence and his indifference to the everyday material aspects of the world – hair lice, the need for food – were proof of his holy state; proof was his effect on people and the knowledge of his compelling prophetic vision and his precocious solitary pilgrimage. People felt joy and peace and assurance in his presence, and returned, sent others, spread the word.

While he remained silent, news or rumours or inventions flew about regarding his former utterances as a juvenile in a small town. There was little to go on – he had once come to blows in a dispute as to the merits of a New York new wave rock group, he had preferred football to cricket.

And once, when his mother had pleaded with him to join her in some ritual observance, he had said that he could not, as he was reading Ambedkar and had renounced the sacred thread with which he had been ceremonially invested. His parents decided he was going through a stage, made an effort to applaud his intellectual efforts, and for a brief while trusted he would come to see the value of their tradition, including its symbolic pujas and the deeper wisdom lying at the core of caste observance.

While he sat silent in his cave, contemplating the Eternal, the nation around him changed. A prime minister became a dictator and later was assassinated. There were reprisal killings of hideous ferocity. The world's worst industrial disaster was caused by a US multinational chemical company. Colour television was admitted to India and consumerism spread. Increasing numbers of young people began to wear jeans. And much remained unchanged. Perhaps even the Eternal.

Finally the saint stirred. He looked around him and into the faces of the devout and the curious who sat, that fine, unheralded morning, in and around the entrance to the cave. He was helped to struggle to his feet, and leaning on his assistants he made his way down the well-tended rocky path to the ashram that awaited him. The faith of those who had expected him, and would have waited ten times as long or to the end of their days, was rewarded.

He was bathed and shaved and dressed, refusing the saffron robes prepared for him and allowing only a lungi and a shawl to clothe him.

He was asked what had been revealed to him in his years of communion with the Absolute.

And finally he spoke. He spoke, in English, the famous words 'Be good'. He then beamed such a smile of joy and beatitude that everyone there felt an answering smile rise up in them, big grins broke out on the grimmest of faces, merriment lightened the heaviest of hearts, a peaceful silliness altered the most melancholic temperaments, benign good humour visited all who had been shaped by bitterness and disappointment.

'Of course that happened before I arrived,' Larry told me. 'But I experienced moments like that in his presence. You know, in other places – the Shakti Estate, the Buddhist meditation centre – I had been told to experience rather than understand. But here that had real meaning.'

People brought the saint gifts, they had brought him gifts while he had sat in the cave and they would continue to bring him gifts to the end of his days, at his feet they would lay baskets of fruit, garlands of flowers, lengths of cloth, radios and cassette players, glass bangles and even precious jewels. He would always point to someone to whom the thing would be given, or signal for it to be taken away, and it would be used for the workings of the ashram. It was understood that the gift had been accepted, just as people ate and distributed the prasad that they gave to the gods. But one gift only he reached out for, took in his hands and put around his own neck.

This was the necklace, a copy of which Larry had seen in Benares, from which hung a number of icons or symbols, some of them with clear or obvious referents, some far more writeable by those who read symbols or by anyone who cared to have an opinion.

He never answered any questions about the necklace, let alone the symbol of the mysterious sphere that had no obvious referent. Some said it signified the planet and its unity, some a reminder that we were only a part, some the perfection of shape we all should strive to create, some the zero or nothingness at the heart of enlightenment, some the Everything.

Often the necklace was all he wore, but for the simple lungi draped over his loins, or, occasionally, a thin blanket someone put over his shoulders against the cool nights even in that southern climate.

The necklace was stolen, somehow, one night, but by then it was being reproduced. The saint laughingly refused to accept a reproduction, but happily placed any that were brought to him on others' necks. It was as good as an endorsement. Later, there would be battles over copyright, a patent, intellectual property.

While the particulars of its symbols were debated, its overall message was clear: all religions were one, if religions was the word to include belief systems that eschewed deity or the supernatural (the hammer and sickle of communism), belief systems that subsumed them to material profit (was the dollar sign a benign nod to capitalism or an irony?), belief systems that enjoined their followers to repudiate all others. Or perhaps all religions were none. Or were mere ornaments. No, its message was not so clear.

'Did you ever wear one?' I asked Larry.

'No,' he said, but as if it was of no importance, and he did not stop to talk about why. He began to tell me about his own journey to the sacred mountain and the saint.

After long dusty hours in local buses, Larry found the ashram. He was shown to a room, quickly bathed and changed, and then was taken to the shala where the saint sat.

The owners of some land at the base of the mountain on the other side from the temple and the central market next to it had some time ago been persuaded by his more assertive devotees to give it over to the building of accommodation for the saint should he ever care to descend, and this eventually became the ashram, complete with a meditation room, and a darshan hall, kitchens, dining hall, and later some dormitories and bungalows.

A daily darshan began soon after his arrival. 'Darshan literally means "view" or "sight of",' Larry told me, 'and it refers to seeing or being in the presence of a revered person, or God, or a sacred place or sacred image. It often implies an experience of inner awakening. The saint simply sat on a couch provided for him and everyone filed past him, simply pausing, or sometimes having a few words. Or they just sat in the hall with him.

'This was about four years after he had come out of his silence. He still observed silence most of the time but for an hour or two in the afternoons. Not everyone in the darshan line tried to talk with him, and he often answered without words. Sometimes he would say something brief, sometimes he spoke at more length. Sometimes he sang.'

'What language did he speak? You said he said "Be good" in English?'

Larry paused. 'Apparently he spoke a number of languages, and there was no explanation for this. Like most educated Indians, he grew up speaking a few languages: the local language, one of the national languages and English, which by now was pretty much accepted as a national language. He also used Sanskrit, an older form of Tamil, and Urdu. But he spoke and sang in many languages. It was pretty much accepted as a kind of divine gift.'

'Were there any tapes made?'

'Electronic devices did not work in his presence. People tried to record him, on all kinds of audio and later video recording devices, on film even. But it never worked. Even electric lights would flicker unbearably or go out when he was in a room. The darshan hall was lit with oil lamps and candles.

'He spoke directly to me twice,' Larry said, 'and the first time was when I had just arrived, and took my place in the line. The people before me did pranaam, bending to touch his feet. He had indicated he did not care for this. I did not care for it myself and only gave a namaste.'

'What did he say to you?'

'He said, "I've been expecting you."'

'And you believed him?'

Larry paused to look at me. We've all known those people who claim prior clairvoyance after events. The phone: 'I knew it was you.' Some news: 'I knew that would happen.' An exposure: 'I always knew, I just could tell.'

'Yes,' Larry said, 'but maybe only when I realized he did not necessarily mean me, Larry Darrell from Australia.

'And then he said, "What have you come here for?"

'I said, "To learn from you."

'He said, "Learn from your sadhana," and gave me a smile I can hardly describe, although it is still clear in my mind. It had understanding, sweetness, forgiveness, tenderness, sternness, as if he saw to the farthest extent of my soul and understood more than I ever could. I fell into a strange state then and don't recall moving from him in the line.'

Larry sat on the floor amongst the others there in the hall, with the few dozen others present.

He felt a sense of rightness and peace. It remained with him.

In the morning he asked how long he could stay and they said 'up to you'. He asked how much the room cost and they said 'no charge'. He asked if he could make a donation to the work of the ashram and they said 'of course'. Every day volunteers came to the kitchen to prepare the food donated by farmers, shopkeepers and housewives. Most of this was then given away to a line of people who arrived to be fed out the back.

Larry spent nearly four years there. A local contact even organized his visa extensions.

'And you were never bored?'

'Never. I meditated. Sat in the shala. Did duties. Talked with people. Bicycled to other towns. Climbed the mountain, or walked around it. Read a few books many times. Sat in the cave. Swept the paths.

'Many times I walked up the mountain – they called it a mountain but you reached the top in a couple of hours easy climbing – to sit in the cave where he had sat for so long.' Larry fell silent for a while.

'I don't know how to describe it, but the place had a very affecting quality. If you sat there silently you felt an incredible sense of peace and rightness, and all sense of time and the outside world fell away. Sometimes I had visions there, sometimes I just felt extraordinarily alert to the consciousness of every cell in my own body and of every living thing around me, trees and rocks included. It was never an experience available to language. And so I could never ask myself at the time if this was to "be good", and still it seemed to be part of the inquiry the saint told us to undertake.'

In the afternoons Larry spent some time in the hall where the saint sometimes sang in various languages that he could not possibly have learnt. Some of the verses were identified as devotional songs from old traditions, some were never traced.

The town still had not seen very many foreign tourists. There was nothing deemed significant there, but for the access to the sacred mountain, to which pilgrims had always made their way, but not in nearly the numbers it would attract as a central place in the growing lore and reputation of the saint. Growing numbers of people came to do the auspicious walk around the mountain, especially at the full moon.

The population of the small town grew. Across the road from the ashram, where there had been one tea stall, there was now a line of stalls with rough benches providing seating, and they began to serve not only local coffee and tea from the north but bottled soft drinks and fruit juices. Other little stalls sprang up to sell snacks, cigarettes, batteries and toilet paper. Travellers could get a good cheap meal at nearby houses. For foreigners not too spicy.

It became part of Larry's routine to go to one of the tea stalls, sit for an hour or two in the late mornings, after many hours spent in work or contemplation. He drank the local sweet, milky coffee, chatted to people, watched boys washing or painting the temple elephant, or the cobbler's industry at the side of the road, or the plodding passage of bullock carts.

Although most devotees were Indian, there was an increasing number of foreigners, from anywhere in Europe, all the Americas, parts of the Pacific. They had heard of the saint in the web of tea stalls, hotels and ashram trails. As a boy the saint had sought out foreigners and now they came to him.

India provided a generous supply of gurus and swamis, of divination and magic, a range of sacred traditions and unholy hocus-pocus, all that assures people that the world they live in is 'spiritual'. Many of them were more accessible practically or theoretically than this saint, and many exposés and even denunciations of the adoption of Indian practice and faith had been written, but people came, and many stayed longer than they ever dreamed they would.

'Now, Larry,' I said, 'where it all began for you was a search for some meaningful principle to live by, the problem of evil, some universal truth. Are you telling me this all came down to "Be good".'

'How I understood that,' Larry said, 'was as a starting point to an inquiry that had to take place for true and total knowledge which comes from knowledge by being. I had come there attracted to the idea that the path of knowledge was the most noble, in any case it was the one that suited me to pursue, as it was knowledge that I was after.'

Of course the meaning of the simple phrase was declared and challenged, debated and contested among the occupants of the tea stalls, among scholars, sceptics, devotees and observers.

Goodness was kindness, some said, and what we were to do was to practice kindness, by caring for all creatures on earth, giving whatever we had to give, not judging, not withholding.

Goodness was beauty, some said, for the glories of nature and of art, the fresh innocence of babies, were most valued by all humankind, and studies show that it's rundown, neglected, filthy places that get vandalized and breed crime and despair. What we are to do is take a block of land, and clear it, and plant things on it, and take care of it, and allow people to use it well and nurture and support art that is about beauty. If you invoke the beautiful you cannot be drawn into evil. All dreams of a perfect world are of a beautiful world.

You can only judge good by its results, not its intentions, said others, and the results of actions must be measured and studied.

Be good meant to be spiritual, to live in knowledge of God.

To be good was to be aware. It was to live in the moment, to see with the infinite eye that did not see other, did not see duality, not good and evil, object or subject, time or space, seed or fruit. What we must do was cultivate the Awareness that dissolved all these.

To be good was to renounce the illusory pleasures and rewards of the world and live in simplicity, as the saint himself did. Is not he a living example? Renunciation was its key.

To be good was to accept and rejoice in all the blessings of your life, all that you had and might have, to envision the best life you could have and thus bring it into being.

Be good meant be good at what you do, be good in your duty and your calling and your gifts. We were to cultivate and perfect ourselves, our talents and skills.

Some people said be good meant caring for the planet, starting with what's in front of you, starting with doing something about the toilet paper. Foreigners would adapt to local conditions as far as sitting on the floor and eating rice and spiced vegetables, but they would not learn to clean themselves with water at the toilet, and few stopped to wonder about the effect of old drains suddenly crammed with soiled paper. The single biggest selling commodity for the stall holders had become toilet paper.

Larry said, 'I had endless discussions on the meaning of "be good". It meant "know thyself", it meant "do as you would be done by", "there is no god but God", "do as thou wilt".'

One day, his mind full of such questions and possibilities, Larry climbed up the mountain. 'It was such a beautiful day that instead of sitting inside the cave I left the path and sat on a rock overlooking the valley, and seemed, in the sharp clear air, to see further to the distance than I ever had. I closed my eyes and without any conscious effort or intention, it was as if there were no more "I", only something that words can only refer to but not describe, intense peace and bliss and clarity. It seemed as if entire universes were created, evolved and returned to the ultimate disorder while I sat there and it also seemed as if it were a mere instant, or, more accurately, there seemed to be no way to measure time. In any case, this experience has been described by others, the mystical experience, unique in each instant yet uniting or unifying all consciousness. When I opened my eyes it was late afternoon.

'I felt that the saint's message was to take the path of knowledge itself, but as usual the human impulse was to turn the message into a universal answer or slogan or dogma, whereas the path of knowledge was to ask not once but always what anything really means. And the experience on the hill was one whose meaning was not available to rational understanding, but as an experience it gave me knowledge that such experience is part of my nature. And I didn't know how I knew but I knew it was time to leave.

'I went back down the hill and into the hall, and rather than just sitting there I took my place in the line to go past the saint.

'When he looked at me I knew I did not need to say a word, and only bowed my head to request his blessing. He put his hand there and said gently, "You have been here long enough."'

'And that's when you came back to Australia?"

'A few months after that.'

'And a few months later you were going to marry Sophie.'

Larry nodded but said nothing to this.

'And you've come back to India for what?'

'I can't stay away. When I left the saint, I went back to a couple of villages I had gone to on an earlier trip. I think I have something to do here, something worth doing. After all it's always the practical effect that I believe counts the most. There's something I'm looking into, something that's basically practical, practicable, pragmatic. If there's anything I have to give others, it's the money I have.'

'Larry,' I said in a sudden alarm of comprehension, 'you're not thinking of giving your money away? Don't do it.'

Larry only smiled at me.

'Are you going back to the saint?' I asked him.

'He died while I was in Australia. No, he wasn't very old at all. Of course, in some sense he has not died, and the ashram and its work are still going strong, I believe. No, there's no point for me in going back. Once he's gone, it'll be different, in a way I don't need to see. Even though it will continue to do good works among the poor and offer experiences of peace and knowledge to many who seek it. For all the value I got from it, it's not going to be the same now. I've heard that caste practices and puja rituals are beginning to dominate the daily workings of the ashram. This country has changed in the last few years and they have appropriated the saint into the ritual framework of a religion that has recreated itself basically as monotheism. It invokes the authority of an invented history. No, I have to do some other work now.'

When we left the hotel dining hall we took an auto to Beach Road and sat for a while watching dawn streak the sky and the fishermen drag their boats out onto the dark water. Bodies were strewn in sleep over the wide expanse of sand, and near us someone stirred from under a pile of coconuts and sold us two fresh green coconuts. We each drank the refreshing and tonic water as the top of the sun hazily emerged on the horizon. A group of men came jogging past us, and a few people appeared on a grassy bank and began to perform loose-limbed sun salutations, a couple of the women impeded a little by their saris. A little way along across the road from us sat the white curves and arches of a building once known as the Ice House – for the building had been planned for the storage of ice – and was now the Vivekananda Illam. I told Larry that just that day I had been taken there, and read how Vivekananda just a century ago had addressed the Parliament of Religions in Chicago, electrified the public and began a craze for Vedanta in America.

Larry said, 'Vivekananda said preaching religion was futile without first removing poverty.'

'Is that what you want to do now, remove poverty?'

'Some of it at least. That seems to me the most important thing there is.'

Before we parted, I said, 'Larry, can I give you some advice? I do not usually give advice, even when it's asked for, and you haven't asked.'

I think Larry knew where I was going. 'I'm not asking for advice,' he said gently.

'I have to say it. Don't get rid of your money. Money saves time. You say yourself it enabled everything you've done. It will continue to enable you. I haven't always had money, so it might seem that it's more important to me than it should be, but I know how its lack can mean your life is dominated by anxiety and humiliation. You've never had that much that you've had to live with the fear and guilt of the very rich, but what good would it do to you not to be able to strike while the iron is hot, go where you want to go, buy what you need?'

'I can earn money,' said Larry, 'and I know it will now do more good elsewhere.' Though he spoke with his usual equanimity, his tone made clear his certainty.

I sighed. 'Then you can pay the driver.' We went in silence back to my club. We said an affectionate goodbye with few words. He pulled from his wallet a card, the name on it, he said, that of a foundation that supported some village-based projects, which would become the recipient of Larry's former material assets. I put it in my own wallet.

I went inside, and woke a couple of the bodies sleeping in the entrance hall and at the foot of the stairs. I could not tell which of them were employed for security and which others were simply allowed to take shelter there. A bleary-eyed man found my key. I don't know if it was any surprise to him that a man of my years should be arriving back at this scandalous hour. I had a long hot shower, got into my pyjamas, and took a melatonin tablet, and, waiting for its soporific effect, began to read an English translation of Romain Rolland's biography of Vivekananda which I had earlier picked up in the small library downstairs.

PART VII

I didn't see why I should be mixed up in it

The following year, I was back in my North Coast home, and busy writing. I never like being interrupted, and was at a crucial stage, so I tried to ignore a knock at my door, but it turned quite insistent, a ruder knock than ventured by anyone who was selling something or seeking converts.

Crankily I went to see who it was and found a policeman.

Concerns about speeding or wrongful parking darted in my mind, or some flashing notion that they were knocking at every door with a photograph in hand of a miscreant at large, or that of an abducted child.

'Sorry to disturb you,' he said amiably. 'We got a call from the officers at Byron. The detectives want to see you.'

He wouldn't tell me what it was about. This, he said, was a 'courtesy call', a request that I go to see them, or else they would come and see me. I gathered putting them to the extra trouble would not be taken well. Infuriated, I went inside to call the station at Byron and learnt no more than that: they wanted to see me. I inferred that I could take the house call by the local officer as either a gesture of decency or a check on my presence and conduct. How soon could I get down there? They could tell me no more by phone.

Seething by now, I got my car out and set off. I tried to guess what this business was about: maybe they'd caught someone who had tried to stalk or blackmail me.

At the police station they showed me into a dingy little office, where I felt pangs of anxiety and guilt and even searched my conscience as I waited alone. I'd had no liaisons with underage boys but what could I do if someone said I had?

A wiry young man with receding fair hair, Detective Someone, finally sat down across from me, thanked me for coming in so readily and then asked me:

'Do you know a woman called Sophie Macdonald?'

So that was it, Sophie was in trouble, I thought, sure to be something to do with drugs, but I didn't see why I should be mixed up in it.

'I have met someone of that name,' I said cautiously.

It was worse, though, than I thought.

I didn't even know she had returned to Australia. I eventually learnt that she had been staying in what they still called a commune on the outskirts of the little town of Nimbin: it was a rundown old farmhouse leased to 'the hippies' by a farmer who had moved with his own family to a new redbrick dwelling over the hill and out of sight. Whoever had signed the original lease had long gone. People who stayed there turned up through a network of connections, and the gathering of the rent and the running of the household depended on various ad hoc arrangements by combinations of inhabitants.

Once so idealistic, was the general sense of the early days of communes, but they now featured an entropy of domestic politics, too many bludgers and drifters and addicts subverting the ideas of sharing and volunteering, not that I had given it much consideration. My subject matter remained the urban and suburban classes.

Sophie had not been seen for some days, not since she set out to hitch to Byron one day. Hitchhiking was a common way of getting around in the area. If you didn't have transport of your own there was no other option, even if you had been willing to pay for public conveyances, which the community of dropouts usually was not. There were enough people generous enough to pick up someone thumbing a ride into town – some of them had relied on hitching themselves once – to make it a pretty reliable means of getting around, especially if you were a woman alone, not generally seen as any threat. Even young people with employment in town relied on it.

Who knows what Sophie's business in town had been; the occupants of the old farmhouse had no information whatsoever. It had never occurred to them to think of her as officially missing when she had not returned, if they had even noticed. By the time police returned with further inquiries no one in the old farmhouse could be found who had been living there during the brief duration of her residence, or who admitted to knowing a thing about her besides her name and that someone she'd met in India had recommended the house as a place to stay.

A body had been found. Nothing on it to identify her. Naked, murdered. It was some days after she had last been seen. Somehow the connection had been made to the woman called Sophie who was staying at the place near Nimbin.

No one knew her next of kin.

At the rundown house outside the edge of town, it was discovered that she had left behind a backpack. She had owned some clothes, cheap Indian jewellery, cosmetics and three books. One was a blank notebook, one was a copy of the Bhagavad Gita, and the third was a book by me which I had inscribed in such a way as to indicate close personal relations with the deceased.

I was easy to find.

And so I had been brought in to assist the police with their inquiries.

It was the only photograph...

Although the grisly MO of Sophie's murder was already known to the police, for she was the sixth known young female hitchhiker to have been murdered in the state in the last eighteen months, the perpetrator was still unidentified.

By this time, though, a Task Force had been installed and they were closing in on a man who had been taken in for one murder and would later be charged with several more.

Eventually, after my story ends, there were horrible revelations on front pages and on television news shows. There were debates about the causative factors of poverty, neglect, dysfunctional families and the association of violence with pleasure. The 'hitchhiker killer' confessed to the murder of all and any young woman who had disappeared in recent years, he was forgotten for a while and then there was a thoroughly reported trial. There were chilling analyses of serial killers who plan their crimes and have no relationship with the victim. There were allegations that the murderer had been framed, convicted on politically motivated fabricated evidence. There were tabloid articles about how to spot future monsters of this type, the predictive factors of persistent bedwetting and torturing animals.

Any one who had ever stuck their thumb out on the side of the road sold a piece to a magazine.

But until then, there were no clues as to what had happened to Sophie. I eventually gathered that she had been in the area for about a month. She intended to return to Goa, and as far as I could tell she had come to Australia to sort out some financial business.

Anyway, she had kept that book of mine I had given her in Goa, and what I had inscribed in the book caused the detectives to suppose that I knew her intimately, and to investigate the possibility that I knew something about her movements, acquaintances and plans, or indeed, though they never said so, that I myself might be under some suspicion.

And that is why I found myself meeting with a police detective at the Byron station, attempting to explain my relationship to Sophie and why I had written a 'love poem' in a book for her.

During this, a detective from Sydney arrived. My detective went off and spoke with him while I was given a hot drink in a Styrofoam cup out of a machine. These places aren't designed to make us comfortable. Then the two detectives joined me again, and we had to rewind, as it were, and begin again.

As the author of the book, I explained to the detective from Sydney, an older man, dark and stocky and sardonic, it is a kind of convention to write a specific message to someone when you sign it.

'It's an old poem that I thought she might have known. It tells us to make the most of the present,' I was obliged to explain.

'I see,' said the senior detective. He looked hard at the page in front of him, but did not contest my succinct exegesis. 'Is this the usual kind of thing you would write in a book?'

'Oh, that kind of thing, some kind of remark or quotation you might think of for that person. She used to like poetry as a young student, and would have recognized that as a quotation.'

'Well, it's obviously a *quotation,'* said the detective. 'I don't have time to read, myself, I don't know the last time I had time to read a whole book.'

I caught the expression of the younger, local detective, who had done a university degree, a qualification that would not impress the old school work-your-way-up code and history of the older bloke.

'And who is this?' they asked me, showing me a photograph.

Of Larry. I recognized him at once, in one of his clean-shaven periods, smiling warmly into the camera, seen from the waist up in what looked like a khadi shirt, apparently sitting at an Indian tea stall. I guessed that Larry had given it to her during the time they were living together.

I don't know, I was going to say, but probably they had already seen that I did know, and God knows where this ghastly business was going. It was not a time to be hiding anything.

'That is Larry Darrell,' I said.

It was the only photograph Sophie had among her scant possessions.

'And what was their relationship?'

'They were childhood friends.'

'This photo wouldn't be a childhood photo, would it?'

'They were both childhood friends of some friends of mine. They all met each other again in Sydney, which is where I met them.'

'And he'd be into the same kind of lifestyle, would he?'

'Er, he tends to live alone and lead a sober, studious life.'

'And where is this Larry Darrell now?'

'I don't know,' I said, and I didn't, but then I remembered the card he'd given me that night in Madras. Better, I thought, to try and contact him at once than let some ridiculous suspicion accrue, adding prejudice to a search for Larry and excusing an end to any other investigation. Though at the time it seemed that whoever did this to Sophie might not be found.

The card showed not only the name of the foundation but its URL. This was the first time – it was the early nineties – I had ever tried to contact someone through a website, and the procedure made quite an impression. The site had been updated recently and included telephone and fax numbers and an email address. It all worked and worked fast. Larry was in New Zealand at the time. Within a couple of hours we had gotten hold of him, I managed to talk to him, to tell him very briefly the ghastly news, and he arrived the next day. I still hadn't gotten over the impact of this amazing new global connectivity.

By then, I had been to the morgue of the local hospital to identify the body. Fingerprints, dental records, the documents she left in her room were not sufficient. A visual identification was required. Arrangements were made, I was met at the hospital foyer, taken down some corridors suffused with that hospital smell. Outside a door two hospital workers in white coats were waiting. Few words were spoken.

Inside, I was shown the body, which had been cleaned up but nothing cosmetic had been done to the wounds I could see though a sheet covered most of her. It was obvious they could only have been acquired by violence. 'That's Sophie McDonald,' I said, finding my voice raspy.

Outside, I said to the detective, 'What now? Will she be cremated?'

'The body will have to go to the Coroner's Court, in Sydney,' he said. 'Then they dispose of it. Unless relatives or friends make arrangements. They haven't found anyone.'

'I'd like to take care of it,' I said. 'I want to.'

He gave me a look, but said, 'Up to you, mate.' It was more paperwork for him, but he took me back to the station. 'It's a bloody shame,' said the senior detective about Sophie, 'and we're going to catch the mongrel that did it, but women should not go hitching on their own. And this kind of lifestyle…They have no idea of the real world, you're only asking for something like this.'

He was talking to me but it was for the benefit of the local chap, who would be more inclined to support freedom of movement for all and deprecate the blaming of victims.

I was signing the forms when Larry arrived.

The two detectives had their little talk alone with Larry. I waited in the front office, reading notices to the public and advertisements for a raffle.

When the detectives brought Larry back to me they all seemed to have got along fine. 'They'll give you lunch at the pub,' the local one said, 'they do great fish and chips if you like that, the Caesar salad is good too. The kitchen's usually closed by now but I gave Vicki a call and she'll look after you.'

We shook hands, said the right things.

Larry had hardly said a word to me. I ordered for both of us – salads, breads, grilled fish, an omelette and a bottle of wine. We had a quiet corner table. A few people at some distance were finishing their lunches. We sat in silence until the food came. Larry seemed to hardly notice it. The table, strangely, was set for three, and the third set of mat, cutlery and drinking glasses was left in place.

'Eat it,' I said, 'and drink some of this. And I might get a conversation out of you.'

Larry rallied enough to say, 'Silence can be a form of conversation.'

'You must know some truly stimulating people.'

But there was nothing pleasant to be said. There was no point in saying much at all. We both just wanted to be done with it and go.

'Look,' he said. 'About the cost of the cremation. I'm hoping you can cover it. Coming over here cleared me out.'

'No worries,' I said. It took me another few moments before I realized the significance of what he'd said.

'You didn't,' I said. 'Not all of it.'

But he had, he'd given all his money away, to the foundation that supported independent village-based development projects in southern India. He liked what they were doing. Small loan schemes, literacy for women, goats. Apparently he had spent some time out in rural areas learning about people's lives, trying to assess their needs without prejudice or presumption, and wherever he could, ensuring funds and expertise were appropriately provided. He had some plans to return to the centres of power to persuade those with means and resources to donate and invest, to bestow and bequeath them where they would best be used.

I know that too often well-intentioned deeds cause harm but I like to think that to some extent he achieved what I like to think all of us want: to make the world better.

He'd just been finalizing the structure of the loans and the management of funds in New Zealand.

'I see,' I said. 'And what are you going to do now?'

'I've been asked to New York to give a little talk on the Foundation,' said Larry. 'I might spend a bit of time there.'

'Presumably,' I said, 'as long as there's a job involved.'

'Yes, I'll be earning my living somehow, that doesn't worry me.'

'You have any idea what that might be?"

Larry said, 'I believe we all believe something we can't prove. I believe that I'll soon know what I will do next. I'd like to see the world from a fresh perspective.'

After the last couple of days, even this couldn't get us started. We didn't say anything for a while, finishing our food. There was some wine left in the bottle and Larry took hold of it and put it aside. Then he said, 'If you want to tell me I'll be sorry, go right ahead.'

'Not what I feel like saying. You're free to give away your freedom.'

'I don't know,' said Larry, 'I've liked being free to go wherever I wanted. But I feel freer now than I ever have. I feel more independent, not less.'

I said, 'But I do wonder, have you never met anyone you wanted to settle down with? Is that kind of thing on the agenda for you?'

Larry said, 'The only person I could ever have lived with, been happy with, shared my whole life with, was Sophie.'

I did need a moment to take that in. 'Are you serious? Do you still think that?'

'She was the most complete, true to herself person. She had a really beautiful spirit. She was smart and funny and tender and open. She was always like that, right from the start.'

'Why didn't you get together with Sophie back then?'

'It just wasn't like that, we were just kids, we were just good mates, we hung out together, secretly showing each other books.'

I didn't mention the time I saw Sophie in Goa and he never told me if he had ever received as much as a postcard from her. Neither of us mentioned Isabel. Larry *never* mentioned Isabel. I think he had no idea just how much of a torch she had kept on carrying for him. It was as if the episode of their engagement had long been resolved by him as a youthful folly from long ago.

I would have to go back to the police to fill in some more forms.

The ghastly business of sending the body down to the coroner meant that at this point there was no ceremonial farewell to Sophie, no honouring of her life and grieving for her death. But it seems as if we did not even speak when we agreed on a drive up to the Lighthouse. The day had turned dark, the sky filled with storm clouds over the sea. We stood side by side in silence on the high cliffs looking out to the horizon beyond the wrinkled grey sea. Larry lifted the wine bottle and poured its remaining contents onto the rocks descending before us.

After a while, 'I want to get back,' was all Larry said then, 'and if you don't need me, there's a coach to the airport in half an hour.'

We parted with few more words. Though I was not sorry for our odd little gesture of closure, it had all been horrifying and depressing, and we both wanted to go our separate ways. There was no point in lingering, nothing more to say.

You killed her

I was going to go straight back home – by now my house on the North Coast had become the place I most easily called home – and straight back to work. I felt the call of an unfinished page and longed to re-immerse myself in my brutally interrupted writing. But after what happened, I couldn't quite immediately resume my new play in the same frame of mind. To recreate that flow, first I had to clear things up. I decided to go down to Sydney and booked the next day's flight. No clearer proof of the cold single-mindedness of the writer than to say that, to me, the greatest impact Sophie's death had was the sense of interrupted writing, the change to what I had been working on.

I rang Isabel and she said I could come and have a drink with her. She and Gray were going out to dinner later. Though I would have to excuse the look of the place.

I'd hoped to talk to her alone, so was glad to find Gray wasn't there when I arrived. He was with his group of mates who took a yacht out on the Harbour midweek. It had been a clear sunny day with a light wind.

Pictures had been taken down, many objects had been removed. Some of the furniture had already gone. Things had been already packed for the move back to Brisbane. There were only days to go before they completely moved out.

Isabel moaned a while about people who wanted to inspect the apartment before they'd left it, about how old-fashioned Elliott's stuff was, about how hard it was to get rid of, it wasn't what people were buying. I heard about estate agents and removalists, auctions and dealers and collectors. Isabel and Gray were going to stay in a hotel in Brisbane until the new house was ready. I heard about her plans for the decoration of their new place – sliding doors, courtyards and water features were already planned. Serious purchases were going down. Collectible new artists were being investigated.

We had decided on a glass of wine and Isabel had opened a bottle of a delectably crisp white from New Zealand. As she went to refill my glass, I asked:

'And have you heard from Larry?'

'No, have you?'

'I was with him yesterday.'

She looked at me very intensely, very alert, very interested to know that this might be why I was here, very eager for me to tell her about that. 'Where?' she asked.

'Nimbin. Byron.'

'What were you doing there?'

'Arranging for Sophie to be cremated.'

'*What*? Does that mean she's dead?'

'That's usually a precondition for being cremated.'

'Very funny. Well. Well. I can't pretend to be grief-stricken. Drugs I suppose.'

'She was found murdered,' I said, 'she had been stabbed a dozen times.' I couldn't help exaggerating.

'Well. When you choose that sort of lifestyle, you're really choosing that kind of death. Some people are just drawn to the dark side. It's basically self-destructive.'

'That's something like what they said up at Byron.'

'I suppose they'll never find what really happened.'

'I suppose they won't but I knew just where to look.'

'What! Where?'

'Here, my dear. Right here. I think you killed her.'

She did this bug-eyed, head-shaking stare at me. 'What are you trying to say? Hey, I was right here, and I can prove it.'

'I happened to see Sophie last year, after she'd left Sydney. We had a nice long talk.'

'With her off her face I suppose?'

'Oh, she was making sense. She told me about the time she disappeared just before she was going to be married to Larry.'

Isabel's face went rigid for a moment. I told her what Sophie told me. Isabel shrugged and fiddled with her beads.

'The thing is, Isabel, I kept thinking about it, because there was something not quite right about it. You are a control freak. You are efficient, punctual, well-organized. And, how many times have I been here in the afternoon and there has never been a bottle of vodka or anything else on a tray on the coffee table with glasses.'

'Uncle Elliott sent that over, you remember how he was raving about it, it was something a bit special, we were going to serve it later.'

'So until then you were keeping it in an ice bucket and not in the fridge.'

'Well, yes, in case Uncle Elliott came around. I wanted him to see we appreciated it.'

'I did notice the great reviews you gave that vodka at that lunch, most unusual coming from you, it's not one of your drinks.'

'Uncle Elliott made the big deal about it, I was only humouring him.'

'I also kept thinking how you were always impeccable about keeping appointments.'

'The dentist called with a cancellation. Do you know how hard it is to get an appointment? Sarah had a toothache. I had to take her first chance.'

'You have a nanny, a housekeeper, a driver, anyone could have taken the child to the dentist.'

'She was so scared, in such pain, she needed me, and anyway I'd picked her up from school myself that day, which sometimes I do when everyone is off.'

'And then, you never said a word about the pilfered vodka when Sophie disappeared.'

'Didn't I? Well, it was all so confusing and upsetting and I didn't realize till later that some of it had gone and by then it could have been anybody.'

'Isabel, you're lying.'

'Why don't you believe me?'

'Because I know it's not true.'

She got up and walked over to the window.

As usual, she was dressed in black, having adopted the Sydney penchant as her current style. She had on some mid-calf-length pants and a matching loose top, black patent slides on her feet, the toenails like a row of rubies. She had some beads on that day, a long string of some kind of black rock polished into marbled spheres. She had graceful moves, an instinct for flattering light and becoming angles. She turned back towards me as if from upstage.

'Look, okay, I'll tell you the truth. I'm not sorry she's dead because I wasn't sorry when she shot through. I did notice that we left that vodka there that day she was coming, and I was going to put it away, and then I thought, what if I'm a bit late, and she has to wait for me while it's sitting there in front of her, and she doesn't touch it, and waits for me, then I'll believe in her, and really try to be friends with her, because basically I have to try and respect Larry. Honestly, all she had to do was wait for me and not touch it, and I wasn't all that late anyway, and I would have been as good as gold to her, she didn't have to do much to just meet me halfway.'

'Oh, nice little confession, but I still don't believe you.'

'What don't you believe?' she said, anger rising in her. She glared at me for a while. I looked back at her steadily. 'All right, look, I did leave the vodka there.'

'If you hadn't she might still be alive.'

'Making Larry utterly miserable as well as herself and anyone they came in contact with. Honestly! You know that! They were not going to be happy, she would try to destroy him as well as herself! How long could she stay sober?' Isabel did not restrain her emotion, beginning to shout and pace about. 'You and Gray weren't going to do anything about it, even though you knew it was a disaster. It was up to me. Did you see the way she looked at us drinking that day? Did you even notice? She couldn't stop watching us drink it with those puffy eyes of hers. She wanted to have some so much and it was only because of

Larry that she didn't have any. Oh yeah, I noticed that, and I carried on about the stupid vodka just to give her a hard time. But that's what gave me the idea. God, he is such a bloody fool, no way was she going to stay sober, what happened was going to happen sooner or later, I really saved him from a lot of grief!' Isabel had worked up quite a passion, sounding outraged and defensive at once. 'I've always been there for Larry, I've always known what he needed most.'

'To take from him the woman he wanted to marry?'

'He didn't *want* to marry her!' Isabel was near hysteria. 'She made him, she fully took advantage of him, anyone could see how she was using him, any *woman* could see that, and I thought you were meant to be perceptive! She wanted something from him, she just wanted him to look after her, she'd even pretend to go straight to get it, and then once they were married she would only...I saved him from that! I put the vodka there, all right? I knew she wouldn't resist it, she had no self-control, no self-respect, no respect for anything. If she did resist it I would have just gone, great, fine, good, and made the best of it like I said, I swear I would have. I did take Sarah to the dentist, but we couldn't get in of course so we did a bit of shopping and came home. And Sophie had gone, she'd drunk half the bottle and run off, proving she's weak, she's an addict, she was never going to make it, and everyone is better off now.'

I said, 'I thought it was something like that. You stabbed her and left her to bleed to death.'

Isabel calmed down and came and sat very close to me. She arranged herself fetchingly and began to stroke my arm. She was like a little puppy crawling to you beseechingly, wagging its tail while half-cringing, wanting to be petted again after a scolding for upsetting its bowl or weeing indoors. 'Will, darling, you never will tell Larry any of that, will you?'

'I wouldn't dream of it. Not that I think I'd have a chance even if I wanted to.'

I told her that Larry had given away his income to some remote subsistence project in the boondocks of India, and could well move on to become more seriously inaccessible. Tears began to form in her eyes as she took it in.

She listened as I told her of his latest deeds, and began to weep. He was now really lost to her. He would not come back, and she would not be able to seek him. Their lives were as separate and far apart as two lives can be. The way she was crying, grief for a sudden loss, made obvious what kind of hopes she still had nurtured, though I could not tell precisely what she had imagined. Maybe she wanted Larry forever to remain close, the perennially single boyfriend of the couple. Perhaps she imagined that Larry had never stopped wishing she had waited for him and she wanted to keep him near still longing for her. Perhaps she had always maintained an expectation that one day, maybe when the children were grown, she might with some mysterious ease find Larry become her life partner.

I let her cry. I stood, and wandered round the room, stopping at the window to look out upon the Harbour.

With the heavy drapes removed, the splendour of the outlook was clearly greater than that of any of the treasures that had been carefully purchased to set inside. There were a few yachts still out on the water taking advantage of the season's long dusk. The light out there was marvellous, the water opalescent, the sky marbled in pink and charcoal. The kind of thing that's always better in Nature.

After a while she stopped crying and went to inspect herself in a mirror. She took out her makeup and began a hasty interim touch-up. 'I'll need an ice pack for my eyes, I'll have ten minutes to lie down before I have to get ready for tonight, lucky I've got those eye drops too,' she said decisively, powdering her nose. She put on some lipstick and came back to sit near me.

'So do you think I am a dreadful, wicked person?'

'Does it matter what I think?'

'It does to me,' she said. 'I want you to like me.'

'I'm not a moral person. If I like someone I like them even if I don't like what they do. Unless they do it to me! And you're good company, you're smart and educated, you have style and spirit, and of course it is enchanting to behold you.' She was smiling at me, well pleased. 'There's only one quality you lack to make you entirely compelling.'

She was still smiling, still listening, wanting more.

'Compassion.'

The smile expired and at that moment Gray arrived, shambling into the room in his heavy-gaited way. He had put on weight and lost more of his hair. He looked well, though, better than I'd ever seen him since they moved here. The recent change in their fortunes had done wonders for him, he exuded the old confidence and vitality as well as a new maturity. He looked pleased to see me, and we chatted for a while. He said he was looking forward to 'getting amongst it again' and said he was feeling 'highly motivated' and 'ready to optimize the situation'. Dear old Gray. You couldn't help liking him, cliché-ridden and imperceptive though he was. He had no pretentiousness in his manner, his frankness and warmth shone through, and it was good to see him excited about the move back north and the involvement in a new career. 'No place like home,' he said.

He told me a bit, frankly a bit too much, about the new company that he would be heading up, about its holdings and ventures, its international reach, more information than I was worthy of but I did understand that a lot of money would be made.

'In town long?' he asked.

'Just the night. Leaving in the morning,' I said.

'Tell you what,' he said, 'Isabel and I can get out of this do tonight, can't we baby? It'd be terrific if you could have dinner with us. Go on.'

'Darling,' Isabel countered, 'we can't really, it's a bit of a farewell for us.'

'Love to,' I said, 'only I've got a dinner date and I can't break it. With Josh Rouvier. Another time.'

'We might see you in Brisbane then.'

'Who's that?' asked Isabel.

'An artist. One of Larry's boyfriends,' I said.

'Yeah? I wondered about Larry,' Gray said genially.

'No way,' said Isabel. 'No way known.'

'Well, have just one more drink.'

Gray got himself another beer and I finished my glass of wine. Just before I left, Isabel, putting on an air of gentle caring and wifely nurturance, as if to perform the quality I had accused of being deficient in her, nuzzled up to Gray and asked him, 'Darling, tell me honestly, you know me better than anyone, do you think I'm mean and nasty?'

'No way, baby, just the opposite, did anyone say you were?'

She stuck her tongue out at me behind Gray's back.

'That's not what I said,' I whispered to her as she came to the door with me. I stepped out and she closed it behind me.

I have never seen her

Next time I was in Sydney, the Maturins had gone. I used to like going over to see Isabel, she was an easy, pleasant diversion. But I suppose I stopped missing her before too long, and in fact I have never seen her again.

She never was a letter writer, and this was before we all began using email to any great extent. She never made an effort to get in touch, not after a Happy Holidays or Season's Greetings card at the end of that year. We'd never written to each other and as time has passed I suppose we can say that we have officially lost touch.

They are no longer 'high profile', not in this new era. I imagine they are well-known in their own circles, and that if I read different publications I'd see more of what they have been up to. No doubt Gray has made a success in the new company or corporation or whatever it is, and if I wanted to I could easily find out, no doubt they'd show up with pages of results in a search engine. I seem to have come across their name in connection with something about new developments in the north of the state, with protests from 'tree-hugging greenies' temporarily delaying progress as they tried to defend some of the last remaining mangrove areas. But I never have found out more, and with Elliott gone, there is no longer any direct connection between us.

I imagine they bought a very nice house and had builders and tradesmen and decorators do their work with swift efficiency. Isabel would have found the right furniture and furnishings, and it would all look suitably elegant. Her Brett Whiteley and her Rover Thomas would be shown to great advantage on large walls in light-filled rooms and would be in good company with new artists that she would be guided to by the gallery owners and art dealers who were all expanding their premises and thriving happily in the rejuvenated city that Brisbane has become. So I hear, though I have had no occasion to return.

Isabel would always look impeccable and by now her grooming customs would include some subtle surgeries. She would hold functions and raise money for victims of natural disasters and terrifying diseases. Her daughters would find her hard to live up to. They would have completed their years at private schools, and God only knows what kind of young women they might be. Isabel would want them to have good careers and find suitable husbands, but perhaps they acquired different ideas in their adolescence, and at least one is a lesbian environmentalist, or has adopted the Islamic headscarf.

But I'm certain that they all like each other tremendously, Isabel and Gray and the daughters, and get together regularly for meals and holidays. Everyone thinks they are very lucky, and so they are.

Advance publicity...

I saw Josh Rouvier from time to time, for a couple more years, but it's been a long time since then. I've always thought I would see him again one day, and I still think I might, no idea how or when.

The last time was when I was spinning round my usual brief orbit in Sydney, meetings and lunches, and had some spare hours. Why not give Josh a call I thought. He said, 'I'm working and I can't stop but come around anyway.'

At his studio I found design versions of market stalls from an Indian bazaar, heaped up with pyramid-like mounds of coloured powder (sealed with lacquer) and piles of glass bangles. Josh was kneeling on the floor, carefully pouring a white powder through his fingers into a line of intertwined curved loops that made up a kind of symmetric design.

'Come in, wait a moment, I can't stop, you're not supposed to have a single break in the line. It lets in evil spirits or some such thing. I'm terrified.' He completed the line. 'It's not easy,' he grumbled, getting up, painfully straightening his legs, dusting his knees, 'when you haven't been trained since you were a three-year-old girl!' We contemplated the slightly lopsided design. 'I'm getting better, I don't want to have to trace a line first and pour over that on the night,' he said with satisfaction. 'How good am I!'

What I saw, he told me, would make up the installation piece that was soon to be exhibited in a show opening in a week as part of the Biennale at the Museum of Contemporary Art. Opening night would feature a one-off performance: Josh would draw the kolam on the floor himself. That's what he was doing now, practising. The pattern would remain on the floor for the duration of the show.

'They have a spiritual meaning,' he said of the kolam, 'but I just love something about the way they look. They do them every day though more so on the big occasions. Kolam or rangoli, and there are other names.'

'The Biennale!' I said. 'That's good going, how did you manage that?' He'd shown in group shows in a couple of insalubrious private galleries by now, but to be included in the Bee, and at the MCA, was quite a leap.

'My outstanding talent and unique style.'

'Yeah right,' I said dryly, 'that's all it takes.'

'Now, now,' said Josh, 'it also takes very good timing and a bit of it's who you know.'

'Tell me all about it.'

He went over to a small kitchen in the corner and began to fill a kettle.

The show, he informed me, was called *Crosscurrents,* with twelve Australian artists displaying works that derived from their experience of other cultures.

'My whole self as an artist was made possible by going to India,' he said. 'I've come full circle.'

'From India to the Biennale is a full circle?'

'All right, I'll just make us a nice cup of special tea. I'm kind of detoxing right now.'

He brewed up some mixture of herbs and offered some honey with it. Apparently these herbs would cure and prevent any tendency to arthritis, allergic reactions or cancer. No doubt for efficacy you'd have to drink more than the one mug I could only just abide.

'Well,' said Josh, 'do you know who Justin Justman is? He's been very kind to *moi,* and in fact we have a very special understanding.'

I did not think I had heard of Justin Justman, but soon learnt that besides being some kind of celebrity investment banker (*O tempora! O mores!*) he was a great frequenter of theatrical and operatic first nights and a great collector of contemporary artists.

Not only that, he had very close personal ties to someone I did know of, who was the curator of the show, and similar ties to one of the happy few who made a living entirely from the business of critiquing and theorizing, and thereby establishing the tastes of many.

He and Josh had been seeing each other in a quiet, intimate arrangement that had soon revealed that their compatibility was entire. 'It's a creative partnership,' said Josh but did not explain the term.

They had not made public the potential for a lifetime partnership, not yet, and in fact I was practically the only person who really knew, now, that they were more than social acquaintances or a passing fling.

Justin did not want Josh to be seen as his trick, his lesser in any way, when they came out as a couple. Justin wanted to present his boyfriend as a recognized, esteemed artist in his own right. 'It's only a matter of time,' said Josh, 'and timing needs some timely help at times.'

Justin's hand was an invisible but crucial element in the planning of *Crosscurrents*. Learning of his curator friend's brief for the Biennale, Justin had told him about Josh's work, told him that Josh was doing exactly the kind of work they were crying out for.

'You were doing this work then?'

'It all kind of consolidated my ideas,' he said.

Some of the artists in this show had been recipients of a travelling arts fellowship that the current government was attempting to abolish. Others like Josh were hopeful applicants, and their inclusion in a show like this, while not exactly a guarantee, would make their proposals all but irresistible.

The attempts to abolish or even diminish the Cultural Linkage grants program had stirred up the arts community and the consumers of arts commentary. The grants had enabled artists in various forms to travel and research abroad, to seek the inspiration of art forms and found art and art discourses from cultures they either had no opportunity to experience directly, or those from which their parental origins derived.

'And of course with my experience of India,' said Josh shamelessly, 'that had such an effect on me, which really is coming out in the work I'm doing now, they wanted me to be part of it.

'This work,' said Josh, indicating his chalk marks and the simulacrum of the market stalls, and striking a pose as he recited, 'is an exemplar of contemporary hybridity, the integration of cultural signs and practices from colonizing and colonized cultures, resulting in new expressions that are positive, enriching and dynamic.'

'What turgid crap can that be?' I asked.

'That, my dear, is the advance publicity.' It must have been a quotation from the catalogue essay by Justman's theorist friend. 'The point for me personally though,' said Josh, 'is that I was ready to do this.'

Josh brought me over to a trestle table by the wall, to show me a small stack of drawings – his sketches for the installation and the kolam. He went on to reveal that although his installation piece for the Biennale was not made to last, a certain minister would buy a couple of the drawings for the Museum.

'Because you're such a great artist.'

'Because I am a great artist and because Justin Justman has always given him very good advice from which he has always benefited.'

Josh didn't mind my teasing. He was quite satisfied with himself, he understood the business of the art world pretty well by now, he did not pretend to extraordinary gifts, he was not unhappy with the idea of a career depending on image management and public relations. The hungry boy from the small town had made good.

'And here's the kicker. Ta da.' Josh revealed the prototype for the limited edition ironic artefact that would be sold at the show. It was a kolam design, Photoshopped, if that's the term, or tattooed if you like, onto a clear plastic mat, so that you could take it home and lay it on your own doorstep, or wherever it felt right to you, as a special welcome, or blessing, or prayer, or marker of occasion, whatever it was that you felt the mat was for.

We have all seen these kolam mats by now, they are gift shop standards and you get them as presents all the time, and there I was witnessing the original prototype. But I had a feeling they would take off and so they did.

'Watch out for copyright lawyers!' I said.

'Bring 'em on, all publicity is good!'

Justin Justman had taken Josh on a trip to Bali, where he was buying a villa, and after the Biennale they would go to live there in aesthetic bliss. For so many months per year and so on.

'Couldn't happen to a better person,' I said sincerely; I was pleased for him.

Before I left, I bought one of his drawings.

'Smart move.' Josh approved. 'Good publicity for you.' Josh gazed upon his work a while. 'It really is a wonderful example of producing something new out of the familiar,' he said with satisfaction, and carefully wrapped the drawing in some brown paper and tied it up with twine.

'And now,' he said, 'I'd better get back to work or the MCA will be one crosscurrent down!'

As he walked to the door with me he said, 'Oh my God, I just remembered, you knew Larry Darrell! What happened to him? I heard he went back to India. I don't know how he could. It's all right for a short while in a nice place but get out into it and it's like, oh my God.'

'Last I saw him he was going to New York,' I said. 'Couple of years ago now.'

'God. New York. He'll do all right.'

At the door we kissed each cheek twice, everyone in the nabe was doing it now.

'In case I don't see you...Stay in touch,' he said.

This is the end of my story

This is the end of my story.

I've never seen Larry again, never run into him, never heard a word from him.

I've been back to India, and New York, and used to imagine that he would step out of a throng in front of me, in a temple or at a concert, in a busy street or crowded market place, in a restaurant or bookshop. Every now and then I thought I glimpsed him but it never was him.

We've had no reason to contact the other, he and I, and no doubt he has simply gone about his own very separate and different work. Even these days you can lose touch with someone.

Maybe he has influenced others, but would he care? Would it be in a way he would care for? It never did seem the point.

I like to think that Larry has fulfilled his aim of finding purpose and meaning, but then I think: *was* that his aim? These things are never finally found, they call for constant scrutiny, constant renewal, that's what Larry showed me.

I believe without being able to prove it that he'll turn up one day, and then I'll know. Not before this book is published I hope or else I'll never finish it.

I wish I could compose a better ending.

In life, there is only one ending: when life ends. In spite of the way plays and stories are constructed, in real life when you get married, or find your love, or lose it, or solve the mystery, or decide what you are, or make a decision, it is not an ending but part of another story, or many stories.

In a written narrative, characters are meant to have a goal, and the story tells us whether or not they achieved it. But I am reluctant to point to each of the people in this story and show that we all got what we wanted, in some way.

Larry might have found some meaning, but maybe only by realizing he would have to create his own, or settle for a degree of meaninglessness. Isabel might have achieved social status and wealth but she never found a way to keep Larry forever. Josh appeared to have achieved his life in the art world but doubtless must make his compromises. Elliott, the old dear, might have brought about the rewards he had faith in, it's a nice thought, but there's no way to know if he got what he wanted. Sophie, ah, perhaps death was what she most really wanted, the only end to the deepest grief, but she could never have the choice of a life that had not brought about that chilling desire.

Those of us still living remain driven by our various objectives and purposes and illusions.

Still, as we go about our separate lives, we are connected to each other by this history.

Who really knows how to be good?